Dear 1

In Bloom

best wishes

SOPHIE CHALMERS

Sophie C.

Published by Sophie Chalmers

This book is a work of fiction and any resemblance to actual persons, living or dead, is coincidental.

Copyright © 2014 Sophie Chalmers

All rights reserved.

ISBN-10: 1494373815
ISBN-13: 978-1494373818

For Phil.

CONTENTS

CHAPTER 1
Empty 3
Gone 8
Wild 13
Broken glass 16
Broken doors 19

CHAPTER 2
Brainwave 26
Brooding 31
Vix's big idea 34
Vix's victory 36
Al's hell 39

CHAPTER 3
Snowdrops 43
Helleborus various 46
Confession 50
Breaking a confidence 53
Seeing in colours 55
A toast to Vix 59

CHAPTER 4
Wrong move 63
Hearing laughter 68
The Jules Effect 73
Balm 75
Reprieve 78
Old tree roots 83

CHAPTER 5
- Stepping into the light — 87
- Letting go — 92
- The sentence — 95
- The cat lady — 99

CHAPTER 6
- Awareness — 104
- Maggots — 111
- Trusses — 115
- The walk home — 118

CHAPTER 7
- The headmaster ducks — 124
- The strong box — 127
- Vanishing budget — 132
- The submission — 136

CHAPTER 8
- Taking the lead — 139
- Emerald queen — 143
- Changing locks — 147
- Initiation — 154
- The community garden scheme — 159

CHAPTER 9
- A walk in the woods — 169
- The competition — 172
- Valuation — 178
- Dark Peak — 181

CHAPTER 10
- Letting go — 186
- Car boot sale — 191
- Courting consensus — 194
- Insight — 200

CHAPTER 11
- Back to front — 206

Small hours — 211
Blood poisoning — 214
Bewildered — 221
The plan — 223

CHAPTER 12
Never-never land — 232
Decoy — 236
Recovering — 246
An invitation — 248
Power games — 250

CHAPTER 13
The sponsorship form — 255
Planting lilies — 262
Downward spiral — 266
Growing up — 268
Impasse — 273

CHAPTER 14
Phoenix — 279
The proposal — 284
Falling out — 291

CHAPTER 15
Revenge — 301
The attack — 303
Broken — 306
A home for a cat — 308
Judgement day — 316

CHAPTER 16
Together apart — 323
Awaiting sentence — 327
The fete — 330
The announcement — 334

ABOUT THE AUTHOR — 337

ACKNOWLEDGMENTS

With thanks to Phil Butcher, Saskia James, Diana Everett, and Jacqui Maples, who all ploughed though early drafts, Caspian James for his cover picture, and Emlyn James for his inspiration for some of the characters.

CHAPTER 1

EMPTY

Discarded tissues lay scattered over the bed, testament to another slide into despair. Ruth's nose was so stuffed with grief that she did not notice the stale odour of her rumpled bed. Her head was thick from crying but the memories kept pushing through.

They met at a party on New Year's Eve. She was eighteen, he twenty-five. 'I'm going to spend the rest of my life loving you,' he said, coming up to her.

Mired in memories, the next line was already forming. Like all the recollections before it, it was too precious to kill and so she let it flood her.

'You don't even know my name,' she laughed, tickled by his outrageous declaration.

She groaned. Through the window she could see the last of the day's sunshine seeping through the trees in the garden. A car splashed through puddles in the lane. Birds sang the last songs of the day – she forced herself to try and pick out the great tit from the evening chorus, but her tormented mind was already focused on the way…

… he took her hands. 'I know all I need to just by looking at you,' he said over the thumping music. 'We've been watching each other all

evening. We've been dancing together for hours, you and I – ever since I saw you arrive.' Everyone started counting down to the New Year while the two of them looked at each other, smiles all over their faces.

For days, an Abba song had been running in a loop in her head. The first single in her meagre, girlish collection, she'd bought *Dancing Queen* when it came out in the mid-seventies. Years later she'd danced to it with Michael, never dreaming how well he'd make good his promise.

Friday night and the lights are low
Looking out for the place to go
Where they play the right music, getting in the swing
You come in to look for a king…

Downstairs, a door opened and closed softly. She lifted her head to listen. Someone was moving about in the hall, but she dropped back on her pillow. If you're coming to murder me, just make it quick.

High heels clicked across the hallway. Not a murderer. Her best friend Vix.

Oh God. In her well-meaning way, Vix would tell her to get up and pull herself together. Ruth could even nail the tone of voice she'd use: soft and kind but relentless. For a mad moment Ruth thought about hiding under the covers but in the end she couldn't be fished and lay awaiting her fate.

A beat of silence followed as the carpet on the stairs muffled the sound of Vix's heels, then a voice from the doorway said: 'I hope you aren't going to make a habit of not answering your phone.'

Ruth closed her eyes and rolled her head away when Vix flipped on the lights. 'Turn them off.' It was barely a whisper.

Vix ignored her.

'Pleeease.'

With the click of the switch, the comforting gloom returned.

Vix came to sit on the edge of the bed, the scent of some expensive cologne wafting around her. Reaching out, she stroked Ruth's hair. 'Why aren't you answering your phone, darling? I know you're here.'

*Anybody could be that guy
Night is young and the music's high…*

Ruth tried to focus. What had Vix said? 'The house is cold,' was all she could manage.

Vix sighed and her breath formed a brief cloud. 'Have you run out of oil?'

'I don't know. Or the boiler's packed up.'

Vix didn't reply. She stripped off her mauve leather gloves and sat fiddling with them in her lap. The colour picked up one of the threads in her elegant tweed coat. Even her nail polish matched.

She'd never fall apart like this, thought Ruth.

Still Vix said nothing. Her silence was so uncharacteristic that Ruth turned to look at her and noticed, inconsequentially, that age was starting to soften her jawline. Poor old Vix.

'You know,' said Vix, 'Jules was worried enough to ring me.'

Even that didn't stir any guilt. She was so tired she just wanted to sleep. Things had been going better and when the children had come home for Christmas, they'd had fun together – but they were gone almost as soon as they had arrived, off to various parties before going back to work, Anna to Leeds, Marty to Aberdeen, Jules to London. The silence following their departure had been crushing, and so she had ventured out to Vix's party in search of company.

'He said he's been trying to reach you for days,' said Vix, breaking into Ruth's ruminations. 'He wanted to say Happy New Year.'

On the twelfth stroke of midnight, he kissed her.

'I suppose,' said Vix, 'you came home from the party and have been hiding ever since.'

Ruth curled up under the covers. 'I'm not hiding,' she began, as the rest of that memory took hold:

His kiss was like a pledge.

She cleared her throat. 'I've been up. I just came back to bed for a nap.'

'Come on,' said Vix at last. 'Get up and we'll have a hot cup of tea together.'

Ruth didn't move.

Vix pursed her lips. 'You can get pills for this kind of thing, you know? Sweet little pink ones. They make you feel all fluffy and light.'

God, Vix was irritating. 'For goodness sake, I don't want pills.'

Vix smiled. 'Fine, then get up.'

'Where they play the right music.'

Ruth rolled away. 'What's the point, Vix?'

Vix's mouth became a tight little moue of exasperation. 'The point is,' she snapped, 'I've had to come over here and find out if you're still alive.'

As if I care, thought Ruth.

'Well, I'm dying for a cup of tea,' Vix continued in a more measured tone. 'I'm going to put the kettle on. Don't make me come back up and get you.'

Alone once more, Ruth curled into a ball again. Michael had been hers for thirty years. At Christmas, nearly a year after his death, the pain of losing him seemed to be easing, but then Vix's party had triggered old memories – one song, in fact.

For the rest of the night they danced slow, sensual dances, pressed against each other, hardly moving, their eyes closed, her arms around his neck, his hands stroking her back.

Outside, clouds shrouded the final rays of the sunset, tipping the room into darkness, although the silver frame on her bedside table caught the last of the light and shone dully. It was too dark to make out the laughing man in the picture. She tilted the frame towards her. 'You'd be so cross with me if you were here,' she whispered to it. Then she made up her mind. She pushed back the covers and thumped downstairs to join Vix, dragging the quilt behind her.

'You've run out of oil,' said Vix, handing her a mug of tea. 'The oilman will be round tomorrow. I lied and said you were ill in bed and that it was a huge emergency.'

'I'm not ill.' Ruth slumped at the head of the table swathed in quilt. The effort of coming downstairs had exhausted her.

'It is absolutely freezing in here. Do you want to come and stay with us?'

'I'll be fine.'

'There's nothing in the fridge. When did you last eat?'

'I had cheese on toast yesterday.'

'You know the bread's mouldy, don't you? I chucked it out,' she added when Ruth started to get up.

Ruth cupped her mug and stared blankly into space. Gradually her gaze focused and she realised how rough and dry her hands looked, as if she'd been gardening, although she hadn't put her boots on in months. She was thin with lank hair seeded with grey. Slightly ashamed, she folded her arms, braced for Vix's next bit of advice. It didn't take long.

'Darling, you've gotta start pulling yourself together.'

How? Was grief apportioned – so many days and that's your lot? Or was it something you just got used to? If so, when did getting-used-to begin to happen?

Ruth got up. 'If I go shopping tomorrow, will you come to supper on Monday? I'll cook something nice.'

'Not cheese on toast?'

Ruth's smile didn't quite work. 'I'm so sick of that.'

'Darling, it's a date.'

After Vix had driven away, Ruth stood in the darkened hall of the Old Vicarage, a red brick mansion on the edge of Elderfield, wrapped in her quilt. Somehow she had sleepwalked through the last year.

GONE

Meanwhile, in the centre of town, in a small terraced house built to accommodate railway workers at the turn of the last century, Rob faced his angry girlfriend, regretting that he'd let William persuade him to have a third pint. 'I'll sort the carpet out this weekend,' he said,

It was a stupid, old argument. 'Whatever,' said Emma, her tone suddenly defeated.

'We'll do it tomorrow. It's Saturday and I'm not working.'

'For once.'

He ignored her tone. 'So we'll go and buy carpets. Promise.'

She shrugged. 'Why do you keep your promises to everyone but me?'

'C'mon, that's so unfair. I'm not that bad,' he cajoled, inviting a smile. 'Ask William.'

'Oh, William'll back me up,' said Emma.

'No, he won't.'

'Whatever. It's a ratty, old carpet, Rob.'

'I've grown kind of used to it,' he said, hoping to coax her out of her mood, but she wouldn't play ball. 'It's not just the carpet,' she said, toeing a heap of material in a bin liner under the hall table. 'I made those curtains six months ago and asked you to help me hang them. My CDs are still in boxes in the loft. Everything's still in boxes. The house looks like it did the day we moved in – total rubbish.'

'Read my lips,' he said, stung.

'Don't get shirty with me,' she snapped, stalking back into

the kitchen.

Rob felt exasperated. He was tired when he got home from work; fixing the carpet was the last thing he wanted to do. What was it that drove her mad anyway? It was just a carpet. He barely noticed it.

The phone rang. 'Hello? Rob Ansell here.'

Emma came back to see who it was. 'Lisa?' she mouthed, reaching for the phone.

He shook his head. 'Don't worry, Mrs Moreton,' he said to the squawking voice. 'Since it's an emergency, I'll come round right away. Give me ten minutes.' He replaced the receiver. 'What've I done now?' he asked, as Emma glowered at him.

Her expression changed to one of hurt. 'I told you, supper's ready.'

'I said I'd pop round. She's got water pouring through her ceiling.'

'You're kidding, right?'

'Don't get sarky, Em. I'm a builder. She's got a leak; I go and fix it. That's the way it works. It's not a big deal.'

'But it's Friday and you promised,' she whispered. 'You said we'd have supper together. For once in your life.'

'Don't exaggerate. We had supper together last night.'

'Yeah, at nine.'

'What do you want me to do? Let her ceiling collapse?'

'I want you to tell her you'll go round in the morning.'

'Look, love, I won't be long.'

'You always say that,' she said. 'And you're always twice as long as you say you'll be. I know you. You'll get distracted. Someone else'll ring and you'll go round to sort them out, too. And I'll be here. Again. On my own. And tonight, I've –'

'Em,' he cut in, taking her hands. 'I'll be back in a jiffy.'

'No, Rob. No. You never pay attention to me. I am sick of being on my own in the evenings.'

This was another old argument. He tried a new tack. 'Times are hard, Sweet Pea. People we know have lost their homes. Customers. Do you think they'll ever pay my bills? I have nightmares that we can't pay the mortgage.'

'We always manage.'

'Yeah, and we're always juggling. Now you want a new carpet.'

She bit her lip. 'But we have the money.'

'Rainy day savings.'

She took a step closer and put a hand on his heart, giving him a pat. 'The thing is, you like being indispensable.'

'Now you're talking rot.'

'Think so? You've become a total workaholic.'

'Have not.'

'It starts like that – feeling indispensable. I should know. Dad's a workaholic and history's repeating itself, only now it's me waiting at home.'

'I took you to the cinema last week.'

'You don't get it, do you?'

'What's to get, Em? We have a bigger mortgage than we can afford.'

'I suppose that's my fault.'

His smile came back and he gave her a beery hug. 'No, Sweet Pea. That one's on me, but we should have bought the smaller house.'

'You liked it, too.'

'What's not to like? We have two bedrooms, even if the carpets are rank.' He smiled to show he was teasing her but she shrugged out of his embrace.

'Look, love, let me sort out Mrs Moreton. She's relying on me. I'll be back before you know it.'

'I'm serious, Rob,' she said, 'I'm not doing this again. We have the same discussion over and over and nothing ever changes. You're out all the time. Every single person gets priority over me, so if you go out on that job, I won't be here when you get back.'

'Don't be silly, love,' he said, pecking her nose and snagging his keys. 'I'll be half an hour, is all.'

'I mean it.'

'Yeah, yeah, yeah,' he muttered climbing into his van.

He knew he'd totally screwed up when he got home because it was after midnight. He was expecting to grovel for a month. He was not expecting to find her gone.

At first he didn't believe it. He tore upstairs, hoping he would find her asleep in bed but it was littered with clothes she'd left behind. He reached for one of her camisoles, pulling its creamy texture to his face to breathe in its scent. He'd given it to her for Christmas barely two weeks before. He remembered buying it, anticipating her smile when she unwrapped it even as he carried it to the counter.

Maybe she had fallen asleep on the sofa. No such luck. In the kitchen, he saw what he had missed before. Emma had prepared a romantic dinner with candles and napkins and red wine already poured, waiting. The candles had burned down; the beef joint in the oven was burned beyond eating; the potatoes were still in the pan on the sideboard waiting to be drained, their water cool.

He stood in the dingy hallway absorbing the deep silence of an empty house. His legs sagged and he sank down onto the bottom step. The orange streetlights shone through the sitting room window casting shadows on the walls. It was so quiet he could hear the tick of the clock in the kitchen. He felt nerveless. Absently, he reached out and stroked the carpet, brushing the stained patterns with a dirty fingernail.

I'm a bloody fool, he thought.

He pulled out his mobile but got her voicemail.

'Emma? Sweet Pea, it's me. I'm really, really sorry. I can explain. Call me, will you?'

He dialled another number.

'Lisa?' he said when the receiver was picked up the other end. 'Can I speak to Emma?... Twelve thirty? Oh, sorry... I want to speak to Emma... Oh.' Now he was really worried. Where was she if not at Lisa's?

'Nothing's going on,' he said. 'We had a kind of fight, words really, about the carpets... Yeah, that old one... No, obviously I don't know where she is. I had to go out on a job and she didn't feel like staying in on her own. I thought she'd come over to yours and crashed on the sofa... No worries. I'll try her mobile... Yeah, yeah, everything's fine. I'll tell her to call you in the morning. Bye.'

He redialled Emma's number. 'Emma? You aren't at Lisa's. Where are you? Please call me. Please.' He couldn't keep his voice from wobbling on the second plea.

He sat on the stairs under the glare of the bare light bulb holding his mobile, waiting.

After an hour he texted her: 'Please call me. I'm so sorry.'

At half past four he texted again. 'I'm worried. Where are you?'

His eyes felt gritty. Even his skin felt tight when he rubbed his face. He looked at his phone. Checked he still had a signal. Checked there was enough battery. Dialled the home phone. It rang. He picked it up in case it was her but heard only his own voice – 'Emma?' – on his mobile. He sat on the bottom step, his head against the wall, his mobile on his knee.

He jerked awake and checked his phone again. Good signal. Plenty of battery. He sat holding it and his eyes slid back to the offending carpet. He picked at a dried patch of mud at his feet. He peeled back a corner of the carpet and found there was only grey paper behind it, not even underlay. He would sort it out in the morning.

For a long time he sat thinking about her. They'd laugh about this at the weekend – what a fright she had given him. She was pretty intense and took life more seriously than he did, but she was usually up for a laugh. She used to laugh a lot.

'Emma, please,' he muttered.

He hunched forward with his chin in his hands, waiting.

The heating clicked on. It must be five. A car approached.

He sat up. It drove by and he sagged again.

He stood up. Oh Christ! How dumb can I be? She's gone to her parents. That's why she's not answering – they haven't got a signal. He almost laughed with relief as the stress drained out of him. He'd drive over first thing and grovel, eat humble pie, whatever it took. Then they'd go out and choose a new carpet. Sod the expense. He'd make it right. She'd see.

Upstairs he crashed fully dressed on top of her discarded clothes, instantly asleep.

WILD

On Monday night, Al's mobile beeped while he was doing his homework. A friend had texted two words: 'Its epic.'

The essay forgotten, he clattered downstairs. In the living room, his mum was hunched in the dark by the window staring down the street. Joining her, he followed her gaze but saw nothing. 'Is it happening again?' he asked.

'Sh,' Vix whispered.

'I thought you were having supper at Ruth's,' he whispered back.

In the distance, a car alarm started wailing. Al went to the front door and looked out.

'Shut the door,' hissed Vix. Two seconds later, she yanked it open. 'I didn't mean with you outside, you nitwit,' she said. 'Come back inside.'

The sound of someone running along the road made her press back into the shadows. A lone figure ran by.

Shit, there was a riot in town. Awesome. Another night of giving the cops the run-around. How cool was that?

'Why don't the police arrest them?' she muttered.

'I'll go and see if everything's OK.'

'You will not.'

The sound of tinkling glass made them both look up the street. 'I'll be right back,' he said, squirming past her.

'Al!' He heard her hoarse call but ignored it. He wanted to be there, to see what was happening close up. He pulled out his phone, texting as he ran. Seconds later, a text pinged back: they were by the square. Glad to be in trainers but wishing he had brought a jacket, he sprinted down a side street, planning to come in from the rear.

Before he could meet up with his mates, Gazzer, who was in his class at school, spotted him and called him over.

'Hey,' said Al, breathing hard. 'What's happening?'

'There's a bunch of cops down there, is'n' there?'

'Ta. You in this?'

'Leading the flipping Light Brigade, aren't I?'

They were crouched, trying to make out what was in the shadows. 'You seen Bob?' whispered Al.

'He's with the rest of your poofter crew, down by the supermarket, watching the action like a bunch o' girls.'

Al didn't rise to the bait.

At the end of the street, the side door of a people mover slid shut. 'Look!' said Gazzer standing up. 'Is that the cops leaving?' A siren whooped and blue light bounced off the walls of the houses and then was gone.

'Bloody hell,' exclaimed Al. 'They've fucked off.' As he went to join Gazzer in the middle of the road, something brushed the side of his head and smashed at his feet. Someone had thrown a bottle at him. He swung round in startled surprise to see a group of young men swaggering towards them, beanies perched on the back of their heads.

Without thinking, he grabbed a bottle from a nearby recycling box and lobbed it back. It shattered harmlessly on the pavement in front of them. They didn't even duck. Hell. There was going to be a fight.

In panic, he flung another bottle but that too landed short. 'Oh shit,' he yelped, grabbing another.

'Give me that,' said Gazzer, snatching the bottle from him.

'Bloody nancy thrower, you are,' he said as he threw it. This one arc'd through the night sky. Al watched it compass the stars seeming to take eternity to reach its zenith.

He was surprised that there was no transition. One moment it was stretching to the horizon, the next, it had smashed into the middle of the group. That's when he realised he had provoked animals. He could taste their hunger. They were out for blood and he was simply prey.

In his imagination, he was always cool in a fight, but as the first fist swung towards him, he understood that he was just a wimpy fat kid. His face went slack, his hands started to swing up to protect his head, and his body softened, anticipating the feel of their callused knuckles driving through his face. They were going to brain him and he was half way to reconciling himself to his fate when he heard Gazzer shout, 'Back off, yeah!' Then there was nothing but pain blasting through his head.

When Al went down, Gazzer went berserk and the other boys turned and ran. 'That's it, run away, you tossers,' he yelled after them while Al scrambled to his feet, gasping and humiliated, and stood with his hands on his knees, snot and blood dripping from his nose.

As the boys ran under a streetlight, one of them looked back and Al recognised him – Paddy. He'd played Paddy at rugby last term. Couldn't remember the school; could remember the late tackles and the studded boot crunching down on his instep when the ref wasn't looking. It seemed Paddy knew him too, because he mimed the stamp again, and gave him the finger.

'I hate that boy,' Al muttered thickly. 'He's a fucking bully.'

'Then let's teach him a lesson,' said Gazzer.

'Leave me out of it.'

'You run along home if you like.'

There were depths of humiliation Al was not prepared to descend to. 'I'll come with you,' he mumbled.

BROKEN GLASS

Rob could not believe his eyes as he drove past the smoking Subaru carcass on Tuesday morning on his way to a job at William's. He'd heard the local youths fighting the night before, but they'd never been this bad. Spray paint defaced walls and street signs. Scores of windscreens had been smashed. The main source of ammunition seemed to have been wine bottles scavenged from recycling boxes: the square was thick with green shards of glass.

Rob's hand tightened on the steering wheel. What in hell was going on? This was no inner city ghetto. This was Elderfield with its shops clustered around the quaint cobbled square, where Middle England queued to buy sausages at Roser's, flowers from Lisa, and nails from Brian's Hardware Store. In the streets off the main road, lawns were mowed on Saturday, and kids washed neighbours' cars on Sunday to top up their pocket money.

Yet even Rob had to admit that Elderfield was now more than a picturesque town surrounded by rural splendour. In the old part of town, posh houses with sprawling gardens, tidy stables and expensive ménages extended westwards towards Box Hill, known locally as Never Ending Hill because of its number of false summits. In contrast, the new housing estate festered along the eastern marshy flank. Hastily conceived and rammed through Planning, the estate was built with even greater speed using cheap materials. Rob knew exactly how cheap – he made a tolerable living from repair work there.

Everywhere he looked, people were picking up rubbish. Geoff Roser, whose face usually wore a cheery smile, looked grim. He was trying to straighten the centuries-old signpost in the middle of the square along with a couple of his lads. Nearby Lisa was sitting on the kerb crying. Someone had thrown a bin through her shop window with its gilt writing offering flowers for every occasion. She wasn't insured for this kind of damage, she sobbed. Rob made a mental note to return later and repair her window. He couldn't do it for free. Emma would have said: 'You have to pay the mortgage just like everyone else.'

Practical, lovely Emma. But Emma was gone. His visit to her parents' house at the weekend had wrecked him. 'We wouldn't tell you where she is, even if we knew,' they said. 'She's well enough. That's all we're prepared to say.'

How he had struggled to rein in his rage at this betrayal. He'd never liked her father but he had expected some sort of support from her mother. Verbalising this gall, however, wouldn't solve a thing. 'Will you tell her I need to talk with her,' he said. 'Please.'

He'd driven home in a blue funk. These were – correction – had been future parents-in-law. They'd spent Christmases together. He'd mended their roof last summer. He'd whiled away hours in the pub with her humourless father.

If they had told Emma of his visit, she hadn't called or texted or reacted in any way. Maybe she didn't trust herself with him. Maybe she was afraid he'd pressure her into returning against her will.

Don't be a jerk, he thought. I'm not a beast. I've never threatened her or been cruel.

The crunch of broken glass under his tyres brought him back to the present and he wondered if he were heading for a puncture. As he drove by, Brian ambled over from his hardware store and crouched in front of Lisa. She listened to him, nodded, and then reached for the handkerchief he held out. Other shopkeepers were more stoical. They worked steadily to sweep up the shambles that was the High Street. Huddled in clusters, everyone else was subdued. The police looked sullen – once again they had nothing to show for their night out: not one arrest, not one caution, not even a satisfactory beating. The hoodied youths had simply melted into the darkness whenever the blue lights had appeared.

Near the Subaru, several men were gathered in an angry conference with Bruce Turner, a man who made even Rob crane his neck. Rob knew everyone by name and raised a hand in greeting but didn't stop. There was no way he was going to find himself sucked into whatever self-righteous decisions Bruce chose to impose on the men around him. That's not to say Bruce wasn't a decent bloke – he was chair of the parish council and proprietor of the local farmers' shop – but his greatest skill was whipping up anger.

Rob knew pretty well what Bruce was saying. He said it to anybody who would listen: 'When will this stop? Why don't parents control their kids better? When will the police get their act together? Why don't people look out for each other any more?'

At least, that was the gist. From the words drifting on the breeze as Rob passed, it sounded like Bruce was on his fourth or fifth iteration; adjectives were beginning to creep back into his harangue, though 'fucking' still framed most sentences. Fucking kids. Fucking car. Fucking police. His words focused frustration and brought out the vigilante in people.

Fifty meters on, the old cat lady stood at her gate in a faded print nightie that reached down to her ankles, her feet bare in spite of the morning frost. Long grey hair straggled round her shoulders. Rob glanced in his mirror at Bruce and then at the clock on his dashboard, before pulling in beside her gate. So much for being on time at William's.

Walking up to her, Rob smiled and put his hand on the gate, resting it there. 'It's Rob, Mrs Mallinson. You'll catch your death if you stand in the cold dressed like that.'

'They broke my window and Georgie flew away,' she bleated.

As far as Rob knew, Georgie, the budgerigar, had escaped three decades ago but he held his tongue. He pushed open the gate and gently put a hand on her elbow to usher her back towards the house. She was a diminutive woman, barely reaching his chest, and bordered on skeletal. She stank of wee.

'Georgie flew away,' she repeated.

Rob sighed. He was going be late for William. Again.

The smell of cat wee and the cloying scent of something

long dead made him gag as he entered her house. A brew of sweet tea helped to settle the old lady's nerves. She sat on the sofa and sipped it while he fixed her broken window with a sheet of plastic and gaffer tape from the van. The house was freezing but nothing happened when he switched on the electric heater.

He flipped the lights. Still nothing.

'What's with the electrics, Mrs Mallinson?' he asked.

She hauled herself up to ferret through piles of papers on the desk. 'They sent a letter,' she said, and rattled a disconnection notice under his nose.

Oh, nuts. He was going to be so late for William. 'Let's start by getting you warmer,' he suggested. 'Why don't you go and get dressed? Then I'll call your daughter and wait till she comes.'

'Not my daughter,' she whispered, ducking as if from a blow.

He remembered the daughter and concurred, 'No, not your daughter. I'll call Social Services.'

'She gets so angry with me.'

'I won't call your daughter,' he assured her. 'I'll call Social Services. They'll look after you.'

'I don't want to go to a home. They'll put me in a home. You won't let them put me in a home, will you?' Her myopic eyes gazed up at him in distress.

'Why don't you get dressed?' he said, not knowing what else to say.

BROKEN DOORS

It was not until lunchtime that Rob reached William's garden centre. He found him sitting at one of the tills reading a newspaper. Without looking up, William said, 'You're too late, Ansell, and you're a bloody loser. I'm a busy man with things to do, so I fixed it myself.'

Rob's gaze swept the deserted garden centre. 'I can explain,' he said, too used to William's tone to rise to it.

William rolled his eyes, which Rob interpreted as glad to see him nonetheless. 'You always can.'

'Chuck us a Coke, mate.'

William pulled a couple of tins from behind the counter. He lobbed one at Rob, and pulled the tab on his own, tipping his head back to gulp as he did so. 'I've been waiting three hours to make deliveries,' he said, wiping his mouth on his sleeve. 'Three hours! Can't you see I'm running a business? You said you'd be right over.'

'This door?' Rob asked, indicating the one he'd come through.

William gave a breezy shrug. 'Might be.'

Rob sniffed. 'Next time, leave it to the bleeding expert. It won't close.'

''Course it won't close,' snorted William, stating the obvious. 'I'm not a bleeding handyman, am I?'

When Rob prodded the door, it peeled from the frame and twisted towards him. He caught it before it smashed into one of the displays. 'You're a bloody loser, Jonesy,' he said, in a deadpan voice.

William's eyes met Rob's and he smirked. 'Well, are you gonna stand around all day or are you gonna fix it?'

Rob rubbed his hand over his chin, pretending to think about it. 'Depends what it's worth.'

William's smile vanished and he sighed.

Rob could have kicked himself. He knew business was bad for William. On the other hand, he had to earn a living too and, lately, lots of his clients were asking for more time to pay. William wasn't just a client, though. He was a pal. 'I need a new plant for my living room,' suggested Rob. 'Swap you?'

But William wouldn't rise. 'You need a plant like you need a hole in the head, mate. And Emma'll bleeding kill me if I send you home with another sodding houseplant. She'll kill me, and tell you you're going soft in the head, and kill you an' all.'

All the energy drained out of Rob. He took a breath to speak, swallowed at the lump in his throat, and then went on: 'Suit yourself.'

He was glad to go out to his van to fetch his tools, rattling around for longer than necessary while he collected himself. *Emma, please come home. I love you so much.* He reached for his mobile and even brought up her number, but put the phone away and picked up his tools. He was beginning to hate the sound of her voice mail inviting him to leave a message. He'd left dozens.

Fortunately his work was blessedly mindless and his brain ticked over in neutral, for once blanking out the endless conversations with Emma he had been rehearsing all weekend. He let some customers in, who wandered over to the seed racks before going to poke through the shrubs outside. Vicky Watson screeched up in her racy Mazda MX5.

'Hiya, Vix,' he said as she tottered towards him in a ridiculously high pair of heels. In her early fifties, she was in good nick and received more wolf whistles than any other woman he knew.

'Hi, darling,' she replied. 'Were you out last night?'

'Me?' said Rob. 'Not on your life! They really trashed the place this time, didn't they?'

'Yeah. I was supposed to have supper with Ruth Dawson, but was too frightened to go out. Al went to see what was happening but didn't come back till the small hours.'

'Was your boy mixed up in it?'

'Al? Nooo.'

Rob screwed a new hinge into the door while Vix watched.

'I had a coup, today,' she offered suddenly, thrusting the local paper at him. 'A full page profile for one of my clients.'

He scanned the headline, impressed. 'Nice one. I bet he was pleased.'

'Not really,' she said in a deflated voice. 'He wanted to be in *The Times*.'

'Bastard. He should be chuffed you landed him this.'

She shrugged. 'Yeah, I suppose. People'll recognise him for a couple of days, so that'll flatter his ego, but it won't be enough. I told him, I'm a PR consultant, not a miracle worker. If he doesn't have an angle, not even Hill & Knowlton could get him the coverage he wants.'

'Hill and –?'

'Big PR company. Big.'

William came up beside her. 'You still here, Ansell?'

'Godda problem with that, Jonesy?'

'Yeah. You're monopolising this beautiful lady and stopping her from finding the plants she wants.'

'Oh, Rob's not distracting me, William,' said Vix coolly. 'I was showing off my latest coup.' Then she added, 'Though it's pathetic really.'

'Give us a gander,' offered William, relieving Rob of the newspaper. *'Designers score a hat-trick,'* he read.

'They landed three big orders with three local authorities,' she explained.

'Not bad. Big picture, too. And,' he said scanning the piece, 'it looks like he's been quoted in every paragraph. *"We are a young company, and most other bidders are more established," said Ward.* Blah, blah, blah, progressive. Blah blah, innovative. That's not pathetic. That's stuffed with enough fancy vocab to make him wet himself.'

'Oh, it's pathetic that I'm satisfied with getting headlines in the local paper.'

'You just need a good story,' said Rob.

'I need a good client. I wish people would stop banging on about the economy. The PR budget's always the first to go and last to come back.'

'Well, you can work your magic on me, if you like,' William suggested. 'Between you and me, it's like a bleeding morgue in here. Christmas was a wash out. It's usually one of the best times of year for me.'

Rob looked around. There were plants piled artfully on

counters. The tables in the café were decked out with crisp tablecloths. The smell of scented candles infused the showroom. Outside, aisles of shrubs waited for spring. Two ladies were weighing up which of two rose trees they would buy. Other than them the place was deserted. It occurred to Rob that there were almost no staff around. Had William fired them? A frown clouded William's face and Rob had a sudden, awful feeling that business was not just bad for William; he was facing ruin.

'Sure, I can work my magic on you,' laughed Vix. 'But I work for cash.'

'What's that supposed to mean?' asked William.

'Well, I'm not a sop like Rob, who'll work for houseplants.'

William looked hurt. Rob pressed his lips together and met William's gaze with a slight shrug, and then turned back to work on the door. Vix never did know how to keep her mouth shut, he thought.

'As if I care anyway,' muttered William and stalked off.

Rob could feel Vix's eyes on his back and ignored her. There was a long, painful pause while she digested the change of mood. 'Sorry,' she muttered.

''s OK.'

'Yeah right. Even you won't look at me.'

Sometimes Rob wondered how she ever succeeded in PR. 'It's him you need to apologise to.'

'I don't think he's in the mood to listen to an apology just now,' she said. 'Listen to him thumping those files around. He'll break his desk if he goes on like that.'

Rob lifted the door into place and began screwing the hinge into the frame. Vix shimmied over to the air plant display and picked one up, looked at it, and then selected another. She wandered over to the till to pay. When William didn't come out to take her money, she went and knocked at the open door of his office.

'You got a story?' she asked softly.

'Nope,' he said, banging away at his PC.

'I can't make headlines without something to say.'

He continued typing as though she hadn't spoken.

'Can I pay for this?' She held out the air plant.

'Take it. It's on the house,' he shot sulkily.

She gave up with a sigh of irritation. 'See you, Rob,' she said, sticking a fiver on the till as she went past.

Rob tightened the last screw. He chucked his tools into the box and straightened up, arching his back. Then he went over to lean on William's doorjamb. William was poring over a lever arch file stuffed with papers in front of him. 'Christmas bills,' he said, gloomily.

'There were loads of people in here over Christmas,' observed Rob.

'Yeah but they didn't buy anything,' said William. 'People generally give rellies something decent for Christmas: a big houseplant, some garden furniture, that kind of thing. This year, they settled for a bowl of bloody hyacinths, and most of those they bought separately and potted up at home.'

'Spring'll be here soon and people'll soon be in to pick up their seedlings.'

'Yeah.' The plantsman didn't sound convinced.

'How long can you hold out?'

William took a deep breath. 'Six weeks.'

'What can I do to help?'

'I don't know, Rob.' William cleared his throat. 'I can't even pay you for the work you did before Christmas. I've given up holding my head up in front of Emma.'

'Emma left,' said Rob.

'What!' William gaped. 'Christ, I'm sorry, mate.'

'Nah, it's fine.'

'I don't understand. You're so right together.'

Rob looked round the shop as he tried to compose himself. 'I er...' He hated that his voice became husky with emotion. 'We had a row.'

'A row?'

'About a carpet.'

'Not that manky thing in your hallway?'

That was not what they had been arguing about, and he knew it. She was fed up because he was never at home. He remembered her threat and winced. He'd completely misread her. That evening, he'd gone out, tweaked a jammed stopcock, and had then driven up Never Ending Hill, where he'd parked in the layby overlooking Elderfield. He'd only meant to be half an hour – just to show her that he still wore the trousers – but he'd dozed off. He hadn't called her bluff. She had called his and he was gutted. 'She says I never keep my promises to her.'

'Course you don't. Women have two complaints about men: we don't commit and we take them for granted. We can't win, Rob.'

Had he taken her for granted? Rob picked up his toolbox. 'See ya, mate.'

'We're a right pair of crocks, aren't we?'

Rob remembered why he liked William. He could talk bollocks with the best of them, but underneath he was a true friend. 'Yeah,' he replied. 'We are. Wanna pint later?'

'If you're buying.'

'If you pay me.'

William made a show of leafing through his invoices. 'OK, after this one, and this one, and – oh Lord.' He became serious again. 'The fucking oil bill. The bastards won't deliver till I pay. Fat chance of that. I'll lose my bloody stock if we have a cold snap.'

'We'll think of something over a pint. Rose and Crown at six?'

William nodded. When Rob looked back, William was sitting with his head in his hands, staring at the mess of bills in front of him.

CHAPTER 2

BRAINWAVE

The night before, Ruth had cooked a meal and then waited for Vix to arrive. Eventually Vix had rung to make excuses.

'Of course I understand you can't come round,' she said, not understanding at all. All she heard were some lame excuses about some boys making a noise in town, and the anticipation of good company over a bottle of wine, which had started building when she went shopping on Saturday, flipped to dejection. The whole evening stretched ahead and Ruth was strangely at a loss what to do with herself. After pacing the house in the gloom she switched on the telly, but there was nothing to watch.

This feeling of frustration was alien to her. For the first time in months, she felt utterly purposeless: Vix was right – she needed another project. Right after Michael's death she had been busy getting her gardening book off to the publisher, with a multitude of editors imposing deadlines on her, forcing her to react. On delivering the final draft, she had sunk into apathy. How feeble, she thought, looking back. Maybe she could write another book.

Her heart sank. Maybe not.

Something easier. She could clear up Christmas. The tree still stood in a pool of needles. Cards hung on ribbons. The children's beds needed fresh sheets. From here, it was a short step to wondering when they'd be down to see her again and...

No, not clearing up, she thought. I'm not having sad thoughts today. Her mind went blank. She picked up an old seed catalogue from the pile on the coffee table. Ah, here was a project. For the last year she had abandoned the garden. Perhaps she could bring it back to its former glory, even open it to the public again.

Feeling lonely but, for the first time in months, not low, she took herself off to bed. She was just dropping off to sleep when she heard a deep boom.

She sat up in time to see the sky over the town light up. Oh my God, she thought. Is that the hooligans Vix was talking about? I've been so unfair to her. Grabbing a cardigan, she went to stand on the doorstep, her feet curling against the cold, where she listened to the feral yells of hoodlums threading back through the town, car alarms whining in their wake. The cardigan didn't afford much warmth; she shivered and wrapped it tighter as she peered apprehensively into the rustling shadows around the house, straining her ears for the sound of running footsteps. Would they come this far? What if they took it into their heads to –?

Just then, a police car glided past her driveway going towards the town, its blue light flashing in the moonlight, and she heaved a sigh of relief. Soon after came the wail of sirens as fire engines raced to put out whatever it was that was blazing.

Gradually the noise from the town died down. Cold and stiff, she went back to bed. Her feet were so cold they ached. In spite of this, she fell into a wonderful dreamless sleep. Next morning, she rose with the sun and went straight into the garden armed with clippers. Her first task was to prune back the clematis and the honeysuckle round the front door, which had become so overgrown that people had to stoop to enter the house.

By lunchtime she had finished. She surveyed the pile of cuttings around her and felt a quiet sense of satisfaction: it felt as though that part of the garden could breathe again having been choked with deadwood for too long. Back in the kitchen, she scooped some of last night's bolognaise sauce into a pan, and turned on the hob. As she reached for a plate, she stroked the framed photograph on the sideboard. 'Michael,' she whispered, 'it's better today. I know what to do now.'

'Hello,' said a quiet voice behind her, making her almost drop the plate in surprise. 'I knocked and pressed your bell, and knocked again,' said Vix. 'The door was open so I let myself in.'

'Oh my!' exclaimed Ruth. 'You gave me such a shock.'

'Here, I bought you a present.' Vix handed her the air plant she had bought at the garden centre.

Ruth inspected it. 'Hm. *Tillandsia fasciculata*. Thank you,' she said, kissing Vix's cheek.

'How do you do that?' gasped Vix. 'I made sure to take the label off.'

'I –'

'I'm sorry I cried off last night. I feel awful.'

'That's –'

'I was afraid. Me, a black belt in badminton, actually afraid! Those blooming louts frightened the bejeezus out of me. They've left the streets in a terrible state. Glass everywhere. They even torched a car. On the corner as you go in. By Susan Mallinson's place.'

'Is that what I heard exploding last night?'

'I've no idea. I swear I'm not becoming a grumpy old woman, but the place has really gone to the dogs in the last twelve months. They were actually trying on shoes in Stead & Simpson last night. Caught on CCTV, apparently. Can you believe it? Absolutely brazen, they were. You know,' she added, 'it's the first sign of madness when you start talking to yourself.'

'I was talking to Michael,' admitted Ruth.

'Same thing. Am I too late for supper?'

'Oh. No.' Vix hadn't let her down after all. 'Of course. Give me a mo. Sit down. Gosh. You know, this was my first proper go at having someone round since… since… It was just the two of us, so nothing major, but I'd planned it, you know. Spag bol. Thought about it. A bit any way. Then, when you didn't come… Oh Vix, I'm so glad to see you. Would you like a glass of wine?'

'Nah. Gotta work later. Want some help?'

'Sit, sit. It's all sorted. Let me just boil some water.'

Idly, Vix picked up a book that was lying on the table and began to leaf through it. Then she checked the front cover before continuing to turn the pages. It was a copy of *The Red Garden*. 'Is this *the* book?'

'Yes,' said Ruth, pride swelling inside her. It was a coffee table book of her red garden, now well known locally thanks to a television programme made by her nephew Jules. In the book, the photographer had managed to capture the essence of the garden, its passion and tranquillity, with its flowers and foliage in every shade of red. The publishers had done a magnificent job.

'Wow,' said Vix. 'I'm impressed. When did it come out?'

'Yesterday. I was going to give it to you last night for being such a good friend. Is it a bit conceited to give you a copy of my own book?'

'Totally, but I love it. Thank you.'

'Thank *you*, actually, for your patience with me, and for getting me out of bed last week after... when I didn't answer my phone. I was a bit down that day.'

'I know you miss him, and I know it's hard, but –'

'– you've gotta start pulling yourself together,' they said in unison, and then laughed.

'Am I that predictable?' said Vix, worried.

"Fraid so.'

'You know, I haven't heard you laugh properly in a long time.'

'Gosh. I hadn't realised I'd become so...' Ruth became thoughtful again.

'You're doing OK.'

Ruth pulled a face. 'I think you're being generous but it's funny, today, in the garden...' She paused as her emotions swam to the surface. 'In the garden this morning, it's silly, I know, but there was this thrush singing. And I listened to it.'

Vix frowned. 'I'll ring up the men in white coats now, shall

I?'

'It was beautiful, Vix. I heard it and it was beautiful.' She put two plates of spaghetti on the table.

'Ri-ight.'

'The point is, I feel alive today.'

Vix was busy grating Parmesan over her bolognaise. 'Well, that's great. I'm pleased for you. I hardly missed Paul when he left.'

Ruth pulled her food towards her, unsure whether to be reassured by Vix's lack of comprehension.

'I missed him in bed, of course, but he wasn't good for much else. No, I tell a lie. He was great at mowing the lawn.'

'I think divorce is a little different,' said Ruth cautiously. 'Actually, talking of lawns, I was thinking of opening my garden to the public again.'

Vix, forking spaghetti into her mouth, did a theatrical double take. 'Things are looking up!' she said with her mouth full. 'You know your lawn looks like a meadow, don't you?'

'Hm,' acknowledged Ruth, as it dawned on her just how much work would need to be done to bring the garden back up to scratch.

'Any idea who you might give the proceeds to this time?'

'Er,' Ruth stalled. The question sounded loaded. 'I suppose Marie Curie Cancer Care. They were so supportive in Michael's last days.'

'Ri-ight.'

'I can tell you have other ideas. Go on. Out with it,' she invited.

Unusually, Vix paused before she spoke, perhaps collecting her thoughts for once. 'I think you need to stop looking backwards.'

Ruth took a breath to speak but it seemed that Vix did have an agenda. 'I'm helping another charity get some publicity for a golf marathon they're organising. Some pro bono work.'

'Oh yes?'

'In aid of the Muscular Dystrophy Campaign. Research into

muscle disease, wheelchairs for kiddies, that kind of thing.'

'And you think I should give the proceeds to them. Interesting. I'll think about it.'

'Everybody'll come and help, the same as always. You know, they're all still there, waiting to see you again.'

Ruth smiled brightly, although tears welled up suddenly. 'Oh God,' she muttered, pulling a tissue from up her sleeve. 'Do you suppose I'll ever be right again?'

'You're gonna set me off in a minute! Course you will. Mourning takes time.'

'A year?'

'Some people get over a death quickly. Others take a lifetime.'

'Oh my,' said Ruth in a stricken voice.

'Hell, I didn't mean it like that.'

'It's OK. I'm laughing. See?' And she was, at least, smiling. 'Oh Vix, I want to move on.' She frowned. 'At the moment, though, I feel I can only inch forward. I'll work on the garden, run an open day and see how it goes, but moving on is a really big step.'

'What you need is sex.'

'Vix!' Ruth was wide-eyed with shock.

'You can't be unhappy when you're having an orgasm.'

'Victoria Watson, you are terrible.' spluttered Ruth.

'But I'm right. You know I am,' Vix replied. 'Oh my goodness,' she added. 'I've just had a brilliant idea!'

'Not to match me up with someone, I hope.'

'No, no. Much better than that.'

BROODING

Later that afternoon, Ruth was once more pottering in the garden when the phone rang. She thought of ignoring it; there was no one she wanted to speak to, needed to speak to, but her knees were aching and she decided it was a good excuse to stop for the day.

'You sound relaxed,' said her nephew, Jules, when she answered.

'Do I, darling?' said Ruth.

'Cheerful, even.' His voice sounded far away, and there was a lot of traffic noise in the background. He was breathing as though he were walking fairly fast as he talked.

'I had Vix over for lunch,' she said.

'Ah ha!'

'What does that mean?'

'Oh the incorrigible Vix. Did you know she seduced my soundman when we came down to film your garden?'

'Er,' she stalled, trying to remember. Had she been oblivious to everything? 'No,' she admitted. 'I didn't know.'

'Well, it caused something of a scandal at the time. Lots of twitching curtains. Elderfield is so locked in the past, it's tragic.'

Ruth thought about youths setting cars alight on the village green and started to enlighten him, but Jules didn't let her get a word in. 'I haven't seen you properly for ages,' he went on, 'so I thought I might invite myself down.'

'You're not worrying about me, are you?

'No.'

His response was too fast. 'Jules, you were here two weeks ago. I'm not falling apart.'

'Am I not welcome?'

''Course you're welcome, you nincompoop. When would you like to come?'

'Saturday week?'

'Lovely, darling. I'll get your room ready. How are you otherwise?'

'Frustrated. My new girl friend is playing hard to get – the one who couldn't come to Christmas lunch – and my producer is pushing me to put together another series for the autumn but the team keep coming up with the same old ideas, which have been done to death. *Jules Dawson*,' he proclaimed in a hushed, pseudo-American accent, '*introduces yet another television series on garden makeovers*. Argh, I'm bored already. I really loved doing the series on themed gardens. It was a brilliant idea of yours. D'you know, people still talk about it?'

'Really?'

'They talk about your garden in particular.'

'I think that one was so good because you did it as a kind of tribute to Michael.'

'Maybe.' There was a smile in his voice. 'I have to go now. I've arrived at my meeting. I'll see you Saturday week. Love you lots.'

'Love you, too, darling,' she replied, and then sat listening to the dialling tone. Jules had become like a son after his parent's messy divorce. For a while he had drifted between his feckless mother and her selfish older brother. He ended up on Ruth's doorstep one half term that both his parents had forgotten about, and never went back. As she replaced the receiver, she realised with dismay that she hadn't known Jules had a new girl friend, let alone that she had been invited to Christmas lunch. Why hadn't she come? And why was she playing hard to get?

My God, she thought. When did I become so wrapped up in myself that I lost sight of my family? In this introspective mood, she made herself some tea, and curled up on a sofa with the hot cup cradled in her hands, staring blindly at her reflection in the window.

That last day, the day Michael died, she had been late home from shopping. She'd stopped in town to buy a new dress that had caught her eye. In her mind, as she ran up the stairs, she was showing it off and already responding to his banter. There were voices in the room: the children and Jules were already there, collecting for a gin and tonic at his bedside.

When she walked in, a gigantic smile on her face, it took a second to realise she was looking her last at her husband. His eyes sought and held hers, but the light was already fading from them. Her cry of despair shocked the children to silence as they realised what was happening. Even now she could still hear herself shouting: 'Michael, stay with me. Please stay.'

Jules had rushed forward to hold her, whispering, 'Let him go, Ruth. Please let him go.'

So she held her husband's hand as he slipped off, stroking it over and over.

He had waited for her to return home before fading.

He had waited for her.

He had waited.

Over the months since his death, she replayed this scene endlessly. 'Michael,' she said desolately, 'this has to stop.' A tear trickled down her face and she wiped it away. 'I don't know how. I miss you so much.'

VIX'S BIG IDEA

Vix was so excited by her idea that she detoured home via the garden centre where she knocked at the entrance door. Although the sign said it was closed, she was pretty sure William was still there – the lights were on and the gates were still open. She rapped again and then saw movement at the back of the store.

'William!' she called cheerily with a wave. 'Cooee. Let me in.'

He stood for a moment looking at her, and then grudgingly came to open the door a crack. 'I'm closed, Vix,' he said.

'Don't be so silly. I've had an idea.'

'It's late, and I'm meeting Rob at the pub in five minutes.'

'Oh pooh. He'll be late. At least an hour. He always is. Come on, let me in.'

Reluctantly he stood back for her to enter. He rubbed the muscles at the back of his neck as he watched her teeter around the store in her impossible heels.

'Oh it's perfect,' she exclaimed. 'I knew it would be. We could turn that into a bar, there's plenty of space, the displays look good, we could move those plants, and –'

'Vix, my dear, are you planning a takeover?' he asked.

'No. I've had a great idea to get people into the shop.'

'Mm hm,' he responded.

'You're going to host a book signing.'

'I am?'

'Yes. You said you needed something to hang some publicity on, and I've come up with the perfectest plan. Ruth Dawson's new book was published last week.'

'She of the *Red Garden* who lives down the road?'

She nodded. She could almost feel his eyes following her as she continued to inspect his displays.

'OK, I'm listening.'

'Wow. I love the enthusiasm.'

He became nonchalant. 'Forgive me, but she gets all the kudos and I get to fork out for the wine.'

'Yes,' she acknowledged, brushing his objection aside with a sweep of her hand, 'but people will come in and meet her, and while they're here, they'll buy your plants and remember you exist.'

'Just in case you hadn't observed, I'm smack on the main road into town, Vix. They know I exist. They can't help but know I exist unless they've collectively gone blind. What's happening is people are losing their jobs and no one's spending money on books, let alone plants.'

She bit her lip, daunted, and then rallied. 'You're such a killjoy, William Jones.'

'I'm a realist,' he corrected, 'and I haven't got a bean to spend on PR.'

Of course he didn't. No one did. She almost ground her teeth, but she wasn't going to back down and loose a third pitch this week for lack of a budget. She had something to prove. 'I need some plants for my house,' she suggested.

He fixed her with a look that made her blush. 'I don't think so,' he said. 'The fact is, my business is dead. I have no money to pay for more heating oil, and in one week I'll run out. Then the plants in the greenhouses will start to die. That's the cold and rather banal truth of it all.'

'Never say die, Will.'

He cocked his head, and she wondered if she'd over stepped the mark shortening his name like that. He took another deep breath and rubbed the back of his neck again.

'You game?'

'I can't pay you.'

'William, just for once, stop being so flipping prickly and accept some help from a friend, will you?'

She could see he was struggling not to tell her to mind her own business, and then he seemed to swallow his pride. 'Never say die,' he said.

Vix's Victory

Next morning, Ruth stood in her kitchen with her arms folded tightly across her chest and her head bent. 'You do this the whole time, Vix,' she said in a low angry voice.

It was all too soon. She wasn't ready to go out and meet lots of people. She liked them in small groups: ones and twos at the supermarket, or in the road where they offered a gentle greeting and let her continue on her way. Now Vix was expecting her to meet a roomful. And not just a little roomful. Forty or fifty people. It was the kind of setting where Vix would be in her element, showing off to the crowd.

Meanwhile, Vix was pacing up and down the kitchen, clearly frustrated. 'It's just an hour of being nice to people and signing some books,' she snapped. 'Your books! And basking a bit in their admiration. What's so hard about that?'

Ruth's heart was beating in a lumpy, uneven way making her feel queasy. She wiped her damp palms down her trouser legs and folded her arms again. 'You assume everyone will drop everything and fall in with your plans, but I don't like being coerced.'

'I'm not coercing you. I'm asking you to sign some books,' said Vix, her voice rising.

'You arranged the whole event without consulting me once. A phone call, Vix. That's all it would have taken.'

'You just don't like surprises.'

'Bingo,' said Ruth steadily. 'I hate surprises. I like to think about things. I like to anticipate things. I like to be consulted.'

Vix brushed the objection aside. 'You've got five days to think about it.'

'You should have asked me first. I might have been busy.'

'Busy?' Vix jeered. 'You haven't been out in a year.'

Love her as she did, if Vix was found strangled to death one day, Ruth would not be surprised. 'I didn't say out. I said busy.'

'You just want it to have been your idea.'

Oh my God, had Vix just accused her of being childish? 'I don't want to fight about this, Vix,' said Ruth in her quiet way. 'I just want to be consulted, not railroaded into another one of your projects.'

Vix swung on her heel and Ruth thought she was about to storm out. Instead she leaned against the sink and looked out of the window to the garden where Ruth had clearly given up on an attempt to strim the lawn. 'I'm sorry,' she said over her shoulder. 'I should've asked first. You're right. You always are.'

How devious, thought Ruth, waiting for Vix's next manoeuvre, but Vix surprised her by saying, 'You see, I wanted to help William.'

Ruth waited. Maybe, for once, this wasn't just about Vix.

'Ruth, his business is going to the wall!'

'It's the wrong season for buying plants, that's all.'

'Where've you been, love? The economy is nose diving and taking William's business with it unless we do something.'

'We?'

'I thought this might be a way to get people into his shop. I saw your book and pictured loads of people in the shop queuing for you to sign it. I needed something to hang a story on, and thought this was the perfect opportunity. I never thought you'd object. You like William.'

Ruth shook her head sorrowfully. 'Sometimes, Vix, you can be so manipulative,' she observed.

Vix bristled.

'Oh, it's always for the best of reasons. *Vix rolls up her sleeves and charges to the rescue,*' Ruth announced. Then she added, 'I bet you railroaded William, too.'

Vix opened her mouth to deny this, and shut it. Her shoulders sagged, and she said in a hurt voice, 'I just wanted to help him. To do something. Nobody else was going to do anything. Nobody!'

Ruth shook her head. 'Ah, Vix. You annoy me to bits sometimes.'

A grin lit up Vix's face. 'I knew you'd do it.'

'Next time,' begged Ruth, 'please talk to me before you bulldoze your way through my life. As it happens, I will be busy. Jules is coming up for the weekend.'

'He can come, too,' said Vix quietly, her eyes unfocusing as she began to tumble another angle.

'Vix, did you hear what I just said?'

'Yeah,' came the abstracted reply.

'And?'

'And, what?' said Vix, coming back to the present.

'Ask him. Vix. Ask him first.'

'Oh. Yeah. Natch. But you can see how we could get more people to come by saying Jules Dawson will be there. Jules Dawson!' she breathed. 'Oh my, this is going to be so great.'

'Please, Vix. Ask him, don't tell him.'

'Yeah. I get it. I'll present it as your idea.'

Ruth looked at her askance – Vix really had missed the point. She clearly thought Ruth was throwing her toys out of her pram in a fit of pique. Nevertheless Ruth decided to let the subject drop. 'I've got mushrooms growing out of the ceiling,' she said. 'Curly, rather pretty, yellow-brown mushrooms.'

AL'S HELL

That night, Al fingered the bruise on his arm and slouched lower on his bed. He didn't care that his shoes were dirty and that Vix would throw a hissy fit for getting mud on the duvet. In fact, he'd almost welcome it.

He felt sick with misery and didn't know where to turn. If he talked to his mother, she'd go off the deep end. He could imagine her white-hot fury; it was no more than he deserved.

He looked again at the picture that had just arrived on his mobile. It was going to go viral, clearly implicating him in torching that car.

Shit, he thought, as he pressed the heels of his hands into his eyes until he saw stars. What have I done?

'Choose a car, choose a car,' they'd chanted, and he'd picked a white Subaru without a clue what they were planning.

Now, every time a car slowed in the street outside, he imagined it was the police coming to get him, making his heart smack against his ribs as he waited for it, willed it, to drive on by.

Vix called him down to supper but he wasn't hungry. He didn't think he would ever be able to eat again. She called once more, impatience making her voice rise, and then he heard the thump of her feet on the stairs.

'Al Watson,' she said, flinging open his bedroom door and flicking on the light. 'I've called you three times. Why are you making me come up and get you?'

'I'm not feeling so good,' he ad-libbed.

'Oh, darling.' She softened and laid her palm on his forehead. 'You feel normal,' she said. 'At least, you don't seem to have a fever.'

'I just feel sick, that's all. Maybe it's something I ate.'

'Do you want some toast to nibble?'

'No, thanks,' he said.

A car was approaching in the street outside, and he felt his whole body tune into the sound of its engine. It slowed and stopped. There was a beat of silence, and then he heard a car door slam. He imagined footsteps pounding up the path. He imagined a hand reaching out for the bell.

When the front door bell rang, he almost whimpered.

'I wonder who that is,' mused Vix, turning away.

'Mum,' he called in panic. 'Mum!' He had to warn her.

He heard her on the landing, then silence.

He listened to the accelerated sound of his breathing and heard a low moan. It had come from him. He curled up and buried his face in the pillow, pulling the covers over his shoulder as if they could hide him for ever. He let the pillow smother his moans before he forced himself to sit up, bracing himself for the sound of heavy feet climbing the stairs as the police came to take him away.

What would he say to them? How would he explain that he'd only gone out to join the lads who, if they weren't the inner circle of Gazzer Turner's gang, were certainly up for a lark? He hadn't been bullied into throwing things. He'd been schizzed out and it had turned into the most exciting night of his life. He had no excuse at all. If the police sent him to prison for his part, it would be entirely justified.

I can't go to prison, he thought. I'm just seventeen. There he'd been, minding his own business and the next minute, everything spiralled out of control. Windows were being smashed, and fences ripped up for ammunition. 'Choose, choose,' they chanted. And he laughed and smacked his hand on the Subaru. Seconds later there was the most almighty boom as the car, just metres from where he was standing, exploded in a ball of fire.

A wall of hot air flattened him. He lay there, unable to hear a thing, watching flames peel the sky. Yards away, Gazzer and Paddy were slapping each other on the back – which seemed strange for deadly foes – and laughing like demented hyenas. They were sharing a half bottle of spirits, their arms around each other's shoulders.

Gazzer tugged Al to his feet and offered him the bottle. Al took a swig and choked on the fiery liquid, which sent the two lads into further guffaws of laughter. When Gazzer shoved something in his face, Al, still spluttering, looked blankly at the photo Gazzer was showing him on his mobile phone. He could see Gazzer's lips moving but he couldn't make sense of what he was saying. He looked back at the phone.

That's when he realised he'd not only run amok, but been photographed doing it. It was as if an electric current had zapped through him, instantly clearing his mind. He looked around at the damage they'd done and was horrified. That was Lisa's shop they were smashing as he watched. He knew Lisa. When he was small, she used to give him a lollipop from the jar when his mother went in to buy flowers.

Suddenly, Gazzer and Paddy sprinted him down a side street, away from what turned out to be approaching police, and then they'd split up. He ended up alone in an area of the estate he didn't know, abandoned. As he wandered aimlessly, trying to find a street he recognised, he was repelled by what he saw. Rotting rubbish rimmed the gutters. Disintegrating sofas and old mattresses, soiled and soggy from months of winter rain, had simply been left on the pavement. In a bus shelter, which leaned drunkenly on its remaining posts, he walked past what turned out to be discarded needles.

He shuddered. He could remember when these houses had been built. How shiny and new they had been, like the Lego houses he used to make all those years ago. When he looked up, two foxes trotted past, making for upturned bins. Something rustled in the gutter on his right, and he saw a rat staring back at him boldly. Picking up his pace, he eventually found his way to the main road and home to his nice, warm bedroom.

Now he sat on his bed rocking backwards and forwards muttering profanities. In prison, they'd rape him. He'd heard that. He'd get AIDS and die, all because someone had thrown a bottle at him.

He sat listening for feet trooping up stairs, one two, one

two, sounding his doom.

Instead, he heard the front door slam and then nothing. Outside, the car started up and drove away. He flew to the window. Dragging the curtain aside, he pressed his cheek against the pane to look, but the car was already at the bend in the road, and he couldn't tell whether it was the police or not.

He slid down the wall in an apathetic heap, waiting for his mother to come, to face him, to annihilate him with a look.

CHAPTER 3

SNOWDROPS

Rob had driven by Ruth Dawson's house countless times – it was an old, rambling rectory on the edge of town – but he'd never been in. Someone had mentioned a television programme about the garden, but he hadn't seen it. Another memory insinuated itself. The garden had been open to the public a couple of times; Emma had wanted to go but he had got home too late to accompany her. At the time, he wondered why she hadn't gone by herself. Now he felt sad to have let her down. This was the first time he had driven through the wide stone gates and up the gravel drive of the Old Vicarage. As he did so, the sun pierced the thunderous clouds and the view stilled his breath. Without thinking, he drew the van to a halt, the better to take it in.

Under trees twisted with age, drifts of snowdrops grew in the short green grass silvered with recent rain. It was so perfect that he felt his shoulders drop. For the first time in days, the ache of Emma's departure smudged and softened. Without realising it, his lips curled in a smile.

Suddenly there was a tap on his passenger window. 'Are you all right?' A woman was peering into the van.

He stopped the engine and climbed out. 'Mrs Dawson?' he asked.

Ruth nodded.

'I was admiring your snowdrops. I don't know why. I've never really looked at flowers before,' he added in a burst of candour. He expected to feel foolish talking with a stranger like this, but she smiled.

'Come and take a closer look,' she invited. She gestured him to go before her and followed him across the grass to the tiny dell.

Was he barking? What was he thinking of, looking at flowers? Yet somehow she didn't make him feel uncomfortable at being caught in a moment of contemplation.

When she crouched at the edge of the drift of tiny white flowers, he squatted down beside her. It was still more beautiful closer up. Moss-covered boulders looked as if they had been there since the dawn of time. Droplets of rain caught the light and he found himself reflecting on a single drop and the way the light sparkled through it. When he looked closer, he noticed each snowdrop had a splash of green at the tip of its three outer white petals, and he was enchanted.

'*Galanthus nivalis* Viride-Apice,' murmured Ruth.

To Rob just then, a man not given to sentimentality, it was like hearing poetry. 'I take it that's a fancy Latin name for something as simple as a snowdrop.'

'I like Latin names. They sort of roll off the tongue.' She chuckled to herself. 'My nephew calls it showing off.'

'It's more like an incantation.'

She blinked in surprise.

He stood slowly, gazing round the tiny glen. He took a slow deep breath, waiting for the peace to dissipate, but it remained. 'I didn't expect this,' he said gruffly. 'It's lovely.' She smiled and he found himself smiling back. She was taller than he expected, with pale blonde hair and the milkiest skin he'd ever seen. Her calm blue eyes seemed to look right into him.

'Vix says you have mushrooms sprouting in your ceiling,' he said, when he recovered his voice.

'I have,' she agreed.

There was that enchanting smile again.

'Rather a lot,' she added. 'I showed them to her yesterday, and she said you'd fix it, what ever "it" is, and that I could trust you to do a good job and not rip me off.'

'Sounds like Vix,' he acknowledged, his eyes crinkling in amusement. 'Over-egging the cake in the name of spin. She rang me to tell me to drop all my other clients and sort you out straightaway.'

'Ah, and that sounds like Vix, too. Are you keeping busy?'

'Busy enough in general, but thanks to these troubles, it seems everyone has broken fences and windows to mend.'

'I've always thought of Elderfield as a dull little town. It seems appearances can be deceiving. I hear they even set light to a car.'

'That's right. Just opposite Mrs Mallinson's.' He paused. 'Turns out she didn't see a thing.'

'Is she all right?'

He scratched his head. 'As far as I know.'

'I must go and see her,' Ruth muttered. Then to Rob she said, 'Did you know she was a war hero? She didn't get a medal or anything like that, but she was in the thick of it. They say she had a couple of close shaves.'

'I didn't know. She just seems like a loopy old lady.'

'Yes, she is a bit dotty, isn't she? But get her onto the old days and she remembers everything. They say you forget what you want to remember, and remember forever what you want to forget,' she mused. 'I sometimes think Mrs Mallinson remembers too much. There are stories she can't finish. Can't bury.'

'It's hard, isn't it, when you keep remembering? But sometimes you can't let the memories go because they're too precious. So you worry them like beads on a rosary, round and round, looking at them from every angle except the one you can't face.'

Ruth shuddered and seemed to turn inwards.

'Do you know if she has family?' he asked, bringing her back to the present. 'She's needing some support and Social Services are, well, Social Services.'

Ruth thought a bit and then shook her head. 'There's an estranged daughter.'

'Apart from her; Mrs Mallinson's frightened of her.'

'I don't think Jennifer means any harm, though it's no secret she can't wait to shunt the old girl off to God's Waiting Room down the road.'

'Maybe that might be a better option.'

'Personally, I'd rather gas myself. For all she's eccentric, Susan's quite capable of looking after herself as well as those foul cats.'

'Hm.'

'I'll go and see her later.'

He nodded. 'That would ease my mind. I fixed her window yesterday and – well, you'll see soon enough. Why don't you show me your mushrooms?'

'This way,' she said heading back to the house, 'but I'm sure they're not that urgent.'

Rob smiled. 'They may not be, Mrs Dawson, but Vix has demanded instant action, and when Vix demands, we'd best jump to.' He smiled to invite her to share the joke.

Helleborus various

Soon everyone was talking about the Book Signing. Stung out of their complacency by the anarchy that seemed to have sprung up in their midst, the towns people as a body embraced anything that smacked of respectability. They were fiercely proud to have an authoress in their midst, and told anyone who would listen about the up-coming Book Signing. Over the next few days, several people made a point of stopping Ruth when they saw her in town to tell her how much they were looking forward to hearing her read.

The first time this happened, Ruth rushed round to Vix's house in panic.

'What do they mean, they're looking forward to hearing me read?' she cried the moment Vix opened the door.

'Well, hello to you, too.'

Ruth took a deep breath. 'Vix, explain.'

Vix swung the door wide and Ruth followed her down the passage to the kitchen.

'Vix, you don't understand. They're expecting me to read. Aloud. From my book.'

'Natch.'

Ruth looked aghast. 'What do you mean, *natch*?'

'Darling, it's a book signing. That's what people do. I thought you knew.'

'Why would I know?' Ruth yelped.

'Well, because you're a sophisticated woman. Your nephew's famous – you've been to his book launches, you know what it's like.'

'He never reads!'

'No, but I bet he talks about the book for a good forty minutes.'

Ruth gulped. 'I'm – not – reading – anything,' she said. 'You talked about signing books, nothing else.'

'Would you prefer to talk about the book?' asked Vix, missing the point.

Ruth huffed and paced round Vix's cramped kitchen, stepping over the laundry piled up in front of the washing machine. 'You don't get it, do you?'

'Darling, I thought you'd prefer that than to talk about how you came to write it. I know how hard you find it to talk about Michael.'

Ruth frowned, groping for the connection. 'Michael? What's he got to do with anything? Vix, I'd rather swallow red hot coals than read in public, let alone speak.'

'Didn't you create the garden as a tribute to him?'

Ruth gaped. 'No, not really. I garden because I garden. Oh, this is awful.' She could almost hear people asking who she thought she was to carry on like this. 'Vix, how could you do this to me? I can't do it. I just – I can't.'

'Darling, you're making a terrible song and dance about

this,' said Vix, laying a fortifying hand on her arm. 'I've heard you read to your kids. You're good. Not exceptional, but good enough. You wanna know my thinking? One or two people will come to a Book Signing, but many, many more will come for a quiet, safe, even slightly staid evening out where they'll be gently entertained over a glass of red wine. Last weekend, those yobs ripped the spirit out of this town. This is the kind of thing that will help people start to feel normal again. All you have to do is read a few pages,' she added, reasonably. 'People will stand around and listen, and then they'll buy your book, and you hang around for ten minutes signing them.'

Ruth put her head in her hands. 'But which bit shall I read?'

Vix tried so hard not to show her elation and became very matter of fact, but Ruth could see she was having to steel herself not to give a triumphant whoop. It seemed that she had already identified three possible passages, but recommended the first because it stood well in isolation. It was about Ruth's hellebores.

> They grow in drifts in the woods at the back of my house. Every winter, they push up through the dead leaves and carpet the bank with their subtle flowers.
>
> These days, they self-seed every year, and I have a hopeless time of it on my knees, grubbing around in the dirt, weeding out most of the seedlings. It feels like murder. A few I pot up to sell when I open my garden to the public. Avid gardeners enquire keenly as to the variety, but my hellebores are promiscuous and thoroughly interbred. All I can say is that they will be handsome. But these are my babies, and I find even the dullest one beautiful.
>
> In the first few years of growing them, though, and short of money at the time, I used to carefully dig up each established plant in late spring, rinse off the excess soil to allow me to see the roots better, and then subdivide each plant, taking care to damage the roots as little as possible. At least, this is what the experts in the books tell you to do. This worked perfectly the first couple of years, when I only had a handful of little plants to divide up.

Then I missed a few years – Michael was sick and the garden was no longer my focus. By the time I came back to the hellebores, it was payback time: they had no wish to be disturbed any more.

Picture me 'carefully' digging up an established plant to divide it. For a start, the blighter had a root ball nearly half a meter across. At least, that's all I left it. It was no longer a quick rootle around with a trowel; the plant dispatched two. I resorted to a garden fork, and ditched that for a spade, slicing through the roots any old how in an effort to uproot it. It cost me blisters, broken nails, and a sore back. I recommend you do not dig up established hellebores unless you are doing penance for some heinous crime.

Once the root ball was free, I then had to get it out of the hole, wash off the soil and divide it up neatly. Those were the days when I followed instructions in books religiously. Today, like any more experienced gardener, I have a go, experiment, and if they die, well, I write it off to experience. On the other hand, many plants are amazingly forgiving. Indeed, some delight in being hacked viciously back to the ground – and push up again next year, stronger than the plants you 'put in their place'. You can almost hear them say: 'Naa naa na naa na!'

Back to the hellebore: a woman of my interesting age cannot lift a root ball with a diameter of half a meter. That's when I did my back in. Oops. I left the blackguard in the wheelbarrow for well over three months while I recovered. I left it under the trees unwatered and unloved. In short, I forgot about it.

It was a hot spring. Ah, but this plant was tough. Abandoned it may have been, but not ancient history. It was slightly wilted, but pushing up new leaves when I returned to it. So I decided to continue my splitting efforts. I discovered washing the soil off had a negligible effect. I was dealing with a compacted root ball, not a ball of roots.

'Ease the roots out taking care not to damage them.' That's what the books said.

Yeah, right. In the end, I went to the shed, got out my biggest saw and hacked hard for ten minutes. I ended up with four pieces of root ball, which I replanted and which

did me proud.
    I had fifty more established plants to subdivide. These I saluted with a glass of wine, and left to their own devices. They continue to flower to this day.

Several cups of tea later, Ruth was fully coached on the art of reading to an audience. She and Vix sat by the fire in Vix's frayed, squishy sofas with photocopies of the relevant pages scattered around, now covered in notes. Ruth took a lot of persuading that she would be good, let alone passable, but even she couldn't help but be carried along by Vix's enthusiasm. With a bit of practice, Vix was sure Ruth would be fine.

Yet Ruth knew it was all very well reading aloud in the comfort of a friend's sitting room. She was afraid of drying up on the night.

CONFESSION

It was dark when Ruth came to leave so Vix insisted Al walk her home. Al came sullenly downstairs moaning that his mother was interrupting his homework, and didn't she know he had mocks soon? Vix looked at him in derision over her glasses. 'I know perfectly well you've been on Facebook all evening,' she commented.

At this, he hunched his shoulders and stood by the front door with his hands in his pockets, waiting for Ruth to put on her coat. Doubtless Vix knew her son but Ruth thought he looked exercised about something – maybe he really was worrying about his mocks.

She and Al walked along the streets towards her home in silence. Hoping to encourage a more accommodating mood, she thanked him for being so considerate, but he just grunted in reply. Having brought up two children of her own and a nephew, Ruth, familiar with the world of grunts, continued blithely, 'What do you think of the ruckus in the town at the weekend?'

Suddenly it seemed Al couldn't grunt let alone speak in response. Instead an 'Er' came out as a high-pitched squeak.

'Vix said you went out that night. Did you manage to see anything?'

'No.' The waver in his voice made Ruth pause and she was rewarded when he said: 'Can I ask you something?'

'Sure.'

'What do you think the police will do to those, er, guys who were, er, you know, who, er...' His voice trailed away.

Ruth thought about his response and the ragged sound of his voice. 'Is there something you'd like to get off your chest, Al?'

'Er, you see, it's complicated.'

'It usually is.' There was a long silence which he seemed to have lost the courage to fill, so she went on lightly, 'I remember when Jules was caught smoking what he thought was marijuana. It turned out that one of his friends was playing a prank on him and it was marjoram. The police read the riot act to him. He was fifteen at the time. I had to go down to the station and collect him. Michael was away and I remember how Jules sat there waiting for me to go ballistic. Of course, Michael would have gone ballistic, but I don't do ballistic very convincingly. Anyway, we talked and together we came to an understanding. To this day I don't think he's ever touched drugs.'

They walked past the memorial cross and up the main road towards the church. When they passed it, Ruth slowed her walk to give him more time. At last he ventured, 'Someone threw a bottle at me that night, and I kinda went ape and threw one back, and then it all went mad and we were all running through the streets smashing things. I – I didn't smash things. Er. Not much. Bottles and stuff. But I was there. And I was in a fight. And Gazzer took a picture of me on his mobile, and I'm –I'm frightened the police will come and arrest me, and I think he might post it up on Facebook, and Mum will go ape-shit when she finds out, and I'll end up in prison just because I threw a bottle at someone.'

When he ran out of breath, Ruth asked gently: 'What did you do?'

'I threw a bottle at the cat lady's house and it smashed her window,' he admitted. When she didn't respond he blurted out in a self-pitying whine, 'I only went to see what was going on, and then suddenly I was in the thick of it. I was there when they torched the car. That's where Gazzer took a picture of me on his mobile. But I swear, I swear on anything you like, I had no part in torching the car.'

She thought about this for a moment. She didn't condone what he'd done, but right now, there was a wild card in the pack. 'Did you get a good look at the photo?' she asked, wondering how much it actually gave away.

'Yeah! Holy moly, it's me filling up the entire screen.'

'And what was behind you?'

'What do you mean? It was me. There. Right smack beside the car with this weird expression on my face, like I was drugged out of my brain, which I wasn't. I don't know what to do. Mum'll kill me if she finds out.'

They reached her house; she unlocked the door, troubled by the wild look in his eyes. 'Will you tell your mum?' she asked.

'No way!'

'May I?'

'No. No!' His voice became shrill with panic. 'Please,' he begged, his eyes wide and the cords in his neck standing out as he sucked in air.

'Your secret is safe with me,' she promised, 'but I need to think about this. Give me a few days. Why don't you come and see me after school on Friday?'

He looked as if he wanted to believe her.

'I won't speak to your mum about this without your permission,' she assured him. 'Shake on it.' She held out her hand. It was a freezing night but his hand was clammy when she took it. 'Al,' she said. 'Relax. We'll talk about it on Friday.'

He jerked his head in acknowledgement and lumbered off.

BREAKING A CONFIDENCE

Over a week had passed since Ruth promised Rob she would look in on Susan Mallinson. There was no answer when she knocked at the old lady's door, so she tried the handle and was not surprised to find it unlocked. Pushing it open, the smell hit Ruth between the eyes; the sweet scent of putrefaction easily outranked the sharp smell of cat pee. Oh God, had she come too late?

Every surface of the house, with its stately wooden stairway sweeping down to the hall into which she now stepped, was coated in dust. Skeins of cobwebs hung from the ceiling.

Her tentative 'Hello' was rewarded with a wavery: 'I'm in here.'

Her shoulders dropped in relief. 'Susan?' she called. Stepping over the cats that came out to investigate, she followed the sound of Mrs Mallinson's voice until she found her lying on the floor by an armchair.

'Oh, Susan,' exclaimed Ruth, rushing forward.

'Hello, Ruth dear,' murmured the old woman, feebly. 'I'm so glad you called.'

'Are you hurt? Shall I call an ambulance?'

'Not at all. I slipped and fell a little awkwardly. I just need help to get up.'

Ruth supported Mrs Mallinson until she managed to get to her feet, and then guided her back to the armchair. 'May I put the kettle on and make us some tea?'

'That would be wonderful,' wheezed Mrs Mallinson, plopping back into the chair and closing her eyes. Ruth folded her lips as she took in the texture of Mrs Mallinson's skin, looking so pasty it was almost translucent, and the long strands of silver hair that had escaped the bun at the nape of her neck, and then went off to make tea. When it was brewed, she stirred in extra spoonfuls of sugar, and put it on the little table at Mrs Mallinson's elbow.

'Susan, your tea's here.'

'Mm.'

Ruth frowned. 'Susan, open your eyes and take your tea.'

'I'm not ill, you know,' said the old woman.

'No,' agreed Ruth, 'but you look dreadfully pale for a healthy person.'

Mrs Mallinson gave a cackle and opened her eyes. 'That's because I'm a daft old crone left on this earth too long.' She took the tea in claw-like hands and sipped. Within minutes the colour started coming back into her cheeks.

'How long have you been lying there?' asked Ruth.

'Not long.'

'Do you need help to get to the bathroom?'

'I may be a loon but I can still piss on my own.'

Ruth smiled. 'I never doubted that, but when I'm stiff after gardening, it takes me ages to straighten my back, so I know what it's like to be a bit tottery when you've been in one position for a while.'

Mrs Mallinson waved a dismissive hand at her and she let the matter drop. 'I've made some stew. I was expecting someone to lunch and they didn't turn up. I can't eat it all so I thought you might like some.'

'I see through you, Ruth Dawson,' said Mrs Mallinson, pointing a knotty finger at her.

'It's still good stew. Are you hungry?'

'It'd be a pity to waste the company.'

'Good. It's in a Tupperware box in the car. I'll go and get it. Then I need your help. I have a problem and I need your advice, but it means breaking a confidence.'

Mrs Mallinson smiled, her eyes becoming unfocused as she gazed on the past, and sipped her tea. 'I know how to keep secrets,' she whispered after a while.

Ruth nodded. 'I thought you might.'

SEEING IN COLOURS

A Mercedes coupé was parked on the gravel outside the front door when Ruth returned from lunch with Susan Mallinson. 'Jules?' she called excitedly, letting herself in. 'Jules?'

There was no answer. She found him in the greenhouse potting up lily bulbs. 'Darling, how wonderful to see you.'

He leaned over to kiss her cheek, and she suddenly realised how true her words were: she was delighted to see him. 'Oh goodness,' she said, hugging him. 'I thought you were coming tomorrow.'

'I had a meeting with my producer but she blew me out, so I came early, looking for inspiration.'

'Potting up bulbs?'

'My most insightful moments come when I'm doing something with my hands.' He bent to resume his work. 'The garden's looking wintery,' he added.

'The hellebores will soon be out, but the sniffdrips are up under the trees.' Chilly, she rubbed her arms with her hands. 'Thank you for making a start on the bulbs. Only four hundred or so to go.'

'They'll look amazing in the summer. Where will you put them?'

'I've just dug a new bed along the road as you turn into the drive.'

'I saw it. They'll look spectacular come August.'

'Won't they? I started with eighteen, which Michael gave me on our eighteenth anniversary. Every autumn, I'd split out the bulblets and pot them on until they were ready for flowering.'

'And this is the result? Wow.'

She shivered and rubbed her hands again. 'Come on, it's freezing out here. Let's go in. Did you bring your new girlfriend?'

'Nope,' he said briskly. He was concentrating on potting up

another bulb so she couldn't see his face properly, but she thought she detected a fleeting frown. She didn't want to pry but she also didn't want to seem disinterested, so she tried a neutral question. 'Does she have a name?'

With a brilliant smile, he dusted the compost from his hands. 'Samantha. Samantha Clarke. I met her when we were filming here – she was the PA who kept losing things, remember?'

'And you met her again in London?'

'She moved up a couple of months ago and gave me a call. And, well, one thing led to another.'

'Of course it did,' she grinned, knowing her nephew. He had inherited her brother's good looks, and there was something whimsical about his eyes that made women fall for him. Somehow he managed to look impish and lost at the same time.

'You're looking... good,' he said, surprised. 'But then it's dark in here,' he added, making her laugh.

Back in the kitchen he made her do a twirl for him. 'Hm. The hair suits you. It makes you look all sophisticated again. I like the colour. Quite brave.'

She was piling toasted crumpets on a plate, but paused to brush self-consciously at her platinum blonde bob. 'Vix suggested I go dark, but I thought, what the hell! and went the other way. It's not too much, is it?'

'Lord, no.' He buttered a crumpet and took a bite. 'Classy,' he said with his mouth full. 'You'd better start saving for the face lift to go with it.'

She gave him a friendly smack on the shoulders as she passed his chair. 'I haven't got wrinkles.'

'Only teeny weeny, little baby ones.'

'Next time you're passing, be sure to call in at Harley Street and find out how much a lift costs.'

He leaned back in his chair, mischief in his eyes and said, 'A blonde goes into the desert.'

'I'm not really a blonde.'

'She looks up at the moon, and says, *Which is closer, the moon or New York?'*

'It's bottled.'

He paid no attention. 'Which is closer?'

'Well, New York, obviously.'

'*Duh*, says the blonde. *Can you see New York from here?*

It was such a foolish joke but laughter cracked out of her. 'Oh dear,' she exclaimed, recovering. 'That's terrible.'

He chuckled. 'That was one of Michael's. He was the champion of silly jokes.' As soon as the words were out of his mouth, he glanced up anxiously, but his aunt continued to smile. Her next words reassured him. 'He was, wasn't he? Blonde jokes in particular, but I hadn't heard that one. Tell me about Samantha. I don't remember her.'

'Yes, you do. My producer spent her time shouting at her because she kept putting things down and forgetting where she'd put them. Important things, like microphones and the clip board with my questions.' He caught her wistful expression. 'Or, maybe you don't,' he admitted. 'You were still in a bit of a lonely place when we made that programme.'

She gave his arm a squeeze. 'Was I wretched company?'

'You seemed to forget we were about to lose a father and an uncle. Anna says hi, by the way. She's told you she's off to Sydney, hasn't she? Anyway, she's well. She asked me to set you up on Facebook so you can chat together. And Marty's got a job looking for natural gas in Argentina? He said he'd try and come home before he leaves, but that it's all a bit hectic.'

Ruth nodded. 'Anna mentioned the possibility of Sydney when she was here at Christmas, and I spoke to Marty a couple of days ago. So now you're here to check up on me.'

'I'm here for a relaxing weekend in the country. And,' he added when she didn't respond, 'I promised the others I'd keep an eye on you since they're so far away.'

'It was wrong of me to behave like that. I'm sorry.'

'It's in the past, Ruth,' he said, making light of it.

She sipped her tea. 'I came a bit unglued, didn't I?' She took a breath and brightened. 'But you met Samantha.'

'Met and fell in love. She has the brownest eyes, gorgeous, thick dark hair, and is adorably klutzy.' He laughed quietly. 'She takes everything very seriously.'

'Not like you, then.'

'I can be serious,' he retorted, pulling a serious face. 'Oh, Ruth, she's The One.'

'Darling Jules, you say that about all your girlfriends.'

'Not all of them. Well maybe Katrina. Possibly Pat. Oh yeah, Charlotte was a One, too.'

'How long have you known Samantha?'

'Nearly four weeks. I met her at the Christmas bash.'

'Hm.'

'It's serious, Ruth.' He put his hand on her arm where it rested on the table. 'I want what you had with Michael. When I remember him, he was always laughing and you were always smiling.'

'Michael coloured my days,' she mused. 'Without him, everything is just grey.'

'Still?'

Ruth looked out of the darkened window. 'Actually, things have coloured up a bit. I don't know what's happened, but the garden seems to have reengaged me. And recently, I've come alive to beauty again. There was this bird singing and, well, Vix thinks I've gone nuts. And Rob – he's the builder who's going to sort out the mushrooms in the sitting room – when he came to give me an estimate, he stopped to look at the sniffdrips beside the drive. He seemed charmed by them, and I found myself seeing them properly for the first time in ages. They were beautiful, Jules.'

'I'm so glad,' he said.

'And now you want to marry someone you've only known for four weeks.'

He waggled his eyebrows. 'Jules Dawson run to ground.'

'Treat her nicely, then,' she said.

'I treat her like a queen.'

Ruth pursed her lips. 'And does she treat you like a king?'

'It's early days.'

'How –' she began, but was interrupted by the doorbell. 'That'll be Al.'

'Vix's boy?'

'That's right.'

'Oh?' He sounded interested, but she didn't elucidate.

'Your room's ready and the paper is in the sitting room. Would you light the fire?'

'Sure,' he replied, his interest piqued. 'Shall I take down the Christmas tree?'

She attempted a smile. Look forward, she told herself. Keep looking forward. 'That would be helpful.'

A TOAST TO VIX

At the garden centre, William morosely shut the main doors. Total takings for today: pathetic! He felt like going down on his knees and praying tomorrow's Book Signing would be everything Vix promised.

As he was about to turn out the lights, a delivery van from the off-licence drew up. William unlocked again and went out to greet the driver. 'Jeff! Good to see you, mate. Delivering in person, I see.'

'It's not because I have to,' said Jeff. 'Unlike some.'

Stung, William swallowed his pride, conscious he had laid off another member of staff that afternoon.

'No, I came round in person to tell you to your face that I'm only letting you have this lot on sale or return because I like Mrs Dawson, and I want her evening to go well. She's a good customer and I liked her husband. Mr Dawson was special for all he were rich. Didn't flaunt his money. Made it himself, too. Clever man, he was, unlike some.'

A white line set around William's mouth as he pressed his lips together and forced himself not to rise. 'Thank you,' he ground out.

'Don't thank me. I expect payment for this lot on Monday morning.'

'You'll have it, even if I have to sell my soul,' said William, forcing a laugh.

'Your soul's not worth a squirrel's fart to me. Right, let's get this lot unloaded.'

Vix pitched up as they were finishing, a swirl of scent and lavender scarves. William couldn't take his eyes off her black patent leather shoes. They had red soles. Jeff eased the last box of wine on to the pile and nodded politely at her. 'Ticket sales going well?' he asked.

'Actually, yes. There's been a sudden flurry. Somehow word's got out that Jules Dawson will be coming, so there was a run on tickets today. We've sold around two hundred and forty and calls are still coming in.'

William gaped and mouthed, 'Two hundred and forty?'

Jeff did some quick mental arithmetic. 'Looks like I won't have to sue you for payment after all.'

Vix bridled but William laid a cautioning hand on her arm, conscious she was about to spring to his defense. 'Stow it,' he muttered.

'I'll see you tomorrow evening, then,' said Jeff. 'Put me down for another ticket — I'll bring my wife to see young Dawson. She's ever such a fan of his. Mrs Watson.' He nodded politely in her direction, ignoring William, and drove off.

'Excuse me, but that was completely out of order,' exploded Vix as the van's taillights disappeared down the hill.

'Checking up on me, Vix?' William asked, ignoring her outburst. He was raging at Jeff's insult, but wasn't going to give Vix the satisfaction of seeing it.

'Don't you start,' she snapped. 'I came to tell you how ticket numbers were doing.'

'Never heard of the bleeding phone, poppet?'

She softened. 'Oh, well, I did want to check everything was ready.'

'Come and look round,' he invited, waving a lofty hand in the direction of the store.

'Shall we start again?'

'What do you mean?'

'Hello, Will.'

He sniffed and looked down at her, and then conceded. 'Good evening, Vix. Thank you for dropping by to tell me about ticket numbers.'

'Two forty's quite something,' she admitted.

He chuckled. 'Actually, it's bloody amazing. I was thinking in terms of forty or fifty, and didn't believe you when you told me to order wine for three hundred.'

'But you did!'

'It's best to jump when Vix gives an order.'

She was delighted by his backhanded compliment and preened. Then her gaze fell on the boxes. 'Let's see what you've got. Reds, whites, OJ, sparkling water.' She opened one of the boxes and pulled out a bottle of red. 'Shall we test it to see if it's OK?'

He looked down at her with a smirk. 'You're not as prissy as you make out, Vix Watson. I'll get a bottle opener. You see if you can find the wine glasses.'

She collected a bottle and two glasses and wandered round the store. He had redesigned the place to showcase the book and found himself unexpectedly tense about her reaction to his efforts. Would it be good enough for her? He'd brought in extra hellebores and arranged them around a podium where an armchair and an angle poise light were arranged. Ruth's books were stacked in twisted pillars on tables around the room. Everywhere, he'd accented red with gold. Even the tables in the café were draped in red tablecloths.

'My goodness,' she gasped, 'it's fantastic.'

Of course it was. This was his gig, wasn't it? What the hell had he been worrying about?

He startled her when he put his hands on her shoulders and whispered gruffly, 'You should trust people not to let you down more. You asked for lavish and I promised it, didn't I?'

'Oh Will,' she said, turning to face him, 'but I didn't expect this. This is... I'm stuck for words.'

'The great Vix speechless,' he mocked, and kissed her cheek. Then, sliding his hand down her arm, he took the bottle of wine from her. 'I might even be able to pay you,' he murmured.

She swung away, clearly irritated. It seemed she hadn't done it for the money. Perhaps it had been a challenge; something to prove to local business people that, in spite of the economy, she could single-handedly turn a business around. A secret part of him hardly dared to hope she'd done it to impress him.

'Come on, Vix,' he said. 'Lighten up. What'll we drink to?'

When she hesitated, he thought she was going to say, 'To you.' Instead she said, 'To success.'

'Ever my Vix,' he said. 'Focused to the last on results.'

He was astonished to see her colouring, but pretended not to notice. She raised her glass sportingly.

CHAPTER 4

WRONG MOVE

Vix was feeling mellow as she returned home. That glass of wine with William had knocked the edges off her day. It was Friday evening. Tomorrow she'd put the house to rights, tootle over to Ruth's for lunch, and come home in plenty of time to pamper herself before the Book Signing. Sorted! As for Sunday, well, who knew what Saturday night would bring? She'd go to the Signing wearing that new bra from Rigby & Pellar. It had cost a fortune but the result was a cleavage worth eying. Would she use the new scented oil from the Body Shop, or would she use the cream that Ruth had given her for Christmas, the one that smelled of old-fashioned roses? Decisions, decisions.

As she drove past Mrs Mallinson's, a tow truck was loading up the razed Subaru. The cat lady was watching from her garden, her hair straggling out of her bun, her gnarled hands resting on the gate. She didn't notice Vix's wave.

Vix shuddered. Every time she saw Susan Mallinson, she wanted to take her in hand, starting with that straggly hair. 'Old' did not equate with 'past it' in her books. She glanced in her rear view mirror, and was reassured her own hair was looking particularly nice today. She checked a couple of angles, trying to see herself from Will's point of view, and was satisfied. Pleased with life, she switched on the iPod she had liberated from the mess in Al's room and drove home singing to Mumford & Sons.

As she swung into her short drive, however, her mood turned to one of alarm when she noticed Ruth's car parked in the road outside. Good grief, she thought, she's going to back out of the Book Signing. Suddenly this and her career seemed terrifyingly intertwined. If Ruth backed out now, she, Vix, would never live it down or get work in Elderfield again.

She tripped into the kitchen as fast as her heels would allow, arranging her face into 'polite surprise' as she did so. Al was sitting at the table cupping a steaming mug, and Ruth was leaning against the dresser, a mug beside her, too. Thank goodness he's made her a hot drink and calmed her down. That's my boy!

'Hello, darling,' she said, too abstracted to worry if she were embarrassing him with her super-affectionate hug. 'And hello to you, darling,' she added to Ruth over brightly, pecking her cheek. 'This is a pleasure.'

Steeled for the worst though Vix was, Ruth's hesitation still filled her heart with glue. 'It's OK,' she leapt in. 'I need you to stay calm. It'll be just fine. I know you find this whole thing difficult, but I'm right behind you on this one and I'm really, really grateful.'

Ruth seemed to relax. 'Then you know.'

'Natch. I've been there myself. I know exactly what it's like to feel you're being judged. It's really scary.'

Al's head sank lower. Trust him to be discomfited by the whole nerves thing.

'I see,' said Ruth. 'Well, this changes everything.'

'Oh, good. I need you to be as courageous as you know how.'

Ruth licked her lips. 'Courageous. Yes. That is a good word for it.'

'All you have to do is nerve yourself up and deliver.'

'Er,' said Ruth, looking perplexed. 'Deliver what?'

'Deliver. Perform. Do your bit, obviously.'

Ruth cocked her head. 'Are we talking about the same thing?'

'Chill, darling. Everything's under control.'

'Ri-ight,' said Ruth. 'Then I'll leave you and Al to discuss this together.' With that, she pushed herself away from the counter and gave Al's shoulder a reassuring squeeze.

Vix frowned. 'What's he got to do with it?'

'Is he not the centre of everything?'

Vix stood a little straighter. 'Now it's my turn to ask if we're talking about the same thing. You're having second thoughts about tomorrow, right?'

'Ah. OK. No, this has nothing to do with tomorrow at all. Sit down and let me make you a cup of tea.'

Vix's heart gave a double beat. Ruth was stalling. Was Al in trouble? 'You – make me – a cup of tea – in my own house?' A question mark seemed to force its way between every phrase. 'What – is going – on?'

'Sorry, that came out all wrong. I wanted you to be sitting calmly so we could discuss something.'

Vix had to clear her throat. 'This sounds pretty bad.' She turned to her son. 'Al?'

Al said nothing.

'Ruth, would you fill me in? My son's ducking, which doesn't bode well for him. What's happened?'

Whatever was troubling her, Vix guessed Ruth's instinct was to leave the two of them to sort it out between them. Ruth never had been one to face things head on; she always claimed that confrontation left her feeling like a blithering idiot. However, catching a passing glance between them, it seemed that Al was begging Ruth for something. To hold her tongue? Vix turned to her son. 'Al? Are you in trouble with Ruth?'

'No,' he croaked.

'I'll make tea,' said Ruth.

'I'll make my own tea in my own house, thank you very much, and then we'll get to the bottom of this.' Vix snapped on the kettle and sat down at the head of the table. 'Ruth, you're obviously part of this. Would you care to join us?' She leaned over and drew out a chair opposite Al.

'Thank you,' said Ruth, and perched as if for flight.

'OK. Would one of you please explain what's going on?'

Al looked at Ruth beseechingly, and Ruth smiled back encouragingly. 'This is Al's story,' she said.

'OK, Al. Over to you.'

'Well...' He sat for a long time clutching the mug in his hands.

'He-llo. I'm still he-re!'

'Yes,' he agreed in a whisper. After another long pause, he added, 'I got in a fight.'

Vix dropped back in her chair. A fight. Gordon Bennett, was that all? 'Well, that's not the end of the world. The way you two were carrying on, I thought you'd killed someone.'

Al looked up at Ruth. 'Go on,' she prompted.

'I think, the other day... I was partly... you see, it was like this... there was a bottle... and anyway... then Gazzer, well, he sort of... but it was me really, you see... so anyway, I sort of lost my rag, and... I didn't mean to, and you know...'

Vix leaned forward in utter bewilderment. 'Al, what are you talking about?'

'That Monday. Two weeks ago. In the street fights. I was part of them. But I swear I didn't torch the car.'

There was a long, awful silence while Vix simply looked at her son with her mouth open. 'You were one of those disgusting hoodlums who smashed up the town?' she whispered at last.

'I only broke one window, but I didn't mean... you see, I was trying to miss, but it was kind of mad, and then it was, you know, the most –'

'You belong to one of those gangs?'

'No. Not at all. Not really. Well, yes. No!'

'You either are or you aren't.'

'I got kind of caught up... I didn't mean... You see –'

This was getting worse and worse. Vix spun to face Ruth. 'And why are you involved?'

'Al came clean when he walked me home after –'

'He spoke to *you* about this?' All the air seemed to rush out of her lungs. She knew she was touchy about Al – being a single parent was hard sometimes – and later she would recognise she was nettled that her son had confessed everything to Ruth and not her. Every time Al got into trouble, as he not infrequently did, she felt exposed, as if people were judging her ability to bring up her son alone. Now this!

Worse, she felt rejected, as if, after all the times she had stood beside him facing the headmaster, he'd turned his back on her when he was in real trouble. She thought of herself as an understanding parent. Obviously not understanding enough. The hurt was like a blow, as if he'd physically punched her.

'Fine,' she ground out. 'Just flipping dandy.'

Ruth's attention was focused on Al, and Vix's change of mood passed right over her head. 'We agreed,' she began, 'that he wouldn't get off scot-free. We agreed that he'll make reparation.'

This was too much. Vix erupted. 'Ho! You agreed, did you? Who the heck do you think you are, interfering in my family?'

Ruth opened her mouth to speak, but Vix cut through her. 'Last time I looked, I was Al's mum. I may be divorced, but I can still manage him by myself, you interfering busy body. How dare you agree his – what was it? – *reparations*? How dare you? I am Al's mother. I will decide his punishment. I will set the terms.'

Ruth glanced at Al, but he was playing least in sight. She said, 'I'm very sorry, I really didn't mean to –'

Vix, however, was beyond being able to listen to anything, let alone an apology. 'Just who do you think you are? You take my breath away.'

Ashen-faced, Ruth put her hands on the table and levered herself up. 'I'll talk to you tomorrow when you're feeling more reasonable,' she whispered.

Vix's eyes widened. 'Feeling more–? Feeling –?' She watched Ruth walk out of the kitchen as calm as you please, and sprang from her chair. 'You're unbelievable. Do you know that?' she yelled down the corridor, and then wheeled on her son. 'Go to your room,' she roared.

HEARING LAUGHTER

Ruth's calm was a front. She dropped the car keys twice before she managed to slot the right one into the lock, just as the heavens opened. She pulled out into the road without looking, narrowly avoiding a white van. It slithered to a halt. In her mirror she saw a hand behind the thrashing windscreen wipers wave her on. She acknowledged it and drove round the corner where she pulled up.

She was shaking. She turned off the engine and leaned weakly against the steering wheel. How dare *she*? How dare *Vix* take her good intentions and wipe the floor with them?

She was startled out of her wits when someone knocked at her window. It was Rob Ansell. The builder. Oh God.

'Mrs Dawson?'

There was a lilt to Rob's voice; a faint, attractive accent she couldn't place. She cracked open her window. Rain had plastered his hair to his head. 'Ruth,' she said, distracted. 'Everyone calls me Ruth.'

'OK,' he acknowledged. 'You've stopped...' he hesitated, wiping the rain from his eyes. 'Let's say, there's quite a chasm between you and the pavement. You all right?'

'I'm fine,' she lied.

'Of course you are,' he agreed, flipping the collar of his jacket up against the rain. 'I was wondering if you'd join me for a drink?'

'A drink?' she repeated, totally bemused.

'You're outside the pub.'

She looked around. 'Ah. Yes.' She couldn't seem to gather her wits.

When she didn't move, he said, 'I'm probably being presumptuous, but you don't look *fine*. And the way you drove off from Vix's house...'

Ruth was mortified. 'That was you? I'm so sorry.'

'You'll probably want to park nearer the kerb.'

'Yes.' She started the engine and pulled in.

'I expect Vix was in one of her moods,' he said, as he ran her to the pub and pushed the door open for her.

She couldn't raise a smile. 'You make them sound like regular occurrences.'

'Well, Vix has a temper,' he said shaking the rain from his jacket and hanging it up.

'I've never witnessed it before.'

'No,' he agreed. 'You probably haven't. She talks about you as if you're a wired bomb half the time. Though you seem all right to me,' he added.

She stared at him. What was he talking about?

'Sorry, I'm probably speaking out of turn.'

Was he talking about her?

'What's your poison?'

'Oh.' She couldn't think. 'A gin and tonic. Thank you.'

'Coming up.' He directed her to one of the seats by the fire. 'Go and warm up.'

Despite the cheery glow of the fire, she sat hunched on the edge of her chair, shivering, her clothes gently steaming. Outside she could hear the roar of the rain.

'You look like you're about to make a run for it,' said Rob, bringing over the drinks.

What on earth was she doing here with a man she hardly knew? She stood up. 'Actually, I ought to go home. My nephew's waiting for me.'

'Absolutely,' he agreed, 'though it seems a pity to waste a good drink.'

Feeling foolish, she plumped down again. 'I'm sorry. That was rude of me. Thank you for this.' She held up her glass. 'You really didn't need to.'

'You seemed distressed,' was all he said. He relaxed back and took a long gulp of his beer.

Distressed? What an understatement. She was all over the

place. 'It's strange,' she said at last. 'Everything feels so odd, like I've just woken up. I'm not making sense, am I?' she added when she met his frank gaze.

'Like you've been in a cocoon?'

She nodded.

'Like you're coming up for air again?'

God, he understood exactly. 'Yes,' she admitted. 'My husband died a year ago. Jules – he's my nephew – he said today that I forgot he'd lost an uncle who was more of a father to him than his own. He made me feel awful. I was so wrapped up in my own loss that I lost sight of other important things like him and my children.'

'Don't beat yourself up about it. You were in mourning.'

'Jules said that, too, but that makes me feel worse. They were, too.'

'You must have loved your husband a lot.'

'Yes,' she admitted, waiting for the tears to well up. She was pleasantly surprised when they didn't. 'He was ill for years – leukaemia – but the last two were horrendous. He was in and out of hospital all the time – even blue-lighting it a couple of times. Those trips following the ambulance used to make me sick. Literally. I'd get to the hospital and throw up in the car park. And every time he came home, I'd nerve myself up for the next crisis. I used to dread them. They made me feel so, I don't know, helpless. And when he died, I felt… relieved. That sounds terrible, doesn't it?'

'It sounds like you were exhausted.'

His answer made her look at him anew. He was unlike her husband in every way. For a start he was over six foot tall; Michael described himself as five foot ten but, when pushed by his children, added 'nearly'. While Michael had a soft paunch, Rob was all muscle and sinew. Michael smiled at everything and everyone, but Rob was all brooding and dangerous. He was also a few years younger than her, she guessed. She shivered. 'I've never told anyone.'

'I'll be as silent as the grave.' Then he seemed to hear what he'd said because he added: 'Damn it, I really didn't say that,' but she was laughing.

'It's all right,' she assured him.

He grimaced. 'Yeah and I'm going to need an operation to extract my foot from my mouth, it's gone in that deep.'

'I expect you'll be in hospital at least a week.'

'That long?'

'I'll bring flowers.'

'I'd prefer grapes.'

'If you wait until autumn, you could have grapes from my vine.'

'That's quite a wait. It might be a tad awkward hopping around town on one foot till then. You couldn't just buy them from Tesco?'

She shook her head and grew pensive again.

'Tell me about your husband,' he invited.

'No, it's boring.'

'No, it's not.'

His voice was unsteady, and she glanced up, wondering what she had said to make him so emotional. Perhaps she had misread him – it wouldn't surprise her – because he sipped his drink, clearly expecting her to say something. Gradually, his calm steadiness washed over her and she slipped off her shoes and tucked her feet underneath her. 'Michael was a good man,' she said at last. 'We laughed a lot, he and I. About a day after he died, it hit me that I'd never hear his laugh again. Then there didn't seem any point to anything. When I look back, I can't remember what I've been doing since he died. That must sound pathetic.'

'No, not really.' His eyes welled with understanding and she looked away.

'But I must be beginning to let him go; today – this week, actually – the pain of losing him doesn't bite in quite the same way. He was my soul mate,' she added. 'Oh, we had fights like any normal couple but, at the end of the day, he completed me. I expected to be with him for the rest of my life, but he left me behind.' She laughed at herself. 'Oh my. How whiney that sounds, but it's not. He left me behind, and I'm beginning to see that I can survive. No! Not just *survive*,' she amended. 'That life will be fun again. Just the other day – with you – I realised that I can still look at a bunch of snowdrops growing under a tree and be moved by their absolute beauty.'

'They caught me unawares, too.'

He was so easy to talk to. She hadn't even talked like this with Vix. 'You sound like you know where I'm coming from.'

'My girlfriend, Emma, she left me recently.'

'And you still love her.'

'I thought she was my other half. Obviously, she doesn't think the same.'

'It hurts, doesn't it?' she said when she could bear the silence no more.

He nodded. 'It's like a knife twisting in your gut, all day, all night, there when you go to sleep, there when you wake.'

She thought about how she woke in the mornings when, for the briefest moment, she didn't remember… then it all came back. 'Those are the worst times of day, aren't they? when there's nothing to distract you. How long –'

Just then, William hailed them and wandered over. 'Chatting up the ladies again, Ansell?'

Ruth watched a subtle change come over Rob as he made himself light again.

'You know Ruth Dawson, don't you?' he said.

'Should do. She's kept my garden centre going practically single-handed over the years. How are you, Ruth?' He shook her hand.

She rose. 'Well, thank you, William.'

'You're looking… different.'

'It's the hair.'

'No, it's more than the hair.' He grinned. 'I'm looking forward to seeing you perform tomorrow.'

'Assuming my nerves don't get the better of me.'

'Ah, you'll be fine. Care for a top up? I see Ansell's manners are as bad as ever and your glass looks as dry as a nun's... looks empty.'

'Thanks, but no. I was just leaving. Thank you for rescuing me,' she added to Rob.

'I'll see you tomorrow, then,' he said, rising.

'You will?'

'At the Book Signing.'

'Gosh. Everyone seems to be coming.'

'I'm looking forward to hearing you read. You have a nice voice.'

Ruth was too confused to reply. She raised a hand in salute and left.

THE JULES EFFECT

William was almost crowing. The garden centre was stuffed with people buying plants and he was beginning to wish he had his full complement of staff again.

The Book Signing last night had been a huge success. Ruth had been magnificent: calm and collected in spite of her obvious nerves, and looking surprisingly beautiful. Surprising, because he was still having trouble shaking off his memory of her as a melancholy husk of a woman. He clearly wasn't alone in noticing the quiet transformation. He'd even caught Rob watching her from the back of the room and had ribbed him about it. However, the highlight of the evening had most definitely been her nephew, Jules.

Of course, the men were keen to shake the lad's hand – trust Jeff from the off-licence to be first in line – but the women went mad for him. They were too polite to mob him, but the fawning had been ludicrous. The funniest thing was their reaction to an accident he'd had earlier in the evening. Jules had cut his hand trying to dig the stone out of an avocado, and had come to the Book Signing with a plaster over it.

Unfortunately, he'd knocked it getting out of the car and the blood had welled up badly enough for William to get out the first aid kit to dress it. Word had gone round, and William had never seen the mothering instinct expressed quite so forcefully by quite so many women at a time.

It did look like a nasty cut to William but they smothered him in concern. They asked if he was OK, thought he looked peaky, suggested he get it stitched, advised him to have a tetanus jab and warned him not to get it dirty when he was gardening. They didn't just recommend he wear gloves for gardening the next day, several women bought a pair and presented them to him. Meanwhile, the lad stood patiently and smiled what seemed a genuinely sweet smile, while the photographer from the local paper snapped him with every single one of them.

What impressed William most was his charm. It wasn't obvious from the way he behaved that Jules was a rapidly rising television personality. The opposite. He was as down to earth as his aunt. Not once did he get frustrated with his admirers. Everyone he talked to came away thinking they were fascinating, which had made William want to roll his eyes. They'd returned today thanks to a throwaway remark that he'd be back to buy some plants for his aunt's garden. William was practically kowtowing to him. Even the photographer was back, this time with his wife. And they didn't just come to gawp. They were snaffling up plants by the truckload.

Vix pitched up when William was at his busiest and winked at him. He wanted to kiss her, he was so grateful. Instead, he gave her a thumbs-up and went on taking payments. The Hellebores were selling like hot cakes. Thank the Lord Vix had given him a heads-up on that one.

BALM

Rob was all keyed up when he turned up at Ruth's house on the following Monday morning for work. At the Book Signing, his gaze had kept sliding back to her. Although William had noticed, he hoped no one else had. This woman was having the strangest effect on him, as if things were building up to a crescendo.

He couldn't decide if he found her attractive. He hadn't fancied anyone but Emma for longer than he could remember. Lisa was pretty but not his cup of tea. Jill was sweet but sexless. Vix was a definite possible, even though she was a little older than him, but he could see she'd be hard work. For the last couple of years, it had just been Emma; she was the most exciting thing he'd ever had in his life. Now he wondered if the fifteen-year age gap between them was the problem. At twenty-five, she was still awfully young. Had she met someone nearer her age and used his going out on that job as a strategic exit card?

Or maybe it *was* his fault. Maybe he had left her alone too much.

No! He had customers, responsibilities. He had a mortgage to pay. Didn't she understand he was out working for her? She'd been completely unreasonable.

Yet the hurt of her departure was nothing compared to the hurt of her deliberate disappearance, which prevented him from talking things through with her – no, be honest: begging her to come back. She hadn't answered her mobile, her friends hadn't heard from her and even her parents hadn't seen her after that first night.

After a grim fortnight he was beginning to get used to the idea that she was gone for good and that there was nothing he could do about it. Yet the feeling of helplessness seared him.

Meanwhile, for some reason, Ruth's presence acted like a balm on him. At the Book Signing, he'd tried to figure out what her effect was, but had come away as perplexed as ever. Somehow she made his pain feel, briefly, like a memory. So he hardly knew what to expect the first day he turned up for work at the Old Vicarage.

As it turned out, things couldn't have been more banal. She was on the phone when she opened the door and stood back to usher him in, talking all the while. Sure, there was a welcome smile, but her mind was on the phone call. She waved a hand to indicate he should get on, and so he shouldered his tool bag and trod upstairs to the bathroom.

This was ensuite to her bedroom. The first time he'd come, he'd hardly noticed this, focused as he was on a quote for the rot in the bathroom. Now he didn't know whether to avert his eyes or look his fill. He indulged himself. A sofa stood at the end of a double bed. Books were piled on every surface of the room, even on the bed. Most were garden reference books but he also noticed a couple of popular economics books – *The Undercover Economist* was one he recognised.

Here and there were photos in silver frames, he presumed of the rest of the family. He picked out Jules straightaway, but there was another serious looking young man, and a girl who looked like she could be Jules' twin. On the bedside table was another photo. Michael, he presumed. He looked like a regular fellow with slightly dissipated good looks and a kind smile. Rob would have liked to have taken a closer look, but it wasn't on the path to the bathroom and he drew the line somewhere when it came to respecting people's privacy.

He was soon carting old linoleum and rotten chipboard down the dust-sheeted stairs to his van. Ruth came for a progress inspection, opened the door to the bathroom, and waved her hand in front of her nose in disgust. 'Euww, Rob. This smells like a public latrine. It's vile.'

'That'll be chipboard, well soaked.' He cleared his throat. 'Ruth, you know I warned you there might be extra expenses?'

She grimaced.

'Yeah, well, you see these beams. I reckon they've had water soaking into them for years and they need replacing. Here, come and look.' He held out his hand.

She looked uncertainly at the holes in the floor and then at the beam he was standing on.

'You'll be quite safe.'

She took his hand and it felt warm in his palm. Her grip was strong but not panicky. She seemed reassured by his smile because she stepped across the beams and came to his side.

'There,' he pointed.

'Yes, I see.'

Her tone was dubious, and he tried to see it from her inexperienced eye. He bent down and pushed his screwdriver into the beam in front of them. It came out the other side. Her eyes widened. 'Oh goodness. I do see.'

'The best thing to do is rip everything out and start again,' he said, handing her back to safety.

She took a deep breath. 'What kind of numbers are we talking about here?'

'I'm going to have to chip all the plaster off the walls down there,' he said, indicating the sitting room below, 'and up here a meter high. It'll need treating for dry rot. Then it'll need replastering and redecorating. We're talking about a new bathroom, two new beams, a new floor, the works.'

'That sounds expensive.'

'I estimate around four thousand.'

'Four...' she squeaked. 'It can't be that bad. Are you sure? Yes, of course you are. Vix said I could trust you, and I do, I do, only it always seems that builders only ever uncover more work.'

He met her gaze candidly. 'I know how it looks, but I hadn't taken up the chip board when I gave you my estimate.'

'Four thousand,' she repeated.

'I'm pretty sure your insurance policy will cover everything.'

'Will it? I suppose so.' She frowned. 'I don't know. Michael dealt with that kind of thing. I wouldn't know where to start.'

'Would you like me to look at your policy and check?'

'Yes, please,' she said in a voice tight with apprehension.

She made tea and fed him biscuits while he thumbed

through her insurance documents. He took his time explaining the relevant clauses. When he finished she sat back looking dazed. 'Tax forms and paperwork always made Michael impatient with me. Usually I don't get them, but you've made it all so simple. I'm going to have to rethink my assumptions on life.'

'I reckon the small print is designed to make you panic so you don't put in a claim. I've just ploughed through more of it than most people.'

She fingered the papers. 'You're very kind, Rob. Thank you.'

Was that disappointment he felt? He wanted to be more than just kind in her eyes, which was weird given he hardly knew her. He gave himself a mental shake. 'You'll want to call them and make a claim,' he advised, standing up.

She got up with him and he towered over her; he'd never felt so tall but he realised he must have alarmed her because she took a step back. 'Thanks for the biscuits. They're my favourites.'

'Will you be back tomorrow?'

It *was* disappointment. How foolish could he be? 'Best get the work signed off first. It's the fault of the last plumber. Remember the pipe work I showed you? Just point it out to the assessor. I'll make everything safe before I leave. Call me when they've given you the OK.'

As he left, he saw her pick up the papers again and bite her lip.

REPRIEVE

William sat with his feet on the desk and looked through the office door to his store. It was the beginning of February, the season to buy seeds and shrubs and to start preparing hanging baskets, but Laura, his part-time assistant, was at the till filing her nails with nothing to do.

The Book Signing had put him on the map again. Or so he'd thought. A week later, with no Jules Dawson to lure them in, it seemed that yesterday everyone preferred to spend the day reading the Sunday papers. Once again his business was running through his fingers like sand. Worse, the bank manager was due in half an hour. He'd sit lumpishly at the desk full of I-told-you-sos – the Book Signing was never a dead cert for him.

William rocked back on his chair. Tonight could be the last time he closed the garden centre. Real men don't carp, he thought sourly. As wondered what he'd do next, Vix teetered through the double doors from the car park. 'Will?' she called.

'In here.' He swung his legs to the floor and sat up, his mouth slightly agape at what he beheld. She wore perilously high heels, a suit that nipped in her waist and a blouse with a completely distracting neckline. The result was all curves and red lips. For a moment, William was utterly diverted.

'You look like the first course,' he said as she minced into his office.

'Argh, I'm sorry,' she said by way of greeting. She wrung her red tipped fingers and he suddenly noticed how pale she looked under her perpetual tan. 'I've ruined everything,' she added. 'I'm so sorry.'

'What have you ruined?'

'I was coming to distract Hugh and – oh, sweet balls of fire!' She buried her face in her hands.

'Who's Hugh, and why are you trying to distract him?'

'Hugh Duffy, darling. The bank manager.'

'Oh, him. We aren't precisely on first name terms, him and me, which kinda says it all in this day and age. Why were you trying to distract him anyway?'

'He fancies me. He's fancied me since school. The creep always has a grope at the Hunt ball. His wife turns a blind eye. She dresses like a frump, the silly cow. If my man strayed, I'd make myself so sexy, he'd go crossed eyed.'

'You're having that effect on me now,' he admitted.

'I knew you were meeting him,' she went on, as if he hadn't

spoken, 'so I thought I'd come along and throw him off the scent so he'd delay closing you down.'

William was gob smacked. This wonderful girl was still trying to rescue him. 'Ah,' he said, finding his voice with difficulty. 'Thank you. I think. So what's the problem?'

'Ah, well, you see, I had a leedle prang in the High Street. Not on purpose, believe me, but his car sort of leapt in front of mine while I was – oh blooming heck!' She screwed up her face in distress.

'While you were what?'

'I was doing my lips, OK?'

'Your –?'

'Lipstick, darling. I was putting on my lipstick.' She pouted at him.

'And you do this while you drive?'

'Well, how was I supposed to know he'd come out of a side street without looking? Anyway, as your diversion, I have a teensy feeling I'm now useless. I'm so sorry. I'll make myself scarce.'

She bent to kiss his cheek and was about to leave when the phone rang. He rested a hand on her hip to hold her there. 'Wait a mo,' he said, and lifted the receiver. 'Hello. Elderfield Garden Centre,' he said formally.

While William listened to a woman on the phone, Vix apparently decided she liked his somewhat possessive hand on her hip because she relaxed back against his desk. Her nerves betrayed her as she fiddled with her bracelet, although she was clearly as alive to him as he was to her because her gaze kept skittering away from his.

At last he let her go to draw a desk diary towards him. 'OK,' he said, scanning the empty columns before him and turning a couple of equally blank pages, 'I can squeeze him in in three weeks. Let's say Friday at 1pm… Yes, I do realise how important this is, but I have a business to run… Fine. I'll see him then. Please send him my good wishes for a speedy recovery.'

He replaced the receiver, stood up and smacked a kiss on her mouth in one fluid motion. 'Sweetheart, you're a wonder. We have our stay of execution.'

As kisses went, it was probably the brusquest kiss he'd ever given a woman but her coy manner didn't deceive him, especially when he leaned forward and experimentally brushed her lips with his again. She moaned so softly he almost didn't hear her. Then she caught his lapels, lightly tugging him towards her. This time the kiss ignited them both.

'You'll need to put that lipstick on again,' he said, his breath fanning her face, when at last he pulled back. 'Bloody hell, woman.'

It was the kiss he had hoped for on the night of the Book Signing.

'It wasn't a very good kiss, was it?' she whispered unsteadily, obsessively stroking the material of his jacket.

'No, it was slightly frayed at the edges,' he agreed. 'Shall we try it again?' he asked, nudging her forehead with his.

She gave a mock shrug. 'I don't know if it's worth it.'

'I'd like to see if I can't do better this time.'

'Goodness me,' she murmured breathlessly a while later, her fingers clenching his lapels.

'Goodness me, indeed.' Lord, she smelled good. 'But I'm going to need a lot more practice,' he said, slightly shakily. He reached for her again, but Vix eased out of his embrace. 'Perhaps,' she said, 'but your lovely assistant's eyes will be popping out of her head if we carry on like this.'

He glanced around for Laura, but she was nowhere to be seen. 'I'll send her home.'

'At midday? No, darling. You have a business to run.'

He gave a harsh laugh. 'No I don't. The Toad may have rescheduled –'

'You can't call him The Toad.'

'Mr Duffy is a conceited toad who suffers from the misconception that bank managers are still important people. If he'd come today, he'd have closed me down. The fact is, I have three weeks to turn this place around. I might as well top myself now.'

'Perhaps I could get some PR for the place, you know, to get people back in again.'

'Ah, the cavalry!' he said bitterly, letting her go.

'I might come up with something, you never know.'

He shook his head. 'I'd rather take you to bed.'

She batted his hands away. 'Be serious.'

'I am. The garden centre can't possibly compete with you.'

'No, no, no,' she said backing away. 'You may be finished for the day but I have work to do so I'll bank that kiss for now, although naturally...' She frowned. 'There is no competition,' she ended in a thoughtful tone.

William touched her hand. 'I think I've lost your attention.'

She beamed at him. 'Ha! I've had an idea. Better, miles better, than the Book Signing. I'm so brilliant.'

'O-K. Now, I made money on the Book Signing, so I'm kinda game, but your ideas, Vix, they're expensive.'

'They work, though.'

'N-yes,' he conceded. 'But it was a one week wonder.'

'Exactly. What you need is sustained publicity and an imperative for people to keep coming back.'

'Uh-oh. I've a feeling this is going to be much more expensive.'

She frowned.

'You're tossing up whether you can charge a lover,' he ventured.

Her eyebrows shot up. 'That's a bit quick, isn't it? One kiss and suddenly we're lovers.'

'Well, we are, aren't we?' he growled, and pulled her close.

'Stop it. I can't think straight when you do that.'

'We're lovers,' he asserted, releasing her. 'And you're going to charge the business not me.'

'Actually, I was trying to remember when the next town meeting was. Is it this Thursday?'

'Yep. And get this! The proposal is to convert the old school into a YMCA.'

'Oh, great timing. That's what we really want around here: more yoof hanging about. Bugger.' Then her head snapped up. 'Actually, I take that back. The meeting'll be packed. Oh my goodness. It's going to be perfect.'

'Are you going to fill me in?'

'Not now. I need to think it through. You'll be the first to hear.'

'That sounds ominously like you're leaving.'

'There's only so much polishing young Laura can do on that till.'

He was not interested in his assistant. 'Later?'

She pulled a face. 'You're a great kisser, William, but I have an impressionable son at home.'

He sucked his teeth. 'That sounds just like a brush off. Suit yourself.' He drew himself up and jerked his jacket straight.

'No. I mean you can't… I can't… Not at my place.'

'You women talk a language I have never understood. Do I get to see you this evening?'

'Yeah.' Her eyes shone.

'I'll book a table at the Pauper's Arms. That suit you?' He leaned down to press another kiss on her lips.

'Assuming you can get a table.'

'The landlord owes me one. Hm. You might want to put some more of that lipstuff on before you leave.'

She gave her lips an exploratory lick.

'Go on, scoot, before I change my mind. I'll collect you at seven thirty.'

She pirouetted and waved at him over her shoulder.

OLD TREE ROOTS

A few days later, the insurance company approved the works at the Old Vicarage, and Rob was back on the job. This time he was more relaxed. Last time he'd been here, nothing had happened. Meanwhile, Ruth hadn't been unfriendly since his return, she just hadn't been around. Mostly she was in the garden. At one point yesterday afternoon, he had stood at the window for the longest time, watching her struggle with some old tree roots. He had been tempted to go and give her a hand but had resisted. Today she seemed no further on and she was having a go with a pickaxe.

She swung it ineptly and missed her leg by a hair's breadth. It set his teeth on edge to watch her raise the pick above her head again. He couldn't bear to watch and went down to the garden.

'You'll do yourself an injury if you go on like that,' he said, walking up to her.

She straightened and blew a wisp of hair out of her eyes, and then snagged it behind her ear, leaving a graze of dirt on her forehead. Now why did that make her look attractive?

'Here,' he offered. 'Let me do that.'

'I shouldn't be taking you away from your work.'

He glanced at her. 'I'd only have to stand at the window to make sure you didn't stab yourself.'

She looked embarrassed and held out the pick to him.

He was careful as could be to tread around her plants, aware that each one was precious, and managed to get away with trampling just one. She was pretty nice about it and claimed it was a waste of space anyway. It was one of her hellebores. He didn't believe her.

After labouring for an hour the root gave way and he heaved it up.

'Thank you,' she said, elated.

He bent to retrieve the pickaxe, his expression thoughtful. He found he liked making her smile, which muddled him because he felt he was being disloyal to Emma, which was crazy given she'd been gone nearly a month.

'Come on. Let's go and have a hot cup of coffee,' she said.

'Not for me,' he exclaimed, wiping the sweat from his face.

'I could murder a glass of cold water, though.'

'I'm freezing.'

He caught hold of her hands and they were indeed cold. He chafed them. 'On the other hand, coffee would be nice,' he amended.

In the kitchen she put on the kettle. How did making coffee seem like a courtship dance all of a sudden? She seemed self-conscious, as though aware of his gaze following her around the room. They spoke nothing but commonplaces until he finished his coffee and went back to work where he thought about her all afternoon.

When he got home, he looked up Hellebores on the Internet. Then he remembered he had her book, and reread the passage on them. However, that didn't help him source them, so he called William and invited him down to the pub.

'What do you want a Hellebore for?' demanded William. 'You don't garden.'

Rob hadn't figured on William's curiosity. 'I just want one.'

'OK. I have loads of Hellebores you can have,' said William.

'No, I don't want anything you have. I want something unusual. Something special.'

'What for?'

'To give someone.'

'Are you going to tell me who, or must I prise the information from you one slow admission after another?'

'It's for Mrs Dawson.'

William raised an eyebrow. 'Ruth has wall-to-wall hellebores. So give.'

'I trod on one of her hellebores today. Damaged it beyond repair, regrowth, whatever.'

'You're killing me here, Ansell. And?'

'I want to replace it.'

'This is like getting blood out of a stone, mate. She slings in a seedling. Job done. So why would you want to replace it?'

'She said it didn't matter, but I could see it did, and I wanted to get her another one.'

William's expression became sly. 'Are you…?'

'Definitely not.'

'Mm.'

'You keep your dirty little thoughts to yourself, Jonesy.'

William laid a theatrical finger to his lips. 'I'll keep mum.'

'Nothing's happening.'

'But it will.'

Rob groaned. 'No it won't. I wanted to be nice. I broke a plant and felt badly about it. She said it didn't matter, and I got the feeling it did. End of story. End of speculation.'

William brayed with laughter.

Rob wished he'd kept his mouth shut. He gulped down his beer and put the glass down on the table with a thunk. 'You can buy the next round.'

'My pleasure,' said William.

'Oh sod off,' said Rob, but he was laughing.

CHAPTER 5

STEPPING INTO THE LIGHT

Bruce Turner had probably been a committee man in the womb, thought Rob as he sat in the crowded parish meeting room on Thursday evening, bored out of his brain. There was nothing Bruce seemed to enjoy more than being at the centre of power: he liked to think he made things happen, or, in this case, not happen. At the front of the room, a hapless developer was trying to make his case for turning the old school into a YMCA. Meanwhile, Bruce was not being as diligent as he ought about giving him the floor.

The scheme's supporters – shopkeepers, the café owner, publicans, craftspeople, and the local garage manager – were all vocal in their demands that Bruce allow the developer to speak uninterrupted. However, they lacked a leader with enough charisma to remind Bruce that his job was to chair the meeting, not be partisan at this stage.

The developer had other supporters who were not so vocal. While Rob was in favour of a YMCA, he sat at the back of the room with his arms folded and kept his counsel. Fighting Bruce Turner on his turf was not the way forward. You only fought Bruce when you were sure you had everyone's backing. Unfortunately no one had explained this to the developer, so he hadn't known to canvass support in advance.

Rob stretched out his feet and clasped his hands behind his head. He angled his head in such a way that anyone glancing his way would think he was giving the events at the front of the room his full attention, but he was actually watching Ruth, who sat in the row in front of him. Yesterday William had assumed there was something going on between them. Was he so capricious that, within weeks of losing the woman he thought he loved most in the world, he was beginning to look around again? By all accounts, Ruth had retreated from the world for a year to recover from her loss.

No! He was not fickle. Comprehensively rejecting someone and then giving them no chance to right any perceived wrongs did not exactly invite loyalty. If he were at fault, so was Emma. If she had felt so badly, why hadn't she said something?

Lisa, the florist, got up. She had fistfuls of dark hair long enough to sit on. Rob imagined running his fingers through it. She was stunning and young and reasonably bright. So why was it an older woman, who had expressed no interest in him to date, who was making his heart beat a tad unevenly?

'You were voted in to clear up the streets,' Lisa said to Bruce. 'So what are you doing about it?'

Bruce blustered and Rob's attention waned again. He wondered why he was here. William had insisted he come but hadn't turned up himself. It occurred to Rob that ninety per cent of the people in the room were from the old town. Only one or two were from the new estate. The gangs came from there; that the estate was so badly represented at this meeting made more clashes inevitable. The people from the estate didn't feel they belonged. Sure, over three weeks had gone by without any thuggery, but that was not unusual. They'd clash again. It was just a matter of time, and nothing Bruce said tonight would make the blindest bit of difference, because, Rob realised, Bruce was a man without vision and without leadership.

Suddenly William was walking towards the front. Rob did a double take. When had he arrived? Uh-oh. He looked as if he had the bit between his teeth. What was he up to now?

A quick glance round the room told him William's progress had taken everyone by surprise. What happened next made Rob drop his head in his hands with a groan. When William reached the front, he turned to the audience and said, 'What this town needs right now is something to juice it up.'

So that's why I'm here, for my support. You idiot, this is not how to get the chairman on side.

'I propose,' William continued, 'that we run a garden competition. I want you to do up your gardens. I'll offer the winner two hundred quid's worth of plants from my shop. Can't say fairer than that, can you?'

A stony silence greeted his announcement. They saw right through the ruse. Rob noticed Vix sitting near the front shaking her head in exasperation. William had jumped the gun in his enthusiasm.

Bruce Turner cleared his throat and folded his arms. 'All those – ' he began.

'Excuse me,' came a muted voice.

Bruce frowned at the interruption. 'All those –'

Ruth stood up quietly. He cleared his throat again expecting her to sit down, but she stood her ground.

'Mr Chairman, I wonder if I might address the room before we vote, please.'

Her profound calm undermined him and there was nothing Bruce could do but beckon her forward. She didn't move and chose instead to speak from the middle of the room. 'As you know,' she began mildly, 'William is very direct.'

A titter ran round the room.

'We like that about William.' She smiled and other people smiled back at her. 'He tells it to us straight.'

William stood up to speak, but Vix jerked him back down.

'But his idea is part of a bigger concept. Let me give you the thinking behind it. Meanwhile, we can vote on the YMCA proposal when we've done more research.'

Rob smiled approvingly. That was neatly done.

'But for now, we live in a beautiful town. As towns go, it's pretty small: little more than a village with a few shops before the estate was built. But it's got history. We're mentioned in the Doomsday Book. We fought for Cromwell. We have one of the oldest and largest village fetes in the country. Our Morris

Dancers are invited to dance around the world. Elspeth Ryder is in *Britain's Got Talent*.'

There was a general cheer.

'I can tell you, I'll be glued to the box every week, following how she does. I reckon she'll get to the finals, and I'll spend my 50p to vote for her when the lines open.'

There was another round of whoops.

'In other words, we've been there, got that T-shirt. This little, insignificant town has survived the plague. It's seen real civil war, and we've seen success. And now this lovely old town, with its creamy stone walls and Norman remains, described in numerous tourist guides as *quaint* and *worthy of a visit*, is being torn apart. Kids burn out cars on the green. They spray graffiti on our walls and fences. They brick shop windows.' She turned to face Bruce. 'Mr Chairman, I know you and the other counsellors are concerned about the mayhem that's taken root in our midst and been wracking your brains to find ways of uniting the town. You want people from the estate to feel this is *their* town, not just *ours*, that it's something precious to every single person who lives here, somewhere we're all proud to live.'

Rob sat forward and scanned the room. Everybody was craning forward to hear her soft voice. This shy person, the one Vix said could hardly bring herself to read aloud in public, had gripped them. Even blustering Bruce was nodding sagely. Rob was flabbergasted.

'While a garden competition might look like an odd idea,' Ruth continued, 'I know Bruce believes this town needs a project anyone and everyone can get involved in. It needs a project to bring us all together. With Bruce and the other counsellors' permission, I propose we enter the whole town into the Britain in Bloom awards.'

Everyone started talking together.

'This is a nationwide competition,' Ruth continued quietly, and the room fell instantly silent to listen to her again, 'which recognises communities that take responsibility and action to regenerate their local environment. We'll have our work cut out for us because, despite our *picturesque* appellation, a gold medal won't be a given. To succeed, the judges will want to see the campaign embrace the entire community, not just the town square.

'To improve our chances, William will be getting in experts to give talks at the garden centre. William, by the way, will be giving his advice for free.'

Again William jumped up and again Vix pulled him down.

Ruth continued diffidently, as though she had not been interrupted: 'As I will give my advice for free… if you want it.'

At this, there was a general laugh. Who would not want her help?

'My nephew, Jules, many of you know. Jules?' She turned to the person on her right. 'Say hello to everyone.'

Jules duly stood up and raised his hand in a self-effacing greeting. There was a collective intake of breath.

'If Bruce and the rest of the counsellors agree, Jules would like to film the transformation, from, quotes, the cradle of crime to gold medalist in the Britain in Bloom Awards, for a new BBC TV series called *Village People*.'

Jules' eyes widened involuntarily, but he kept his mouth shut.

'Now, Mr Chairman, when we discussed this, you felt, given the right leadership, a townwide competition would go a long way to help heal the rift between the us-es and the thems, between the old towners and the new towners.' She looked round the room slowly. 'So I urge you to vote with the chairman on this.' She nodded at Bruce. 'Thank you for allowing me to speak, Mr Chairman.' With that, she sat down.

The room erupted in talk, each person animatedly developing the idea with their neighbour. The level of excitement was palpable.

Rob gazed at Ruth in awe. In front of him, Jules leaned towards Ruth. 'Great idea,' he whispered, 'and what if my commissioning editor thinks otherwise?'

'You'll say he changed his mind.'

'Seriously, it's a gem.'

She glanced at him. 'Do you mind that I'm using you?'

'Blatant exploitation. But I wish we'd had cameras here to film this.'

'There'll be time for that later.'

'We'll line up an interview with you –'

She held up her hand. 'It's not my idea, Jules. It's Bruce's.'

'Bruce Turner's?'

'Yes. Remember that.'

'O-K. When did you speak to him about this?'

'I lied. This is about them, not me, Jules. It's what we need to bring the town together.'

'But aren't you going to lead them?'

'I'm not a leader, Jules.'

He shrugged. 'OK. You're the boss.'

She laughed. Rob sat transfixed by the excitement that shone from her.

LETTING GO

That weekend, the phone rang as Vix was stuffing clothes into the washing machine. 'Hello?' she said.

'Vix, it's Jules.'

'Hello, darling. How the devil are you?'

'I'm good, thanks, but I have a problem and wondered if you might be able to help.'

''Course!'

'It's Ruth.' She bit her lip and he went on cautiously, 'I don't know what happened the other day. Ruth hasn't said a word, but she came home really upset after seeing you. She seemed OK but now she's sitting on the floor in her bedroom surrounded by Michael's clothes, just staring into space. I don't know what to do.'

'I'll come round. Anything to get out of housework.'

'Thank you.'

Vix's car now looked much better than before – the garage had straightened out all the dinks, not just the bonnet. She drove to Ruth's house slowly, not out of concern for her car, but because she was thinking. She had to admit that Ruth had saved William's bacon on Thursday and that Ruth's idea was bigger and better than hers, but she still felt sore, although her anger had dissipated. Beside her Al glared out of the side window. He was gated and sulked in his room most of the time. She'd brought him along with her because she wasn't ready to let him out of her sight. Naturally this peeved him and he was being tiresome. Tough! He could strop at Ruth's house as well as anywhere.

Jules greeted her warmly when she arrived and pointed upstairs. Ruth was sitting exactly as he had described. She scratched at the open door and Ruth looked up.

'May I come in?'

Ruth stared at her. 'Gosh. I thought I was in purdah. How are you?'

'I'm well.' Vix sat on the bed.

Ruth nodded. 'Good.'

'You?'

'Good.'

'Good.' Vix looked around the room unsure how to go on. She'd spent many an evening in here playing backgammon with Michael until he had become too weak to sit up. She used to come round a couple of nights a week, drink her after-work glass of wine, and reflect on the day with him. He'd given her many insights, and without his encouragement she would never have felt confident enough to approach bigger clients. When he died, she'd missed him as well as his guidance.

She missed Ruth, too. The last couple of weeks had been lonely without her; it was ridiculous to have been so touchy about Ruth's good, if irritating, intentions.

'I'm sorry –' they both began.

Then together: 'You first.'

They both laughed.

'I'm sorry I interfered.'

'I'm sorry I got so angry. I was hurt that he spoke to you not me.'

Ruth nodded. 'He was too ashamed.'

'Yeah. How do you think that makes me feel?'

Ruth bowed her head. 'How's it going between you two?'

'Badly. We're not speaking at all. What's happening here?'

Ruth picked up a shirt and dropped it. 'I decided to Oxfam his clothes. It's time to move on.'

Vix looked at the numerous piles and took a fortifying breath. 'Need some help?'

'Yeah. I find it extraordinarily difficult. I can't choose what to pack in boxes and what to keep.' Ruth drew an old jersey to her face and inhaled. 'You know the worst thing? His clothes don't smell of him, any more. They have that sweet Oxfam scent about them. I wish I could remember his smell.'

Vix slid off the bed and gave her a massive hug. 'Oh, darling.'

'Don't. You'll have me in tears,' said Ruth, her voice cracking.

'Then we can cry together.'

'Jules'll think we've gone mad.'

'It's a girl thing.'

'Life's not fair, is it?'

'No, said Vix. 'The best of men die, and the worst of men push off and leave you saddled with debts.' Then she added: 'But things change.'

Ruth wiped her eyes. 'I suppose so.'

'No, darling. They *really* change.'

'What do you mean?'

Vix waggled her eyebrows suggestively.

'Oh?'

'Yep.'

'I'm all ears.'

'Will Jones is a very good kisser,' Vix whispered.

'Ah.' It was amazing how much curiosity could be crammed into one little syllable.

'Pass that box over here.'

Ruth chucked the box in Vix's direction. 'You going to 'fess up, or what?'

'I'll put these sweaters in here, shall I?'

'Vix?'

'Sweaters?'

'Do what you like, but don't leave me like this. I want to know everything. What's going on between you and William? When did it happen? How? Where?'

THE SENTENCE

By the end of the morning, boxes containing Michael's clothes were piled high in the hallway. Ruth ran a hand over them. 'I don't know if I can actually take them to Oxfam,' she admitted. 'It's like the point of no return.'

'It can't be me,' said Vix, putting a comforting arm around her shoulder. 'It's something you have to do.'

'I'll do it later in the week.'

'Al's here. Let's get him to load your car now.'

'Really, there's no need.'

Al slouched against the window, looking out into the garden and ignoring them both.

'He'd be happy to help,' said Vix.

'Thank you. It's just…' Ruth tipped her head back, determined not to cry.

Vix held out a wad of hankies but Ruth shook her head. 'I'm fine.'

Jules put his head round the door. 'Coffee, anyone? I've made a fresh pot. Oh, and I've found where Ruth stashes her chocy bikkies.'

'Those were for...' She stopped. 'Thank you, sweetie. Let's have a break.'

'Al?' Jules called, as the boy began to follow the women to the kitchen. 'Help me load this lot in the station wagon, would you? It'll be quicker with the two of us.'

Ruth paused in the doorway. 'I'll do it later,' she protested.

Her nephew pretended to misunderstand her, and they both knew it. 'Really, it's no trouble. It'll take two ticks.'

She grimaced but turned to follow Vix to the kitchen, where she found her wilting in a chair. It seemed neither of them had expected to find sorting out Michael's clothes so emotionally draining. Ruth pulled out a chair at the other end of the table and nibbled apathetically at a biscuit.

'You talked about reparations,' Vix announced suddenly.

'Oh God, Vix, don't bring that up again. I've said sorry. I haven't got the energy to discuss it. Just take it from me, I was out of order to suggest anything.'

'I'm not beating you up again. I'm stuck,' said Vix. 'I can't communicate with Al. He only opens his mouth to be rude to me. It's horrid at home. He says these vile things. I'm sure he doesn't mean them, but somehow he seems to hit the jugular every time.'

The two young men ambled into the kitchen. Al grabbed the plate of biscuits and helped himself.

Vix sighed, and Ruth could see she was deciding whether to pull him up for his bad manners. It turned out that she didn't need to. Her sigh was apparently enough to elicit a reaction from him. He curled his lip and demanded: 'You got a problem with something, Mum?'

'Yes,' she said. 'You're behaving...' She gave up. Now it seemed was not the time for another battle, which made Ruth angry. 'You're being rude, she means.'

Al looked abashed. 'I'm sorry, Ruth. May I have a biscuit?' he said, spitting crumbs as he spoke.

'Don't apologise to me. It's her you ought to be apologising to. She's worked hard to give you a nice life and you're behaving like a pig.'

'You don't know anything about it,' he said.

'I know bad manners when I see them.'

'Al, just leave,' said Vix, jumping up. 'Go away. I'm sick to death of you.'

'How do you think I feel?' he challenged.

'I couldn't give a rat's arse. You're behaving boorishly. I don't know why. I didn't run riot. You did.'

'Will you shut up and listen, Mum. There is nothing you can say, nothing, that I haven't already told myself.'

'I think,' began Ruth in her low voice, 'you've had it easy for too long, Al.'

Vix opened her mouth to speak, but Ruth held up her hand. 'My turn, Vix. Al, I think you've been an idiot. I also think you got caught up in events outside your control. You should have walked away and, maybe, next time you will. I hope so. But for now, grow up. Your sulks are boring and childish.'

'I'm not sulking.'

'Yes, you are.'

He pointed to his mother. 'She doesn't let up! Ever! She bangs on and on about it.'

'Be glad, Al,' said Ruth, suddenly fierce. 'Be very glad. I'd give anything to be able to have a good shout at Michael right now.'

'I don't know what she wants me to do.'

'For a start, you can bite your lip and show her some respect.'

He hung his head.

'You owe Mrs Mallinson. You broke her window and you terrified her.'

'I'll pay for her window,' he muttered.

'That's not enough. How do you compensate for fear, Al?'

He thought about it. 'Dunno.'

'You comfort.'

He looked perplexed.

'She's very old. Over ninety. She was active in the war. Did you know that?'

'You mean one of those Land Girl thingies?'

'A bit more active than that. She's known real fear, the kind of which I hope you'll never have to face. Do you think it's right for a ninety-year-old woman, who has faithfully served our country, to be terrified out of her wits by some stupid boys who should know better?'

'I didn't mean to frighten her.'

'And that makes it better?'

'Well, yeah.' He took in her appalled expression and changed his mind. 'No it doesn't.'

'I should think it doesn't. So what have you done about it?'

'Nothing,' he mumbled.

'Yep. Nothing. You haven't gone round and offered to pay for her window. You haven't even said sorry. You holed up in your room and sulked because your mum, for once in her life, can't make things right for you. And for some reason beyond my comprehension, you think that justifies your anger at her.'

He sat lower in his chair. 'I felt embarrassed.'

Her voice softened. 'That's a good place to start, Al. So what are you going to do?'

'I dunno. Go round and make amends. Pay for the repairs.'

'Nice start. But, I don't think that'll cut it. Not after all this time. No, I think something more is required, don't you?'

'Like what?' he asked warily.

'I'm going to suggest you give up your afternoons after school and spend them with Mrs Mallinson –'

'The old cat woman?' he exclaimed.

'– for the next three months,' she finished.

'Three months!'

'You reckon it should be more?'

'No!'

'You weren't going to suggest less, were you?'

He hunched a shoulder and huffed, 'What will I do there?'

'Keep her company.'

'Three months.' he groaned. 'What if I say no?'

'Are you sorry, Al, or is this apparent regret all a huge sham?'

He reddened and worried the hem of his shirt. At last he said, 'I'll go.' He reached sulkily for the plate of biscuits, thought for a moment, and then whispered, 'May I have another?'

Ruth pushed the plate towards him. 'Help yourself.'

'Do I have to go in the holidays?'

'Especially in the holidays. Weekends, too.'

He bit his biscuit unhappily, brushing the crumbs onto the floor.

'You can start this afternoon. I'll drop you off on my way back from Oxfam. I'd appreciate some help with Michael's... with those boxes.'

He nodded miserably.

Vix relaxed for the first time since the discussion began. 'Thank you,' she mouthed at Ruth.

THE CAT LADY

Ruth dropped Al off at Susan Mallinson's gate.

'You aren't coming in?' he asked.

'No.'

'What do I do?'

He could see Ruth's smile was meant to be reassuring. It wasn't. 'You walk up to the door and press the bell.'

'Duh,' he said, only half joking.

'You'll be fine.'

He pulled a face. His memory of Mrs Mallinson was of a smelly old woman who farted in the supermarket.

He pressed the bell as instructed and waited. And waited. No way was he going to press it again... but what if it hadn't rung properly? Shit, he didn't remember hearing it himself. He pressed the bell again and heard it clang faintly in the distance.

He looked at his watch. You've got one minute, you old dingbat, then I'm history.

He counted the seconds off and then turned back down the garden path.

'Yes?' It was a threadlike call but loud enough for him to hear. He turned unhappily and saw Mrs Mallinson leaning on a Zimmer frame in the doorway.

'Ah. I'm, er, I've come round, and, er…'

'Come in, dear boy. I've been expecting you these last couple of weeks.'

'Oh?'

'I saw you throw that bottle.'

'Ah.'

'Mighty fine throw. My father bowled for Somerset, you know.'

'I, er, didn't know.' He took a breath, and then choked as bile rose into his mouth. A sour smell of dried urine emanated from her. This, combined with the nauseating, sweet smell of death coming from the house, made him hesitate.

'Close the door after you,' she said over her shoulder as she shuffled away into the gloom.

Behind him, it started to drizzle: horrid wet stuff that made everything feel damp through and through. Back down the garden path, beyond the overgrown garden, was the street; he could see where he'd stood that night. He remembered how the bottle had arc'd through the air. It was not a fine throw. There was a good reason he wasn't on the school cricket team. That bottle was never meant to break a window, but to smash harmlessly against the wall, making him look like one of the brethren but without doing any real damage. He turned back to the darkened house. What am I doing here?

A cat wound its way through his legs, pressing against him, and he shoved it away. Dirty, foul thing. Two more cats trotted ahead of him, their tails high, as he followed the alternating clonk of the Zimmer frame and the shh shh of her slippered feet on the wooden floor. In the sitting room, two more cats sat on the table. One leapt off and skittered past him, disappearing down the passage. He began to lower himself into one of the armchairs, then realised it stank of wee and leapt up. There was just one hard chair in the room, and yet another cat lay curled up asleep on it.

'Don't disturb him,' said Mrs Mallinson, as he bent to tip it off the chair. 'There are plenty of other seats to choose from.' Her Zimmer frame caught in a hole in the carpet and she struggled for a moment to free it.

He hesitated before moving over to stand by the window.

'Now, don't be standing over there. I can't see you without craning my neck. Come and sit opposite me.'

Anger rose up inside him. This was ridiculous. He didn't have to be here in this loathsome house with this raddled old woman who sported a fuller moustache than his own. Nothing was keeping him here. He was a free agent, wasn't he? He pushed past her and ran back down the corridor to the front door, flung it open and bolted down the path to the gate. Out in the road, he loped in the direction of Gazzer's house. He'd wash his hands in disinfectant when he got there. When he thought about sitting in that repulsive armchair, his flesh crept. He slipped and staggered on the wet pavement, and slowed down.

Nothing would induce him to return to that house. Nothing. He may be sorry for what he'd done, but going there was beyond the call of duty. He'd pay for a new window and be done with it. But as he walked along, a memory nagged him. He remembered knocking into her. Hardly touching her really, just barely brushing against her. What dogged him was the memory of the old woman in the first split second of over balancing, just reaching the tipping point.

He remembered her shambling through the house and the clunk of the Zimmer frame.

He remembered how feeble she had looked.

He slowed and stopped and wiped the rain off his face. He took a couple of steps forward, then stopped again. For several long minutes he tussled with himself. At last, he swung round and jogged back the way he had come.

If she'd fallen – shit, it didn't bear thinking about. He picked up his pace.

The front door was still open. This time, he hardly noticed the smell as he burst into the sitting room. He stood there, all out of breath, his chest heaving, and took stock. She was sitting calmly in an armchair. Slowly she looked up.

'Dear boy, I thought you'd gone.'

'I had, but I thought you'd –' Fallen, he wanted to say, but couldn't say it.

'Did you close the front door?'

'I'll close it now,' he said dully, and retraced his steps. He was inclined to slam it, but swallowed his frustration and shut it quietly instead.

'Have a seat,' she said on his return. 'Push the cat off the chair and draw it closer so I can see you.'

'What about the cat?'

She raised an eyebrow. 'The cat can find somewhere else to sleep.'

The small black and white cat flexed lazily in his arms when he picked it up. Until then, he'd thought of her cats as vermin, but this one had particularly silky fur, and he brought it up to his chest for a fleeting hug. In the corner of the room, there was a hair-covered armchair, and he gently deposited the cat there. It looked at him with large green eyes, and then closed them and started purring.

What was he supposed to do? Where was he supposed to begin? He pulled the chair slightly closer to the old crone.

'Would you make us a cup of tea?' she asked, no sooner had he sat down.

He nodded, relieved, and scouted round until he found the kitchen. This was as disgusting as the rest of the house. He ran the hot tap to wash some mugs, but it remained obstinately cold. Then he noticed the house was freezing. It was February and there was no heating on.

He carried the steaming mugs through to the warm sitting room, placed her tea on a small table beside her, and immediately forgot about the rest of the freezing house.

The mug gave him something to do with his hands. He sipped slowly, glancing at the clock every few moments; the minute hand seemed to have stalled. At last, five o'clock chimed. One more hour.

Mrs Mallinson seemed content to look out of the window. Her farts were audible and added to the pungent odours in the room. He bit his nails. He ruminated on the wrongs of life and how he was being imposed upon, and how unfair it was that he had to endure this. None of the other boys was being punished. He'd been a mug to own up. A flipping mug. So what if there was a picture of him on Gazzer's phone. Gazzer wouldn't shop him. Now this. They'd laugh at him on Monday if they learned he was babysitting the cat lady just because he'd broken her window.

At one minute to six she looked at him over her glasses. 'Time's up. See you tomorrow.'

He stared at her, his mouth open. She didn't really mean it. He had hoped against hope that she would be bored and suggest he needn't come after all. Shit. He had three more months of this.

As he shut the front door behind him, he heard soft laughter.

What the hell! She thought this was funny.

A red mist descended and his reaction was to stomp on the snowdrops that grew beside the path. He was in a towering rage by the time he got home.

CHAPTER 6

AWARENESS

William was fed up. 'But it was my idea.'

He was lounging at the far end of a sofa from Vix in Ruth's sitting room, surrounded by the Sunday papers, at what was probably an unspeakably early hour on Sunday morning for him.

'If we're being strictly accurate, it was my idea, actually,' said Vix. 'Which Ruth developed,' she added as an afterthought, hearing Rob's slight intake of breath from across the room.

In the two days since the parish council meeting, Jules had worked manically to rope in the support of his producer to make the documentary, and call in favours to assemble a film crew. Now William, Vix, Rob and Ruth awaited Bruce Turner's arrival so they could start filming.

Ruth was not sure why Rob had been invited, but presumed Jules wanted a tame builder on hand; Rob himself had been very laid back about coming along. He had plunked down in Michael's old armchair, which strangely hadn't affected her at all, and was flipping through the sports section, but judging by the way he seemed to keep rereading the feature on yesterday's rugby international, his concentration was as shot as hers.

She sat apart from the others at the small table in the centre of the room, trying to ignore Vix and William's bickering. She was thinking about the tree roots, and how Rob had helped her get them out. Since then, it was almost as if he had been avoiding her, which was, of course, totally silly. Why would he?

'Anyway,' Vix snapped at William, 'what do you care, so

long as people come and buy their ruddy bedding plants from you?'

'I care, I care,' said William, jabbing himself in the chest with a finger and half launching himself from the sofa as he did so, 'because that stupid moron couldn't organise a piss-up in a brewery. He's going about it all the wrong way.'

'Oh, and you never do that?' retorted Vix. 'What was it? Now, let me think. Ah yes, I have it. *What this village needs right now is something to juice it up.* Well, he-llo. You should listen to yourself sometimes.'

'We haven't all got your way with words, Miss Perfection.'

Vix and William had been sniping at each other since they'd arrived. Afraid that she would snap at one of them if they didn't let up soon, Ruth got up. 'Would you like a cup of tea, Rob?'

He leapt up so fast that she almost laughed. It seemed he couldn't bear the petty squabbling any more than her. 'I'll come and help you carry it through.'

Behind them, the row escalated until the sitting room door swung shut and cut off the sound. They walked through to the kitchen, Ruth aware of Rob's every soft step behind her. She wondered what he was thinking and whether he was watching her the way he sometimes did, the way that was beginning to make her feel out of breath.

In the kitchen, the film crew slouched in chairs with empty mugs in front of them. The garden door was open and the cameraman was smoking in the doorway, flicking his ash onto the doorstep. In a corner of the kitchen table, the soundman was playing cards with Al and the production assistant; judging by the pile of coins at his elbow, the PA was winning.

Jules swung his feet off the table and sat up. 'Is Bruce here?'

Ruth shook her head.

Jules pulled out his mobile and scrolled through his contacts, and then went into the hallway to make a call.

'Here, let me,' said Rob, taking the kettle from Ruth and filling it up. It was a while since anyone had helped her with anything so mundane. She glanced round but no one else seemed aware of anything momentous. Cards continued to slap the table. The cameraman ground his butt into the doorstep, came in and shut the door behind him.

Rob plugged the kettle in. When he turned to lean back against the counter he caught her studying him. His smile in response was unexpectedly winsome, but it faded as his gaze dropped to her lips, where it lingered. After what seemed like a season, he raised his dark eyes back to hers, his expression slightly stunned.

She turned away abruptly to sort out a tray with mugs and milk, her mind in a flat spin. It felt as if he had kissed her.

When she glanced back, he was staring at the ceiling, worrying his bottom lip with his teeth. He cleared his throat. 'William and Vix. Not an easy combination,' he said.

Ruth had to force her mind back to the present. 'I expect, when they've known each other a bit longer, it'll settle down.'

'It'll go on until she understands he wears the trousers.'

He obviously doesn't know women very well, she thought. 'Pray it happens quickly, then.' This time it was he who looked away, busying himself with the teapot.

'Thank you, Rob,' she said, when he picked up the tray.

He gestured her to go before him. They crossed the hallway again, each conscious of the other, and each not knowing quite what to do about it. Ahead of them an ominous silence was coming from the sitting room.

'D'you think she's killed him?' said Ruth, in an attempt to lighten the mood.

He played along. 'Maybe he's scarpered.'

She opened the door, and said, 'Or maybe not.'

Vix and William were locked in a clinch in the middle of the room. Perceiving they were being observed, the couple broke apart sheepishly. Rob set the tea tray down and retreated to the window.

Ruth wondered, from the way he stood so still, whether he was still in shock from that surreal moment in the kitchen, and as confused about it as she was. 'Tea, William?' she asked, preparing to pour.

Vix, blind to the change of mood between Ruth and Rob, started laughing. 'Oh dear, Ruth. This is embarrassing. We come to your house and scrap like teenagers. Then the moment you're out of the room, he jumps on me.'

'Actually it was the other way round,' put in William.

Ruth was not interested. 'Any idea where Bruce is? He's normally so punctual.'

The doorbell rang. It seemed to be a signal for action because suddenly everything was happening at once. Rob, William and Vix followed Ruth, who went to open the door for Bruce, just as Jules came out of the kitchen followed by Al and the film crew, who were all shouldering bits of equipment and checking clip boards. As she put her hand on the door, Jules reached out and stopped her; he wanted to film the greeting.

The bell rang again. 'Wait up, Ruth. We're just sorting sound,' he murmured.

Ruth glanced at Rob and found him watching her with a brooding look in his eyes. She dropped her gaze, strangely shy. 'Jules, I can't leave him on the doorstep.'

'Just one more sec – Pete, are you turning over? Great.'

When Jules finally gave Ruth the go-ahead to answer the door, Bruce was no longer on the doorstep but half way back down the drive.

'Blimey, is it always this chaotic?' asked William, as Jules trotted down the drive to catch Bruce. The two men shook hands and conferred. Then Jules returned, shut the door and spun a finger in the air. The film crew took their cue and turned on their various recording devices.

'Doesn't he say "Action"?' asked William, just as the doorbell rang. Jules raised his eyes to heaven. 'Give me patience. Cut,' he called.

He opened the front door. 'Give us a minute and do it again,' he asked Bruce. Then he retreated to the back of the room. 'Quiet, please,' he said, and immediately there was silence.

Jules looked at William. 'Action.'

Someone's mobile rang just as Bruce rang the bell.

Jules folded his arms. 'Whose phone just killed my scene?'

'Mine, sorry,' said Al. Jules pretended to cuff him. He opened the door. 'Sorry, mate. Do it again.'

Bruce beamed. It was clear he was perfectly happy to reshoot as many times as Jules wanted. Indeed it took all morning, and many retakes as Bruce fumbled his words, to film Ruth greeting Bruce, their preliminary discussion about running the competition and then Bruce filling out the entry forms. William gnashed his teeth and fumed. 'This is my project,' he muttered. 'He'll get all the glory and I'll end up with all the donkeywork.'

'Your chance will come,' said Ruth, carefully avoiding looking in Rob's direction.

William looked balefully at her and continued pacing up and down the sitting room. 'You know why he was late, don't you?' he whispered loudly to Rob. '*I can't wear this,*' he minced across the room pretending to fling clothes aside. '*Do these trousers make me look fat? I look like a chav in that colour. What I want, what I really, really want is some bling to wear nestled against my manly chest.*'

Vix shoved him playfully and he frowned and stopped clowning. 'Seriously, Vix, does my bum look big in these trousers?'

'Shh,' choked Ruth, as Vix giggled girlishly and patted his bottom. 'He'll hear you.'

In the end, they skipped lunch. Jules, twitchy about losing the light, insisted they work on. He walked down the High Street planning the shots with his cameraman, and then they clipped microphones to William, Rob and Ruth, before Bruce led them down the street as they discussed how to bring the town up to scratch.

By the end of the afternoon, William was almost foaming at the mouth. Rob laid a steadying hand on his shoulder and William allowed himself to be guided off to the pub. Ruth was about to turn for home when Rob invited her to join them on the pretext of planning what needed to be done.

'What about you, Vix?' asked Ruth. 'You joining us?'

'I've got to get back for Al,' she said regretfully. 'It's his second day with Susan Mallinson.'

'Remember what we agreed if he bottles it.'

Vix nodded and was about to leave when William stepped forward. 'A pint of the usual,' he said to Rob. 'Give me fifteen minutes.' He held out his arm to Vix.

'No one told me you were a gallant knight,' she said.

'Can't have you walking home alone on a night like this. It's not decent.'

She squinted at the sky. 'A night like this? But it's perfect.'

'Exactly,' said William. 'Pity to waste it.' Then he put on a frog-like Bruce voice and said: '*Oh yes. I'm very important. And what I have to say is Important because I'm an Important Man in this town. And what's Important is the Town. Oh yes. Young people should clean up their own Mess. When I was young, young people were Deferent. They showed Respect for their Elders. Respect is the Thing. That's what we Want in this Town. The Loathsome Yoof, Scum of the Earth, will be Brought to Heel.* Tell me, does he realise what a pompous ass he is?'

It was early and the pub was nearly empty when Rob and Ruth walked in. He ordered a gin and tonic for her without thinking. 'I'm sorry, I didn't ask what you wanted,' he said when he brought it over to where she was warming her hands in front of the fire. 'You cold?'

She shook her head. 'This is fine, thank you.'

He nodded and sat opposite her. 'Filming went well.'

'Didn't it?' she said. Is that all she could come up with? She couldn't remember feeling this jittery for years, and all because she was having a drink with a man on her own.

'I thought Bruce was heavy going.'

Rob didn't seem affected at all. Maybe she had imagined that almost-kiss. 'He's not precisely eloquent.'

He gave a crack of laughter. 'Mumbling and tongue-tied, more like. It was supposed to be his big idea but you had to keep feeding him his lines. Honestly, you'd think he could remember, *I had an idea and it just mushroomed.* It's not that hard.'

'That's because you've got mushrooms on the brain.'

'He's a fraud, Ruth. Seriously, it won't work if he leads us. What was that business about inspiration? Something about spring coming, and daisies? He didn't make sense. You've got more inspiration in your little fingernail than he could summon up if they put a gun to his head. I thought, at one point, Jules would punch him – you remember when he put his hand on Bruce's arm and just squeezed it?'

Ruth had never heard Rob so vocal. The exchange seemed to clear the air between them again, and their conversation became animated as they discussed the rest of the day's filming until William's return.

Later he offered to escort her home, but her reserve inhibited her and she insisted she was happy to walk home alone. Vix, when she heard this the next day, scoffed. 'You silly woman. He fancies the pants off you.'

Ruth gasped. Though not immune to Rob, it was something else entirely to have someone else notice it. 'That's crazy. He's much younger than me.'

'Well, hello to you, Mrs Robinson!'

'No really, Vix.'

'Darling, he doesn't seem to mind, and it's *younger*, not *much younger*.'

'Jesus, Vix.'

'Oh for goodness sake, Ruth. Every woman needs a toy boy when she gets to a certain age.'

Ruth coloured.

'I told you,' Vix continued, without noticing Ruth's reaction, 'what you need is sex. Don't let him slip through your fingers because you're finicky about your age. You're still shy of the big five-oh, unlike me. Besides, you don't look your age any more. You were right.' She flicked Ruth's hair. 'Platinum is much better than light brown. It's knocked a decade off you.' She fingered a lock of her own hair as if contemplating what blonde would do for her.

'Think about it, girl. And next time, don't be so bloody independent. Allow him to walk you home. He might even kiss you on the doorstep. A tongue in your mouth will stop you thinking for five minutes. When Will kisses me, I can't unscramble my brain for hours.'

Ruth couldn't even formulate a reply.

'Don't tell me you haven't thought about kissing Rob.'

Ruth thought back to that breathless moment in the kitchen. The feeling of him having kissed her was so strong that she could almost taste him. 'Maybe,' she conceded.

'That's my girl. So?'

'I'll think about it.'

Vix groaned. 'I give up. With you, that's like saying no.'

'No, no. Really. I'll think about it.'

'Yeah. Right.'

MAGGOTS

Al griped and wheedled when he was sent off to Mrs Mallinson's after the first day of filming. He wanted to hang out with Jules, but his mother said he'd be late if he didn't hurry.

Late? What did the old hag care if he was late? She wouldn't care if he never turned up at all. About to be defiant, he had made the mistake of glancing Jules's way, who raised his eyebrows as if he couldn't believe they were having a discussion about this. Shamed, Al let himself out.

In Mrs Mallinson's garden, he hurried past the crushed snowdrops with barely a glance. The witless old woman wouldn't know anyway. She wasn't going anywhere with that stupid Zimmer frame. He hammered at the door and leant on the bell just to be sure she heard. At least, that's what he told himself. Eventually, he heard her clonk and shuffle and was suddenly tempted to run away and hide, the way he and his friends used to when they were younger, then watch her sound off to thin air from their hidden vantage point, each convulsed by stifled sniggers. They used to press her doorbell over and over. It must have driven her mad.

'So you stayed to face the music,' she said by way of greeting.

He turned from his contemplation of her garden to see her framed in the doorway, so lost in memories that he hadn't heard the door open. 'Good afternoon, Mrs Mallinson,' he said formally.

'When you were younger, you used to hide under that big Ceanothus by the front gate.'

He was startled that she seemed to have read his mind but wasn't about to let on that he'd been one of the punks involved.

'It took me ages to make the den in there.'

'The – the den?'

'Well, you didn't think that great big cavernous space in the middle of a bush was natural, did you? Lovely bush,' she added. 'It turns powder-puff blue in spring, with thousands of little bottlebrush flowers, d'you remember?'

'But...'

'I was younger then, and more able to wield a saw. Even so, it took me several days to make it.'

Al found himself laughing. 'And there we were with our escape route all mapped out for when you called the police on us.'

'Up through the juniper, along the back of the box bush, under the holly –'

'And out over the back gate,' he finished for her, realising even that had been her work.

'I needed help with the escape tunnel bit. Rob Ansell helped me drag the branches away. Nice man, Rob. Well, are you just going to stand there letting in the cold?'

'I'll come in,' said Al, diffidently, seeing this crazy old woman with new eyes. Far from calling the police out on them, she had been the architect of whole summers of daring adventures. Troubled, he wondered if another generation of small boys would be out to taunt the old cat woman again this summer. What a seriously sad way to get yourself company.

The house smelt worse than before. She invited him to make tea, and he peeled off to the kitchen while she clonked slowly through to the sitting room. When he came in bearing two steaming mugs, she was sitting in her chair with her eyes closed as if she were meditating. It was only when he placed her mug on the little table beside her that he noticed the snowdrops in a jam jar.

Oh shit.

He looked up and found that she was watching him with her little beady eyes.

'Sorry,' he said.

'Speak up.'

'I said I'm sorry.'

'No need to shout, I can hear perfectly well.'

Of course she could. She just wanted him to say it properly. 'I'm very sorry I broke your snowdrops,' he said in a more measured tone.

'Saved me the bother of having to pick them.'

'I was feeling —'

'Don't make excuses, boy. Your apology was pretty, and came from the heart, but I can't abide people who make excuses as though that makes their behaviour acceptable. We've all had a belly full of thieving politicians who build duck houses at tax payers' expense and who don't know how to say sorry when they're caught.'

'What?'

'The expenses scandal?'

What the hell was she talking about? He tipped one of the cats off the hard chair and sat down, got up and pulled it closer, and sat down again. He wasn't sure what to do for the next two hours. The old bat looked as if she'd nodded off. After about ten minutes of her farting gently, she gave a little snore and started but settled again. Bored, he toured the room. The more he looked, the more his fingers curled in disgust. He wasn't going to touch a thing if he could help it.

Dust and cat hairs coated every surface. He could see where the toms sprayed the walls. In the grate, the cold ashes of a long dead fire served as a litter tray. The real litter tray he discovered behind the sofa. It had more cat shit than cat litter, and most of it, so old it was desiccated.

A little snort from Mrs Mallinson startled him, but she was still asleep. Then he felt something squishy underfoot.

'Argh yuck,' he moaned, gaping at what was suspiciously like cat vomit. He heeled out to the kitchen and held his trainer under the tap, but the glutinous mess obstinately remained in the cleats. Rifling through her cupboards for cleaning materials all he found was a few tins of cat food. He ended up using the dish brush. When he'd finished, he was left wondering what to do with it. His instinct was to put it back where he had found it. As soon as he had done that, he realised the next time he drank tea here, his mug could well have been cleaned with this brush. He opened the bin, and nearly puked at what he saw there. Here was the dead thing that was stinking out the house, heaving with maggots.

He couldn't take any more. He ran out of the kitchen and kept running all the way home. Vix smiled when he banged breathlessly into the house, then looked at her watch and frowned. 'Why are you back so early?'

'Mum, it's gross. I'll die if I go back there.'

'You gotta go back.'

'But Mum. The bin's full of maggots. Thousands of them.'

'You've still got another hour and a half.'

'Seriously?'

'Yeah.'

'But Mum!'

'If you don't like it – '

'I shouldn't have thrown the bottle,' he finished sarcastically.

'– you can always do something about it,' she corrected.

'Like what?'

'I dunno. I've never been inside. That's for you to decide.'

He chewed his nails and then remembered what they'd touched. 'Argh yuck,' he moaned. He barged through to the kitchen and scrubbed his hands, carelessly knocking his mother's washing up gloves into the water. Serves her right. Nevertheless, he fished them out and hung them up to dry. As they dripped onto the draining board, an idea began to form.

He yanked open the cupboard under the sink and pulled out the bucket he found there. Into it he piled all the chemicals and cloths he could lay his hands on: furniture polish, bleach, oven cleaner, window cleaner, cream cleaner, a blue liquidy cleaner in a squirty bottle, bathroom cleaner, tile cleaner, loo thingies, disinfectant, and lime scale remover. He helped himself to a new pair of gloves, and lastly opened drawer after drawer until he found where his mother kept the black bin bags.

'If I die, they'll send you to prison,' he said as he stalked past the sitting room door with his haul. Vix didn't move from where she sat curled up with the Sunday papers. 'See you later,' he heard her call after him.

Back at Mrs Mallinson's, he angrily pressed the doorbell and waited for her to let him in.

'Hello, Al,' she said slightly perplexed. 'Haven't we done this already today?'

'Your house is repul – your bins need emptying and I went to get some bin bags,' he said, holding them up.

'Wonderful,' she said, stepping back to let him in.

TRUSSES

Although Rob had submitted a quotation, Ruth had the uneasy feeling he was going to go way over budget. It was two weeks since he'd been back on the job. In the garden, the daffodils were coming up. While she pruned and cleared, she had a lot of time to think about his reaction to her in the kitchen on the day of filming, but either the whole thing had been a figment of her imagination or he had changed his mind. It was flattering to know she was still an attractive woman, though.

Meanwhile, Rob worked so slowly that some days she couldn't see any apparent change to the bathroom. When asked, he'd always point out something new that he'd had to stop and make good, which he attributed to the state of the guttering, or the poor workmanship of a previous builder.

'Would you look at that botching?' he'd say, and she'd dutifully follow the line of his finger and obediently concur with whatever he said; she had no idea what he was talking about. One day, however, she couldn't help herself. He'd gone up to the attic above the kitchen to check something, and she'd followed him up.

The attic was a repository of broken furniture, old mattresses, bags of outgrown children's clothes, forgotten toys and battered kites. She hadn't been up here in years. There was surprisingly little dust, as if everything was waiting in suspended animation for her return.

Rob had gone ahead and was inspecting the roof. 'Oh my goodness.'

She put down the hobby horse she had made for one of the children and went to see what he was exclaiming about.

'Would you look at that!'

It wasn't a question but she hesitated slightly too long while she tried to work out what he was showing her.

'Can you not see it?'

She looked at him, her eyes wide, and her shoulders rose an eloquent millimetre. So he invited her deeper into the attic to point out a mangle of trusses nailed together. 'Be careful,' he murmured. 'Here, lean on me while you step over the beam.'

She couldn't remember the last time anyone had been careful of her. Michael expected her to be independent, so she had been. That afternoon, Rob solicitously took her elbow. His nearness flustered her. She glanced up at him, and found him looking down at her.

'OK?'

He smelt of woods and gentle rain after a long dry spell, of wind and sky and drying haystacks.

He didn't seem to expect an answer. He continued his tranquil study of her face, and then raised a hand to brush her cheek before running his fingers through her hair. 'Cobwebs,' he said. He raised his hand to show her.

She nodded, struck dumb by his touch.

'But no spiders.'

She found her voice. 'I'm OK with spiders.'

He nodded, his eyes dark as night. ''Course you are.' His breath fanned her face. 'Over there.' He bent slightly and pointed over her shoulder into the dim recesses of the loft. 'Now d'you see?'

'Yes, I see.' Then, 'What am I actually supposed to be looking at?'

He frowned, perplexed and then laid a hand on a beam. 'This truss here, you see how it's not butted in?'

'Yes.'

He stepped across the room and laid his hand on another beam. 'And this truss here, you see how it's not butted in either?'

'Yes.' Then, 'Oh! Nothing's holding this part of the roof up but that old beam, which...' her voice trailed away before she added, '... is full of wormholes.'

'It's rotten.' He pulled off a bit of the beam and crushed it to powder.

She gasped. 'The roof could come down.'

'It could be good for another ten years or it might come down in the next big wind.'

His patience was a revelation. Michael would simply have blown out his cheeks in frustration and walked away, bored with the whole topic, but Rob was leaning into her and talking as if her understanding really mattered.

'And you could fix this?' she asked.

'Yes, but it won't be cheap. I should be concentrating on your bathroom, but the wall has a huge crack running through it, and I think the stress comes from up here. You just need a new I-beam.'

'Does that mean you'd have to take the roof off?'

'No, no, no.' He explained how he'd slot in the replacement beam, his tone affable.

'I see,' she said at last. And, surprisingly, she did. She understood everything he said. Then she stepped back and tripped over a box of papers. He caught her hand before she fell, steadying her.

'Here, let's go back to the light, shall we?' he said.

He guided her back to the door, ready to help, but this time she was determined to be more self-sufficient. He had nothing of Michael's majesty. Before he was ill, Michael used to sweep through doors, expecting people to fall back and let him pass. In Rob, though, there was an old world charm that took her breath away.

THE WALK HOME

Ruth arrived at the pub the next evening for a meeting of the Elderfield Special Interest Group in time to witness William needling Bruce Turner.

'There you are.' Bruce boomed, walking up behind them as she stood beside William at the bar.

William's startled jump was so hammed up that Ruth had to hide her smile in her hand.

'Oh hello, Counsellor,' he said. 'Good to see you.'

'Where've you been? I've been waiting over an hour for you,' said Bruce, completely ignoring Ruth.

'I wasn't expecting to see you this evening,' said William.

'Not expecting –? We were supposed to do a tour of the town to sort out an action plan for the Award.'

'Really? A gin and tonic for the lady,' William said to the barman, winking at Ruth. 'But you asked me to sort that out,' he added to Bruce.

Ruth looked at the floor. She would laugh if she looked at William. He was really hamming this up, but then the power struggle between the two men was ever so slightly ridiculous.

'I am the horticultural expert around here, am I not?' continued William, all condescension.

'But this whole award thing is my responsibility. It must work. We must get a gold,' said Bruce, and ordered a pint.

'You know a gold isn't the only thing that matters,' said William.

'Getting a gold doesn't matter?' demanded Bruce, skewing round to look at him.

'Sorting out the town is what matters.'

'Well, yes, we all want the hooligans to go away.'

Ruth wondered about that. She thought he rather liked being photographed by the local press having long conversations with the police, his white teeth flashing and his cheesy smile never quite reaching his eyes.

Bruce carried his pint off to a table just as Rob walked in. Tongue-tied, she summoned up a bland smile for him and dug in her pocket for some change.

'Allow me,' he said and held out a note to the barman. 'And a pint of my usual,' he added.

'Thanks,' she said.

He smiled at her vaguely. 'What's up with you?' she heard him ask William as she carried her drink to the table.

'He just walked away expecting me to pay for his sodding pint,' said William.

'Who?'

'Bruce Turner.'

'What d'you expect? Ah, here's Vix. What are you having, my lovely?'

He's kind to everyone, thought Ruth, disappointed. When she looked up, he was looking right at her with that inscrutable expression of his, and she dropped her gaze in confusion. He was deep in conversation with Vix when she steeled herself to raise her eyes again. Oh God, I'm being a perfect ninny.

Meanwhile, Bruce sat at the corner of the table quaffing his beer and drumming his fingers. 'Right,' he said, when everyone was seated. 'Is everyone here who should be? Good,' he said, answering his own question. 'Let's call this meeting to order, shall we?'

William made a face, and Ruth saw Rob kick him under the table.

While Bruce made a show of ticking off people present on his list, Ruth looked round the motley group, noticing how close William sat to Vix, and the gulf between Rob and herself.

'William,' began Bruce, when he'd penned his last tick, 'I asked you to do an inspection with me to sort out an action list.'

Was he trying to make William look like an idiot? Surely they'd just covered this at the bar?

'Done,' said William smugly.

'When?' blustered Bruce.

'This afternoon,' said William, drinking deeply.

'But you were supposed to do it with me. You were supposed to meet me here,' Bruce consulted his watch, 'an hour ago so that we could do it together.'

'Why?' asked William insolently.

'Because, as chairman of the parish council and chairman of the Special Interest Group for Elderfield in Bloom –' there was a faint sneer on William's lips as he watched Bruce dropping titles – 'I'm responsible.'

'Yeah, but you asked me to sort it.'

'With me, William. I'm in charge. What you don't realise is that we're dealing with a sink estate. They're hoodlums in there.'

'They're not *all* hoodlums,' put in Ruth.

Bruce gave her a withering look. 'They're out of control hoodlums. You don't know anything.'

Most were not, she wanted to say, but didn't think he'd understand the distinction. They were ordinary people who were demoralised and angry about being frozen out by the rest of the town, but he was right about one thing: she didn't know, so she shut up.

'Do you really think anyone in the estate sees this competition as a priority?' he sneered. 'You're just a bunch of amateur do-gooders poncing about with secateurs. It's my job to sort this town out and it's a full time job. This Bloom thing is a bloody distraction. Nevertheless, I take *all* my responsibilities seriously.'

Vix suddenly laid a hand on William's arm. Even Ruth could feel his irritation rising. 'There's no doubt about that, Bruce,' said Vix. 'William appreciates what a lot you have to manage.'

'So being in charge,' Bruce added, talking right over her, 'I must be allowed to manage things as I see fit. If everyone takes it into their heads to do their own thing, it'll all end up in a terrible mess.'

William's temper boiled over. 'You –' he winced, as Rob kicked him again under the table, cutting off whatever disclosure he was about to make. 'Will you stop it?' he said, rounding on Rob.

Rob didn't say anything, but Ruth was interested to see how William backed down in the face of Rob's quiet authority.

'You see,' said Bruce, William's little eruption going completely over his head, 'the buck stops with me. Everyone has to do their bit, for sure, but it's vitally important that I supervise every aspect to make sure they're doing it properly. So since you took it into your head to proceed without me, William, I expect you to have a fully comprehensive list of what needs doing.'

William looked like he was about to explode.

Ruth leaned forward; perhaps Bruce really did care. 'I think William may need time to write up his conclusions, you know, officially, so you can present them to the council. I suggest he drops them by your house tomorrow, if that's acceptable. Now it's late, and we wouldn't want to keep you from your dinner.'

'That's considerate of you, Ruth. My wife's expecting me. But if anything's been missed out, we'll all know who to look to,' added Bruce frowning at William.

'It's a huge responsibility you've taken on,' said Ruth.

'Yes, a huge responsibility,' said Bruce, mollified, accepting his dues, 'and this competition has added substantially to my workload, but it's vital to get it right. There are procedures to be followed. People need to be told what to do and it's my responsibility to make sure everyone knows that. Naturally, it takes up a lot of my time. Nobody appreciates the work I put in to make these things happen. I have a business to run.'

'Likewise,' muttered William, but Bruce didn't seem to hear him.

'We'll see you at the next meeting, then,' said Ruth. She stood and held out her hand. Bruce shook it automatically. Then there was nothing for him to do but leave, so he left.

'Wow!' said Vix, as the door closed behind him. 'I love the way you dismissed him.'

'Does he realise he's a caricature of himself?' spluttered William.

'Oh, so are you,' Vix ejaculated. 'For goodness sake, learn how to manage him.'

'What the hell does he know about plants?'

'Nothing, but fighting with him won't help any of us. Let him be in charge if he wants to be.'

'Yeah, I noticed you sucking up to him.'

'Will, you can be such a jerk sometimes,' said Vix, jumping up.

'Did you listen to yourself? *Oh, William appreciates what a lot you have to manage*,' he mimicked.

She stormed out of the pub with William close on her heels. Ruth reached for the list he had left behind on the table, and started to go through it. Rob watched her. 'They'll make up,' he said.

She put the list in her pocket. 'Hm.'

'Here,' he said, draining his glass. 'I'll walk you home.'

'Thank you,' she said and then regretted it. What if he tried to kiss her? What if he didn't? Did he want to kiss her? Did she want him to try? Her stomach knotted as each question threw up another. All the way to the door she considered changing her mind. Once in the street, braced by the frosty air, she felt calmer. She was being silly. He wasn't going to try anything. He certainly wouldn't pounce. She glanced up at him.

Like her, he was walking with his hands in his pockets and his collar was turned up against the cold. He seemed so self-contained. When they left the streetlights behind, he pulled out a torch and switched it on, then off again; above them, stars shone in a half-moon sky lighting up the road in an ethereal ribbon. For the first time in years, Ruth walked along the short road to her house seeing it through someone else's eyes. It was beautiful but seemed to meander on unendingly. How still it was. Not a leaf stirred. It was so quiet she could hear Rob's crepe-soled desert boots treading softly in time with her own footfall. She felt... she didn't know what, but nervous, gawky and tense were all in there. What would his kiss be like?

'It's kind of you to walk me home,' she blurted out.

'I should have driven you.'

'Now I feel bad. You'll have to walk all the way back.'

'It's a nice night for a walk.'

'Yes, it is.' There seemed nothing more to say. As conversations went it scored ten for banality. So why had it escalated the tension between them? She racked her brain for something interesting to say, but could come up with nothing beyond observing the moon looked beautiful, and she drew the line at uttering inanities twice in an evening.

Rob did not, as Vix predicted, attempt to kiss her on her doorstep. Instead, he left her at the gateway and watched her walk to her front door. When she had let herself in, he waved and called: 'Goodnight. See you tomorrow.'

She felt strangely let down, even though she knew it was madness to go down that road.

CHAPTER 7

THE HEADMASTER DUCKS

When Ruth put the idea to Mr Sharples, headmaster of the huge secondary school on the outskirts of town, the following day, he was set against involving pupils in designing posters to promote Elderfield's entry to the Britain in Bloom awards. A thin, weedy man, he spent the entire meeting bending and unbending paperclips until they broke.

His nickname was Buggins, which said it all, and he had a reputation for secreting himself away in his office while everyone else prepared for the arrival of the next set of school inspectors. Every time they came, the local media gleefully reported the school's conspicuous decline. 'Headmaster faces detention' was this morning's headline, which he had no doubt read. The piece went on no less sensationally: 'With Special Measures a hair's breadth away, Tom Sharples, dubbed Buggins by his pupils, spends his time checking risk assessments, ticking boxes, and filling in forms while his teachers wage war in the corridors.'

Thanks to the new estate, the school had doubled in size since Ruth's last visit as a parent. Bubblegum wrappers and crisp packets swirled listlessly in corners of the playground. Ramshackle portakabins with doors that rattled accounted for the increased number of classrooms, no doubt freezing in winter and boiling in summer. Many old town parents had lost patience with the institution and had removed their children, leaving mainly children from the estate, who, the headmaster was quoted as saying, 'are uncontrollable brats.'

'Parents,' the article continued, 'far from deferentially

deferring to him, ignore the no smoking signs and blow cigarette smoke in his face while they challenge his right to give their children detentions after school. Teachers patrol in twos, and prefer not to go out at all. They are habitually abused, spat at, or, what is somehow worse, completely ignored. Breaks are often punctuated with chants of "Fight, fight, fight" and staff routinely call in the police.'

Ruth could see Mr Sharples thought she was a fool to propose the school get the children involved in poster designs. He didn't quite say it, but the phrase 'Are you on another planet?' hovered unspoken between them.

'Their style is graffiti, and not of the Banksy kind,' he said. 'Banal rubbish that means nothing and adds nothing. They'd look on your flowers as an invitation to yet more destruction.'

He listened somewhat impatiently to all Ruth had to say about trying to unite the two halves of the town, but he was more concerned about trying to stop playground bullying, staff absenteeism and pupils trashing the toilets. 'I simply don't have the energy to devote to this folly. The teachers will revolt if I ask them to get involved.'

'Could they not do it in their art lessons?' asked Ruth, doggedly.

'There's no room in the timetable for such a project but thank you for coming in,' he added mechanically, and rose. Defeated, Ruth took her cue from him and left.

As she approached the front door, a great lunking hunk of a boy with a black eye tried to push past her. She stared him down. Unexpectedly he took a step back and opened the door for her. 'Sorry, Mrs Dawson,' he murmured. 'Didn't see you there.'

Surprised, she paused in the doorway. 'Do I know you?'

'No, but me mum watches your Jules on the telly every week. I saw the one of your garden, just after your husband… Made me Mum cry, it did. Dead sentimental, me Mum. Just like our Maggie.'

'Well thank you for opening the door.'

He grinned. 'I'll tell Mum I met you. She'll be that envious. She likes to garden, 'n' all.'

Slightly less downcast, Ruth called in at Doodlepad to buy greetings cards for various birthdays coming up. The shop was an Aladdin's Cave of artists' materials and, though she never bought any, she liked to browse the shelves of paints and brushes, imagining that one day she might take up painting in her spare time. 'Yeah, what spare time?' she could hear Jules mock. However, she was disheartened enough by her interview with Mr Sharples to mention it to Lucy and her husband, Terry, who ran the shop.

'He what?'

'No way.'

'He always was a stupid, unimaginative git, even when he was at school,' said Lucy. There was something of the artist about her long flowing, colourful dresses, and silk scarves wound around her head. The effect was subtly bohemian; she was not someone who would ever have had much time for stolid Mr Sharples, Ruth imagined.

Then she had a brainwave. 'So,' she said, pausing for effect, 'I was hoping perhaps you might know someone who could organise a poster competition.'

'I'm up for it,' exclaimed Lucy.

'Oh, I don't know,' countered Terry in his lowland lilt. 'It'd involve a lot of work.'

'Yeah but think about it, love. Think how many people would come into the shop to collect an entry form.'

'They wouldn't buy anything,' he said.

'I could do a leaflet-drop advertising the competition,' piped up their son, Charlie.

'On the new estate, as well?' said Ruth.

'If you want.'

'We haven't got any money for printing,' said Terry.

'Perhaps Elderfield Printers will sponsor it. I'll talk to Guy,' said Ruth.

'I'll call him now,' said Lucy. 'Save you going round.'

'Hold up, Luce. When will you have the time to do all that work?'

'What are you on about? Anything's better than sitting in here day after day watching dust settle on the stock. We should have thought of this ourselves,' said his wife, ignoring his objections and flashing a toothy grin at Ruth. 'It's a terrific idea.'

'And you could give over the gallery upstairs to hold an exhibition of the winners,' added Charlie.

'Aye, we could,' murmured Terry. 'Obviously the winners will want their pictures framed,' he said, fingering the case of mounts by the till.

Suddenly, where there had been despondency, Ruth could sense the germ of an idea taking root. She collected her cards. 'I'll send Vix Watson round to get the story for the local paper.'

'I could do that,' said Charlie.

His parents stared at him.

'What? I've always wanted to be a reporter.'

'I thought you wanted to run the shop.'

'And spend my life mouldering away?' he said. 'What would I want to do that for? I just like doing the Warhammer workshop on Saturdays.'

'Warhammer?' asked Ruth.

'Over-priced plastic soldiers,' said Lucy. 'They paint 'em and have battles.'

'They're not over-priced,' said her husband. 'We hardly make any margin on them.'

Ruth left them arguing the merits of Warhammer's pricing strategy, and drove home with a jaunty grin on her face.

THE STRONG BOX

It took Al several days to clean Mrs Mallinson's house and it smelled a lot fresher when he'd done the kitchen. The tom cats still sprayed in the sitting room, and the worst culprit he dragged off to the vet to be neutered. It never sprayed again, and without his lead, the other toms did not feel the need to mark their territory so diligently.

Al ended up paying for half the operation from his own savings – the old bag clearly hadn't a clue how much such an operation cost these days. However, when it came to buying cleaning materials, he didn't draw on Mrs Mallinson at all. He snaffled everything he needed from under his own kitchen sink. It was a small, petty rebellion which neither he nor his mother mentioned.

That first afternoon, he started work on the kitchen. Maggots weren't the only things that made him want to vom, and he was relieved he'd never eaten anything in the house when he discovered quantities of mouse droppings in all the cupboards. Meanwhile, he chucked out several packets of food too far gone to be healthy for anyone.

Mrs Mallinson found him still on his knees cleaning out a cupboard at seven. 'Dear boy,' she said, 'isn't it time you were home?' Then she looked around her kitchen and took in the pots and pans and bowls and plates all over the floor. 'Ha! What a terrible mess you've made of my kitchen,' she said, and clonked away with her Zimmer frame. Tired and dispirited by her comment, Al chucked his cloth in the sink, shoved everything any old how back in the cupboards, and left without saying goodbye.

After school the next day, when he went to make tea for Mrs Mallinson and himself as usual, he found a magazine on the kitchen table, *Mountain Bike Rider*, and snatched it up. It was only after the kettle boiled that it occurred to him that this was a strange magazine to find in a pensioner's house.

'I found this in the kitchen,' he said as he handed her her tea, and bringing out the magazine.

'Have you read it?'

'No! It's the latest edition and I haven't had a chance to go to the newsagents yet. How come you have a copy?'

'I wanted to give you a present,' she said.

He frowned. 'For what?'

'For having the courage to come back, and for your hard work yesterday.'

'But... but... thank you. *MBR*, you know, it's kind of a specialist magazine. How did you know what I'm into?'

'I have a phone, and I used it to find out what you like to read. The newsagent told me you come in every month for that. If you'd gone in to collect it today, he was going to tell you it hadn't arrived yet.'

Al was overwhelmed. He opened his mouth to speak but no words came out.

'I must say, it's rather a dangerous sport. It has pictures of young people leaping into the air on their bicycles. Things have changed since I last cycled.'

'It's really fun and you do all these jumps and things, and race through woods and... Would you like to see some of the stunts?'

'I'm a little old to go traipsing through the woods, don't you think?'

'I could show you on the Internet. Do you have Internet here?'

'Dear boy, I don't actually know how to work the telly.'

'Oh. Well, I can show you how to do that. And tomorrow I'll bring my laptop and dongle and show you some stuff on YouTube. You'll love it. It's really amazing.' He pulled up a chair and started to talk her through the magazine.

His mother had never shown the remotest interest in his biking, but Mrs Mallinson was so full of questions that he was soon enthusing about his heroes, his hopes and plans. He was all fired up by an idea to build a bike track near the village. He even drew her a plan of some of the elements he might include, like jumps and berms, and spoke of his fancy, when he found a suitable site, of hiring a mini digger to get it started. He was astonished when she told him it was time to go home.

'I'll see you tomorrow,' he said cheerfully, and then stopped to wave her goodbye as he passed the window from the path.

Having set himself the task of cleaning the house, Al set to work diligently. The results pleased him no end, and he frequently went back to admire the gleaming windows and polished wooden floors in rooms he'd completed. Oh but it was slow. The house was enormous. Every day he swept and rubbed and wiped and sponged.

Mrs Mallinson superintended, watching and instructing and pointing out bits he'd missed, which he took on board with barely a grunt: she was old and dotty and couldn't help it. The weird thing was that he came to enjoy her company, and together they moved from room to room, him cleaning and polishing and her endlessly finding fault. He actually missed her acid tongue on the days when she remained dozing in the sitting room.

Upstairs, he counted six double bedrooms and three bathrooms. These, except for her own bedroom, which was furred with cat hair, turned out to be fairly clean as the doors were kept shut. Their only occupants were spiders whose cobwebs he quickly hoovered up.

'What's with the pictures?' he asked one day, alluding to the dark patches on the walls. 'Last week, there were a few left in the bedroom at the end, but they're gone now.'

Mrs Mallinson looked unsurprised. 'Jennifer must have been to visit.'

'Your daughter? But surely you'd know if she had.'

'Not if she didn't want to be seen.'

'You mean, she's nicking stuff?' he asked, shocked.

'I don't think Jennifer thinks of it as nicking. After all, it will all be hers one day.'

He looked troubled. He couldn't imagine taking anything of his mother's without her express permission. Then he thought about the cleaning materials, and resolved to ask before he took stuff from home again.

'My daughter has expensive tastes. She lives in an expensive suburb in an expensive house, and sends her sons to Eton, none of which she can afford on Simon's salary.'

'Why doesn't she move into a smaller house, then?' he asked naively.

Mrs Mallinson cackled. 'Because she is silly and vain.'

'You don't like her much, do you?'

She seemed to consider her response carefully. 'No,' she admitted at last.

Towards the end of his bout of spring cleaning, about three weeks after he had started coming to her house, Al came across and old metal strong box in her study. She was dozing on a chair in the corner and he was tempted to have a squint inside. Lifting it onto her desk, he wiped years of dust from the lid and tested the catch. It gave easily and inside he found letters and papers and dozens of curling black and white photographs: young women in uniform, a group of young pilots by a Lancaster bomber, a man smoking a pipe looking seriously at the camera with a dog at his feet. Dull stuff, he concluded, and closed the lid again. When he looked up, Mrs Mallinson was watching him.

'You should put the photos in an album,' he gabbled in embarrassment.

'I haven't looked at them for years. Bring the box here.'

He lumped it across the room and was about to put it on the floor when she pulled him up. 'Bring a table over, boy. I can't reach the damn thing on the floor.'

When the strong box was on a low table in front of her, she turned to him and said, 'You can go now.'

'Home?'

'Yes, home.'

'But it's only half past four. Mum'll send me back.'

'Go now,' she commanded.

'Suit yourself,' he said and left.

When he looked back, her hand was resting on the strong box and her eyes were closed.

VANISHING BUDGET

Towards the end of February, Vix invited Ruth to supper. She found William had arrived before her, along with Al's girlfriend, Olivia, who was hogging the conversation.

'I finished the puzzle but there was a bit missing in the sky,' Olivia told Ruth as she flipped her long, straightened hair back over her shoulder. She giggled. 'Derhahahaha.' The giggle sounded like a demented horse whinnying.

Al looked mesmerised, William like he'd been hit with a brick.

Ruth was astonished. This woman-child, with her super long legs and sensuous feminine curves, talked like a 14-year-old but looked as if she had come out of the pages of *Cosmopolitan*. Her face was immaculately made up and her clothes revealed, well, everything – a huge cleavage and acres of orange thigh, courtesy of a bottle of L'Oreal's finest. Apparently she and Al were catching the bus to the cinema after supper.

Olivia dabbed at the corners of her mouth with her napkin and then continued, 'I searched everywhere for the missing piece, yeah, but it wasn't in the box or anythink. Derhahaha.'

William bent his head and stolidly munched his way through the plate of shepherd's pie in front of him. Ruth smiled and said, 'How frustrating,' which was a mistake because the girl took it as a cue to go on.

'I really like doing puzzles, derhahaha. They're dead, you know, interesting, yeah, and some of them have really cool pictures.'

William snorted and Vix dug his ribs with her elbow, at which point he choked on his food.

'Mum's taking me shopping on Saturday, yeah,' Olivia said to Al. 'I need more, you know...' she waved a hand vaguely over her chest. 'And anyway, I was thinking, yeah, that you could come too.'

Al's reaction was half yelp, half gulp. 'To buy bras?'

'Well, you wouldn't be helping me buy those, yeah.'

'OK.' It was more of a squeak.

'Yeah, and maybe, yeah, we could go out after 'n' have a pizza, yeah, and then go window shopping together. Derhahaha.'

William eyebrows popped up as if he couldn't imagine a more boring way to spend an afternoon. Ruth had to look down at her food to avoid looking at Al's bewitched expression, or she would laugh.

'OK,' Al managed at last. 'But I have to be back by 3.30.'

'Okelydokely. I'm having a sleepover after, yeah, and we'll be painting our nails.'

Al's mouth dropped open.

'Shall we go?' she asked artlessly, getting up.

'In a minute,' gasped Al.

'Why don't you go and refresh your lipstick?' said William, taking pity on him, 'and Al will be waiting by the front door when you come down.'

'Okelydokely.' The girl pranced out of the room.

Al flashed him such a smile of gratitude that Ruth was optimistic that William would grow to like the boy, given time. 'OK, lad?' he asked.

Al nodded.

'Wait outside. It's raining and cold.'

'Yeah,' said Al, and fled.

Ruth, Vix and William sat with knives and forks suspended, studiously avoiding each other's gaze, until they heard Olivia's high heels clump down the stairs and out of the front door, at which point they erupted into gales of laughter.

'What did Al say to her to persuade her to go out with him?' asked William when he caught his breath.

Vix was mopping her eyes on her napkin. 'Al's nice. And tall. He's nice.'

William shook his head. 'Vix, did you actually look at her?'

'She does rather take your breath away, doesn't she?' conceded Ruth.

'My goodness,' said Vix. 'That giggle is insane. And she's so thick. Her conversation will bore Al in a week.'

'I shouldn't think conversation's high on his agenda,' mused William. 'That cleavage makes your eyeballs slither down the slope of bad intentions. And those legs! They're long enough to wrap around your worst fantasies. Her mother must be barmy to let her dress like that. She's jail bait.'

Vix started to clear the table. 'Coffee, anyone?'

Ruth shook her head and pushed her chair back, reflecting that this was her first time out to supper in over a year. She was surprised at how much she had enjoyed herself, Olivia's limited conversation notwithstanding. She'd expected to feel uncomfortable coming out on her own, but not a bit of it. 'Sorry to break up the party but I have to be going.'

With Al gone, she felt *de trop*. It was the first time Vix had invited William to supper, and she thought she knew why she'd been invited. She was a foil to distract Al – not that Al turned out to need distracting. Nevertheless, she thought she would slope off and leave these two lovebirds to enjoy their evening alone.

'Did you hear what Bruce Turner's gone and done?' asked Vix, coming over to say goodbye. 'He's just approved a budget of £5,000 for a video to teach children how to catch a bus. It'll be in the paper tomorrow.'

Ruth's jaw dropped. 'But, but – I don't understand.'

'What's not to understand, darling. The council has just approved a 90-minute video to teach 11- and 12-year-olds how to catch a bus. I think it's a very important life skill,' she added.

'Yes, but...'

'But because the timetable is so full,' continued Vix, utterly deadpan, 'too full even to design a poster in their art lessons – the kids will be allowed to skip an English lesson to watch it.'

'Well, that's OK,' said William. 'They'll be able to catch a bus, but won't know where it's going.'

'They made it because Recycling won't accept shredded banknotes,' Vix concluded.

Ruth spluttered.

'Bruce Turner will be on record tomorrow saying, and I quote: *It's not just about teaching children to use a bus, it's also about behaviour and vandalism, which can be very costly for bus companies.*'

'Excuse me,' burst out Ruth, 'but last time I looked, how children behave on a bus was down to parents, not the ratepayer. Did you know I'd asked the council for funding to print Elderfield-in-Bloom posters?'

'Yep,' said Vix.

'Bruce Turner said there was none.'

'Not any more.'

Ruth put her head in her hands. 'I don't understand. Doesn't he want us to get a gold? Doesn't he want to promote the award and get people pulling together?'

'Darling, the poster competition was truly inspired, but it wasn't *his* idea. By the way, do you want to go into business with me? I could get filthy rich putting just half your ideas into practice.'

But Ruth would not be deflected. 'I didn't think he was that petty.'

William guffawed.

'This is war,' muttered Ruth.

'I'm glad you're taking such a reasonable view of the matter,' said Vix, clearly finding her reaction hugely entertaining.

Ruth moaned. 'Five thousand pounds?'

Vix nodded.

'I must try and talk him round.'

'You can't argue with that man. He's right,' said Vix.

'No, he's not.'

'He's the kind fool who will ruin a good argument because he knows what he's talking about,' interjected William. 'Talking of which, you know who called me today?'

'Bruce?' asked Vix.

'Why would he call me? No, The Toad.'

'If he heard you calling him that!' exclaimed Vix.

William leered at her. 'The bank has approved a loan to tide me over till June. Things are turning round.'

'Oh, Will.' Vix flew across the room to kiss him.

'I'll just let myself out,' said Ruth, tiptoeing theatrically towards the door.

Vix giggled. 'That's the kind of line they have in bad soaps.'

'Is it? Maybe I'm more current than I thought,' Ruth replied jestingly. 'Anyway, I've got things to do and if I go now, I get out of doing the washing up. Too slow, William,' she said as he got up. 'Looks like you're wearing the washing up gloves tonight.'

'Actually...' he began, an arrested look on his face.

THE SUBMISSION

What started out as something to generate interest in the Britain in Bloom awards morphed into a scheme in its own right. Entries for the poster competition poured in, and every time Ruth dropped in at Doodlepad, she found Lucy host to dozens of children buying art materials and collecting entry forms.

As if the huge notice in the shop window wasn't enough to advertise the poster competition, the local paper devoted the whole of page five to it, complete with a teaser on page one. Charlie must have done some fast talking because he landed this without his mother even needing to bribe the editor by taking out an advert for the shop. Whether it was the poster, the media coverage, or something entirely unconnected, entering the competition gradually gained currency in the playground.

Ruth took to having a coffee with Lucy a couple of times a week to help sort out the submissions; the two of them left Terry sitting dourly at the front of the shop listening to their whoops of laughter at the back. One day, Mr Sharples unctuously dropped in to find out how the competition was going and Lucy showed him the growing pile of entries. He left thoughtfully, and then tried to seize back the initiative by announcing the school was holding its own competition.

Ruth found herself having a giggle with Lucy when she told her that everyone, including the teachers, had ignored him. 'Apparently he slunk back to his office and hid,' said Lucy, rocking back and forth with glee. 'No one's seen him since.'

'Perhaps he's wasted away in there,' said Ruth.

'How could you tell?' said Lucy, with a shriek of laughter. 'The po-faced git is certainly wasted out here.'

Meanwhile, Al had spent hours thinking about his entry. As the closing date approached, he racked his brain for inspiration. He couldn't draw to save his life (although his mother fondly described him as artistic), but that didn't stop him hankering for first prize. When Gazzer Turner lorded into the playground one morning declaring: 'I'm in, I'm gonna win,' Al bit his nails and got into trouble for doodling design ideas in his exercise book when he should have been taking notes on some boring poem.

Mrs Mallinson brought him up short one afternoon by remarking that he couldn't win if he didn't enter. He grunted and bit his nails. The next day, he borrowed his mother's camera to take photos of the square. These he manipulated on his laptop, Mrs Mallinson at his elbow gazing at the screen in amazement, until they looked as though they were drawn with coloured pencils. When he got home, he printed them out onto the best paper he could find in his mother's office.

At school he pinched a large sheet of poster paper from the art room. He took it from right under Miss Jenkins' nose. Miss Jenkins usually got pretty antsy about students nicking stuff, but it seemed she was turning a blind eye to the current spate of petty thefts; by then word had got out that Mrs Dawson had approached Mr Sharples first about the competition and Miss was livid he hadn't bothered to consult her.

Back at Mrs Mallinson's, he laid the sheet of paper on the kitchen table and dropped the printouts on top. Mrs Mallinson leafed through them while he made tea. 'They're not bad,' she commented.

He looked sideways at her – that was something coming from her. 'They'll do,' he said.

Mrs Mallinson sat perched beside him as he spent the rest of the afternoon creating a collage. On the blank walls of buildings, he stenciled 'Elderfield in Bloom' graffiti-style. In the street, he stuck old sweet papers so they looked as if they were rolling across the square like leaves in the wind.

'I need a small square piece of glass,' he muttered.

Mrs Mallinson disappeared and came back with an old compact mirror from her dressing table.

'Perfect. Can I keep it?'

'Do I look like someone who needs to look at herself in a mirror any more?'

'But your face is full of character,' said Al.

'Oh, you talk as much baloney as your father used to.'

'He lives in New Zealand, now.'

'I heard.'

'Stupid bastard.'

Mrs Mallinson sniffed, evidently agreeing.

He took the mirror, taped the back with Sellotape, and then smashed it under his heel before sticking it over the window of Lisa's Florist.

Finally, over the next couple of days he and Mrs Mallinson cut out pictures of flowers from old magazines he brought from home. He arranged these in a huge wave up the side of the buildings.

The result was quite shocking, capturing the worst of Elderfield while the flowers hinted at better things to come. He dropped his entry in on the closing day of the competition and walked home pensively when he found out that there were nearly fifteen hundred entries.

His mum went on to everyone about 'the staggering response'. The local paper raved about what it meant for the town. Then a boy was knifed in a street fight the following night, and the poster competition was old news.

CHAPTER 8

TAKING THE LEAD

Two weeks later, Bruce Turner had called an Extraordinary Meeting at the town hall to formalise the Special Interest Group and discuss an action plan to prepare the village for the competition, or, as Vix said, 'To order people about.' It seemed, however, that in his enthusiasm, Bruce had failed to promote the event properly and only people from half the town turned up. Once again, almost no one represented people from the estate.

Rob sat at the back of the room with half an ear on the conversation in the hall, which was focused on the boy who had been knifed, as it had been in almost every home for the last fortnight. Some people knew his neighbours, others his family.

'He's a good boy. He puts my bins out every week,' said one woman.

'Why was he knifed? What did he do?'

'He refused to hand over his wallet.'

'I heard they wanted his mobile phone.'

'They were high on drugs.'

'They were drunk.'

'The police said they were glue sniffers. They used to hang out in the rough ground behind the Seven Eleven.'

'The police. What do they know? They haven't arrested anyone. All they've done is gone door-to-door with an artist's impression which my five-year-old could have drawn better.'

'A wallet! Is that all they wanted?'

'I don't like to go out at night any more.'

'No one does.'

It took Bruce several minutes to wrench their attention back to his agenda. Rob slouched with his arms folded and his legs stretched out in front of him, his mind drifting as the big man droned on. Essentially Bruce's message was: 'It's the middle of March. Time is short. Do up your front garden and plant loads of hanging baskets.' This he repeated several times in different ways, occasionally adding an adjective.

Then someone stood up and interrupted the monologue. 'What I'd like to know is what you intend to do about sorting out the estate?'

'Yeah,' came a thin chorus of voices.

'A boy was stabbed in this town a fortnight ago. Stabbed!'

'The police haven't caught anyone.'

'What's the point of this competition? As soon as I paint over the graffiti on my shop wall, another lot is sprayed on.'

'My insurers won't cover me for another window. What should I do when it's broken again? I can't go on like this.'

Just when it looked like the whole meeting would disintegrate into recriminations, a gentle voice spoke out. Rob swung his chair back onto four legs and sat up to listen. He hadn't seen Ruth, though he'd looked for her. He couldn't help looking for her these days. It was like his body was tuning to her, and it was a deeply unsettling feeling.

'We all know something's not right with our town,' began Ruth, 'and the result seems to be a growing cycle of destructive behaviour. And before you leap on me for just accusing youths from the estate, I'd like to say, there are, to my certain knowledge, youths from the old part of town who are equally responsible. It's up to us parents to come down hard on our children when they do wrong. It's up to us to give them clear guidelines about what is, and what is not, acceptable. It's not just for the police to catch these yobs.'

There were murmurs of assent around the room.

She's doing it again, thought Rob. She's got them. She's

bloody got them. How does she do it? She's so mumsy and middle-class-polished, yet they're hanging on her words. *I'm* hanging on her words.

Maybe it was her gentleness. Could you be ruthlessly gentle? He shook his head at his own joke.

'A boy was stabbed a fortnight ago,' she was saying, 'and people are afraid. The police will catch the culprit. Maybe not today, but they're not incompetent. They're hampered by a wall of silence. Vandalism is bad enough but stabbing someone is different. I don't care if the Harris boy was innocent or whether someone thought he deserved it. Somebody knows something and needs to come forward and shop a son or a brother before they kill someone – maybe someone in this room.

'Meanwhile, Bruce said we need to do up our own front gardens. Why? you ask. Why on earth are we bothering with front gardens at a time like this? Two reasons. The first is that life goes on.' Her voice shook and she paused. 'I've learned that.' She stopped again.

The woman beside her opened her handbag and passed her a tissue.

'Thank you,' Ruth whispered, taking it and dabbing her eyes.

Around the room there were murmurs of support. They waited patiently for her to go on.

Was she thinking about Michael? She talked about him sometimes when they had coffee together. For all he was gone, Michael was still a huge presence in her life. Rob wondered what it must have been like to be loved like that for so long. He shifted uncomfortably in his seat. Was that envy he was feeling?

Ruth tucked the tissue up her sleeve and looked up again, her expression tranquil. 'Second, this town is broken,' she continued. 'We let our children break it. We need to repair it. We need to get out hammer and nails, and glue and paint, and put it back together again. Our front gardens are part of that glue and paint. They're about pride. Until we have pride in our own homes, we can forget civic pride.

'The problem is, many people haven't got the know-how, let

alone the time, to do something with their front gardens. So may I propose, Mr Chairman, that we set up some community gardening groups?'

'What are those?' asked Rob.

She smiled at him gratefully, and he felt his heart accelerate. 'Well, as you may know, Rob, I open my garden to the public. To get it ready, I work in it almost every day. Most people haven't got that luxury.'

'I know I haven't,' he said, guessing what she wanted from this interaction, and playing along.

'So what if, this Sunday, I said I would come round and help you for the morning?'

He chuckled. 'Bring it on.'

Seeing where this was going, Vix piped up: 'I could come too. And I can bring Al. He's got muscles and can do the heavy bits.'

Lucy from Doodlepad stood up. 'I'm normally so fagged by the weekend that I just want to put my feet up on Sunday, but I reckon it could be fun. If you lay on a shedload of beer, I bet I could persuade Terry to come, too.'

There was laughter at this suggestion.

'And I could bring Charlie with me. He can help Al,' Lucy continued.

'How about me? I have a garden full of rubbish from the last owners,' came a voice from the back.

Within minutes, several people had volunteered to go round on Sunday to help him, too.

Vix nudged William, who got up genially. 'I'll put up a notice board in my garden centre to get some of these community garden groups going. Just sign up there.'

Ruth said, 'And one lucky gardener per week will receive the benefit of William's advice in their own garden.'

'They will?' asked William.

He took the wisecracks that followed in good part. 'Fair do's. I'll start with your garden on Sunday, sir.'

The man beamed.

At the back of the room, the local reporter started making notes.

A woman at the side stood up. 'I saw an idea on the telly the other day. In one town, they had an adopt-a-verge scheme.'

A chorus of voices thought this idea didn't have legs. It was the council's job to mow the verges.

'Who said anything about mowing grass?' put in Ruth. 'Nick the verge and plant an extra garden. I know some people would love to do that. I have. I'm going to plant four hundred lilies along the verge outside my house. It's called guerrilla gardening – war against neglect and abandoned spaces.'

'I'm not sure the council will approve that idea,' said Bruce, at which point several people shouted him down.

'Could I grow vegetables in it?' the woman asked.

'Like a little allotment?'

'People would nick the stuff.'

'They might.'

'The kids will trash it.'

'They might not.'

'I'll give it a go,' said the woman.

'I hear there's no money to print posters from the poster competition,' said Rob. Ruth started as though he'd touched on something that was exercising her. The hullabaloo that followed had Bruce running for cover saying he'd try and find some money in the budget. Rob looked at Ruth and shrugged. They both knew it was an empty promise.

EMERALD QUEEN

The next day Rob dropped by the garden centre on the way to work. It seemed other people had the same idea, because, early as it was, a small crowd was gathered around a new notice board, and already half a dozen community gardening schemes were getting underway that Sunday.

He studied the rules. They looked simple enough: you got help with your garden if you promised nine hours in other people's.

That was just three Sunday mornings. Perhaps it might work, as it seemed lunch was included.

'No cooking for several Sundays,' said William, sidling up to him.

'You said it,' said Rob. 'Hang on! Does that mean I have to do lunch at my place?'

William had lost interest. 'I have that Hellebore you wanted for Ruth's garden,' he said.

Later, while Rob worked in the loft, he pondered on what Ruth's reaction might be when he gave her the plant. Now that it came to it, he felt iffy about handing it over. He was worried she might read too much into it. Ruth was an attractive woman but she was a customer and right now he didn't need a complicated life. And then there was Emma. Or not. She was obviously gone for good so why wasn't he going out and getting laid?

When he went down to make himself a coffee mid-morning, he expected to see Ruth in the greenhouse pottering. She was in there most days 'supervising' the four hundred-odd lilies she had growing in pots. They were already about an inch high and she fussed them like a mother hen. Apparently she was waiting for the last of the frosts to be over before planting them out in the new bed by her gate. They'd look dead classy when they flowered – a block of sweetly scented, dusky pink, bell-shaped flowers nodding in the breeze.

But she wasn't in the greenhouse. He spotted her at the far end of the garden struggling with yet another heavy plant, and watched her working while he waited for the kettle to boil.

'Need a hand?' he asked a few minutes later, strolling across the lawn towards her.

She did that thing with her hair again, leaving another streak of mud across her temple where she'd caught up a stray strand of hair to curl it behind her ear. 'Thank you but I feel I'm taking advantage of you. I shouldn't be taking you away from your work.'

'I'll swap some muscle-power for a favour,' he offered.

Her grin made him catch his breath. 'Give,' she invited.

'I don't know what to do about lunch on Sunday. I have to lay on a spread for the garden scheme thingie at my place.'

'Warm up some sausage rolls, hand out some bags of crisps, and Bob's your uncle.'

'Is that all? Nah. Sounds too easy. There must be a catch.'

'There is. I should have told you after you helped me with my plant.'

'You could help me boil some potatoes,' he suggested.

'Are we being a tiny bit chauvinist here?' she said, arms akimbo and her head cocked on one side. 'On the other hand, if you were to help me roll this palm into that hole, I'd be really grateful. It's incredibly heavy.'

'Does it come with a fancy name, too?'

'*Trachycarpus fortunei.*'

'Another incantation.'

'In a way.'

He looked at the hole and the plant, automatically gauging heights. 'Mind if I check the depth first?'

'Be my guest.'

He dug out a few more spadefuls. 'Gives us more room to manoeuvre,' he said.

'You'll just think I like making you work,' she replied.

'I just didn't fancy having to lump it out again,' he countered as, together, they rolled the plant down a plank. 'I'd rather sit in the kitchen and have coffee with you.'

Had he just said that aloud? Jesus, what an idiot. Her only reaction was to try and align the plant without his help. Damn, he'd embarrassed her. 'Here. Let me,' he said, climbing down into the hole and turning the plant. 'Is that the way you want it?'

'Yeah. That'll do.'

It clearly wasn't right but she wanted to get rid of him.

Damn, he really had embarrassed her. 'I've put my foot in my mouth with you before,' he said. 'You promised to bring me grapes last time.'

It cleared the air between them instantly because she chuckled. 'You wanted them from Tesco because you were in too much of a hurry to wait for the ones on my vine.'

'Tell me how you want the palm.'

'Can you turn it a quarter to the right?'

'It weighs a flipping ton,' he grunted, twisting it carefully. 'How the heck do you do this alone?'

'I am very slow,' she said. 'The catalogue said 50kg.'

He looked at her amazed, and then started to backfill the hole for her. When it was done, they stood back to admire their work.

'Hats off to you,' she said. 'It's at just the right depth. Come on. Let's go and have that coffee.'

Back in the kitchen, sitting in the middle of the table, was Rob's hellebore. Ruth went straight to it, pulling off her gardening gloves as she did so. 'Is this for me?'

He nodded. 'I broke the other one last time I helped you.'

'Oh, Rob, you are sweet,' she said automatically reaching up to kiss his cheek. Then immediately she busied herself with the kettle looking more than a little confused.

He pulled out a chair and sat down, his heart hammering. His hands, when they reached for the plant, felt like they were trembling, though they looked steady enough, thank goodness. 'It's a *Helleborus orient* "Emerald Queen",' he said, reading the label, 'whatever "orient" means. William says the flowers have red lines radiating from the centre. Oh, and it prefers semi shade, so it turns out to be useless for that spot.'

'You really didn't need to, but thank you,' she said, bringing coffee over. When she sat down she seemed collected again as she nudged the plate of biscuits his way.

'My favourites,' he said, reaching for one.

'I know.'

Of course she knew. Just as he knew her favourite drink at

the end of an afternoon was weak jasmine tea. 'Well, it's important you know. I've a sweet tooth. Feed me a few of these a day and there's no knowing how many bushes I'll plant for you, though I hope they aren't all as big as the one we did today. I'll do my back in and –'

He stopped, conscious that he was rambling, and got up. He'd have liked to spend the rest of the afternoon talking with her, but suddenly it felt too intimate, though he was hard pressed to say why. All she'd said was that she knew what biscuits he liked. 'I'd best be getting on,' he said gruffly, picking up his mug.

Ruth nodded, blowing on her coffee to cool it. 'See you later,' she said.

He paused in the doorway. It was funny how such a neutral phrase seemed laced with meaning. 'Yeah,' he replied, and was gone.

CHANGING LOCKS

Two days later Ruth was on her way home from Lucy's where she'd been invited to offer advice on the garden. It was just balmy enough to make-believe spring was on its way: white wood anemones carpeted the narrow belt of woodland between the town and the estate, and the tips of the hawthorns were bright green as if they were savouring the warmth before fully breaking into leaf.

Continuing up London Road past the cheap stores, the car repair shops, the Job Centre, the bookie and the tattoo shop with its sign telling passers by 'No-one under 18', she drove along the edge of the estate.

Having gone to Lucy's via Vix's, she was driving the direct way home. It was a while since she'd been in this part of town and she was overcome by the decay that had set in. The estate had not been up five years and already there were signs of rotting windows and peeling paint. One boarded up property bore signs of a recent fire, the streets were rimmed with soggy litter, and rubbish leaked from front gardens. Judging by the number of black plastic bags oozing on pavements, the rubbish men hadn't been for weeks. Meanwhile, at regular intervals along the way, abandoned building sites were already ankle deep in nettles, docks and thistles. Come summer, the plots would be impenetrable.

Was this all in William's report?

Then, past a narrow, bramble-infested strip, rows of neat terraced houses indicated she was back in the old part of town. It was like reaching a park after stumbling about in the wild woods – gardens looked cherished, daffodils were shooting up, crocuses were in flower, people had made an effort to disguise their recycling bins, cars looked polished, front doors smart.

Yet, in spite of her unease about the mountain of work that lay ahead of the Elderfield in Bloom team, Ruth was relaxed and curiously happy as she entered the one-way filter system into town. She drove up the narrow street to the junction at the main road reviewing her morning with Lucy.

Lucy had taken the day off work and had plied her with coffee and muffins while they explored her chaotic front garden. Ruth rather liked the way everything grew through everything else, but she could see Lucy's frustration. She knew exactly what it was like to lose heart when faced by a mammoth project, and advised Lucy to set herself tiny projects, aiming to complete each one in a couple of hours. They'd made a start by pruning the Pyracantha, and now the mop of a bush was trained back against the house leaving space for other plants to come up underneath. The effect was instant and the garden already looked tamer. Ruth had left Lucy sweeping her driveway clear of last year's leaves.

Now, as she drove home, she was planning what to do in the sunken garden at the back of the house. This year, she wanted to do something more theatrical with it, more formal and less cottage-garden, like a living flame of red, and she wondered how Rob might react if she offered to pay him to help her with the heavy work. She had a plan involving a ton of Heuchera Fire Chief with its lush leaves the colour of summer sun though a glass of merlot, and Verbascum Caribbean Crush with its tall spikes of ruffled smoky-caramel flowers rising from a rosette of velvety leaves, and pondered calling into the garden centre to discuss the project with William.

At the junction ahead, two boys waited on bicycles. How nice, she thought, remembering her own childhood messing around on bikes. The boys seemed to hesitate. The main road wasn't that busy – it was just a bit challenging to slip into the traffic – but they didn't move. As Ruth edged past them to wait for a gap in the traffic, one of the boys rapped hard at her side window as if to call her attention to something. She started to wind it down and, as she did so, the other boy opened the passenger door and grabbed her bag. Together they flipped their bikes round and pedaled hard down the one-way street, disappearing round the corner, leaving Ruth stunned, then furious.

Her reaction was to reverse hard down the road, turn the car and race after them, but they had gone, along with her mobile, her purse, everything. She looked left and right down the side streets as she drove, but nothing. They might as well have vanished into thin air. Then she spotted Rob's van parked outside a house.

'Hello!' she called urgently when she banged at the door seconds later. 'Is Rob here?'

She heard footsteps, then Rob was there standing on the threshold. She felt a rush of relief just seeing his familiar face.

'Ruth, are you all right?' he asked, all concern.

'I'm fine but some bloody boys just nicked my bag and I wanted to call the police.'

'When?'

'Literally two minutes ago.'

He stood back. 'Come in.'

'Do you live here?' she said, completely distracted as she

followed him along a dark passage into the kitchen at the back of the house. 'I saw your van and thought you might be able to help. I was driving home and they just took it from the passenger seat while I was waiting to pull into the traffic. I thought they wanted to ask me something. They looked young. Nice. On smart new bikes.'

In the kitchen, he offered her a seat before dialing the police and speaking briefly. 'They'll be right round,' he told her replacing the receiver.

She nodded. 'I'm fine,' she reassured him when he abruptly crouched beside her, closing a comforting hand around hers.

'You're very pale.'

'It's the shock of it, that's all. I'm not going to cry all over you.' But she wanted to; maybe then he might give her the hug she craved right now.

'You can if you want,' he invited with a smile, as if reading her mind.

She shook her head. 'I'm not frightened. I'm so angry I could spit.'

He gave her hands another squeeze just as there was a knock at the door. 'Blimey, that was quick. The cops must be taking it seriously for once in their lives,' he said. He seemed reluctant to let her go.

It turned out that the police wanted Ruth to go with them to see if she could spot the boys as they drove around town. 'Can I leave my car here?' she asked Rob.

'I'll be here when you get back.'

'Thanks,' she said, 'you've no idea how good that sounds.'

Two fruitless hours later, the police dropped her back at Rob's house. He opened immediately and invited her back in. 'How was it?'

'A complete waste of time,' she growled. 'Apparently there's been a string of thefts just like mine. I still can't believe they had the audacity to take my bag with me in the car like that.'

'Would you like a drink?'

'Yes, please. I'm parched.'

This time, as she followed him through the house, she had time to look around her. Downstairs was carpeted in smoky green. The walls were either papered in bold patterns or painted in garish colours that just worked – quite a contrast to her house, which was white throughout. Beautiful curtains hung to the floor in all the windows. The kitchen looked brand new, and the quarry tiles looked as if he'd spent all morning buffing them to a dull shine. But then, she supposed, he was a builder and it made sense for his home to double as a show house. Meanwhile, it seemed Rob had green fingers because the house was chock-a-block with thriving houseplants. How could she have missed this the first time? 'Wow,' she said. 'This place is like living in a jungle.'

'I can do the inside ones easily enough. The outside ones are trickier. Tell me what happened.'

So she told him everything, from her time at Lucy's house and what they had planned there, to when the police had picked her up. 'And the last two hours were completely useless,' she concluded. 'They drove aimlessly around the estate and any time they saw a child on a bike, they stopped him and asked me if that was one of them. I thought it was insulting. I bet all of them were nice children. There was no proof those two boys came out of the estate. It could have been anyone from anywhere.'

'Pity you didn't catch up with them yourself.'

'Just as well I didn't. I'd have rammed them and then spent the next year in prison for aggravated assault, or grievous bodily harm, or some such hugely punishable crime no one thinks small, pathetic women are capable of.'

'I've seen you manhandle enormous plants, Ruth. There's nothing pathetic about you at all.'

She sat a little taller. 'That's a really nice thing to say. Thank you.'

He toasted her with his coffee. 'How much did they get away with?'

'Ouff,' she sighed in vexation. 'Almost nothing. They've got my camera with some vital garden pictures, which irritates me but it's not the end of the world. My purse with about five quid in it. Credit cards – but they're useless without the pin numbers. A gas bill, my house keys...'

He met her eyes and they both stood up together.

'I'll come and change all the locks right now,' he said. She was trembling again. He put his arms around her. 'Is that fear, now, or anger?' he asked.

'Definitely fear. I don't want to go in there alone.'

He held her gently and dropped a kiss on the top of her head. 'I'll be with you. Don't worry.'

He followed her home in his van and flashed his headlights at her as they approached her house. She pulled over and he got out and ran up to her. 'Stay here,' he whispered. 'I'm just going to have a shufty round. If they're here, I'll call the police.'

'Rob, it's not safe.'

'You'll be OK, I promise.'

'No, I meant you.'

He looked at her askance. 'Ruth, look at me. I could bash those boys with one hand tied behind my back.'

'Don't do anything that'll land you in jail. It's not worth it.'

'I won't. Wait here till I call you.' With that, he ran along the road, climbed over the fence into her garden and jogged through the undergrowth to the back of the house. It took him seconds to confirm the place was deserted, so he loped back down the drive. 'All clear,' he said when he drew level with her, 'but I'll change the locks anyway.'

She opened the front door with a spare key and leaned against the wall while he worked. All through the alarm of the robbery and the trepidation of coming home, Ruth had been aware of the tension building up between them and now Rob's silence was getting to her.

'I was thinking of developing my sunken garden,' she announced. 'I want to put in a small pond with a fountain, one of those dribbly Japanese plinky things.'

'Would you like some help in it?' he asked in his calm way,

glancing up.

'I'd love some. But I'd like to –'

'Please don't say you'll pay me for my time. I'll help you as a friend.' He reached forward and kissed her cheek. 'There. Now we're officially friends.'

Oh goodness. She couldn't breathe let alone think straight. She pushed herself away from the wall and, before she knew it, she was half way across the hall going – she didn't know where.

'Sorry. I didn't mean to overstep the mark,' he said gruffly.

She took a breath to speak, and then another. 'You didn't ov...' she said over her shoulder. Come on, girl, get a grip. You're friends talking about gardens, that's all. The thought settled her and she turned back. 'I don't want to take advantage, Rob. You're so kind to everyone and –'

'Not everyone.' He seemed to come to a decision because he crossed the hall to where she'd retreated and put a hand on her cheek. 'Only people I care about.'

She couldn't help it: her shoulders dropped as she turned her cheek into his warm hand, like a cat arching its back into a stroke. His breath fanned her face as he bent towards her but then he seemed to hesitate because he paused, his steady blue eyes studying her face. In the end, it was she who closed the gap between them, brushing his lips with hers.

His kiss in return was neither sensuous nor assertive. It was so diffident she had to rein in the hunger threatening to overwhelm her.

'I've never done this,' he whispered against her mouth.

'Neither have I,' she gasped and felt his lips smile against hers.

'It's not something I make a practice of, seducing customers,' he added, pulling back slightly as if to check she believed him.

She did. Part of her was conscious of being Ruth Dawson, faithful widow of Michael Dawson. Another part of her just wished he'd kiss her again. That first, all too brief, kiss had been like pouring champagne into her blood but initiating another was beyond her – she was all out of practice at courtship.

He appeared to sense her dilemma because he tentatively kissed her again, and this time he reached past her parted lips to touch her tongue with his. Electrified, she moaned into his mouth, kissing him back. It was as if he'd been waiting for permission because he cupped the back of her head and pulled her not so gently into the line of his body as he lost himself in her mouth. He was so not immune to her.

Then all of a sudden he eased back and stood cradling her against him. 'Come and show me what needs doing in the sunken garden,' he suggested.

Now she was embarrassed. She had wanted more but he was pulling away. Had she done it wrong? Oh God! He must think she was just a sad, middle-aged woman with a crush.

Just when these thoughts threatened to paralyse her, he led her out into the sunshine. The way he took her hand, his fingers entwined tightly, almost painfully, in hers made her realise that, far from not wanting her, he was giving her the space he thought she needed.

Her heart seemed to skip a beat. God, he was nice.

INITIATION

Meanwhile, on the other side of town, Bruce Turner was livid. Al could hear him through the floor, thundering down the phone at someone about mud all over the streets – word had got round about the adopt-a-verge scheme and several mad gardening enthusiasts in the old town had taken rotovators to the verges outside their houses.

Nervous, bordering on terrified, Al perched on Gazzer's bed while Gazzer himself sat at the desk texting. Yesterday, Al had been truly shocked by Gazzer's behaviour. Consequently, when Gazzer 'summoned' him this morning, he had biked over without a second thought.

'You going to be texting all day?' Al asked as nonchalantly as he could.

'No. Just getting one of the crew round.'

'Oh yeah?' Al had officially met The Crew after school the day before when Gazzer had swaggered up to him and asked without preamble, 'Is that him?' and pointed to a boy who had been bullying Al for the last six months.

Al shrugged, not sure what Gazzer could do about it. He himself had grown used to keeping a low profile whenever Neal was about.

'Well, is it?' Gazzer demanded.

'So what if it is?'

'Watch and see how we look after our own,' Gazzer promised, and gave a slight nod to a bunch of boys who were lounging against the cars parked outside the school gates. The boys seemed to ignore Neal as he passed, but he must have sensed something because he picked up his pace.

He looked back when he reached the corner of the road, but Gazzer's crew were idly lighting fags and blowing smoke rings. The moment he had gone, the crew arranged their hoodies over their heads, taking time to adjust their gelled hair in car windows, and set off after him, keeping their distance at first as they threaded through the streets towards Neal's home. Then, in a street filled with litter and half finished blocks of flats, Al spotted more boys coming towards them. Neal saw them too and looked around in panic.

'Now it gets physical,' said Gazzer. 'Watch.'

'Not for me. I don't want this,' said Al, but he might as well have saved his breath because Gazzer ignored him, intent on his quarry.

Neal wheeled, running up one of the paths to a house where he hammered at the door, never noticing it was boarded up. When it was obvious no one was coming, he cast about, jumped the low garden wall, and tried to sprint around Gazzer's group, but Gazzer had a runner ready for him, who tackled him to the ground. The youths closed in, armed with thick sticks.

Gazzer seemed content to observe. He held a long hunting knife and seemed entirely focused on caressing the blade, but Al could see his attention was all on the boy.

For a long moment nothing happened. Al realised the crew was waiting for orders and his blood seemed to curdle.

'Do 'im,' Gazzer said, and the crew moved as one, like a pack of wolves.

'Please, please,' screamed the boy, roiling and twisting in a frenzy to get away. 'Don't shank me. Please don't shank me,' he begged.

As the crew set upon the boy with their sticks, Al was sick in the gutter and then looked on helplessly, too afraid to run away and too afraid to help Neal.

'Stop it,' he said weakly to Gazzer.

'He shouldn't have fucked with you,' replied Gazzer.

'OK but enough.'

'You reckon?'

'Yeah,' whispered Al.

Gazzer gave a short wolf whistle and instantly there was calm. The boy lay in a bloody, unmoving heap. Several of the crew fished out their mobiles and took photographs. 'Trophies,' said Gazzer to Al, before walking up to the boy and grabbing a fistful of hair. 'See this?' he said, shoving the knife in his face. The boy was crying, Al was relieved to see, crying but alive, with snot trailing from his nose.

'Do you see it?' demanded Gazzer.

'Yes,' the boy choked.

'You fuck with my crew again, and this will pin you to the wall. See this? This is blood. Remember the boy who got slotted? This is his blood, so don't think I don't mean it. Whoopsadaisy! I think he's just pissed himself,' said Gazzer, standing back and braying. The crew cackled with derision and took more pictures, some of them moving in for a close-up of the darkened patch spreading on the boy's trousers.

They left him in the road.

Al plodded home in a stupefied daze beside Gazzer, who

kept up an endless stream of chatter about girls and music as if nothing had happened. There were no sirens or blue lights. At one point, Al spotted a CCTV camera. 'Taken out,' said Gazzer, noticing Al duck his head. 'No fret.'

Al couldn't stop shivering. He was so cold he thought he would never warm up. 'Be cool,' said Gazzer when they parted. 'Lots of people get the shakes the first time. Fight or flight. Remember Mrs Patel telling us in biology? He won't fuck with you again, you'll see. OK?'

Al could barely nod.

The next day, sitting on Gazzer's bed, Al was gnawing his nails when he heard footsteps on the stairs. They paused and a deep voice said politely, 'Good morning, Mr Turner.'

'Paddy, good to see you. Gary's upstairs. You go on up.'

'I thought you'd like to see my stash,' Gazzer said to Al casually, as Paddy walked in. 'Go and make us tea,' he told Paddy, 'and ask my father if he wants one while you're about it. Give us five minutes.'

Paddy stomped back down the stairs, and Al heard him respectfully address Mr Turner and ask if he could fix him a cup of tea.

Gazzer turned to Al. 'Look!' He opened his desk drawer and revealed a gun.

Al's heart started to hammer. Was it loaded?

'She's a beauty, isn't she? Want to hold her?' Without waiting for a reply, Gazzer picked up the gun in its protective cloth and tossed it at Al, who caught it automatically.

It was surprisingly heavy and slightly oily.

'And this is the knife that did Harris,' Gazzer breathed, pulling it out from the back of the drawer. 'Go on, take it. Now *that* is sweetly balanced. See what I mean?'

Al took the handle and weighed it, his heart in his mouth. Harris had been knifed in the riots last week. A young man of about twenty, he'd been found by the police lying in a gutter holding his stomach together. He was still in hospital.

'I lied to Neal about blood on the blade yesterday,' said

Gazzer. 'Only a wanker would leave blood on a blade, but he didn't know that, did he? Stupid twat.'

Al held the knife in limp hands, revolted that Gazzer might actually have stuck it into someone.

'Look, I don't want no aggro, so if you breathe a word about this to anyone,' said Gazzer in a friendly tone, 'including the crew, you're a dead man. Got that?'

Al managed a faint nod.

'See, you owe me for Neal.' Gazzer gave him a light shove. 'Ah, lighten up, mate,' he joshed as he put the gun and knife away. 'Oh will you look at that?' he muttered. 'You've got 'em all dirty. They're covered in your fingerprints.' He sighed and smiled at Al, whose stomach heaved. 'Never mind. I'll clean 'em later.'

Paddy came up with mugs of tea, which Gazzer lightened with a shot of whiskey from a bottle secreted behind his chemistry textbook. 'How d'you reckon you'll do in the exams?' he asked.

Al stared at him, wide eyed. 'I dunno. All right, I suppose.'

'Good man. Listen, on your way home, drop this package off at Pitt's, will you? Here!' He stuffed a fiver in Al's shirt pocket. 'That's for the bother. You'd be doing me a favour – I want to watch the footie on the box with me dad.' He put a small package in Al's hands. It was well sealed.

'What's in it?' asked Al, knowing he shouldn't ask.

'DVDs. Porn. Wanna see?' asked Gazzer.

'No. I'll take your word for it.'

'Good man. See you at school on Monday.'

Al was subdued when he went round to Susan Mallinson's house that afternoon where he set his hand to mindless cleaning. Later, when he got home, his mother hardly noticed he was monosyllabic. She thought he didn't know she was shagging William Jones. He couldn't think why she bothered hiding it from him. Grown ups didn't have a clue, he thought.

Meanwhile, he was having nightmares at the thought of his fingerprints all over the gun and knife. He'd been a mug.

THE COMMUNITY GARDEN SCHEME

That Sunday, all over town, strangers turned up at people's houses and were let in. They had all volunteered nine hours of their time to the community garden scheme. Al, along with his mother and Ruth, pitched up at Rob's house, where Rob was worrying he was abusing the system because he didn't have a front garden; his door opened straight on to the street.

'It's about gardening, not the competition,' Ruth reassured him as she concentrated on watching Vix park. Had he slept as badly as she had?

'You're probably right,' was his laconic reply.

Was he being nice yesterday in not rushing her with a second kiss, or had he really been trying to let her down gently? She risked a glance at him and was rewarded with one of his slow smiles. She couldn't hold his gaze, feeling even more jumbled than before. Was that a friendly smile or a lover's smile? He was still smiling at her when she looked up again and, though neither of them moved, it suddenly felt like they were circling each other in a slow dance of courtship so subtle that no-one else would notice – unless they happened to be Vix, she amended. Ruth pretended not to notice Vix's raised eyebrows and nonchalantly kissed her cheek in greeting before shaking hands with Al.

Then she ruined it by uttering, 'Beautiful day, isn't it?' which made Vix titter, and echo, equally brightly, 'Yes, beautiful, isn't it?'

Ruth couldn't help herself – she laughed. A glance at Rob told her that this exchange and her reaction to it had thoroughly perplexed him.

In all, about ten people turned up. Rob made them all hot drinks and someone passed round a packet of biscuits. Sitting in his living room was tricky, dominated as it was by enormous potted plants, but eventually everyone found themselves a space. Ruth sat cross-legged on the floor and led the discussion about what Rob wanted to achieve in his garden, in the same way as she had primed all the other homeowners to do.

It was a matter of pride to her that the community gardens project got off to a smooth start, so during the week she had gone round to each house being visited that Sunday and toured the garden with the owner, making suggestions when requested on how to manage a bunch of enthusiasts who might know nothing about gardening.

It turned out flowers didn't interest Rob at all; he wanted to grow vegetables.

'It's too early to sow seeds now, but we could prepare the beds,' suggested Ruth. 'Why don't we go and see what needs to be done? Has anyone got a camera? Mine's been nicked.'

Charlie piped up. 'I could use my phone.'

'Great. You wrote up the piece for the poster competition, didn't you?'

'Yeah,' he beamed. 'They didn't pay me or nothing, but they put my name at the top. "By Charlie Sullivan". Dad was dead impressed.'

'I was, too,' interjected his mother.

'You're pleased about everything,' he dismissed. 'Nothing ever excites Dad, but he kept showing my piece to everyone who came in the shop that week.'

'Great,' said Ruth. 'We need something to encourage other people to get involved.'

Charlie's face lit up. 'I can do that.'

'We'll need some before- and after-pictures and a team photo,' added Vix.

Charlie nodded and raced off. He returned almost immediately and asked to take photos from upstairs. Rob showed him the way.

'Give me two minutes,' Charlie called, 'then send people out. Then I can have them arriving like they do on the telly.'

'Another Jules in the making,' murmured Vix.

Ruth grinned. 'I'm having fun.' She did indeed look a different person to the one Vix had bullied out of bed at New Year. Vix beamed back. 'I'm so glad, darling. You deserve it.'

Everyone drank their coffees and then surprised Rob by trooping into the kitchen to wash their mugs, before donning boots and coats, all the while apologising for mucking up his kitchen floor with dried mud. One or two looked at an elegant mosaic coffee table in the sitting room with interest and asked where he'd bought it. They were fascinated when he admitted to 'knocking it up' himself. After the others had gone outside, Lucy spent a little longer inspecting it and considering what she could sell it for. She caught up with Ruth to ask her opinion about getting Rob to make another one so she could test the market.

'Ask him,' replied Ruth.

'D'you think so?'

'Definitely.'

'I'm not sure. He's so, you know…'

'What?'

Lucy shrugged. 'Distant.'

'Rob?'

'Yeah.'

Ruth felt exasperated. 'Just ask him.'

'OK. Later.'

Rob joined them on the back door step and the three of them watched the others wander around the miniscule space. 'I did warn you,' he said.

'You did,' said Ruth, 'and I can see why Charlie wanted to take pictures from upstairs but I bet it's bigger than you think. You just need to sort out that massive hedge. What d'you want people to do?'

'Can't I put you in charge?'

'I can get you going. Do you want to keep the hedge?'

He shook his head.

'OK. Let's get rid of it.'

'Just like that?'

'Yep. It'll give you at least ten foot of extra garden along three sides. That's a heck of a lot of new ground. Are you going to leave the fence? It's quite high.'

'I can sort that out later.'

'Let me know if you want help.'

In answer he put an arm round her shoulders and gave her a gentle squeeze.

It turned out to be fun. Everybody pitched in. The men threw themselves into the task of hacking down the hedge and soon had a bonfire going. Then, at the back of the garden, they found an old compost bin.

'How long's that been here?' asked Ruth.

'Emma mentioned it just after we moved in,' said Rob. 'She must have…' He stooped to pick up some hedge clippings and threw them on the bonfire where they crackled loudly, drowning out whatever he might have said, and then stood warming his hands against the blaze.

Now Ruth understood Lucy's 'distant' epithet – it felt as if he'd switched the lights out. She smiled brightly at the group. 'Well, compost is just what we need to nourish the garden. Let's empty the bin and see what we find.'

It took both Al and Charlie to tip the bin on its side and up-end it.

'Oooh, look at this happy compost,' exclaimed Lucy, bending down and raking her fingers through the tilth. 'Charlie, come and look.'

Ruth directed people where to put the empty bin and then stooped to dig up a plant. 'There's a ton of weeding to do. For those that don't know, this is a dock. You'll need to dig up the roots, too. Put it on the fire. If you put it in the compost bin, it'll think Christmas has come. This,' she said pulling up another plant, 'is Herb Robert.'

When she looked up, Rob was watching her with that quiet way of his.

'It's er –' What had she been going to say? She took a breath and focused on Al. 'It's an annual, and later in the summer it'll have lots of delicate pink flowers which are really pretty. It has these feathery leaves – see? – and these lovely pink stems. It's dead easy to pull up and you can put it on the compost heap. This, on the other hand, is a dandelion. The young leaves are nice in salads, but if you leave them, they'll grow so strongly that Rob'll end up with a dandelion patch rather than a vegetable patch. You have to dig them up because this long tapering root,' she held it up, 'will keep growing back and back and back.'

'Why don't you just poison it?' asked someone.

'You might not want to nuke areas you're about to grow vegetables in.'

'Good point.'

They worked in companionable groups all morning, chattering away and gradually the garden opened up.

'I've got so much to learn,' said Lucy coming up to Ruth later.

Ruth grinned. 'Me too.'

'What? If you don't know it all, there's no hope for me.'

'Oh, I regularly rip things out because they don't work. Experiment!'

'Nah. I just want a tidy garden. I should be working in it now, but it's lonely by myself. It's not really Terry's cup of tea, gardening. He'd pave the lot over, and put in a giant barbeque and a fridge to keep the beers cold.'

'Well, he's got a point,' said Rob, coming up behind them. 'I'm going to have to keep this lot looking tidy once you've all gone. Paving it over suddenly seems like a great idea.'

Ruth pretended to look affronted, and he laughed and held up his hands in mock surrender. Someone started up a chain saw and he turned away to supervise cutting up the final bits of hedge.

'Thank you for being so supportive,' Ruth said to Lucy. She was thinking of the wider context of Elderfield in Bloom, and Lucy's part in the poster competition.

'You're all right, you know, Ruth?' said Lucy. 'You've

changed. You used to look so withdrawn and stuck up, but you're good for a giggle, aren't you? And this community thingie. It bloomin' works! I've met Parvati Chopra over there.' She waved and a small, dark haired woman waved back. 'She doesn't have a garden but she's going to come and help me in mine as often as she can.' She reached over and gave Ruth a hug. 'Thank you, sweetie.'

Ruth swallowed and beamed back, her eyes shining with emotion.

Everything was going wonderfully until, just before lunch, Rob went to answer the door and found Bruce Turner on the doorstep. It seemed he wanted to see for himself what was happening with the Community Garden Scheme. 'Poking his nose in where it's not wanted, more like,' Vix said, with a sniff.

Rob went round proudly showing him how everyone was helping out, but Bruce looked affronted. 'This isn't going to help us win the Award,' he said. 'Where's that woman?'

Rob stiffened and paused mid stride.

'You've got all these people down here on false pretences,' Bruce went on.

'A word in your ear, Counsellor,' said Rob, trying to lead Bruce back into the house.

'I expect that woman is behind it all,' said Bruce, his booming voice carrying. By now everyone had stopped work and was watching to see how Rob would react. 'She was quite happy to waste tax payers' money printing fancy posters,' Bruce continued, 'but I put her right on that one. Now she's wasting everybody's time on this back garden. It's a shameful abuse of the Scheme.'

Ruth came out of the house, her mouth tight with anger. She was about to say something when Lucy stepped forward. 'We're having fun here, Mr Turner.'

'Fun?'

Lucy faltered. 'Yes. We're meeting new people, making friends. Rob's garden will be ready to plant vegetables in by the end of the day.'

Bruce raised his eyebrows and was about to speak when Rob butted in. 'I'm fully aware no one can see my garden from the road, but –'

'But nothing,' said Ruth. 'This scheme is about helping people in their gardens.'

'In their *front* gardens. To help the town win the Award.'

'To build the community. That's why it's called the *Community* Garden Scheme.'

'Look, I'm not going to stand here and argue with someone who has no authority to make decisions. I'll get the rules amended right away. If the Council's to back this, then it's right and proper that everyone is working to a common purpose, which is not poncing about planting vegetables that no one can see.'

Ruth looked as if she wanted to retort. Then she shrugged. 'I can see your point,' she said, taking the wind out of his sails. 'But I disagree.'

'That's your prerogative, undeniably. I'm sorry, Rob,' said Bruce slapping his shoulder and turning back into the house, 'but you can see how it is. We can't have everybody making the rules up as they go along. I'm in charge and I decide.'

Rob let him out. When he came back, Ruth could see he was fuming.

'You are not That Woman.'

'Forget it, Rob,' she said. She was unwrapping packets of sausage rolls onto an oven tray. While he had gone to let Bruce out, she had had to take a couple of moments to recentre herself – she was no saint, and God knew how much she had wanted to fight for her principles, but arguing with Bruce in public would not help the project in the long run. 'There are other, more important battles to fight, and arguing with him is a waste of time.'

'No, Ruth –'

'Rob, please drop it.'

'But the way he treated you.'

'Hm. His manner is unfortunate.'

Rob huffed. 'Unfortunate?'

'Hm. I think so, don't you?'

He was unhappy but he let her have the last word and carried a table into the garden, which they laded with enough food to feed an army. Bruce's visit left everyone subdued, but Ruth went round smiling and chatting as if he were quite right to object, and soon people began to feel soothed. Before long they were tucking into hot sausage rolls, crisps, and coleslaw still in its tub from the supermarket. The men made a beeline for the beer and the women huddled in groups with paper plates on their knees, nattering.

'I'm so glad William wasn't here,' said Vix softly to Ruth. 'I feel so cross with that man. He'd have had something to say about this, all right.'

It took Ruth a couple of seconds to work out who was who. 'Forget it. In a way, he's right.'

'You don't really believe that, do you?' asked Vix, skewing round to look Ruth in the face.

'No, but it won't help anyone to jump to my defence. I need the town pulling together.'

'But, Ruth –'

'Not you, too?'

'Who else? Everyone played dumb.'

'Rob was equally cross.'

'Oh.'

Where's William?'

The distraction worked. 'He's at another garden on the other side of town.'

'Yes, I remember now. You two have become very close. What's happening there?'

'I think I'm in love.'

Ruth sat up. 'Really?'

'Oh goodness, his kisses! I remember the first one,' mused Vix. 'I thought I'd died and gone to heaven. What's Rob like?'

Ruth looked at her sideways. 'He's nice.'

'Come on, darling. Anyone can see you two are –'

'I sincerely hope not, 'cause we're not.'

'You've kissed him, though, haven't you?'

Ruth was not ready to talk about this yet. It was all too soon. She hardly knew herself where things were going: Rob was younger than her. If I were a man, and he a woman, she mused, no one would blink at the age gap.

'You need a new hair style,' said Vix surveying her critically. 'Something to jazz up your image. And stop wearing roll neck sweaters and frumpy anoraks. Give your cleavage an airing.'

'I look fine,' Ruth retorted. 'You said blonde was good.'

'Yeah, but the style – you look... widowish.'

Ruth was hurt.

'Look, darling. Michael's gone and you've got years and years ahead of you. You don't want to spend them alone. Trust me on this one.'

'Hm.'

'No one can replace Michael, darling. But to spend the rest of your life without sex. Goodness, I'd rather cut my throat.'

'I gather William's OK in that department.'

'Phwor.'

'I'm not like you, Vix. I take things slowly.'

'Well, don't hang around too long. You'll lose your confidence.'

'Thank you for that, Vix.'

'Oh don't get hissy. You know what I mean.'

'Yes, I do,' acknowledged Ruth. She knew exactly what Vix meant. She felt off balance with Rob. He was out of her league yet for some reason he seemed attracted to her. What the heck did he see in her? She tried to look at herself dispassionately, and saw only the livery, widowish woman Vix had described.

Images of Susan Mallinson flitted through her mind. Well, she was not going to end up like her. Michael had not been perfect but he'd been hers. Now he was gone. Get on with life, she told herself.

Fine in theory. In practice, it was harder.

'Well? Did Rob kiss you yet?'

Ruth patted her arm. 'That's none of your business.'

'He looks like he'd be a great kisser. Part of me has always fancied Rob. He's just, I dunno, sexy.'

Ruth picked up Vix's plate. 'We've got a garden to finish. I'll put these in the bin.'

'Well he is! Imagine taming all that smouldering moodiness.'

'Vix. Shut. Up.'

Vix grinned.

CHAPTER 9

A WALK IN THE WOODS

Ruth was aware she was being elusive. She was out having a hair cut when Rob turned up for work on Monday morning. On her return, she scurried into the garden and remained there most of the day, timing her visits to the kitchen when she knew he wouldn't be there. She did the same on Tuesday and Wednesday. More than anything, she wished she hadn't had her hair cut.

Part of her didn't know how to handle the situation. For so many years the faithful wife, now she felt like a teenager experiencing her first crush on the coolest boy in the school. Part of her could not think what he saw in her, and part of her was just getting used to the idea that she was not being unfaithful to Michael. That part felt strangest. She couldn't escape the feeling that she was betraying everything they had had together simply by looking at Rob.

Without a doubt, Vix would have set her right if the two of them had discussed it over lunch when they were at Rob's on Sunday, but she'd avoided that, too.

Michael was never coming back. Logically, she knew he would not want her to turn into a lonely old widow, but it was never something they had talked about when he was dying. How do you bring up a discussion of moving on after someone's death when they are still alive and have been your soul mate until then? It would have been like gross disloyalty.

Till death do us part. That was the vow she had taken.

And after death? What then?

She was alive. And Rob was nice.

He was more than nice.

He was also a good kisser.

She moaned, savouring the memory of his kiss.

Get a grip, she told herself.

How long she would have gone on evading Rob, she had no idea, but on the fourth day of being avoided, he carried a mug of tea out to her at elevenses.

He approached over the lawn, his footsteps muffled by the grass, but movement caught her eye as she dug up a dandelion and tossed it over her shoulder onto the growing heap behind her.

'If they had weeding races, you'd be in a class of your own,' he observed as he got closer. 'It's like you're possessed. I've never seen someone work so fast.'

She feigned surprise. 'Oh, you startled me. Morning, Rob,' she said, resuming her weeding. She just could not face his grave, thoughtful eyes as he told her that kissing her was great but that they needn't repeat the experiment. For sure, he'd be politer than that.

'There's so much to do and so little time,' she said by way of excuse for not stopping.

'I brought you some tea.'

'Thanks,' she muttered, knowing how graceless she was being. 'If you put it over there, I'll get it when it's cooled a bit.'

He put it on the edge of the flowerbed as she'd indicated and stood back. Her unease was rucking up the air between them and she was fully aware that her weeding must look almost frenzied, but these rollercoaster feelings made her brittle with anxiety.

'I like the new hair.'

It was short and spiky and terrifyingly sexy. He would think she was trying to attract his attention. 'Hm.'

'Ruth,' he said softly, 'stop a minute, will you?'

She stopped mid dig but remained kneeling where she was, bent over her trowel. 'I'm sorry,' she whispered without looking up. 'I'm being rude.'

He crouched at the edge of the flowerbed, studying her. Then he picked up a handful of soil, crumbling it in his fingers. 'It's warm,' he said, disconcerted.

'It's going to be a good spring. If you walk through the woods, the wood anemones will be starting to come out, and the hellebores'll be looking good.'

'Will you show me?'

She hesitated.

'It's OK to feel like this,' he said. 'Awkward. I feel it too.'

She dug half-heartedly at another dandelion before venturing to look at him. He was smiling, his brooding eyes full of understanding.

'I...' Awkward was exactly how she was feeling.

He stood up and held out his hand and, without really thinking about it, she took it.

'Of course, I'm really hoping you'll do that Latin bit for me again,' he said, making her chuckle as he tucked her hand into the crook of his arm.

In the woods, the tips of the beeches were purple and swollen with the promise of new leaves. Drifts of wood anemones edged the path and, under the trees in all directions, hellebores bloomed in every shade from green to white, through pinks and reds to black. Some were single, some double, some were plain, some freckled and others were banded. The flowers nodded in the striped light of the pale spring day.

Ruth and Rob took their time wandering through the woods, pointing out flowers that caught their fancy. Rob had never seen anything quite like it; there were flowers as far as they could see under the trees.

'You should open these woods to the public,' he said. 'People would pay a fortune to see this. It's beautiful.'

'Next year, perhaps.'

'This is way better than the pictures in your book. They don't do justice to it.'

'I'm glad you made me come and see this,' she said as they meandered back towards the house. 'Sometimes I garden so hard, I forget to stop and look.'

'I meant what I said on Saturday,' he said, drawing her to a halt. 'I don't make a habit of seducing my clients. You're very special, Ruth, and I don't want you to feel awkward with me. Ever. If we can't be anything more than friends, that's OK and I'll always look back on that kiss with pleasure. But I want – I'd like…' He ground to a halt with a look of admiration in his eyes. It made her feel breathless and brave enough to do something she feared she would regret if she turned out to have misunderstood him.

She stood on tiptoes and lightly touched his lips with hers.

His reaction was all she could have wanted but not what she expected. He took a deep breath and let it out on a sigh, and stood there with his eyes closed and his head bent. His hand came up and threaded through her hair as he gently laid his forehead against hers. 'Oh Ruth,' he whispered, watching her as he slowly, so very slowly, tipped his head to find her lips with his.

The competition

For three weeks after the closing date nothing was heard of the poster competition. In the town, the talk was still of the knifing. Then Lucy invited Ruth, Bruce Turner as chair of the council, as well as the vice chair, Peter Davies, round to choose the winners. They arrived after closing on Monday, Ruth armed with a bottle of wine.

'I remember you like Italian,' she said, as Lucy passed round paper cups. 'I thought this might be a teensy reward. I didn't realise it would be so much work.'

Lucy, who had been thoroughly dispirited, brightened immediately. 'There were so many entries and it was so hard to choose the best ones. These are the rejects if you want to have a look,' she said, indicating the neat piles around the room.

Bruce and his vice chair ignored these, but Ruth picked up two piles at random and flipped through them. 'Gosh, these kids have so much imagination.'

'I know. It was nearly impossible to come up with a shortlist of ten. You'll have to choose the winners, Ruth.'

At this, Bruce huffed and his underlying resentment of Ruth instantly curdled the mood. His antagonism was so palpable that she could almost hear the way his mind was running: 'Who does she think she is, proposing competitions like this? She isn't a member of the parish council or leader of the Special Interest Group. She didn't even stand for office.' Looking at Bruce working himself up into a rage, she realised how galling he must find it that everyone kept putting her in the driving seat. She wished they wouldn't; all she wanted was to work peacefully in her garden. However, she wasn't one to shirk her responsibilities, even those thrust upon her, and if that meant playing politics, so be it.

'Mr Chairman,' she said formally. 'How would you like to proceed?'

Bruce was preposterously pleased she had conceded to him, and went on an on about how he was, after all, the people's representative.

Did he really think she wanted his job? Frankly, he could pick the winners by himself as far as she was concerned. No doubt he considered her an interfering busybody and would have ignored her if he could. That he did not, she suspected, was down to her relationship with Jules; Bruce's reaction to being filmed was almost farcical, as if being on television somehow underpinned his status. Surely it was a man's standing in the community that gave him eminence, not his dubious ability to entertain a wider audience for half an hour, after which no one would remember him ever again.

Eventually, after what seemed like hours of meaningless debate about her position in the Special Interest Group, he suggested the obvious solution that they all choose a picture from every pile and then vote on a winner for each age group. He chose a picture at random and the vice chair, after a brief hesitation, spinelessly did the same. He then drummed his fingers while she agonised over her choice.

Half way through the proceedings, Vix turned up with William and Rob. 'How's it going?' she asked Lucy.

'Really well, I think,' said Lucy, flashing a toothy grin at her.

'We're off to the pub afterwards. Wanna come? Of course, you're welcome to join us, too, Mr Chairman. And you, Peter,' Vix nodded at the vice chair.

Lucy was torn but decided she ought to go home and cook supper. Bruce looked down his nose at Vix. 'I've got more important things to do than sit in a pub all evening,' he said.

Vix raised her eyebrows and was about to say something when Ruth trod hard on her foot. Vix gave her a dirty look.

'Sorry, Vix. Didn't see you there.'

More polite, the vice chair, after a nervous glance at Bruce, said: 'Thank you, another time perhaps.'

All the while, William was poking through the piles of paintings. He frowned. 'There's so many,' he commented.

'Yeah,' agreed Lucy. 'It took me two weeks just to sort them into categories.'

'Wow,' he said. 'Hard work.' Then to Ruth he added with a leer: 'Luscious hair cut. Love it.'

Startled, she smoothed the curls at the nape of her neck self-consciously. Rob, who had obviously heard, was amused by her coy reaction.

When it came to voting, the vice chair cravenly copied his chairman again and together they outvoted Ruth each time, which Bruce carefully minuted in his notebook with a silly simper. She had to force herself not to look at Vix or she would have rolled her eyes at such behaviour. Nevertheless, she was happy with the result – all the shortlisted paintings would have made worthy winners. The overall victor was a thirteen-year-old called Emlyn James who came from the new estate.

'Mr Chairman,' said Ruth, 'about getting a poster printed –'

'I've told you already,' he said, all geniality wiping from his face as he cut her short, 'there's no money in the budget for that.'

'But how will we promote the competition to the wider town? We need everyone to understand that we must pull together in this.'

'You pull together all you want, but you went ahead with this competition without consulting me or the Treasurer. There won't be a penny in the budget for printing posters.'

'And yet you managed to fund a video on how to catch a bus,' Ruth pointed out, unable to help herself.

'That money was applied for using the proper channels.'

'But it's a ridiculous waste of money.'

'Ridiculous is it, Mrs Dawson? Ridiculous? I am doing my best to try and stop vandalism occurring on those buses and you presume to call it ridiculous. If you want posters printed, you'll have to find the money yourself.'

'We could raise it,' suggested Rob from the back of the room.

'How's that?' Bruce demanded.

'We could hold a car boot sale on the playing fields.'

'Those are council property. You'd have to apply for permission to use them in the normal way.'

'I presume you could arrange for the fee to be waived,' said Ruth.

'I don't hold with waiving fees. Who's to say your cause is better than the next one?'

'It's not *my* cause. This is for the whole town,' put in Ruth.

Bruce affected to look astonished. 'And you'd have me steal revenue from the town? That's ripe, that is.'

Unseen by Bruce, Rob put his hand on Ruth's back and she subsided. 'We'll apply in the usual way,' he said. 'Thank you. And thank you for your time here this evening. Vix, can you get a picture of Bruce and Peter together? The paper's asked her to write up how you chose the winners,' he added confidentially to

Bruce. 'Ah Ruth. I suppose you should be in the picture, too. Here, you stand at the back, like that.'

Ruth looked at him as if he were out of his mind, convinced that Bruce would see through his blatant sucking up, but it seemed Bruce expected people to be creepy because he simply turned to the camera and beamed.

Rob, unable to repress a snigger at Ruth's grim-faced pose, prodded her and she smiled too, although it was more of a grimace.

'We'll see you at the next meeting, Bruce,' said Rob as Vix put her camera away. 'Were you going to propose leading a group to see what other towns are doing to prepare for the awards? I only ask in case you needed me to find out how much a minibus might be. I could give you costings to present at the next meeting, if you like.'

'You're a mind reader, Rob. I was just going to ask you that and you took the words right out of my mouth. Good man. You find out how much it'll be. The proceeds of the car boot sale should cover that, too, so make sure you keep money aside for it. Can't be seen to be wasting taxpayers' money gallivanting around the countryside, can we?'

As Lucy closed the door behind the two departing counsellors, Vix turned on Ruth. 'You're a fine one to be treading on my toes to shut me up.'

'Arghhh,' shouted Ruth. 'I'll bloody kill him.' She made a fist but Rob caught it before she slammed it into the table. 'Easy, now,' he said.

Thoroughly intrigued, Vix's anger evaporated.

'Doesn't he want this town to pull together?' demanded Ruth, refusing to acknowledge Vix's look of enquiry.

'He wants to get rich,' said Rob.

She gaped at him. 'What?'

'He's buying up property from people who default on their mortgages. Rock bottom prices, too. I reckon it suits him to have the town down at heel for a while.'

'You're not serious.'

'Yep. Prices are lower here than in the rest of the county.'

She turned to Vix. 'Did you know about this?'

Vix shrugged. 'It's common knowledge.'

'Can you expose him?'

'For doing what?' asked Rob. 'For helping people out and letting them stay on in their houses for a nominal rent?'

'He's a crook!'

'He's on the bleedin' highway to heaven,' said William. 'They've practically set up a shrine in his driveway. He's the Good Samaritan, the Prodigal Son and Elvis Presley all rolled into one.'

'Elvis?' gulped Ruth.

'He's a businessman,' said Rob.

'Whose side are you on?' she demanded.

'This isn't about sides, Ruth. This is about getting rich.'

'But it's not right.'

He shrugged. 'On a positive note, he didn't veto the idea of a car boot sale.'

Ruth scowled. 'I started out this evening feeling so high-minded, but I can't help myself – I won't let him win.'

'That's my girl,' said Rob, patting her on the back.

'Just give the word and I'll have him sweating like a priest in a boys changing room,' William put in.

She shook her head. 'No, I'll get Jules to expose his shenanigans.'

Rob soothed her. 'You do want to live here afterwards, don't you?'

'This is so unfair.'

'I know, love.'

'Vix, I have a horrible feeling I'm turning into a grumpy old woman.'

'You and me both, darling.'

Valuation

The doorbell rang and Susan Mallinson ran to answer it, already knowing who would be there. She found him on the doorstep, that smile on his lips, that slow steady blink as he kissed her with his eyes. He was there. He'd come. She felt a burst of joy as she launched herself into his arms and felt them close around her.

'Mother!'

Mrs Mallinson woke up as rough hands squeezed her shoulders. She looked into her daughter's eyes as she bent over her, and shuddered.

Jennifer straightened up. 'Honestly, I've been ringing the bell for ages, haven't I, Mr Eckhart?' The last was in a foolish, girly voice. Mrs Mallinson wasn't deceived. She said nothing.

'Mother's a bit senile,' said Jennifer to the man standing in the doorway. She turned back to her mother. 'We've come to look at the house,' she said slowly, in the kind of voice one uses to the very stupid or the very deaf.

'I can hear perfectly well,' muttered Mrs Mallinson sullenly.

'Course you can, you silly old bat. I must say, Mother, the smell of cat pee is not as overpowering as usual.' Her hand closed on her mother's arm and squeezed it, her talons sinking into the flesh at the back. 'Has the council sent someone in?' she whispered, her eyes fierce. 'They have no bloody right. If they charge you, you can bloody tell them I didn't authorise it and to mind their own fucking business.'

Mrs Mallinson's courage wavered but her voice was strong enough when she asked, 'Why do you want to look at the house?'

'Mr Eckhart's from the local estate agent. He's going to value it,' she said loudly. 'Do you understand?'

Mrs Mallinson frowned. 'Why? It's my house.'

'Just ignore her,' Jennifer said to the man. 'Bit gaga, as I said. We'll see you in a minute,' Jennifer shouted at her mother, bending down to be level with her face. 'You'll be OK here, won't you?'

'I thought you said she couldn't look after herself,' said the man, hopping from one foot to the other in a kind of nervous dance as he looked round the immaculate room.

'Well, she can't. The council must have sent someone round to clean up. It was a serious health hazard a month ago. Come on. I'll show you round.'

'This is my house. I want you to go.'

'Just like I told you,' said Jennifer to Mr Eckhart, shaking her head pitifully. 'She'll be saying that all day now, like a scratched record.'

Mr Eckhart looked unsure what to do. 'Is it her house?'

'Yes, but she's going, you know, down the road.' Her voice became conspiratorial, and Mr Eckhart nodded as understanding dawned.

'Ah, St Benedict's Nursing Home.' His eyes softened. 'They say it's quite expensive… but nice, too. I can see why you want the house valued.'

Loser, thought Jennifer, and led him back down the passage. 'Let's start upstairs, shall we?' she said, trotting out the coquettish tone again, aware of Mr Eckhart following her up, his brow glistening in spite of the cold, his eyes fixed on her swaying hips and feasting on her bottom. Jennifer walked slowly, drawing out his anticipation.

Upstairs, she opened door after door. The place shone. Why would the council bother cleaning up here? If they sent a bill, she'd tell them where to shove it. Mr Eckhart took notes, goggled at her from behind his glasses, measured and asked if the curtains would remain. Jennifer almost snapped at his stupidity. Duh. Why would she want the curtains? They were old and faded.

He muttered something about them being antique, but she had other things on her mind. On the way back downstairs, she deliberately turned and looked up at the estate agent on the step above her. 'Mr Eckhart,' she breathed, 'about your commission…'

She had timed it so that he would have a perfect view of her cleavage from this angle and he stared down at it, open-mouthed. Jennifer could almost hear the cliché 'perfect, ripe peaches' float through his mind.

She'd dressed carefully in a low cut bra and a sweater bordering on vulgar. The boob job was worth every penny. She took several deep breaths, letting her chest rise and fall with each one, and was pleased to see his eyes widen. He wanted to touch.

'I'm sorry, did you say something?'

She leaned forward. 'I knew you'd understand. When I first saw you, it struck me straight away what a kind, understanding man you were.' She licked her top lip and gently put a hand on his where it rested on the banister. 'You see, the fees at St Benedict's are so high.'

Ever so gently, she rubbed her thumb on the back of his hand.

'I…'

'You and I could come to a little understanding, I thought.'

She tried that thing with her tongue again, licking her lip, and he watched mesmerised.

'Ah, yes.' He glanced back upstairs. There had been beds up there.

She shook her head slightly and took a step up so she could stand on tiptoes to whisper in his ear, 'Not now. Not with Mother downstairs. You understand, don't you?' She laid a hand on his chest and smiled up at him.

He nodded.

'Later,' she said, drawing her hand down his chest and watching as his eyes seemed to pop.

He nodded again and made as if to kiss her, but she was already turning away and there was nothing to do but follow her downstairs.

When he'd finished measuring up, she showed him the garden and then to the gate. 'You are too good, Mr Eckhart,' she said. 'I really appreciate all you're doing for me,' she added, ignoring the hand he held out and kissing his cheek. 'In France,' she whispered, 'they do it four times, like this.'

On each kiss he tried to turn his head so his mouth might touch hers, but somehow her cheek always landed squarely on his.

She waved him off with a saucy smile, waggling her fingers, and he reeled down the road to his car in a complete daze.

When he'd gone, Jennifer heaved a bored sigh and left, pleased with her day's work. She didn't bother to say goodbye to her mother.

DARK PEAK

The old cat lady was distracted all week. She was picky and mean and plain nasty at times. Once Al had the courage to snap back, but she glared at him so fiercely that he backed down. However, he was too full of his own worries to be concerned about a dotty old woman's bad temper.

For a start, he didn't know what to do about his fingerprints on a gun and a knife. And second, it seemed Gazzer was using him as a courier. In the first week, he asked Al to run a couple of packages across town for him. Even though he asked as if it was a big favour, Al wasn't deceived. He recognised an order when he was given one and there was nothing he could do.

He hadn't a clue what was in the packages and thought they might be drugs, but he wasn't about to open the well-sealed bundles to find out. One thing for sure: he took care not to leave his finger prints on them, and arrived at his destinations breathless from hard pedaling, convinced the police were going to stop and arrest him at any moment.

He couldn't sleep, let alone eat, from anxiety. In spite of this, he was careful to act as normally as possible at home. Unfortunately, his fear kept getting the better of him at school and came out in the form of cheek, to which teachers took a dim view. Twice he was sent to the headmaster, who gave him the same interminable lecture both times on 'The Importance of Complying With Teachers' Requests.' Calmer by then, having kicked his heels outside Buggins' office for half an hour, Al knew how to play the game and said 'Yes, Mr Sharples' and 'No, Mr Sharples' at all the right times. Next time, Mr Sharples warned, he would call Al's mother. Such threats, while they had had results in the past, had no power to frighten him now. Yet if his mother were called, he knew he would be gated. Half of him wanted to be, but the realistic half of him knew Gazzer wouldn't care; he'd still expect him to be his gofer.

Then, in the second week after the initiation, nothing. Al's phone fell silent and Gazzer was away from school. Now Al was having worries of a different sort: that the police had arrested Gazzer. Would he hand over the knife and gun with Al's fingerprints all over them as a sort of bargaining chip? Some days, it was all Al could do to get through them, but he continued to drag himself to Susan Mallinson's. Somehow, that part of the day, despite her iffy temper, was the easiest.

Then, over the weekend, while he was having a go at cooking under her supervision, he remembered the trunk and asked where it had got to.

'I hid it.'

'Why?'

'Because I think Jennifer wants it.'

That didn't make sense because, while the last of the gilt framed paintings had suspiciously disappeared, along with all the silver, he hadn't remembered anything of value in the trunk itself. Nothing except photos.

'Where've you hidden it?'

'In the garret.'

'In the garret?'

'Didn't I say so?'

'Yes, but...' He couldn't imagine how she had got it up there; he'd found it heavy enough. 'Why would your daughter want it?'

'Because she'll want a weapon.'

'A weapon?'

'Do stop repeating everything I say, boy.'

'I don't understand.'

'It's got stuff that's precious to me. If I don't do as she wants, she'll probably shove it all in a bin bag and take it away.'

'What does she want you to do?'

'Move into a home.'

'What? Why? She can't force you.'

'If she had the box, it wouldn't really matter any more.'

Bewildered, he asked: 'Would you like me to keep it safe for you?'

'What would be the use of that? I couldn't look at it then.'

'It was an idea.'

'A pretty rubbishy one.'

'Yeah,' he agreed. 'How did you get it up there?'

'With difficulty.'

He gave up and stirred the bolognaise sauce. 'How long did you say this should simmer?'

'An hour.'

He glanced at his watch. That would be half an hour past the end of his allotted time, not that it mattered much but he had an essay to write for tomorrow.

'I'm not helpless, you know? I can take a pot off the stove all by myself. Funnily enough, I've been able to do it all my life.'

He laughed. 'OK, OK. I was being over protective.' Steam rose from the saucepan, which he stirred from time to time. 'What were the photos of?' he asked, then added: 'You can tell me to mind my own business, if you like.'

'I could. Go and get the box down. I'll show you.'

He obligingly dragged the box down from the loft, and dropped it on the table with a bang. 'Sorry,' he said. 'It's really heavy.'

She opened it and drew out some photos, flipping past some, lingering over others. 'They're of my time in the war. This is me in my uniform.' She handed him a black and white photo of a pretty young woman. It was a formal portrait but it captured a look of determination on her face. 'Here I am again,' she said, handing him another photo. 'And this is me with some of the girls.'

'Someone said you were a war hero.'

Her mouth twisted. 'Poof. I had some adventures. Once I nearly crashed a plane.'

'I didn't know you were a pilot.'

'Women sometimes flew planes between bases. Sort of glorified delivery girls.'

'How come you nearly crashed?'

'I was flying back across the Pennines in a Lancaster. Big, heavy, brute of a plane, but solid.'

'And?'

She was silent so long he feared she might have forgotten the question, but her eyes were looking inward: she was reliving that day. 'It was a really wet afternoon,' she began. 'The cloud was low and I got lost. Get it wrong in the Pennines and you ended up buried on the Dark Peak. It's like the Bermuda Triangle, only it's in Derbyshire. Planes went in there and never came out.'

'What happened to them?' he breathed.

'I presume they flew into a hill,' she said prosaically. 'Pilot error.'

'Why didn't you use the auto pilot thingy?'

She looked at him pityingly. 'There was no auto pilot.'

'So what did you do?'

'I flew in circles and consulted my road map.'

'And in low cloud...'

'Precisely. You might not even see the hill. So there I was, having filed my flight plan. They waved me off, and then, just when I reached the Pennines, the clouds came down and I got lost.'

'Couldn't you just ditch the plane and parachute down?'

'No parachute.'

Al looked horrified. 'What happened?'

'There was a break in the clouds. For barely a second. And I saw it. This huge hill and I was heading right for it. It was so close I could almost touch it. I forced the plane into as steep a climb as I could and banked hard. I think God breathed on me that day. When I landed at the base, there were leaves in the fuselage.'

Al was impressed. 'Wow, that was really brave.'

'That wasn't brave, boy. Brave was going out on bombing raids again and again and again, knowing you had a rubbish chance of making it home after each run. Imagine it. You've beaten the odds so far... will this be the time you don't come back? The more successful runs you do, the more frightened you become until you almost can't get into the plane with fear.'

'Refuse to fly.'

'Sometimes your naiveté delights me Al. You think they had a choice?'

He thought about Gazzer asking him to deliver packages and about the consequences of refusing. 'No. Sometimes you just godda play the cards you're dealt, even if they're shitty ones,' he muttered.

She frowned.

He pulled another photo from the box. It wouldn't do for her to ask questions – she was old and wouldn't understand the intimidation and dark ethics of gangland culture. 'Who's this?' he asked.

CHAPTER 10

LETTING GO

Rob worried the incessant rain would ruin the car boot sale. Then miraculously the rain stopped, the clouds cleared and the first Saturday of April dawned unseasonably warm with rinsed blue skies.

The verges were verdant with wild flowers – violets, cowslips, primroses, colts foot. Cow parsley was shooting up everywhere and soon its frothy blooms would sway in the spring breezes. As he drove to Ruth's house, the first bluebells were bravely showing their colours.

His relationship with Ruth was evolving slowly, sometimes more slowly than he would like, but he was content, for now, to let her manage the pace. He kissed her in greeting every day. Sometimes, when they met up in the kitchen for coffee at elevenses, he would grab her and swing her into his arms making her laugh. It felt immensely peaceful to sit with his feet up on one of the kitchen chairs, talking over a coffee. Eventually he would return to finish plumbing her bathroom and she would disappear back into her garden. Last weekend they had worked together on the new scheme for the sunken garden; she had showed him how to plant up the dozens of Heucheras that William had delivered on Friday, and they worked companionably side by side until the last one was watered in.

When he parted from her each evening, he'd hold her in his arms and kiss her. She responded warmly but never quite let go her control. Yet in spite of wanting more, he was caught in a dilemma: he just couldn't help checking his answer machine every night to see if Emma had called. And every night, when once again there was no message, dull disappointment unraveled inside him. So it suited him that Ruth wanted to take things slowly – at night, it was still Emma who dwelled in his dreams, though she'd been gone for four months.

Maybe Emma really didn't love him any more. Such thoughts used to send him into a spin when he allowed himself to think about her in the early days after her departure, but slowly he was becoming accustomed to the notion – each day it hurt slightly less. Now, on his way to Ruth's house to help her load up her car with stuff for the car boot sale this afternoon, he felt exhilarated. They had all morning free, and planned to finish installing the fountain in the sunken garden. He couldn't wait to see it in all its glory.

The front door was open when he arrived, and he went in and called her. She appeared at the top of the stairs looking radiant. He bounded up to her. 'Hello,' he said, smoothing her hair back from her face and kissing her. 'You smell nice.' He kissed her again, desire suddenly flooding him. Today, however, there was none of her usual tentativeness.

'Ruth,' he whispered against her mouth. 'Come with me.' He led her towards the attic. Last weekend he'd helped her cart stuff from the attic down to the hall to sort through: tip or car boot sale. Anything sellable was in boxes ready to load into his van.

'You know we cleared the attic? Well, I kind of rearranged it.'

She looked puzzled.

He cleared his throat. 'I might be taking a huge liberty,' he said.

Puzzlement changed to intrigue. 'Maybe,' she said. 'What's going on?'

Biting his lip, he reached shyly for the handle and opened the door. Inside, the attic had been swept clean. It smelled musty, of legions of memories locked away, but clean. Even the skylight was clear of cobwebs. Below the window, in a small patch of light, lay a double mattress spread with sheets filched from the linen cupboard, and with piles of pillows banked up. It was somehow sumptuous. The sight of it left Ruth trembling. She stood with her mouth open, unable to move.

'Have I taken a huge liberty?' he asked huskily, looking down at her as she stared at the bed.

She took his hand. 'Please kiss me.'

'Oh Ruth,' he breathed, moved by the angst in her gaze.

Later, after they made love, he fell asleep without meaning to. As he surfaced, though, it was Emma who filled his thoughts. He could not get her out of his head, and the feeling that he had been a philandering snake was like poison leaching through him.

Then anger bubbled up. No, he wasn't a two-timing bastard. She'd gone. Accept it, damn it! He'd just spent an hour making love with the most incredible woman, and here he was, like a jerk, thinking of Emma. This was so unfair to Ruth. She deserved a man who loved her unreservedly, not a man who was, deep down, still holding out for a woman who plainly no longer wanted him.

Ruth was gorgeous. Her skin was creamy soft and she was slim to the point of boyishness but all he could think of was skin like velvet and a body so voluptuous and ripe he would find himself disappearing until they were nothing but two souls joined together.

Why had she left him?

How many times had he asked himself that?

Why?

Then gradually, through the haze of his own confusion, he began to remember Emma, her exuberance, the rich way she laughed, the way she looked at him, the way she held him, the way she melded into him at night. He had believed she loved him with all her heart. So what had driven her away? Was there someone else? He didn't think so. No, it had to be something he'd done to drive her off. More than that – to hide, abandoning her job, her friends and even her parents.

Oh Emma.

He almost wept with longing for her.

How ironic that he was in another woman's bed, a woman still mourning for her husband. He smiled to himself. Ah, Ruth had changed so much in the last few months. She had filled out again into the woman he remembered seeing about town. She had lost that hollow-eyed, invisible look that rendered her almost insubstantial. Why, only last Christmas she used to scuttle out of the supermarket when anyone greeted her, polite, but determined to run away. Now she was taking on Bruce Turner.

Rob rolled onto his side and found Ruth watching him. He rolled all the way over and lay on his front.

'Mm,' he murmured. 'You're lovely.'

He did not want to be there, yet she was like a port in a storm. The calm and quiet he found in her soothed the ache in his heart.

He felt her hand stroking his back and he turned and pulled her into the line of his body, spooning himself against her… the way he used to with Emma.

'It's OK to feel guilty,' she said, obviously remembering their conversation in the pub all those weeks ago.

He gave a dry laugh. 'That's my line.'

'I feel it too.' She took a breath as if nerving herself up, and said, 'She's called Emma, isn't she?'

He nodded and without warning tears scalded his eyes for the first time since Emma had left. Ruth stoked the arm he had tucked around her.

'I can't do this,' he said suddenly, rolling away and looking up at the ceiling, anywhere but at her. 'I'm so sorry. I'm not ready.'

She propped herself up on an elbow and leaned over him, one hand resting against his chest. He felt another betraying tear slip down his temple and disappear into his hairline.

'I'm not being fair to you.' He muttered thickly. 'You

deserve so much more than this, and yet I want you. You're a very beautiful woman.'

She reached forward and lightly kissed him. He kissed her back, equally lightly, and then more insistently as desire returned.

In the dim light of the attic, they made love again, feverishly, consumed with an urgent need for each other, both aching for another person, both finding a level of peace and comfort in each other. Afterwards he turned over on to his back. 'We're both completely fucked up, aren't we?'

She hooted with laughter. 'That's one way of putting it.'

He chuckled, hearing the pun, and scooped her against him again. However, as he lay there he realised she was less 'fucked up' than he was, that she was letting Michael go, albeit slowly, while he still clung to hope. He patted her hip. 'Come on. We've got a car boot sale to sort.'

'I suppose.'

He blew a raspberry on her shoulder. 'Can I use your shower?'

'Is it ready?'

'I finished grouting the new tiles yesterday.'

'Me first!' she said, leaping up.

He caught her at the door and crowed as he picked her up and tipped her back on to the bed.

'You cheat,' she giggled. He pinned her arms above her head with one hand and drew his other across her body, until she was squirming and laughing so much her sides ached. 'Stop, stop, you're tickling me, please stop,' she gasped.

'Do I win?' he asked.

'Yes, yes, you win,' she said breathlessly.

'Good. You go first,' he said, flopping back on the bed. Emma is gone, he thought to himself as Ruth opened the attic door. Life goes on.

CAR BOOT SALE

Over a month had passed without a single incident: not a riot, a knifing or even a broken window. No one marked the moment. No one was keeping a tally. On the other hand, Bruce Turner was conscious that his photograph was not appearing in the paper so often, alongside an insightful comment on the state of the town. He looked at his diary and turned back page after page. There were whole days with no clippings. Had peace broken out?

If so, he should make a statement at the meeting tonight. It was his duty, as chair of the parish council and chair of the Special Interest Group for Elderfield in Bloom, to come up with solutions and lead the town back to prosperity. Naturally, his policies and leadership were responsible for this peace, although some people would, no doubt, try to put it down to the gardening craze sweeping through the old town.

He pondered his strategy for handling this inaccurate assumption and started rehearsing a little speech designed to show people how wrong they were. First he would win them over by telling them how hard he was working for them. Next, he would allow himself to become thoughtful and modestly iterate all his policies, like commissioning the bus video, which were small but crucial cogs in the wheel. Finally, he would good-naturedly point out that the riots tended to start on the estate, and that Elderfield in Bloom was having a negligible impact there. Having done that, he would invite people to draw their own conclusions and humbly accept their acclaim. He practiced bowing his head a few times to different parts of the room, and then remembered to smile and practiced again. He tried the effect of lifting his hand in acknowledgement and decided it added the right kind of regal effect.

When he had the speech off by heart, he went upstairs for a shave, where he took time to study his reflection in the mirror. His was the face that stared out of countless front-page articles, the face of the people, and he was proud to be their champion. He wasn't bad looking – not pretty like Jules Dawson, but manly and strong. True, his hair was thinning a bit, but being a modern man he was not one to turn up his nose at the dozens of hair products that helped it look thicker, although he always reminded his wife to tell the pharmacist that these were for her use. The grey wasn't a concern – it conveyed just the right degree of dignity and maturity.

He gave a satisfied sigh and took care over his choice of tie: nothing too flashy or dull, something contemporary but not arriviste. Young Dawson would be filming tonight's meeting and it was vital to convey the right impression. In the two months since that woman had proposed they enter the In Bloom awards, spring had arrived, and with it, Jules Dawson to film some of the community garden schemes. At the weekend, the boy had filmed the car boot sale. Tomorrow, he would film the award ceremony for the poster competition in the town hall especially hired for the event… at full price, naturally.

Of course, being a managing kind of person, that woman had got her posters printed and put up in double quick time on the Tuesday after the car boot sale. They'd fussily explained why the town had been entered in the awards, how to join in, key dates and contacts, as if people were completely stupid. She thought that everyone knew about Elderfield in Bloom thanks to her poster campaign, when really it was down to the full-page advertisement the council had placed in the paper the day before. As chair of Elderfield in Bloom, disseminating information in a timely way was his responsibility, but there were always people who thought they knew better.

The car boot sale had had some success in spite of being disgracefully badly advertised – relying on word of mouth was always risky. That tiresome woman was fortunate that the rain had held off – if he had organised it, he would have arranged the cars in straight lines and at right angles to the road. The haphazard way people were allowed to park was shockingly irresponsible. What if it had rained and they had needed a tractor to pull people out? – there would have been no room for it to manoeuvre at all.

He had turned up halfway through proceedings and strolled up and down the drab lines of cars making helpful suggestions, shaking hands and holding the occasional baby, which mothers never could resist thrusting into his arms. Obligingly he always posed for the press photographer – the paper made a little extra from selling such pictures to doting parents and it was pleasing to consider how many family albums he was surely featured in.

Balloons bobbed from the aerials of cars that had goods for sale, supplied by Lisa the Florist and branded with her logo – another of his helpful suggestions the week before, which she had been unnecessarily off-hand about, claiming she'd already thought of it herself. There was a raffle with some sad bottles of wine, boxes of chocolates and gardening 'consultancy' as prizes. Even so, people were surprisingly loyal and bought strips of tickets, and then played up to the camera in an absurd way when all they won was the consultancy.

'The day has been an inspired way to bring together both parts of the town,' he overheard a man from the estate tell Jules in an interview half way through the afternoon. Of course, the speaker had been coached by that woman: he'd spied them talking together before the interview.

A smell of hog roast pervaded the air. Several women, including his wife, had banded together to sell delicious cakes and he made a point of buying hers, easily the most skillfully decorated with thick chocolate fudge icing whipped into little crests. Regrettably that woman had permitted professional traders to attend and they were selling jewelry and other crafts, which wasn't in the spirit of a proper car boot sale. She, needless to say, was selling plants along with a load of old junk, presumably from her house.

It was as he was studying her tiny Hellebore seedlings in trays around her car that Jules Dawson caught up with him and they filmed a gratifyingly long interview – easily three times longer than anyone else. As Jules asked his final question, the icecream man had jingled his jangle, which made them all laugh. He hoped young Dawson would use that in the final cut – it portrayed him at his most genial.

That was five days ago, and he was bored of hearing people reminiscing about what a good day it had been. Now, though he breezed in early for the Special Interest Group meeting, the hall was already crammed. He was astonished to see large numbers of people from the estate, no doubt drawn by Jules Dawson's appearance. Whatever their reason for turning up, trust Vix and that woman to be mingling hard. Most people from the estate collected at the back of the room and sat with their arms folded, an expression of indifference on their faces. The stupid numpties clearly hadn't yet been won over to the idea of Elderfield in Bloom. Bruce smiled complacently. Here was his chance to show that woman she was not the only person who could spur people into action.

COURTING CONSENSUS

The filming was low key. Jules himself only materialised at the meeting when it was well under way. Ruth had seen him filming a piece to camera outside as the last people hurried in behind her. Then he came and stood at the back beside her with his arms folded, listening. At the front, Bruce was hardly paying attention. He kept looking round for someone, and then spotted Jules. That distraction cost him control of the meeting because, by turning to beam at the cameras, he ignored a woman from the estate who demanded to know why she was expected to turn her front garden into an advertisement for the garden centre.

'I don't think that's fair,' said William jumping up before Vix could stop him. 'No one's asked you to advertise anything.'

'You and your fancy ideas,' retorted the woman, confronting him. 'It's all a big con to get us to buy stuff from your shop. I work. I've got three small children. Where would I find time for gardening on top of everything else? I'd like to see you try.'

Jules shifted, glancing over his shoulder to check what the film crew were doing, clearly delighted with the interchange. He always said bickering was good on TV – it added colour and depth to what would otherwise be banal sweetness and light.

'We all need to pull together,' William was saying in a soothing voice. 'If everyone makes a bit of effort, we'll end up with a town that's enjoyable to live in again.'

'By making sure you do right well out of it,' said a voice from the back. 'This is a conspiracy to make us spend money at your garden centre.'

'You can buy your marigolds from the sodding man in the moon, for all I care,' snapped William.

'Like I have time to garden,' said the man sarcastically.'

'There are plenty of community gardening schemes for you to join,' said William in a bored voice.

'Will you shut up,' Vix hissed at him.

'No, I won't. They're attacking me.'

'They're not. They just don't like being badgered.'

Ruth glanced at the soundman, who gave her a covert wink. They had it all on tape. She took a fortifying breath and spoke quietly into the silence, addressing the woman who had spoken first. 'What would you like to do?'

'I don't want to *do* anything. They're always saying how we should let wild flowers grow. Why can't this be my patch of wild flowers? What do you think, Mr Dawson?'

All eyes turned on Jules. 'This is your town,' he began diplomatically.

'He fucking ducked the question,' growled a voice from the back.

Jules struggled to hide a smile and answer the question seriously. 'You want to encourage wild flowers. Other people might just want a plain patio with space for a car and nothing to do. The point is, I can't tell you what to grow. Gardening is about expressing yourself. Having me tell you what's right for you would be like me telling you to paint your living room purple.'

'My wife did,' said someone.

A wave of laughter swept the room.

'Well, I'm sure it's very nice.'

'I can tell you it's not,' came the reply.

'Martin!' exclaimed the woman next to him.

'Well, it's not.'

'There you go,' said Jules. 'The point is, if you want to grow wild flowers, then I think you should. I think what the committee wants is for everyone to make their garden somewhere they're proud to come home to. If we all planted annuals in serried rows, we'd end up with a town looking like a ghastly 50s advert for the good life. So, go on. Leave your garden to run riot. Make it into a haven for wild life. Encourage butterflies and bees and it'll be a pleasant change after other people's "nip and tuck".'

Pandemonium broke out as everyone started talking at once, some endorsing what he said, others disagreeing vociferously.

'I'm not convinced that was helpful,' Jules whispered to Ruth. 'Sorry.'

'Actually, I don't care. All I want is people to come together again so this town heals itself. D'you know, we've not had any violence here for over a month? The competition's a red herring. It's simply the way to get people to change their mind-set about the community.'

'I thought it was to help William turn his nursery around.'

'That's Vix's agenda.'

At the front of the room, Bruce tried to call everyone to order. Ruth wondered if he been looking round for the film crew so they could catch him stamping his mark on the meeting. If so, he'd missed the boat. Now he faced a dilemma. Did he endorse Jules' perfectly commonsense answer, or did he come up with something radical of his own? The problem was, he was a man of few ideas.

'So if I want to grow wild flowers,' came a voice from the back, just as Bruce opened is mouth to say his piece, 'how do I go about it?'

Jules turned to William. 'You're the expert here. Over to you.'

William stood slowly, and cleared his throat. 'The thing with wild flowers is that they like poor soil. Now most people spend years improving their soil. And before you say it, I've got loads of products that can help you do this... there, I got my plug in.' At this, the atmosphere in the room seemed to ease.

'But there's nothing so good as old-fashioned compost, which you can make yourself,' he continued. 'For a really good crop of wild flowers, though, I suggest you hire a mini digger from George over there, and remove the top layer of soil. Then I can sell you a range of wild flower seed mixes. It needn't cost the earth.'

Conversations broke out as people discussed the idea among themselves. Bruce put his head in his hands. Even Ruth could see it now. People everywhere digging up the top layer of earth from their gardens, dumping it, and then losing interest. It would end up like the verges people had started reclaiming so enthusiastically – which had had Bruce frothing at the mouth thanks to the mud on the roads.

Meanwhile Jules was touring the room talking to people, trailing the film crew in his wake. Everyone was flattered to be asked their plans for their gardens on camera. He listened, and shook hands and chatted with them while his people filmed. Every person came away believing they were key to the competition. Jules behaved as if the town was behind the scheme, and one by one they fell under his charm.

On the stage on his own at the front of the hall, Bruce had been side-lined completely. Not once had he had an opportunity to show the lead and he seemed to suppurate with frustration.

That night, as he walked his wife and son back to his car after the meeting, he was heard sounding off about how ungrateful people in the town were.

The next day, the town was, once more, on its knees after another night of rioting. Having gone round to Vix's house for a nightcap, Ruth only nerved herself up to drive home in the small hours. Jules stumbled home soon after, exhausted after a whole night of filming the masked youths. He set his alarm early, wanting to film the town in the dawn light.

She got up and followed him in, parked, and then stood alone in the square as she surveyed the damage, her hands in her pockets, crushed by disappointment. Glass lay everywhere. Dozens of windscreens had been smashed. Lisa's florist had escaped for once, but other shops had been broken into. What's more, almost every poster promoting Elderfield in Bloom had been torn down.

She bent to pick up one of the fliers. The picture promised such hope. She struggled to comprehend the kids who had done this. They were destroying their own town. Didn't they understand that? She screwed the flier into a ball and threw it away.

'They'll fine you for littering if you do that.'

Ruth scowled at Vix sauntering towards her in high heeled boots. 'How could they do this?'

'It's not that bad.'

Ruth kicked at a tin can and it rattled away down the gutter. 'Vix! Look at the place.'

Vix shrugged. 'It's been worse.'

Bruce was righteously devastated, though Ruth was convinced he was secretly jubilant – his expression flipped too quickly into 'grave' to be unrehearsed when Jules invited him to comment. For five minutes he sounded off about 'the hoodlums who had done this to Elderfield'.

Ruth and Vix bought themselves a latte at Coffee One and stood around talking to people in the streets as they turned up for work. 'A sorry business, this,' the printer John Dunant told them when he arrived at his office. He offered to reprint the posters at his expense if Ruth would arrange to post them around the town again.

If the hooligan's aim had been to disrupt Elderfield in Bloom, they failed. For the moment, enough people had taken

Vix and Ruth's number down for the pair of them to be busy all day dealing with enquiries, most of which came from the estate. It seemed no one was prepared to bow to thuggery. The result was more community gardening schemes started up that day than the pair had hoped for in the entire project.

Some people even wanted to get involved at committee level. Mary Adkins in particular, who turned out to be the manager for the local supermarket, volunteered to spend her weekends working on the project 'doing whatever needed doing'. Ruth invited her to join them on their scouting tour.

Jules filmed Vix taking calls for a while, and then did a piece to camera with her handling more calls in the background. After that, he went off to film the posters being printed. John Dunant subsequently retained Vix to handle his PR. Her first coup for him was a picture on the front page of the Saturday edition of the regional daily, portraying him with the posters coming off the presses in the background. The headline ran: 'Dunant Printing rallies Elderfield to defeat hooligans.' Not to be outdone, the local free sheet devoted four pages to Elderfield in Bloom. This also carried a small photo of John Dunant watching posters come off the presses, with the unwieldy caption: 'John Dunan (sic) of Dunant Printers refuses to bow to yobs and reprints Elderfield in Bloom posters at his expense.' This publicity resulted in several local businesses putting work his way – 'their bit to beat the punks'.

On the evening after the yobs had swept through the town, even while people were still clearing up, the town hall was packed. Hundreds of children and their parents turned up to the awards ceremony. Lucy had been generous and was offering Doodlepad gift tokens to the winner of each category. She had also wheedled Terry into framing the winning pictures at the shop's expense. This went down really well – several parents came up at the end of the evening and asked to have their own children's pieces framed. Lucy couldn't resist flicking Terry a told-you-so smile, to which he shrugged a shoulder in his usual dour manner and continued taking orders.

But it was during the awards ceremony that Ruth and Vix really noticed the sea change. True, a few people from the estate had turned up to the Special Interest Group meeting the night before, but they turned up in droves to watch Emlyn and his fellow winners collect their prizes. They were of one mind: fed up with the yobs. One parent even confessed to Ruth that she had caught her daughter sneaking home the night before, and had threatened to turn her over to the police if she ever went out on the rampage again. '"It's our town you're trashing," I told her,' she said to Ruth.

People were beginning to see the point of Elderfield in Bloom, and Ruth, Vix, Rob and William worked hard courting them and persuading every person to do their bit.

INSIGHT

Three weeks later, Vix discovered that Mary Adkins, the latest volunteer to join the committee, meant her six-month-old baby to accompany the group on its scouting trip to Newport. Her heart sank and she braced herself for Williams' reaction when he turned up to catch the minibus.

'You have got to be kidding me,' he said, right on cue.

'Ha ha, very funny,' Vix replied in a dampening way.

'I'm serious.'

'So am I.'

'It goes, or I do.'

'Suit yourself.'

William started to walk away and Vix hurried after him. 'Honestly, Will. One small baby is not going to ruin the trip.'

'Yeah right. Projectile sick, stinky nappies, wailing for hours.'

'What do you know about it?'

'Enough never to go down that road. I like 'em big, like Al. At least I can take him to the pub and we can get drunk together.'

Secretly she was pleased with this answer, but her maternal voice couldn't help the tart reminder: 'Al is under age.'

'Good Lord, woman, how you take me up. You know what I mean.'

She did. She reached up for his kiss and instantly he was putty in her hands again. 'Honestly, you're one big baby yourself sometimes. I promise you, she'll be fine. Go on. Get on the bus, will you? Ruth and Rob'll just have to miss the trip. Pity, but I don't think we can wait any longer. Bruce's been champing at the bit these last ten minutes.'

'She'll ask us to carry her nappy bag, you'll see,' William tossed at her over his shoulder as he climbed aboard, 'and the next thing you know, you'll be dangling a baby on your arm wondering how soon you can put it down.'

As William took his seat, Rob swept into the car park with Ruth on his heels. They parked side by side and he greeted her with a nod that gave nothing away, certainly not that they had spent the night together. They climbed aboard the minibus offering profuse apologies for keeping everyone waiting. Bruce gave the signal and the driver started up.

The night before, Rob had worked late to finish off the bathrooms, and when he came downstairs with his bag of tools, Ruth had dinner waiting on the table. 'Thank you,' he said as he brushed a kiss on her lips. It was meant to be a light hearted, thank-you kiss, but he got carried away; he lifted her into his arms, and carried her off to the attic, leaving dinner on the table getting cold. Later, driven by an attack of the munchies, they'd come back down to raid the kitchen and discovered the lasagna congealing on plates. Rob sat at the table and dug in. 'Sorry,' he said. 'Maybe I should have let you give me supper first. It's stone cold.'

Ruth vowed she loved cold lasagna but Rob was full of chagrin. In his book, lasagna was one of those meals too complicated and long-winded ever to bother with. 'You could ping it,' he said, nodding at the microwave.

'I could,' she admitted. 'Would you like yours pinged?' she asked, getting up and reaching for his plate.

'No thanks,' he replied, tugging her down into his lap and nuzzling her neck. However, he reached over and shoved her plate into the microwave. 'But I insist we heat yours up.'

After he had eaten, to his surprise, she took his hand and led him back upstairs. This was the first time she had invited him to stay the night. He was even more surprised when she walked past the door to the attic, which had been their secret haven for the last few weeks, and led him to her bedroom.

'Are you sure about this?' he asked.

'I've never felt surer.'

However, once in the bedroom, she sat on the bed unsure how to proceed. Rob tipped her gently back onto the bed and followed her down, and her moment of awkwardness seemed to pass. Much later, just before he switched out the light, he noticed the photos of Michael had gone. Rob was touched; Ruth had obviously thought a lot about this.

He woke hungry for her, and they made love tenderly until the sun started to rise. Then they fell asleep and were lucky to wake up in time to catch the minibus. Now sitting side by side on the hard minibus seats, Ruth's head began to nod and she gradually slumped against him. When he looked up, he caught Vix watching them and he smiled non-committally at her raised eyebrows. Against his chest, Ruth sighed, and he bent to smell her hair, feeling a wave of affection sweep through him.

In Newport, they split up into groups: they all had their tasks. Vix was to grill the editor of the local paper. Bruce and Peter, his vice chair, were meeting up with local counsellors. Ruth, Rob and Mary Adkins went off to meet with community leaders, but not before William nudged Vix. 'I told you she'd palm her clobber off on someone.' And indeed the baby bag, stuffed with the excessive paraphernalia new mothers think they can't do without, was hanging on Rob's shoulder as they walked away down the street.

The trip was uneventful but useful. They gleaned a lot of

insights, but Ruth thought possibly she had come away with the greatest. It had been a revelation to spend the day with Mary and her baby. Rob was besotted with it. The moment Mary started flagging, he offered to carry the baby. While he was clumsy from ignorance, he was eye-blinkingly protective. He wanted to feed the baby and showed off the sour patch of sick he soon sported on his shoulder with ridiculous pride. He was even happy to learn how to change the baby's nappy, which he did with an expression of wry trepidation on his face. He spent hours with the baby cradled in the crook of his arm during interviews, to the point where most people assumed he was the father. 'Your baby' and 'Your wife' cropped up over and over, only it was Mary who was assumed to be his wife. Rob tactfully set them straight, but Ruth watched with interest, and not a little sadness, the longing in his expression whenever he looked on the baby.

Later, when they were being given a tour through some rough ground where some boys were playing football, he sidled off leaving Ruth and Mary to continue on alone. They found him half an hour later best friends with all the boys, who ranged from twelve to fifteen, and joining in their game of football. He left it reluctantly when Mary said they had to be getting back to the minibus, and the boys all followed him to the gate, crowding round him. Ruth had never seen him smile as he did with those boys. It was the most uncomplicated smile she had ever seen on any person. It shone with humour and fun. It also radiated calm and peace. Rob looked as if he belonged with the boys. Clearly they felt the same, because it took ages to pry him away. Just when they thought they were ready to go, another boy would pipe up with something, and Rob stopped to listen. Really listen. To listen as few people ever bothered to. Unjudgementally.

He listened that way with her, hearing all the unsaid quiet bits. Ruth knew just how appealing that was, so she couldn't blame the boys for their hero worship. What astonished her was the speed of the boys' acceptance. Here was a complete stranger, and they had completely taken to him, as he had to them.

Meanwhile, Mary Adkins, with her management training, was keen to make her mark within the group, and was soon being ultra efficient about collecting all the ideas everyone had come back with. In this she was aided by Rob, who appointed himself chief baby distracter. William pointedly nudged Vix when he saw this. On the other hand, Rob did seem to be the only one with the knack of persuading the baby to smile and gurgle whenever it grew fractious.

'Sorry about abandoning you with Mary,' he said to Ruth just before they parted. 'She's so bossy, I thought I might just explode if I stuck around.'

'And it was OK to run out on me and leave me with her?' she jested.

'Nope,' he admitted. 'But you knew I'd come back.' He flashed her one of his disarming smiles and she melted. 'Anyway,' he went on, 'the boys were fantastic – full of ideas for getting the school involved. They have vegetable plots at their school and they grow stuff, which they use to top up the canteen. Lettuce and beans and... stuff. They tried radishes and weren't too keen on those, but they said the peas went down a treat. Their headmaster arranged for the school to take over a couple of empty allotments that back on to the playing fields, and the kids get really involved. Some of them even come in during the holidays to keep the allotments going. It's amazing. They took me down to see them and they are as neat as pie. Then we got distracted by a game of football.'

'I can't see Mr Sharples having the energy to get anything like that going at our school.'

'Maybe if parents got involved, he might. That's how the headmaster in Newport got going.'

There was a shout from the other side of the car park: William called goodnight to them both, then drove off with Vix at his side.

Rob felt envious. Clearly things were going well between

William and Vix, while he, Rob, was going back to a dark and empty house. He'd have liked to go home with Ruth – it never occurred to him to invite her round to his place – but didn't feel he knew her well enough yet to invite himself round to hers. 'Last to arrive, last to leave,' he said. 'It's been a great day, Ruth. You were wonderful last night.'

'Would you like to come round for supper later?'

He breathed a sigh of contentment. 'I'd really like that. When shall I come over?'

'About eight. That gives me time to have a bath in my new bathroom and unwind.'

He smiled and leaned over to kiss her. 'See you later,' he promised. 'Let me know if anything leaks.'

CHAPTER 11

BACK TO FRONT

Rob swung the car out of the car park dwelling on how he would make love to Ruth and then lie with her in his arms, curled around her while she slept. However, when he got home and found his front door unlocked, prickles of alarm shivered up his spine. Then he heard the radio playing and it was almost with a feeling of resignation that he clumped down the dark corridor to the kitchen. He knew what he would find at the other end, and for some extraordinary reason – extraordinary, because until this moment he would have sworn he had craved this – he felt bleak.

'Hello,' he said from the kitchen doorway.

There she was after all those months away, with her long, red pre-Raphaelite hair coiling down her back.

He thought his memory was playing tricks on him because he'd forgotten how beautiful she was: there was a bloom in her cheeks missing when he had last seen her, when she had looked, now he thought about it, sour and gaunt. He didn't remember her looking like this – ever! This stunning, this breath-stealing. She had filled out a bit and, oh, how it suited her. Yet as he studied her, an inexplicable anger began to course through him. All those weeks of feeling let down coalesced into a river of bitterness.

'Hello,' she responded, getting up from the table.

She moved as though she were unsure of her reception. His greeting was obviously not what she'd expected. He didn't know what she had expected. Perhaps for him to rush into her arms. Perhaps to shout at her. But this fury cascading through him also made him guarded with her, as if touching her would somehow tip him over the edge. So he backed away when she came up and lifted her face for his kiss.

'What do you want?'

'Er,' she quavered, 'I've come back. If… you'll have me.' The last sounded like a question.

'I see.' He ignored her and took his time making himself a mug of tea, then dragged out a chair on the other side of the table from her and sank down. Hesitantly, Emma sat, too.

'You don't seem very pleased to see me.'

'You don't say.'

'Lisa said William said you were unhappy.'

He held up his hand. He didn't want to hear any opinion of William's, and certainly not on the subject of his, Rob's, feelings for Emma. For the whole day, William had been boorish about the baby on the minibus, and Rob was fed up with him. It was Rob's nature to make the best of things, and so William's loud and continual banter about bawling babies, when the baby hadn't bawled at all, had been irritating. What had the girl been supposed to do? Leave the baby at home? Rob didn't think William had grasped what an asset Mary would be to the group. A natural organiser, she would take the mundane tasks off Ruth's hands and do them well, albeit in a more heavy-handed manner than Ruth or Vix, but you couldn't fault her enthusiasm.

'How long are you back for?' he asked.

'I want to marry you,' she rushed, and then, as he raised an eyebrow in disbelief, she flushed and said, 'That came out all wrong. I'm sorry.'

'How come I'm man-of-the-moment all of a sudden?'

'Rob, I'm –' she got up and paced the kitchen, though she made no attempt to come round to his side of the table. 'If you only knew how angry you look. You're making things really hard.'

'That figures. As usual, somehow it's my fault. What?' he

demanded, catching her expression of helplessness. 'Is this not going how you rehearsed?'

'Rob, I'm pregnant.'

'Woopdedoo. I suppose the father left you, did he? Or have you done another runner and left someone else wondering what hit him. Well, never mind: *Rob'll see me right,*' he said in a sneering, cruel imitation of her. 'Fuck off.'

'It's yours.'

He smashed the mug that was halfway to his lips down on the table with enough force to make it break. Tea pooled around the shattered shards. He was momentarily ashamed by the fright in Emma's eyes, but the anger scouring his insides frothed to the surface in white-hot rage, the incandescent kind that burns all in its path. He felt ripped apart. He wanted to smash everything in this kitchen, everything of hers and sweep her from his life.

How dare she do this to him? How dare she waltz in and expect him to be overjoyed at her news? Even a month ago, he'd have fallen on his knees at the news and sobbed for joy. Now he felt like killing her.

'Do you have anything to say?' she asked.

He got up and walked to the door, dragging together every ounce of self-control he could muster. 'I need to think,' he whispered.

'I'm pregnant with your baby,' she sobbed.

'You've been pregnant for *four* months,' he snarled. 'You've been gone for *four* months. I've rebuilt my life without you, and you think you can just dance back in here and expect me to fall at your feet?' He'd never felt so angry, so hurt, so disappointed.

'I'm sorry. I was in such a muddle.'

'Was there someone else?'

'No.'

He just looked at her.

'OK, there was. But I didn't go *to* him, if you know what I mean. I met him after. We split up about a month ago. It didn't work out.'

'And that makes it all right?'

'He just wasn't you, Rob. I love you so much.'

Rob had always considered himself a magnanimous sort of person but he couldn't summon up one ounce of forgiveness.

'Rob?'

'Just shut up, will you? You clearly don't understand the meaning of the word "love".'

'Where are you going?' Her voice was pitched in panic.

'Out. Away from you. Don't be here when I get back.'

'You don't mean that,' she said, running after him and putting a restraining hand on his arm.

'Let go of me,' he said, repelled by her touch and shaking her off. He got into his van and locked the door when, sobbing and pleading, she tried to open it. He couldn't look at her but the sound of her beseeching cries made him hate himself even more. He fired the engine and careened off down the road.

He drove without thought and ended up at Ruth's driveway where he stopped just inside the gateway and turned off the engine, shaking all over. Ahead of him, the headlights shone a path across the curving driveway lighting up the little fountain in the sunken garden. He sat there, every muscle taut, staring at the little putto with his urn pouring water into the pond, his mind oddly blank. Though the fountain wasn't switched on, he could almost hear water dribbling into water. He listened to his breathing, strangely divorced from the sound, as though there were someone else in the car with him. Long regular breaths. Gradually his hands unclenched from the steering wheel. Then he saw Ruth walking along the beam of light towards the van. He switched off the lights and got out, but leaned against the van and waited for her to come to him.

What on earth was he doing here? Part of him felt remorse – this woman liked him, maybe even loved him, and he was bringing her his dirty linen. Part of him wasn't feeling anything at all.

Ruth didn't need to be a mind reader to know something was wrong. It was washed into every line of his face in the moonlight. Nevertheless, she was unprepared for his bald statement when it came.

'Emma came back.'

Not 'Emma turned up' or 'Emma came to see me' but 'Emma came back'. She knew, even if he didn't yet, that her time with Rob was over. Whether it would work out with Emma, she doubted even he knew. Whatever happened, he needed to move on. The pied piper effect that afternoon, with small boys hanging on his every word, had revealed to her, if not to him, exactly what he needed in his life. Children. Lots of them. Meanwhile, she did not want motherhood again. Shuddered at the idea. She just hadn't expected her time with Rob to be so brief.

'How do you feel about that?' she said carefully.

He reacted as if she had thrown a glass of water in his face, waking him out of his stupor. 'Oh fuck, Ruth. Stop it,' he said, reaching for her. 'Stop putting on a brave face. I'm so sorry. You're the last person I should be talking to about this.'

'Well, I'm glad I'm the first,' she said. 'It makes me feel special.' She willed her voice to remain firm, but it didn't and she cleared her throat before asking: 'What about Emma?'

'I don't know. Just now, I could fillet her. You want to know the big joke? She's pregnant. She says by me.'

She pulled out of his embrace and rubbed her finger absently over some dirt on the bonnet of his van, shivering. It was a cold night and she had felt so warm with his arms around her.

'Ruth, stop pacing, please, and come here.'

She stopped. Had not even been aware she had been pacing.

'Please come here,' he repeated after a moment.

'I don't think I can,' she replied, keeping her distance.

He pushed away from the van and came up to her, catching her fluttering hands, and turning her to face him so he could hold her. 'I've been falling in love with you,' he whispered. He kissed her neck, his breath hot on her skin, and she suddenly relaxed into his arms.

When they made love, he was achingly tender and they spent hours stroking each other, kissing each other, lips on lips, tongue against tongue, tasting each other's sighs and gasps. Ruth could not still her hands, even when he dozed after coming the first time. It was as if they were determined to learn every contour. Before long, her gently stroking fingers roused him again. When he sank once more into her body, it was like swimming in her. He didn't think he had ever felt like this, ever felt so released from himself.

After he had gone, some time in the small hours, Ruth lay in bed curled around one of the pillows. Nothing had been said but they both knew he wasn't coming back. He'd said it in the kisses tasting salty from his tears, in the way he had dressed and then come back to crush her in his arms until she could hardly breathe.

'Oh Rob,' she whispered to the dark when she heard the front door slam.

She felt more alive than she had in years.

SMALL HOURS

Rob expected the house to be empty when he returned, but the front door was still unlocked. Emma wasn't in bed or in the kitchen. He found her curled up in one of the armchairs. The embers of a fire glowed faintly in the grate.

He took himself off to bed where all he could think about was Ruth. He lay wide awake, his exhaustion leaving him prey to every second thought and regret. In desperation, he padded down to the kitchen to make himself a hot drink, and looked in at Emma as he passed the sitting room door. She would have such a crick in her neck in the morning, and he was moved to put a pillow under her head. He didn't understand why being kind to her should make him feel so base. Now it felt as if he were being deceitful to Ruth. In the end, though he brought a pillow for Emma, he didn't take the final step of slipping it under her head. He left it on the arm of the sofa opposite.

In the kitchen he ran himself a warm glass of water, and then another. His mouth was so dry he thought he would never quench his thirst. His eyes felt gritty. He sat at the table waiting for the kettle to boil. Emma found him there asleep with his head on his arms when the crick in her neck woke her.

She could not get over the changes to the house. Everything was so perfect. The night before she had wandered around marvelling at everything he'd done, saddened they couldn't have done this together. She'd have enjoyed it. He'd laughed at her desire to 'nest' but he'd done more than she had ever envisaged. The bed was mended, there was a new bathroom with a shower that practically drilled holes in her skin, and he'd almost finished converting the loft. As for the kitchen. Wow. That vile, cracked lino was history, as were the old cabinets with doors that used to fall off when she opened them. It may be a small terrace house, she mused, but it was just beautiful.

For hours last night she had run her fingers around the patterns on the mosaic coffee table, and wondered if he'd made that, too. He'd always been a closet furniture designer. She wondered if he'd had any help with the decorating. Had Lisa given him a hand? Regret washed through her again. What had she been thinking of, running away?

His hair had grown, she noticed. It curled over his collar. How streaked with grey it had become. Or maybe, she acknowledged, she had not looked before. While he was older than her by nearly a decade, she'd never been aware of the gap between them. They had been simply a man and a woman who loved each other.

She loved him. Sure, there had been three grim months when she had been furious with him, and had shouted at him in every imagined conversation that never took place. Before then, she had spent months silently raging at him before summoning the resolution to leave. He was no monster. The reverse: he was so kind it made her heart ache, but his kindness was towards other people. In every transaction, she came last in the pecking order.

He never noticed her growing anger. He had brushed aside every impatient snap with an admonishment not to be so silly. Did he want her to leave Mrs Mallinson all alone in a helpless muddle until Social Services deigned to turn up? Did she want Lisa to have no shop window, leaving her premises open to every thief who wandered down the High Street at night? It went without saying she didn't, and such comments only ever left her feeling more like a spoiled child than ever. But sometimes, just sometimes, she wished he would put her first.

He never did. Then one day, she just walked out. She knew if she didn't go then, she never would, because, while she loved him, he was also bad for her. At least, that's what Lisa had convinced her: Rob was selfish, always putting himself and even his clients before her. She deserved a man who adored her and put her first.

Why had she listened to Lisa's poisoned tongue? True, Lisa hadn't meant to cause a rift. She'd imagined Emma giving Rob 'a piece of her mind'. Ha! Lisa didn't seem to understand the she, Emma, was never able to get her point across because he always had a reasonable justification. Emma realised, with the sombre clarity of hindsight, she had needed to grow up, that 'happily ever after' had to be worked on, and there had been nothing to stop her sorting out the carpet, or hanging the curtains, herself. Meanwhile, in the four months away from him, her memory of Rob had grown to such proportions that no one measured up to him.

What a fool she had been.

She remembered that last evening as if it were branded into her soul. They were arguing over the stupid carpet, then he'd gone out to old Mrs Moreton. Of course he'd gone out to her. Mrs Moreton was doddery and there was no way she could cope with water flooding through her ceiling. It was typical of Rob to fly to the rescue and assume she, Emma, backed him, because for her not to was unthinkable and transformed her into the kind of person she despised.

She never knew what time he'd actually come home. She'd stormed around the empty house ranting at him: was she of so little account he could never spend an evening with her? She cringed at the memory. She knew he'd returned after midnight because she'd sat on the bottom step until the Cinderella hour, then grabbed her keys, picked up the bag she'd packed, and walked out.

What she wanted to do now was to curl her fingers through the long hair at the nape of his neck. He looked... how did he look? Well? Buff? How could she convince him of her love?

She reached for a scrap of paper, wrote him a note, and left.

Rob slept on, oblivious, until he woke from discomfort. He lifted his head, bleary-eyed, and all the memories of the day before rushed back: the ache of parting from Ruth, the anger at Emma. Then he saw Emma's note and pulled it towards him, blinking to focus on the words. When he'd read it, he scrumpled it up and tossed it in the direction of the bin.

BLOOD POISONING

Al decided he wanted to be a gardener when he grew up. His girlfriend Olivia thought it was a good idea too, which encouraged him. He liked the cool earth crumbling in his hands, and messing around with plants. The roses that he had hacked back inexpertly and rather too enthusiastically were already showing leaf, when he thought he had killed them. Around the edge of the pond at the back of the house, which he had painstakingly cleared, flag irises were coming up. It seemed all he had to do was to 'shove 'em in and watch 'em flower'; the primulas and pansies that he had planted in the old bag's garden had bloomed within two weeks. Mrs Mallinson drily pointed out the plants had come with copious buds and said it was only a matter of time before they came out, even if he had completely neglected them. Al brushed aside such mundane insights. He liked to sit at her window admiring 'his' flowers and the sweep of 'his' new bed at the edge of the path.

That particular curve had been his especial design. Together, he and Mrs Mallinson had planned what to put in it, pouring over gardening books with faded black and white photographs and thumbing through catalogues, and he was confident it would be an unmitigated success, visible from both the road as their bit towards Elderfield in Bloom, and, more importantly, her window.

When he arrived that Sunday, the old lady was standing in the doorway leaning on her Zimmer Frame while she surveyed her garden. He fetched a chair for her and the tools for himself, and then weeded where she directed, tussling diligently with dandelions, carefully digging up every piece of ground elder and bindweed root, and carelessly ripping up trailing speedwell. After an hour, he gathered up the fruits of his labour, which he tipped on the compost heap, then returned to marvel at his handiwork. The soil was a fine tilth just begging to be planted up.

'Bring the chair in,' said Mrs Mallinson, getting up. 'Let's have tea.'

He looked at the plants waiting to go in. He'd have liked to get stuck into planting those. 'Can we have a look in the strong box again?' he asked, hopefully. He found the contents of her strong box more and more fascinating. Each time they looked at it, there was a new story of death and daring about people she had known in the war. It was a world away from what he knew, yet romantic and full of adventure.

'Maybe.'

He knew her maybes by now. Maybe meant yes, eventually. From time to time over the last couple of weeks, he had climbed to the garret to fetch down the strong box, and together they had gone through her old pictures. She had a profound knowledge of the war years which time hadn't dimmed. Al grew to know all her friends and was beginning to understand how they interconnected. One person she continually passed over was a handsome man in a captain's uniform. Three days ago, Al had caught up one of his pictures for further inspection.

'Who's this?'

'That's David,' she'd said. Shortly afterwards, she had put away the photos for the evening. He assumed the young captain had been killed, but when Al chased down that theory, she told him it was time to go home.

Now, chilled from their weeding, Al made tea for them both, and arranged some biscuits on a plate. He found her in the sitting room sifting through the photos again, lingering over some, skipping others without a glance. Then a photo of David found itself at the top of the pile, and was equally quickly shuffled to the bottom.

Intrigued, Al asked, 'Who was he?'

'Just an infantry captain,' she said, returning to the photograph reluctantly.

'What happened to him?'

'He had a good war.'

On a hunch, he asked, 'Did you love him?'

There was a long pause. 'Yes.'

'Did he love you?'

'Yes.'

'What happened to him?'

'For various reasons he and I were separated. He thought I was dead and married someone else.'

'But you weren't.'

'No.'

'Couldn't he leave his wife and get together with you?'

'By the time I found him again, he had two small children.'

Al thought about his own father who had left years before – his childhood had been none the worse for it. 'Kids aren't the only reason to stay together.'

'We used to write each other long, passionate letters, but when it came to it, he couldn't leave them. Apparently, he got as far as the station. He even bought a ticket. Then his wife turned up.'

'How come?'

'He told her he was leaving her, silly chump, but I suppose she wasn't ready to be left.'

'What happened?'

'I don't know. I suppose the train came in and left without him. I only know I got a telegram saying he wasn't coming.'

'I'm sorry,' he said, inadequately. 'Why did he think you were dead?'

'After my time with the Women's Auxiliary Air Force, I did a spell with the Special Operations Executive.' In response to his perplexed frown, she added, 'A bit like MI6.'

'You were a spy!' he exclaimed.

'I gathered intelligence.'

'That's so sick. A real spy. Did they give you cool gadgets and things?'

'It wasn't like James Bond, Al. It wasn't glamorous at all. Most of it was boring. Half the time, I was crawling with lice. Some days I'd have given anything for a bath. Besides, intelligence work is incredibly dull. You spend a lot of time counting stuff in and out and saying what direction it's going in. I once spent a month disguised as a peasant, though. That was pretty interesting. I learned about sheep, and then herded the scraggy things up and down roads in the middle of France, reporting on German troop movements. Sheep really are incredibly stupid, you know.'

'But you had a wireless thingie and sent dispatches in code and stuff.'

'Yes, I was trained in all that. Later on, my job was to set up sabotage groups and supply them with money and equipment.'

'You mean, guns and explosives?'

'Yes, that too.'

'Did you go out and blow up railway lines and things?' he asked, memories of old war movies flicking through his mind.

'No. My job was to organise other people to do that.'

His shoulders drooped. 'Organising' wasn't exciting at all. 'So it was boring stuff, really.'

She became thoughtful. 'There were times when I feared for my life.'

'Ruth says you're a war hero, but I thought she was exaggerating.'

'Oh, I was no hero. I just wanted to do my bit like everyone else. I wasn't even brave. Maybe that's why I was scared all the time.'

'Was it really dangerous?' he asked, his eyes brightening.

'About a third of the women who went to France for the SOE never returned.'

'A third? I mean – shit!' he said, shocked, picturing what it would be like if a third of his class were killed. Which ones wouldn't he miss? When it came to it, he realised he'd miss all of them, even that cow Sandy.

'So when I disappeared and didn't immediately come back after the war, David assumed I was dead.'

'That's terrible. Why didn't you come back?'

'I was in prison. I don't know how they found out about me, but I was captured.'

'Didn't they, you know, shoot spies?'

'Many of them, yes.'

'But not you. Did you tunnel your way out?'

She shook her head and collected up the photographs of David.

'Did they, you know, force you to name names?'

'No, I didn't do that. I think that's why I survived. They were questioning me but I was lucky. I was captured right at the end of the war; one morning I woke up and found the gates were open and my interrogators had gone.'

'So why didn't you come back then?'

'I was in hospital with blood poisoning.'

She said it so matter-of-factly that at first he didn't take on board what she'd said. Then he felt a chill run through him – 'questioning' was her term for 'torturing'. 'They didn't… they didn't...' He couldn't say the word. 'Why didn't you just tell them what they wanted to know?'

'It would have meant giving them David's name. He was working with me at the time and he needed time to get out.'

Al was disgusted. 'And he didn't wait for you to come back? What a bastard.'

'Never say that, Al. He thought I was dead, remember?'

He wanted to ask what they had done to her, but thought it too ghoulish. Instead, he asked: 'Why didn't you go and find him when you got back?'

'I tried but his street had been bombed and everybody had dispersed. When I went to his bank, which is the only other place I knew might have his address, that was bombed, too. The army didn't know where to find him – the war had been over a year and I was just one of thousands of people trying to find displaced loved ones. What made me so special?'

'But you were, you were... You'd been...'

'I wasn't the only one to suffer, Al. I was alive. I was fit and healthy.'

'He should have waited.' Then his curiosity got the better of him. 'What did they do to you?'

She patted his hand. 'It's in the past.'

'I think you're amazing to have stood up to them.'

She cackled. 'My timing was lucky. The war ended and I survived. It's that simple.'

Something seemed to fall away from her as she said this, and Al found he was able to peel back years of aging and see her as she would have been at the end of the war – broken but defiant. There was a moment when he even found her beautiful and he could imagine himself falling in love with her. No one could have resisted that look.

And then his phone vibrated to announce an incoming text, breaking the mood. He tried to recapture that moment, but it was hopeless and he could no longer see past her crumpled body and moustachio'd upper lip. All he saw now was a frail, wizened woman profoundly at peace.

'Is it important, dear boy?' she asked, poking the phone on the table.

'No.'

'You don't even know who it was.'

He glanced at it. It was a text from Gazzer. 'Can you come?' it said. 'I need some help with Chemistry homework.'

Another drop.

'Is it bad news?' asked Mrs Mallinson.

He sat comparing her life with his and felt ashamed. 'If I'd... I... It's a friend asking for help with Chemistry homework.'

'Well, you tootle along and give him the help he needs.'

'He doesn't want help with Chemistry. It's his funny idea of a code.'

She must have formed her own conclusions because she said, 'Is this something to do with you lobbing a bottle at my wall?'

He looked at his feet, unable to meet her gaze. 'It started then.'

'I won't pry. You're a man now, and know the right thing to do.'

'I would, but I can't,' he muttered. 'You don't understand.'

'No, I don't suppose I will unless you explain.'

'It's not very... er, I don't, er...'

'They broke my toes.'

For a long while he digested her bald statement. 'I wouldn't make a good spy,' he muttered at last, with a sniff. 'I'm not even being tortured.'

'Pain isn't the only hold people can have over you.'

'I suppose not.'

'Why don't you tell me what happened?'

That's how he found himself telling her about Gazzer, and Gazzer's part in the local hoodlums, and his growing 'chemistry' business on the side and how he, Al, had ended up becoming a runner for the crew, all because he'd got his fingerprints on a gun and a knife. 'You know,' he concluded, 'the police would never believe me. It'd be my word against his, and the rest of the crew's, who would all say they'd seen me lance him, even though I wasn't there.'

'Go and do what you have to do, and I'll think about it.'

'But it's wrong.'

'Al, stand up and be a man, or be a coward, I don't care, but I'm not a miracle worker. Give me a day. If you end up in prison, I'll come and visit you.'

She would, too. He got up and gave her a hug.

She suffered his embrace passively, then said, 'Stop being mawkish. Off you go. I'll see you tomorrow.'

'Thanks, Mrs Mallinson,' he said, dropping a kiss on her papery cheek. How on earth could an old woman help him? Even so, her words cheered him.

BEWILDERED

Rob sipped his tea and looked around. Susan Mallinson's house sparkled. Was that down to Al? If so, he was impressed. The boy had obviously worked magic.

'Did you see Al's new flower bed?' asked the old woman.

Rob nodded. He felt tired to the bone and almost incapable of making coherent conversation. He'd gone so far as to award himself another sickie, but when Mrs Mallinson rang and said she had a problem, he'd come round without a second thought.

'You're looking dreadful, Rob. Haggard.'

He laughed. 'No beating about the bush, then?'

'I hear Emma's back and staying at Lisa's.'

The old bat! he thought wryly. Straight for the jugular. 'Yeah,' he acknowledged.

'You sound over-joyed,' she said ironically.

'Mm,' he replied and sipped his tea.

'She's put on weight. It suits her.'

He sighed. 'She's pregnant.' He hadn't meant to say it, had

meant to keep his cards close to his chest, but it just slipped out.

'Ah.' There was a wealth of understanding in that syllable. 'How do you feel about that?'

From any other person he'd have found such directness rude, but Mrs Mallinson, who'd had more than her fair share of troubles over the years, had earned a response, even if it turned out to be a little wanting in substance. 'I don't know any more. I'm a bit muddled.'

And he really didn't know. For three nights he'd not slept properly as he churned things over in his mind. He must have slept, because he dreamed, but his dreams were of deep tiredness and people preventing him from sleeping, which left him even more wrung out.

'Al pointed out recently that children aren't the only reason for staying together.'

'Did you ever meet his father?'

'Can't say I did.'

'Al's one of the ones better off without his father. Given a choice, though, I don't think I want my child to grow up without me.'

'And yet you haven't swept Emma back into the fold.'

'She left me, you know. She walked out.'

'Do I detect a whine?'

Stung, Rob struggled not to snap at the old woman.

'Did you try very hard to find her?'

Rob thought back over the last months. He'd tried her friends and her work. His reception by her parents had been mortifying the first time, and frustrating the second. Where else could he have looked? Who else could he have asked?

As he sat there, he began to see he could have tried harder: for weeks he'd expected her to walk back into his life and had simply waited. Later, when she hadn't, he had begun to find comfort in Ruth and was no longer interested in searching for a woman who didn't want to be with him, however much part of him ached for her.

Then his thoughts drifted back to that last evening. What had been going on in her head for her to walk out that way? What had he done that she couldn't talk to him about it? Once more, he came up without a reasonable answer. She wouldn't have left without exceptional cause, because the Emma he remembered was kind and loving and forgiving. Or was she? Was he seeing her through the rose-tinted glasses of loss?

Mrs Mallinson sipping noisily at her tea brought him back to the present. He said, 'I thought I'd tried to find her, but I could have tried harder.'

'I know what it is to search for someone you love. Believe me, everyone always thinks they could have tried harder. The truth is, it may not have been just one more search; it may have been a lifetime of searching.'

'Aren't some things worth that?'

'You tell me.'

'The truth is, I'm so tired I can't think straight any more.'

'The truth is, you could have tried harder and you have to forgive yourself for that before you can move on. So I'll give you something else to think about in the meantime. Al and I got talking yesterday. Nice boy, Al, but weak. He's got himself into a muddle and needs a helping hand to straighten things out. And you needn't feel obliged to tell Vix. This is his secret.'

'Fair do's,' he said.

She leaned forward in her chair, fixed him with her beady eyes, and began in a hushed voice, 'Al's a drug runner.'

THE PLAN

Later, as Rob sipped a beer in the pub waiting for William to turn up, he reflected on what Mrs Mallinson had told him. The wicked old hag. She certainly knew how to capture someone's interest. And she was as sharp as a knife. That moment of incoherence at the beginning of the year when she'd got confused about her budgerigar flying off seemed to be a thing of the past. What's more, she looked almost kempt. Clearly, Al was good for her. He wondered what would happen when Al's 'punishment' came to an end in early May.

William strode in, spotted him, waved and headed for the bar. A few minutes later, he ambled over carrying a couple of pints, and handed one to Rob.

'You look like shite.'

'I haven't shaved, is all.'

'Take it from me, you look like something my dog would turn his nose up at.'

'Touch of insomnia.'

'Too busy playing with yourself, more like.' He sniffed. 'When did you last eat?'

Rob couldn't remember and it was on the tip of his tongue to tell William to mind his own business, when William grumbled, 'Oh, I could murder a basket of chips. That woman's got me eating weeds.'

'You mean salad.'

'I grow it. I know what I'm eating.'

'I thought you were your own man.'

'You know me, Rob. Anything for a quiet life.'

'Yeah, yeah. Next she'll have you popping the question.'

'I've been considering it.'

'You're kidding!'

'Don't sound so surprised.'

'Happy for you, mate. Honest I am,' added Rob when William frowned at him. 'So what's stopping you?'

'It's like this,' began William in a confidential tone. 'I like to order pizza and eat it from the box in front of the rugger, with my feet on the table, the lights off, and a six pack at my elbow. Women's understanding of the finer art of living like a slob is quite narrow. I actually like my clothes on the floor. I want to find the loo seat up, the way the good Lord meant it to be left. I like my space. I like living alone.'

'Come off it, Will. When was the last time you spent a night in that flea pit of yours? Even your dog knows where you doss. I saw him trotting home alone the other day and it wasn't towards your flat.'

'Yeah, well, the thing is, she keeps saying she doesn't want to get married, and who am I to row against the current?'

'Rubbish. She's scared stiff she'll frighten you off. 'Course she wants to get married.'

'The thing is, I like the dolly bird. Here, have a look at this.' He pulled out a jeweler's box and opened it. Inside was a diamond and emerald ring.

Rob's jaw dropped. 'Damn, you're serious,' he muttered, reaching for it. When he handed it back, William stroked the stones with a finger. 'Bit of all right, isn't it?' he said. 'Never been so happy in all my life.'

'I never thought I'd see the day you were shackled.'

'I'm not shackled. I just happen to be hanging my clothes on hangers and whatnot. I can live with clothes on hangers. I thought I couldn't, but I can. I can even put them there myself sometimes.' He blew out his cheeks. After a couple of moments of introspection, he roused himself and added. 'You wanna know what she does at night?'

'Not really. TMI, mate.'

'Tea what?'

'You should listen to your prospective stepson more. TMI. Too much information.'

'She puts her arms around me and holds me,' said William, ignoring him. 'I never want her to let go.'

A memory of way Ruth used to hold him imploded in Rob's mind. It was almost a physical effort to shut it away. He forced his attention back on William. 'I can't imagine you with a basketload of kids.'

William, blithely oblivious of the way Rob's voice cracked, exclaimed, 'No kids! I'm not wearing that T-shirt. I'll take Al to the pub now and again and tell him everything I know. If he's wise, he'll ignore every word. But no kids. I'm gonna keep my dolly bird to myself.'

'And the rabbit food?'

'It's not so bad.'

'I'm going to get a basket of chips,' said Rob, getting up, 'cover them in red sauce, and eat them in front of you, slowly, one by one.'

'I said it's not so bad. I didn't say I had to live on rabbit food alone.'

Rob went over to the bar and ordered two baskets of chicken and chips, and two pints of Doom Bar with whisky chasers.

'We're settling in, then,' said William, when Rob placed the drinks on the table and the bar man followed with the food.

'She expecting you back for supper?'

'I'm a free man.'

'You might want to let her know, though.'

'I was going to text her.' William pulled out his phone and tapped out a message. 'See?'

'Emma's back.'

'Wondered when you'd mention her,' said William pressing Send, and turning off his phone.

'Coward,' said Rob, flicking the phone with a finger.

William ignored the jibe and pocketed the phone.

'You seen her?' asked Rob.

'Nah. Vix saw her in town this afternoon. Can't miss that red hair.'

Rob smiled. Emma's hair was something he used to like twisting round his fingers when they were watching TV.

'I gather she's not back with you.'

'It's complicated,' said Rob in a ruminative tone.

'Always is with women.' William munched on a chip, watching Rob through narrowed eyes.

'I know what I'm going to do,' Rob went on eventually. 'I just can't bring myself to do it yet.'

William continued to eat in silence, watching his friend.

'Don't do that,' muttered Rob, unnerved by William's inspection.

'Not doing anything, mate,' said William, but he dropped his gaze nevertheless.

'So I'm not happy. So what's new?'

'You have been these last few weeks,' contradicted William. 'Happy, that is.'

Rob winced. 'Was it so obvious?'

'You see my nose?' said William, pointing to it with a chip.

'Damn. Now I feel badly.'

'It was only obvious to people who know you.'

'Do me a favour?'

'If I can.'

'Find an excuse to deliver some plants to her. And... you know.'

'Sure. Hellebores?'

Rob didn't rise to this. 'I'll pay for them.'

'No need for that.'

'I said, I'll pay for them.'

'Keep your shirt on! I've got stuff to deliver anyway.'

'When are you going to pop the question?'

William accepted the abrupt change of subject with equanimity, as Rob knew he would. 'I'm trying to think of the right place,' said William.

'What have you come up with so far?'

'The garden centre.'

Rob gave a snore as though he were dropping off to sleep with boredom.

'It's where we first kissed.'

'No,' said Rob, categorically.

'You think not?'

'Definitely. Take it from me, these things matter to women. They'll bring it up every year on your anniversary. They'll talk about it with their girlfriends, savouring it, showing off a bit, puffed up by your imagination, and going over every insignificant detail you never thought was important. Trust me, it really, really matters.'

'So not the garden centre?'

'Not even among the orchids.'

'I can't think of anywhere else.'

'Ah come on, man. Take her away for a romantic weekend somewhere. Wine her and dine her. Make her feel special in a fancy hotel where the bill makes you gasp. Take her for a romantic walk along the cliff tops with a view of the sea exploding on the rocks below, and then, with the wind in your hair –'

'I'm a bit short on that front.'

'With the wind in your hair,' Rob persisted, 'you put your arms around her and whisper in her ear.'

'Not bended knee then.'

'Break a few rules. Vix'll like that.'

'You've thought about this a lot, then.'

'It just came to me.'

'So this is not what you're planning for Emma?'

'No.'

William sipped his beer. 'Proposing on a cliff top sounds dead romantic.'

'It does, doesn't it?'

'What are you going to do about Emma?'

'She's…' He stopped, for some reason unwilling to admit that Emma was pregnant. Emma's pregnancy was colouring everything and stopping him thinking straight. Were she not pregnant, he'd be able to decide what to do easily: take her into his arms, or send her packing as she deserved.

Or maybe she didn't deserve – he wasn't cruel. He didn't bear grudges. At least, he didn't think so.

However, Emma was carrying his child, which made his decision clear cut in one sense. He wanted that child. Ached for it. But his anger with Emma was growing not dissipating. He felt angry enough to walk away, despite the child, which he found strange given his desperate yearning at the beginning of the year for Emma's return.

He found himself repeating Ruth's name in his head like a mantra.

'When did you last see her?'

'Ruth?'

'Emma.'

He struggled to focus. 'Saturday night.'

William did a double take. 'That's four days, Rob. What's going on?'

'I met someone else.'

There didn't seem to be anything to say to that.

'I know what to do... but I don't.'

'I can't tell you, mate. Do what your heart tells you.'

'My heart's telling me two things, equally strongly, both opposite.'

'Maybe you should talk to Emma. You two, you were good together. Ruth makes you calm but Emma used to fizz you up. You were like a bottle of pop all shook up until you bought that house and became Mr Dead Boring. Then you spent your whole time fretting about money.'

'I've never had such a big mortgage.'

'Do I look interested? Talk to her, for Chrissake.'

'Maybe, but I got you here to talk about something else completely,' said Rob. He knew he was being cowardly, but he couldn't face any more scrutiny. 'It's about Al.'

'Ri-ight,' said William, instantly side-tracked, and drawing out the word uneasily.

'He's got himself an unsavoury friend... who happens to be the son of our friend Bruce Turner.'

'Unsavoury?' asked William.

'A nasty piece of work, from what I hear. You know these hooligans?'

'What about them?'

Rob sucked his teeth and then said: 'He's orchestrating them, apparently.'

'What?' The word seemed to explode into the room. 'Are you sure?' gasped William.

'We've only Al's word for it.'

'Does Bruce know?'

Rob shook his head. 'Dunno. Shouldn't think so. He thinks too highly of himself to get his hands this dirty.'

'Stupid boy.'

'It's worse.'

'How can it be worse?'

'Al's a courier for the boy.'

William's face went red. 'I'll fucking thump him,' he roared, banging the table and leaping to his feet.

'Sit down, Will,' said Rob quietly.

'I will not. I'll teach him a lesson he'll not forget.'

'So you think he's doing this willingly? Hm.'

William stopped blustering, registered the serious expression on Rob's face, and settled back down. 'He's a good boy, Al. What's Bruce's boy got on him that's frightened him so much?'

'Fingerprints on a certain gun and a certain knife belonging to Gary Turner.'

William sat very still with a frown growing on his face. 'What –? How –? I mean…'

'Here, catch!' said Rob suddenly, chucking the empty chip basket at him.

William caught it automatically. Then the penny dropped and he sat staring at it. 'As simple as that? He just tossed it at Al, and he caught it? Oh Lord. But Al's a nice boy. The police'll believe him.'

Rob looked at him. 'Sure they will.'

'Bloody hell. What's Vix going to say?'

'Nothing. You're never going to tell her. Ever. Now, I've thought about this. Guess what day tomorrow is?'

'Thursday.'

Rob ignored the sarcasm. 'And the Special Interest Group meets at 6.30. We'll all be there. Ruth.' He took a breath. 'Vix. You. Me. Bruce…'

'What are you thinking?'

'You and I might be late.'

'You mean, we could break in and –'

'I'm a builder, William, not a burglar.'

'Amen to that. So…?'

'As a builder, I sometimes change locks for people who lose their keys and have got themselves locked out.'

William stared at him. Then a slow smile spread across his face, and he took a gulp of his beer.

CHAPTER 12

NEVER-NEVER LAND

The next day, Vix drew up outside Ruth's house. Ruth heard the car crunch over the gravel, realised it wasn't Rob, and sat at the bottom of the stairs waiting for her friend to go away. Vix, however, was not subtle. After pressing the bell three times, she leaned on it. Goaded, Ruth opened the door a crack.

'I'm out. I'm busy. Just, just go away.'

'You're doing that thing again,' said Vix. 'Not answering your phone.' When Ruth said nothing she asked: 'Are you all right, Babe?'

'I'm fine.' Ruth started to close the door.

'Will asked me to deliver some plants. He was with Rob last night at the pub. Came home completely strapped.' Ruth's feeble smile did not appear to impress Vix, who continued, 'So Rob asked him to deliver some plants.'

'I'm confused. I thought you said William asked you.'

'Rob asked Will, and Will asked me, and I said there was no need for subterfuge, that I'd just come and see how you are.'

'Uhuh. As you can see, I'm fine.'

'Can I come in?'

'I'm busy.'

Vix's face fell.

'I'm fine, Vix,' said Ruth, softening her tone. 'Really I am, but I don't want to see anyone right now. Not even you.'

'Rob's worried about you.'

'Well, he's got no right to be,' said Ruth, firing up.

'He's hurting, Ruth. He's really unhappy.'

The incredible feeling Ruth had had the night he left, of feeling vibrantly alive, had flipped. Now she felt worse than when Michael had died. 'I don't care,' she lied, and began to close the door.

Vix bit her lip. 'I didn't know you two were quite so...'

'We weren't.' Again Ruth started to shut the door.

Vix pushed lightly against it. 'Ruth, darling, let me in.'

'Not now. I'm busy. Good bye.'

'Will you be there tonight?' asked Vix, clearly casting about for something, anything to stop the door shutting.

'Tonight? Where? Oh. The Special Interest Group. Maybe.' She closed the door, leaving Vix outside. Short of busting it down, there was not a lot more Vix could do, except perhaps hope Ruth came to the meeting. It seemed, however, she wasn't satisfied with hoping, because she pressed the doorbell again. And again.

Vix wouldn't give up. 'Ruth,' she shouted through the letterbox, 'we need you there. Tonight. Will and Rob will be late, and without you, there may not be a quorum, so...'

Ruth yanked open the door and glared at Vix, who took a step backwards. '... so Bruce could take it into his head to do nothing about Mary's report from our visit to Newport,' her friend finished in a more measured tone.

After what seemed an age, Ruth made the sullen pronouncement: 'I'll be there,' and closed the door again. She leaned back against it listening to her friend walk back to her car. She felt like screaming. How dare Rob worry about her?

As the engine started up, Ruth opened the door once more. Vix switched off the ignition hopefully as she wound down her window. 'Coffee?'

Aching for Rob, Ruth held the door wider,

'Yes!' muttered Vix triumphantly under her breath, and locked the car for the second time.

In the kitchen, Ruth busied herself making coffee while she shored up her defences and stiffened her resolve not to break down in the face of Vix's sympathy. Finally there was nothing more to do but place two mugs of coffee on the table. Then she remembered biscuits, and got up to get them.

'I'm sorry it didn't work out with Rob,' began Vix, when Ruth eventually settled.

Back in control of herself, Ruth admitted, 'Yeah. So am I.'

'If it's any comfort, he doesn't look so hot himself.'

'No, it's not.'

Uncharacteristically, Vix held her tongue and let the silence run. She was duly rewarded when Ruth continued, 'I'm trying hard to get a perspective on things. When he left, I thought I could handle it. That feeling lasted for less than five minutes. I don't know what happened between us, but I feel I have never fallen off such a high cliff onto such hard rocks in my life. It's almost as bad as when Michael died. Vix, how can that be?'

Vix moved round the table, but Ruth leapt up, anticipating her. 'Don't you dare give me a hug. I'll fall to pieces if you do.' She retreated to the end of the kitchen and began pacing. 'Ah Vix, this is so unexpected, and yet I could hardly say he was ever mine.'

'You fell in love. It's that simple.'

'I didn't think I had. I thought I just liked him.' She smiled wryly, acknowledging Vix's sceptical expression. 'OK. I really liked him. Vix, I miss him.' She pressed the heels of her hands into her eyes. 'Ah, this is nuts. Is this what it's like, falling in love? I'd forgotten. Michael and I were married for nearly quarter of a century. He and I, we were easy together. When he died I swapped a looming sadness for a lingering sorrow. But I'd forgotten the falling in love bit. Not sure I ever experienced it, actually. Not like this. Not this horrible feeling that I've been ripped up.'

She sat down at the table and dropped her head in her hands. 'You know what I'd started to do?' She laughed softly to herself. 'I'd started to plan again. I stopped planning, you know, when Michael became ill. You can't make plans when someone's dying. It's just not right.

'And then Rob comes along. And for the last month – is it a

month since the car boot sale? I think so. Anyway, for the last month, I've been planning.' She chuckled. 'Little things, like dinner out. He likes Irish music – did you know? – and I found a couple of pubs in London with Irish music. London's not that far away. We went up for the night, and stayed in a small hotel in Paddington. We had dinner in a little Italian round the corner – he likes pasta – and… We went off to look at a couple of gardens two weekends ago. You know, spring bulbs. Stayed in a B&B. And we were planning what we'd do in the garden together.

'I was making plans, Vix. We were making plans. I know he won't come back but I really want him to. And if he does, God help me, because I'll have to turn him away. I'm wrong for him. I can see that now. He wants children. For God's sake, can you imagine me with children again? I've got that T-shirt, done the sleepless nights and all that. My kids are grown up, Vix. I simply can't start again.'

With her chin in her hands, she looked at Vix and smiled wanly. 'You know what?'

Vix shook her head.

'I wouldn't swap this feeling for anything. I'm not being masochistic, but looking back, I felt loved by him. We had a great time. And now he's going to get back together with Emma. We were – I was – living in Never-Never Land, and it was wonderful while it lasted.'

Vix reached over and squeezed her hand. 'Do you want some distraction?'

Ruth shrugged. 'Yeah.'

Vix pulled a handful of papers from her bag and pushed them across the table. 'Mary wrote up our trip to Newport. She came to some conclusions and has made a string of recommendations. I think they're pretty good, actually. Imaginative.'

'Let's have a look,' said Ruth, reaching for her glasses.

Decoy

'You know the odds of this working are shorter than a mouse's dick, don't you?' muttered William.

Rob ignored him and drove on.

'Al's better at scratching balls than throwing them,' persisted William.

'He'll be OK,' Rob insisted.

William looked glum.

The whole plan was so contrived Rob didn't think it had a chance in hell of working either, but it was the best they'd come up with. At least it was better than William's idiotic idea of breaking in. Rob's plan involved getting Bruce to open the front door and let him in.

Oh, but what a rotten spy he'd make. Deception was not part of his make-up. He drew his van up outside the meeting hall. 'Don't forget to ring me if Bruce leaves early,' he muttered unhappily. 'I'll need time to get out.'

'Got my mobile,' said William, holding it up, and jumping down from the van. 'You sure about this? We've still got time to think of something else.'

'I'm listening.'

'I don't have ideas now, you nonce!'

Rob drove away slowly, feeling nauseous. This was the stupidest idea in the world and it was bound to go wrong. When it did, his reputation would go up in flames. On the other hand, he couldn't leave Al to sort this one out alone. In the road behind Bruce's house, he spotted the gangly teenager sitting on the kerb rolling a cricket ball from hand to hand in the gutter.

'Where've you been?' said Al leaping up and rushing over to him when Rob pulled up. 'I've been waiting ages.'

'Relax. We have all the time in the world,' drawled Rob, getting out of his van and patting Al on the shoulder.

'I'll miss.'

'You'll be fine. You know what to do?'

'Yes,' croaked Al.

'Before you throw, picture the ball going right through that pane of glass in the front door. Picture it so hard you can feel the glass as it shatters. It's all of two meters, Al. You can't miss it. Is Gazzer primed?'

'I told him I'd nicked fifty quid off William and that drinks were on me. Half the crew will be there.'

'Good thinking. And if Gazzer leaves the pub?'

'I'm to ring you immediately.'

'Don't let me down, Al.'

'I won't.'

There was a tongue-tied moment as Al stuffed his hands in to his pockets and studied the cracks in the pavement as if to draw courage from them. At last Rob said, 'Off you go then.'

'Rob?'

Rob looked up.

'Thanks.'

'Thank me after. Go on.'

Al loped off down the road. Rob called after him. 'Al? Forgotten something?'

Al looked back, perplexed.

'You muppet,' sighed Rob. He bent down and picked the cricket ball out of the gutter, tossing it straight to Al, who missed it. The boy grimaced, then went to get it.

'You'll be fine,' Rob assured him. He climbed back into his van and waited until he thought Al had had time to get to Bruce Turner's house, ring the bell and get Gazzer ready to leave. He wanted them out of the house on the front path as he arrived.

After five minutes, he judged it was time to get going. He drove round the block and pulled up about a hundred metres from Bruce's house. From the glove box, he pulled out a clipboard and pretended to consult this while keeping an eye on the Turner's front garden.

There was no sign of the boys. Where the hell were they?

Come on Al, thought Rob. I'm beginning to look sus sitting

here doing nothing.

Rob flipped slowly through the papers on his clipboard again, and then equally slowly opened the glove box and replaced everything. At last, having drawn things out as long as he felt able, he climbed out of his van and sauntered up the Turner's front drive.

This wasn't like the films. Though he looked nonchalant enough, it took all his nerve not to look round to check which curtains were twitching. With his heart hammering, he wiped his damp palms on his trousers and pressed the doorbell.

Oh balls, he thought as he pressed it. What have I come to talk to Bruce about?

He heard footsteps across the hallway.

Come on, loser, think. Think!

The front door opened. Bruce stood on the threshold.

'Ah, Bruce. I was hoping to catch you at home.'

'Evening, Rob,' said Bruce. 'What can I do for you?'

Rob cleared his throat. 'I was wondering. Are you planning on coming to the meeting tonight?'

'I'd of thought that was obvious, given I chair it,' said Bruce, wiping his mouth on a napkin. 'We're just having supper. Will this take long?'

That's why Al and Gazzer were still inside. No question, they'd invited Al to join them. Balls.

'I don't want to take up your time,' said Rob feebly and followed Bruce through to the kitchen. 'Hello, Al. Gary. Mrs Turner, are you well?'

Al leaped up before Mrs Turner had a chance to reply. 'They invited me to supper,' he expostulated.

'How nice,' said Rob as blandly as he could.

'What was it you wanted to talk about?' asked Bruce, resuming his seat.

'It's nothing really, and I feel a bit stupid bringing it up at all.' Rob looked around helplessly.

'Don't mind the family. Everything's confidential here,' said Bruce confidently.

'Actually, I think it's better if I bring it up in the meeting,' said Rob, still racking his brains for something to discuss.

'No, no. Much better to discuss it now. Then I can think about it before I get there.'

Mrs Turner began gathering up the boys' plates, scraping the leftovers onto the serving dish. As Rob watched her, an idea ping'd into his mind. 'It's about the litter,' he said.

'Oh yes?' asked Bruce, warily.

'Rob,' interrupted Al, red in the face. 'You said you'd toss a ball about with me later. I really want to get in the cricket team this year.' He got out the cricket ball and hefted it in Rob's direction.

Rob caught it just before it hit an indescribably ugly vase. 'Not now, Al.'

Mrs Turner frowned. 'We don't throw balls at the table, do we Al?'

'No, Mrs Turner.'

'About the litter,' Bruce prompted.

Slightly on the hop, Rob *ad libbed*. 'There are quite a lot of houses on the estate with tons of rubbish in their front gardens.'

'Are there?'

'I wondered what should be done about it?'

'Well, people must take their rubbish to the tip.'

'I don't think everyone will. I don't think they notice it any more. I think they've got used to it.'

'Got used to it? I think not.'

'What's the colour of your garden path?'

'What? I don't know. Grey, I suppose.'

'They're yellowish paving stones,' interpolated his wife. 'To match the local stone.'

'And your point is...?' asked Bruce.

'That you don't see them any more, the same as they don't see the rubbish.'

'So what do you propose?'

Rob quietly deposited the ball at Al's elbow. 'Nothing. I

wouldn't presume to propose. That's your job, Bruce. You're the chair. But I was thinking... what if we could get the rubbish men to drive it all away?'

'At council payer's expense?'

'Yes!' agreed Rob. 'Yes,' he added more soberly after gauging Bruce's expression. 'Provided it doesn't accumulate again.'

'Like a sort of temporary amnesty?'

'That's right.'

'Old mattresses don't go into the back of rubbish lorries.'

'Anyway, it was a thought. The council probably hasn't got the money anyway.'

'I don't hold with squandering council funds on something people should sort out themselves.'

'There you go, then. I knew I shouldn't have bothered you. I'll leave you to your supper.'

'No, no. We're finishing now,' said Bruce, pushing aside his half eaten supper. 'We can go together.' He pecked his wife's up turned cheek. 'Enjoy your cards.' Everyone knew Bruce's wife played whist on Thursday evenings.

'Shall we go?' Al asked Gazzer, getting up.

'I want some pudding,' said the boy, sullenly.

'There isn't any, Gary. There never is on cards night,' said his mother, folding her napkin and rising.

Gazzer humphed and got up from the table gracelessly, leaving his mother to stack his plate in the dishwasher. They all moved towards the front door, with Rob practically making sweeping gestures behind their backs to usher them out. Al and Gazzer walked down the path towards the gate. Rob watched Al go in disbelief. The boy had forgotten the plan. 'Al?' he called as Bruce locked the front door. 'Cricket? I'm free tomorrow evening if you want.'

'Oh yes,' said Al turning back and chucking the ball at Rob, who stood with the glass front door framed beside him. The ball plopped into Rob's hands without him moving a muscle.

Rob threw it back again. 'You can practice bowling, too,' he said.

'Right you are,' replied Al. This time, when the boy casually bowled it back, it smacked into the ground at Al's feet.

'Not towards the house,' cautioned Bruce. 'You'll break a window.'

I wish, thought Rob, as the ball rolled to a halt at his feet. The boy was useless. He picked up the ball and, as he made to throw it back to Al, he noticed the Turners' had their backs to him. Glancing left and right to ensure the coast was clear, he lobbed the ball through the front door himself.

There was a tinkle of glass and everyone turned.

'I told you not to throw the ball towards the house,' Bruce shouted at Al.

'I didn't.'

'Oh, Al. What a silly lie,' said Rob. He frowned hard at the boy.

'I –'

'Apologise,' barked Rob.

Al looked alarmed. 'I –' He gulped. 'Sorry. I'll pay for it.'

Bruce swore at him. 'Bloody right, you'll pay for it. Gary, you'll have to stop home. We can't leave the house open like that. We'll be robbed.'

'But –'

'I said –'

'Bruce, I happen to have some glass in the van,' volunteered Rob. 'I can fix it for you now, if you like.'

'You're supposed to come to the meeting.'

'It'll only take ten minutes.'

Bruce considered this for a nanosecond, then said, 'Gary, you wait until he's finished and lock up when he's done.'

This was not something Rob had planned for. 'If you like, I could lock up and bring the key with me to the meeting,' he suggested.

Faced with the possibility of having to deal with a recalcitrant son, and a volunteer who seemed willing to sort everything out, Bruce took the rational course of action. 'If you're sure?'

'You go ahead,' said Rob. 'Al can pay me back tomorrow.'

'Right you are. Do you realise how lucky you are, lad? That was a really stupid thing to do, now, wasn't it? Everyone knows you can't throw to save your life. And if you think you're going to get onto the cricket team while I'm coaching it, you can think again.'

Al gulped and hung his head.

Good boy, thought Rob. Now make yourself scarce.

'I'm really sorry. Would you like me to stay and help, Rob?'

Rob almost rolled his eyes. The boy was no good at subterfuge at all. 'What, and have you break the next pane. No thanks,' he said harshly. 'Get on with you. I'll expect payment in full tomorrow. Twenty five quid.'

'Twenty five quid?' yelped Al.

Rob looked at him quizzically, and Al got the message. 'I'll bring it to your place tomorrow. Sorry, Mr Turner.'

'You great nancy thrower,' Gazzer said to Al. 'C'mon. Let's go before they change their mind.'

'Got your phone, Al?' asked Rob.

'Yes,' the boy called over his shoulder.

Bruce held out the front door key to Rob. 'If you're sure.'

'Leave it to me.'

Bruce shrugged, and then he and his wife climbed into their respective cars and drove off.

A huge sigh of relief escaped Rob. So far, so good.

Quickly, he measured the frame and cut a new piece of glass to fit it. He knocked the old glass out and his fingers worked fast as he slammed putty around the new pane. Though he had a perfectly valid reason to be here, his nerves were still shredded. He hated lying and he worked in constant fear that someone would return and catch him skulking around their house poking his nose into places it had no business to be. As he was picking up the old glass, something brushed against the back of his leg. Startled into crying out, the glass slipped through his fingers as he leapt forward.

A soft 'Miaow' made him week-kneed with relief.

'Hello, cat,' he said. 'You gave me quite a surprise.'

When he bent to pick up the glass again, he realised he'd cut his hand and it was bleeding copiously. Suddenly it started to hurt. Blood dripped freely as he went into the kitchen to find a paper towel to wrap his hand in. Nothing. Just fancy tea towels folded over a rack to dry. He couldn't use those. He'd ruin them. In the end, he found an old rag in his workbox and used that to staunch the bleeding.

Meanwhile, time was slipping away. He tried to think how long he'd been. Ten minutes? Half an hour? Get a move on, he thought to himself. He took the stairs three at a time, and paused on the landing to get his bearings. The cat followed him up. It took seconds to identify Gazzer's room but seemingly hours to find the weapons. All the while, the cat twined through his legs, purring loudly.

He was coming out of Gazzer's room when he heard the front door open. He froze. His mind blanked. Had Gazzer's door been open or closed when he'd arrived? He dithered, and shut it. In two soft strides, he was in the bathroom easing that door shut too. Ever so gently, he turned on the tap until water was running freely over his hand. Ouch. Now it was really hurting.

He felt rather than heard the bathroom door open. 'What are you doing in here?'

Rob straightened up and allowed his bloody hand to show.

'Oh, you poor dear.' It was Mrs Turner.

'I was looking for some Detol. I keep it in the bathroom at home and I presumed you might, too. Forgive me for making free with your house.'

'But that's a terrible cut.'

Rob looked at it; it was deeper than he'd thought. 'Mm,' he conceded. 'Detol?'

'In the cupboard. Here, let me.' She reached past him and rummaged in the cupboard, emerging with a bottle of yellow liquid.

'I thought you were out,' he muttered, and sucked in his breath as she poured neat TCP over the wound.

'Elizabeth's got some sort of fever and I'm dreadfully worried it might be that dangerous new flu going round. You know, it's very contagious and I don't want to take any chances, even though they have a vaccine for it. You never can tell whether you might be the one person who gets an allergic reaction to it and dies. And I worry about Gary, if he got it. And if he got it, Bruce would go down with it in a trice because he always seems to catch every bug around. Some people say he suffers a lot from man flu, which isn't true at all. You should see how poorly he gets. Naturally he's very demanding when he's ill. Intelligent people are always demanding, don't you think? Elizabeth says I shouldn't pander to him, but I think she's jealous – she and her husband are getting a divorce. They claim it's all very amicable but you should hear them fighting when they think they're alone, and he gets all antsy when she puts her foot down, and accuses her of being controlling… although she is a little bossy. It always has to be her way. I'd like to have the girls around here for cards one time, but Elizabeth insists we play at her place, even though she turns out to be ill this week. I think it's rude of her not to have called everyone, don't you?'

She seemed to require an answer this time. 'Er,' said Rob faintly.

An hour and a half later, Rob turned up in time for the end of the Special Interest Group meeting and popped his head round the door. Ruth was addressing the room and didn't see him.

He studied her for a moment, and then slipped away before anyone noticed him. William found him in the car park ten minutes later as everyone piled out of the meeting. Though Rob had taken care to park well away from Ruth's car, he could still make her out as she walked towards it in the soft spring night. Her head was bowed, and then for some reason, she looked up, right in his direction. Had there been light enough, Rob liked to think their eyes met across the car park. As it was, he could barely make out her shape. Nevertheless, they stood frozen for what seemed like an endless moment before she dropped her head and opened her car door.

'What kept you?' asked William, pretending not to notice Rob's expression in the dim light.

Rob ignored him. Ruth drove away without looking his way again.

'I thought everything had gone wrong when you didn't turn up. Did you get in?'

'Yeah.' The adrenalin high had left Rob feeling listless and flat.

'Clever bastard. Any problems?'

'I needed four stitches.' He held up a bandaged hand.

'You stupid nonce. What the hell d'you do?'

Rob wasn't about to explain how the cat had given him a fright, making him drop the glass. He shrugged. William wasn't interested in his response anyway.

'Let me see them.'

Perhaps he'd been wrong to make assumptions about William's level of interest. 'They're taped up,' said Rob, inspecting his hand.

'Not the stitches. The gun and the knife.'

'I haven't got them.'

'I thought you said you were successful. Where are they?'

'Where he left them.'

'What?' William leaned closer to Rob. 'I thought you were going to go in and get them?'

'Keep your voice down.'

'You were supposed to go in and get them.'

'We're not thieves, Will.'

William frowned. 'I don't get it.'

'I went in to wipe off Al's fingerprints, that's all. I thought the police might like to investigate. Feel like calling them?'

A look of glee filled William's face. 'Give us your phone.'

'Call them on yours.'

'It's not charged, is it?'

'You mean –'

'You got out safely, didn't you?' said William, slapping him on the back.

Rob's lips twitched impatiently. 'I suppose. You can buy the first round.'

RECOVERING

When she got home from the Special Interest Group meeting, Ruth couldn't banish the memory of the way Rob had stood beside William in the car park, all hunched up. There was something desolate in that stoop.

Ruth tracked from room to room forcing her mind to think of other things. Over there, they used to put the Christmas tree. On that bookshelf, the last of the chocolate eggs had been found the year the Easter Egg Hunt was rained off and Michael had hidden the eggs around the house. She forgot who found it. Here was Jules' room, empty for the longest, and most bare of personal effects. Here was Anna's, serene and peaceful with cushions strewn over the sofa, and a teddy bear propped up on the pillows. Marty's walls were festooned with posters of mountains he wanted to climb. In her own room, books lay open on every surface and she started putting them away. She had been thinking of writing another gardening book, and had been casting around for ideas, but her mind couldn't settle on anything.

On her way downstairs, she went by the door to the attic, and passed on. She was sad but not maudlin. The bed would look exactly as they'd last left it: the sweat-soaked bottom sheet rucked up and the duvet flung back. They'd made love in there for hours. She could almost hear his deep voice murmuring to her and see his smiling, olive-green eyes sharing some joke with her.

She'd told Vix that she had been living in Never Never Land; the return to reality was painful. The house was hollow; the sound of her footsteps seemed to make the walls whisper back, 'Alone again.' Everything looked grey and tired. The curtains were disintegrating. The armrests on the threadbare sofas had brown shadows from multitudes of hands settling on them. The carpets were faded and worn. In the corners of rooms, dust collected in ancient fluff. This was not the elegant, refined house of her memory, but something worn down and neglected.

As she put the last of the books away, she realised the room no longer echoed of Michael. It was just her bedroom – where Rob had stayed a few nights.

She trailed into the kitchen and turned on the radio, but it wasn't company. She opened the fridge but it was empty – she'd forgotten to go shopping. She reached for the gin but decided that it was pathetic to drink alone, so she put it back. It was too dark to garden and, anyway, she didn't feel like gardening.

She wanted companionship.

She picked up the phone. Vix was laughing when she answered.

'Hello? Vix?'

Vix sobered instantly. 'Ruth? Is everything OK?'

'Yeah. Everything's fine. I felt like company and wondered if I could invite myself round.'

There was a moment of stunned silence. 'Yeah.'

'Are you sure it's OK? It's quite late.'

'Half past eight is not late.'

'It's not inconvenient or anything?'

'Darling, come round straightaway.'

'It's not convenient, is it?'

'Darling, you've kinda taken me by surprise. You inviting yourself round, it's one for the books. We'd love to see you. William's struggling with a barbeque and I'm pouring fat gins. I'm pouring yours as I speak.'

Ruth drew a circle in the dust on the windowsill with her finger. 'Pour mine thin. I have to drive home.' She added two dots and a smile to make a face.

'Rubbish. You can stay the night and we can watch DVDs, ooh, til ten o'clock.'

'We'll see. I'm leaving now. I won't be long.'

'Hurry. The ice is melting.'

She stood for a moment listening to the dialling tone, and then trudged upstairs to put on a fresh blouse. She was low now, but company would lift her spirits.

AN INVITATION

Rob looked at the email's From line. It clearly said Emma Don. Yet the subject line said: 'Inaugural Elderfield in Bloom walk'.

At first he didn't understand. He thought this was a new initiative he'd somehow missed as a result of not attending today's meeting. But how? And why was Emma involved?

Then he read it again and as he did so, wonder filled him. This was not the approach he'd expected from Emma. He'd anticipated angry words at his failure to contact her at Lisa's… which he thoroughly deserved. He smiled wryly; she was trying so hard to set up a meeting with him, and doing it in such an imaginative and good humoured way.

From: Emma Don
To: Rob Ansell
Subject: Inaugural Elderfield in Bloom Walk

To raise money to help with the Elderfield in Bloom Awards, you are invited to join the Inaugural Elderfield in Bloom Walk on Saturday. The walk will start at Elderfield in the Crown car park at 10am and will end, around lunchtime, at the Pauper's Arms.

Walking boots advised though trainers will suffice.

> Funny hats optional.
>
> If you wish to take part in the Inaugural Elderfield in Bloom Walk, there is a team briefing at the Pauper's Arms at 8pm on Friday evening.
>
> Teams will muster at the Coffee One cafe on Saturday morning from 8.30am, where lattes and croissants will be served.

No signature. But then this was an official notice inviting him to join an Inaugural Walk. He hit Reply.

> From: Rob Ansell
> To: Emma Don
> Subject: Inaugural Elderfield in Bloom Walk
>
> Some people are interested in joining the Inaugural Elderfield in Bloom Walk but are concerned there was no sponsorship form attached in order to start the process of raising money.

He hit Send. Was he expecting an instant reply? If so, he was disappointed. In the end he went to bed, his hand throbbing in its dressings now that the painkillers had worn off. Staring unseeingly up at the dark ceiling, he thought briefly about what the police might find when they arrived at Bruce's house. Then his mind shifted to dwell on Emma.

When had the fun gone out of their relationship? In their last two months together, all his memories were of her sniping at him: silly, hurtful remarks. Then he thought about William's comment. Had he really become a bore?

That he had loved her had always seemed a given. She was beautiful and bright and bubbly, but his memories of Christmas and the months leading up to it were of an angry woman. Why had she become so angry with him?

When he woke on Friday morning, the first thing he did was check his email. There was a new message in his In Box.

From: Emma Don
To: Rob Ansell
Subject: Inaugural Elderfield in Bloom Walk

The organisers of the Inaugural Elderfield in Bloom Walk appreciate the concern of some of the participants regarding sponsorship forms. These will be handed out in due course.

They hope to see as many participants as possible at the briefing tonight.

Rob sighed. This was the Emma he really remembered. The one who laughed and played with him. However, leaving him in the cold way she had, had been a bad idea. It had broken his faith in her. The question was, could she rebuild it? More importantly, did he want her to?

POWER GAMES

Susan Mallinson had faced down military interrogators during the war, yet now her daughter's bullying was too much for her. The slaps Jennifer dealt her would never show up as bruises and the vicious way Jennifer twisted her flesh between her fingers in mean little pinches merely reddened the skin but would also leave no trace. But that wasn't the worst of it.

The worst of it was that this was Jennifer, her beautiful daughter – albeit a grown-up version of the sly, manipulative child Mrs Mallinson had always found hard to warm to. She liked to think she had been a good mother, but was this savage, cruel woman before her of her making? Had her inability to love her daughter made her like this? Was this, then, her payback?

Jennifer's red face looked almost crazed with anger. Her fingers gripped her mother's arm and her fishy breath wafted over Mrs Mallinson's face. 'You will sign the papers.' She enunciated each word through clenched teeth.

Her mother's resolve wavered. Then she put up her chin. 'You can't do anything to me. And even if you do, I'll tell everyone you bullied me into it.'

Instantly, Jennifer was sweetness and light. 'Me? I wouldn't hurt a flea.' Then she sneered, 'Think they'll believe you?'

'Yes.'

'You dotty old woman. You haven't got any friends. There's never anybody here. You're all alone. You stink of piss. You've got hairs growing out of your chin and blackheads in your nose. You smell as if you haven't bathed for a year. Your hair is knotted and filthy. You're foul. It makes my flesh crawl to touch you. You need to be in a home where they make you wash every day. Anyone can see that. And what you don't know is that I have a doctor who'll swear you have dementia. That's all there is to it. Old and senile. Past it. Better off in a home. I have debts, you know? The sale of this house is going to pay them off. There's no discussion here, Mother. Just. Sign. The papers.'

Mrs Mallinson stared over her daughter's head.

Jennifer folded her arms and waited, then gave an infuriated sigh and left the room.

Her mother's resolution wavered as she looked anxiously after her.

The clock struck the hour. Al would be here soon. No friends! She'd show her no friends!

Twenty minutes later Mrs Mallinson heard something. It was a sort of shh, then the step of a high heel, and another shh. Something heavy was being dragged along the corridor towards her sitting room. She knew what it was.

She looked again at the clock. Al would be here in ten minutes. She could hold out that long.

Step. Shh. Step. Shh.

At last Jennifer stood in the doorway, triumphant. 'Ha! You thought you'd hidden it, but I searched the whole garret. The whole garret, you old witch. And I found it.' The strong box lay at her feet, all the memories locked inside.

'I don't know how many times you used to show me the pictures in this bloody box when I was a child, and you never understood I didn't care. Hours you'd spend going over the pictures. Hours and hours. I grew to hate this box and all it stood for. It meant you wallowing in stupid war memories. "This is what I did with this girlfriend. This is what I did with that one",' she taunted. '"She died. She survived." Did you think I cared?' she yelled.

Mrs Mallinson blinked, transfixed by the box. She tried to persuade herself the memories were etched in her mind, but the photos of David were irreplaceable. He was her soul mate, for all he couldn't face leaving his wife. Today, courtesy of hindsight, Mrs Mallinson understood how that could be. It had taken Anthony in her life to make her understand David's dilemma. She had loved Anthony, truly loved him. *And* she had loved David. What's more, she could imagine David feeling the same way about his wife and her. Had their roles been reversed, she would have stood by Anthony because he was her husband, her lover, and the father of her child. Because she loved him. For all that, David was just David and nothing else quite measured up to all he stood for.

She glanced again at the clock.

Jennifer flicked her long sleek hair back over her shoulder. 'If you think that lanky oaf will rescue you, think again.'

Mrs Mallinson's eyes widened in panic.

'Cal, is it? Well, Cal isn't coming. I want some time with Mother, I said. I hope you understand. Mother-daughter, you know, needing to talk.'

'He'll come.'

'He won't.'

Mrs Mallinson stared at the box.

'Mother, what did I do wrong?'

Jennifer's wail startled Mrs Mallinson and made her look up. Her daughter's face was twisted with unhappiness.

'Why couldn't you even pretend to love me? I tried so hard to please you.'

'I do love you.'

'No, you don't. You never did. And I wanted you to. So much. Years ago Daddy said you found it hard to love anything after the war, that they broke you, that you were never quite whole again. But I was your daughter. I deserved your love.'

Mrs Mallinson looked down at her hands, ashamed. She did love her daughter but she also recognised that she was no good at it. Today she knew all about postnatal depression and bonding. At the time, her doctor told her to 'pull herself together'. He didn't seem to understand she couldn't, that she was no more in control of her emotions than a passenger on a rollercoaster at a fairground. And like the passenger at the fairground, there was no getting off – she was on that ride for the duration and the black pit of despair she faced was as bad as anything she had felt with the wartime interrogators.

Jennifer interrupted her wandering thoughts. 'I think I deserve this house. Yes, I think I deserve some kind of compensation.'

'I live here, Blossom.'

'Don't call me Blossom. I was Daddy's Blossom. I was Daddy's little girl. He loved me.'

Mrs Mallinson raised tired eyes to her daughter. 'I love you, too.'

'You can't even lie convincingly. I deserve this house. So are you going to sign the papers, or must I burn this lot first?'

Her mother picked up the pen. No sooner had she signed than Jennifer snatched the papers from her. 'Thank you,' she said ironically. 'Now watch me burn this lot.'

'You said –'

'What? What did I say? Daddy hated this box. He'd bury himself in his study every time you got it out.'

'That's not true.'

'Yes he did. It made him sad.'

'It made him sad because his fiancée was killed in the blitz.'

'It made him sad because you were in love with another man.'

'That's not true.'

''Tis, 'tis, 'tis,' ranted Jennifer.

It wasn't but Jennifer was beyond understanding the finer nuances of love. Everything was black or white to her, but there were many shades of love. Anthony had understood that, just as she respected she could never quite replace his dead fiancée.

Jennifer pulled a lighter from her bag and lit the first photo, watching the paper curl and blacken. However, she had not accounted for how hard it was to burn paper. Even so, she burned every photo and document in the strong box, shoving her mother to the floor when she desperately tried to save just one photo of David.

When she'd gone, Mrs Mallinson knelt beside the strong box, trying to gather up the charred bits of paper as if she were raking up the ashes of a loved one after a cremation.

CHAPTER 13

THE SPONSORSHIP FORM

That evening, when Rob parked at the Pauper's Arms, he was still in two minds about coming at all. As he crossed the car park, he was greeted by the proprietor, who was serving some drinks to a group of smokers shivering around a table in the garden. They shook hands.

'You well?' Patrick asked Rob.

'Well enough.'

'Your girl's been here an hour, jumping up every time someone walks past the window in case it's you. I told her, "There's no way Rob'll be here early."'

Rob couldn't even bring himself to smile.

'It's taken all Lisa's nous to get her here as calm as she is.'

Unhappy to be the subject of gossip, Rob frowned. 'Really?' he acknowledged with polite disinterest and started towards the door.

'Emma's falling to pieces, mate,' Patrick called after him.

Rob turned on his heel and went back to Patrick. It seemed the whole world was party to his private affairs. If such a conversation were going to be forced on him, it was not going to be shouted across the pub garden for everyone's entertainment. 'She told you this, did she?' he said softly.

'No, mate. She's been staying with me an' Lis' these last few days. She an' I, we've been living together a couple of months now.'

Slightly mollified, Rob mustered up a 'Thanks.'

Together they walked towards the pub. 'Her pacing drives

me nuts,' Patrick confided. 'She's like a caged animal going mad. Can't eat, can't sleep. Lis' has got her to nibble on something now and again, but only on account of the baby.'

Rob's heart sank. He was in for an evening of tears and hysteria.

At the door, Patrick slapped his back in an overly familiar way that set Rob's teeth on edge. 'Let the bar staff know when you want drinks. They're on the house. I'll give you two quarrelling lovebirds some space now.'

It took several moments for Rob to calm his irritation. Quarrelling lovebirds? What the blazes had Emma told them to make them think that this was a little spat?

A party of noisy business people pulled up in open topped cars, blaring music making the air pulse. They parked and filed past him into the pub. He still hadn't fully made up his mind whether he wanted to see her when he followed the last of them in.

And there she was at a table by the fire, looking fantastic: her hair, make-up and clothes all perfect. She was turning heads, yet he was the only person she had eyes for.

'Hello, Rob,' she said in her husky voice.

'Hello, Sweet Pea,' he said, leaning down and kissing her cheek. 'You look wonderful.'

He'd assumed he would kiss her lips the way he always did, but at the last moment, he couldn't bring himself to, and kissed her cheek. There was a fleeting look of hurt in her big expressive eyes. However, she didn't break down. Instead she put her arms around him and gave him a bright hug. 'You, too. You scrub up really well.'

He was freshly showered and shaved and in a suit, which he'd only worn under duress once before. The tie was strangling him.

'You're early,' she exclaimed, in the same super-bright tone.

'You're important,' he said, sitting beside her.

'I wasn't bef–' she started and then seemed to regret her words, because she pulled herself up.

Perhaps it wasn't going to be an evening of hysteria, after all. 'You were,' he contradicted gently. 'I was just disorganised.'

Rob looked around at the crowded bar. Couples and groups sat at tables piled with drinks. The noise was deafening with everyone chatting at the tops of their voices. They all looked happy, even if half of them didn't look old enough to buy a round. Bottles and glasses clinked in the bar. Plates were being stacked noisily in the corner, and someone was pouring cutlery into a drawer while someone else scraped a plate into the bin. The bar staff seemed to be everywhere, taking orders and bringing drinks and food. 'They do cocktails here,' he said.

'It's quite swanky, isn't it? And if you decide to stay and eat, the restaurant's really good.'

His heart gave a skip. It seemed she'd made no assumptions and he was grateful because his emotional self was still outside in the car park somewhere. Meanwhile he recognised she had come to fight for him, albeit more subtly than he'd expected.

'What are you drinking?'

'I was waiting for you.'

He ordered drinks for them both, and while they waited for these to arrive, they chatted about Elderfield in Bloom. When the waiter had gone, Emma, instead of immediately begging for a reunion, slipped a sponsorship form onto the table.

He chuckled, as he was meant to. 'Will you sponsor me?' he asked, pushing it back.

'Sure,' she replied. 'It's seven miles.'

He frowned. 'Will you be able to walk that far?'

'Hey, I'm pregnant not an invalid.'

'So what will you sponsor me per mile?'

He expected her to say something clever like: 'A decade a mile.' Instead, she said: 'It's a long way. What would be fair?'

He hesitated, taking time to study her properly. She was striking rather than conventionally pretty, and proudest of her long, flaming hair, which made girls in shampoo adverts look like they'd had bad hair days. He'd lost count of the number of evenings he'd spent brushing it before bed. His gaze swept past her breasts, which seemed fuller than he remembered, to her tummy, which was still flat, although he believed her waist was slightly thicker than it used to be. 'Why did you leave me?' he asked at last.

She shook her head. 'I was angry with you.'

'That's all?'

She grimaced. 'At the time it seemed like a big deal.'

'And now?'

'I'd give anything to have the last four months over again.'

He nodded. 'I'm not saying this to hurt you. I just want you to understand,' he said. 'I fell in love with someone else.'

Under her make-up she went white and for a moment he thought she was going to faint. Gradually her colour returned and after swallowing convulsively several times, she managed a strangled: 'I'm happy for you.'

He rewarded her with a withering smile. 'Are you really?'

'No, not really, but it seems polite.'

'I think we need to get beyond manners right now.'

'Yes,' Emma replied, playing with the bowl of pistachio nuts on the table. She took several fortifying breaths while she struggled to keep her expression neutral. Her eyes shone; tears were near the surface. 'Now you know why I took so long to come home,' she said.

'No. I'm still completely in the dark on that one.'

'I've been caught up with similar, huge decisions, though I didn't fall in love with someone else.'

He looked sceptical.

'No, I didn't. And in the end, the decision was simple. I really love you. I always did. That's never changed. All that happened was that I was really angry with you. I was angry for months before I left. And when I came out on the other side of my anger, all I could think of was you. You're in me wrapped round my soul. I love you so much.'

Rob pursed his lips, irritated at her hyperbole, and not remotely convinced she loved him. People who loved didn't disappear. 'Why did you leave like that? If you loved me, why didn't you talk to me, explain what the problem was?'

'I did. Again and again.'

'Then it's not something I remember. You left me in the cruellest way imaginable, without any explanation, and not giving me the chance to make things better. I was worried about you. You didn't leave me. You disappeared.'

'I'm sorry. I'm so sorry. I feel so badly —'

'Stop right there,' he interrupted. 'You're not getting the chance to feel better about this with a quick "Sorry". I was devastated. Maybe you should start by explaining why you felt you had to leave the way you did.'

'I was angry.'

'No kidding,' he jeered. He was livid. Did she have the least conception of what she'd done to him?

'You're doing it again.'

He stared at her. 'What?'

'You're dismissing my anger again.'

He rubbed his face and then folded his arms tightly across his chest.

'That's what you did. You kept dismissing me, kept rubbishing my anger. My anger was real and you never seemed to understand it, no matter how hard I tried to explain it. "Don't be childish," was a phrase you used more than once.'

Rob sucked his teeth. He remembered saying that. 'Do you want to explain it to me now?'

'No, now it's passed.'

'No, you can't do that any more,' he barked, and then looked around, aware that his voice had probably carried further than he'd intended it to. No one paid him any heed, and he began again in a calmer tone, 'If you want me back, you need to explain it to me so that I understand what happened. You need to talk to me and not huff and imagine I can read your mind, because I can't. And it's no good snapping: "If I have to explain it, you'll never understand." I can't read minds. It's a guy thing. We just can't do it.'

She sat hunched with her hands caught tightly between her

knees. 'It's simple really. Sometimes – not all the time, but sometimes – I want to come first in your life.'

He waited. She reached for her cocktail and twisted it round and round on the drip mat. 'You're such a good man, Rob. You're kind and caring, but everyone takes advantage of you. They call you out at stupid times of the night for a leaky pipe. Well, get this, Mrs Customer! "Turn off the mains and put a bucket underneath it!" It's not hard. But you? You go round and fix it. And before you say it, of course you had to go out to Mrs Moreton that night. I get that now. But she wasn't the only one. You'd always go round and fix things in the middle of the night, or at the weekend, or even when you were supposedly on holiday. And you'd spend hours and hours doing it, after we'd planned to go out to the pub, or the cinema, or for a walk... After I'd taken so much trouble to prepare a special meal for you,' she ended.

'You threatened me,' he whispered, his mind zooming straight to that night.

'I didn't threaten. I warned you of the consequences.'

'I don't take well to threats.'

'Is this about you or me? You asked. I'm telling you.'

'Fair enough,' he said, backing down.

'The night I left, I asked myself why I always seemed to come last in the pecking order with you? Why didn't I ever come first? I come after everyone – your friends, your father, even your flipping customers, for Chrissake.'

Emma stopped abruptly and then continued more steadily: 'It's a question that's been going through my mind for months. Why did you always put everyone else before me?'

Rob became thoughtful. Had he taken her for granted? For the first time, she seemed to need him in some indefinable way. Emma was so self-contained he found it hard to get his head around that bit. Did she need him? *Really* need him? He knew she wanted him, but needing was something altogether different.

'Are you going to comment on what I just said?' she asked.

'I was waiting for you to go on.'

She gulped convulsively at her drink. 'Things have to change if I come back. Us getting back together isn't a done thing, Rob. I'm not on my knees begging you to take me back. You have to change – we both have to change –' she amended, 'if I'm to come back.' She took his hand and kissed his knuckles.

She looked up into this face properly for the first time, her gaze serious. 'I love you so much, Rob, but I'm also worth loving. I'm worth putting first. I don't *need* this child to have a father. Being a single mum isn't such a big deal these days. Don't get me wrong. I'll never stand in the way of you seeing him – her – whenever you want. If you want this other woman you fell in love with, fine. I can't fight that. I know that may be the price I have to pay for my stupidity. Rob, darling,' she put up a hand and cupped his cheek, 'you're my best friend. I miss you. I came back because I don't want to spend the rest of my life without you. But I can if I have to.'

Rob sipped his drink, savouring the peaty taste and the burn of the whisky down his throat. 'Do you mean that?' he asked quietly.

'Yes. I love –'

'That you'd let me see the child if I went off with another woman?'

The glow drained from her. 'I think so. I mean it now. It might be harder, you know, when…' Tears were close and her voice became huskier than ever. 'I was never a mean person, Rob.' She looked away over the crowds of people and he could see how she was forcing herself not to cry.

He had to admire her spirit. She was going to come back forgiven, or walk away. He changed tack. 'I thought you said you didn't want children.'

'I always wanted children,' she corrected, looking back down at her hands. 'One day. What I wanted first was you, and I never felt I had that. Not your full attention.'

Out of nowhere an image flitted into his mind: him stretched out on the floor beside a toddler as she reached up to put a brick on the top of a wobbly tower. He closed his eyes against the barrage of emotion threatening to undo him: fear, anger, relief, hope.

'You know what?' she added, bringing him back to the present, 'I have weird nightmares that I won't be able to feed it. You know, really horrible, wake-up-in-a-sweat nightmares? It's funny how the brain works, isn't it?'

He wanted this child. He put his hand on her tummy. She cradled it protectively, saying, 'He doesn't kick so you could feel yet, but I can feel him moving inside me.'

God help him. He still loved her.

Yet he couldn't quite bring himself to forgive her for walking out. A huge part of him worried that, if there were another rough patch, she'd bolt again, and maybe this time for good.

Meanwhile, loving Emma hadn't stopped the way he felt about Ruth. Maybe he did not love Ruth in the same way, but his feelings for her hadn't been make-believe. Parking these thoughts, he leant forward and brushed Emma's lips with his. 'Hello, Emma. It's good to see you.'

PLANTING LILIES

Ruth was wheeling a barrow full of lilies out to the road when Jules arrived on Saturday morning. She heard his car sweep up the drive spinning gravel onto the lawns; he had already let himself in when she rounded the corner. She called out but he didn't hear so she mooched on to her new bed.

She was feeling proud of herself. Although she ached for Rob, she was getting good at focusing on the moment. Two nights ago she had laughed until tears had run down her cheeks watching *Some Like it Hot* with Vix and William. Reflecting on it now, she winced at the slightly deranged tone in her laughter and she was determined to be sensible and calm for Jules.

A robin perched on her spade watching for worms she might unearth and then flew off with a frrt of its wings, making her look up. Jules was ambling towards her, inspecting the garden as he came.

'My back is killing me,' she said after they'd greeted each other. 'I've set myself a ridiculously big project here,' she added, pitching her tone a little more upbeat and delighted-to-see-him. 'But they'll look stupendous when they're in flower. I'm crossing my fingers they'll be out for Judgement Day.'

He searched her face. Did she look tired? Oh God, he was going to start quizzing her.

'You should hire a young lad to help you,' he said, his eyes running over the work outstanding.

'Oh goodness,' she replied, inspired. 'Why didn't I think of it before? I bet Al could do with the extra pocket money.'

'How are you?' he asked.

'Fine.'

She almost smiled at the way his face fell. That was naughty of her, but what a lovely catch-all word 'fine' was. It could mean anything, and, said with finality like that, it had the power to end all discussion on the matter if you were talking to a man.

'Good,' he said. He wanted to probe, she could see, but he chickened out. 'I'm here for a week, if that's OK.'

'There's lots of stuff for your guys to film,' she replied.

'Oh? Talking heads or photogenic?'

'Definitely photogenic,' she said, stabbing the trowel into the earth and scooping out another hole for a lily.

'Great. My producer'll be pleased.'

'Then you'll be teacher's pet by the end of tomorrow, because tomorrow – "For One Day Only",' she parodied Bruce, 'there'll be an amnesty on rubbish.' She thumped the earth down around the newly planted lily and scratched out another hole.

He passed her a lily from the barrow. 'Did I tell you, she, my producer and I are –'

'Of course, people are being encouraged to take stuff to the tip themselves.' She turned the pot over and smacked out the plant.

'She's my new girlfriend.'

'What happened to the last one? – the one who was playing hard to get.'

'I lost interest. Couldn't persuade her to take us seriously.'

'Oh well. On Thursday, I got lots of people to step up and offer to load trailers. They've been pooled from all over the town for the day.'

Had she overdone the perky tone? There was that cautious expression of his again, but once more he evaded the issue. 'That's good. Anyway, the moment I lost interest, she was all over me again.'

'They'll collect anything on the pavement that won't fit into a car.'

He started clearing up, tossing her empty pots into the wheelbarrow. 'But I really had lost interest in her. You see, Harry and I got talking one night over a bottle of wine, and, well, we get on so well.'

Ruth started back up the drive pushing the wheelbarrow and then paused. 'Harry?'

'Harriet. I call her Harry.'

'Ah. Did I tell you, Freecycle are coming with a removals van to take away anything that can be reused?' she said over her shoulder to him. 'Passable sofas, that kind of stuff.'

He ambled after her. 'Harry's been my producer for three years now. She confessed she's always liked me.'

'Everything will be carted away. Old mattresses, the lot.'

'I've fancied her for years, but she's older than me, so I always felt a little, you know, tongue-tied about asking her out.'

'Silly thing. You're –' Even from an aunt's fond perspective, she could see how handsome he was and how he charmed people, but she was distracted. 'How old?'

'Age doesn't matter.'

She plonked the wheelbarrow down by the greenhouse and together they started refilling it with pots from the bench. 'No,

I don't suppose it does, but it does.'

'You were younger than Michael.'

'Believe me, it matters if you want children.'

'It's just ten years, but it doesn't feel like it.'

'It never does,' she said, thinking of Rob. There were just ten years between him and her, but one huge, insurmountable barrier. A hysterectomy six years ago meant children were no longer an option. Would she have given him a child if she had still been able to? Yes.

No.

Maybe.

What she'd have done was irrelevant, though. Rob was too honourable to live with her while another woman bore his child. He'd want this child yet be loyal to her, and this tension would become unbearable for him. Eventually it would sour everything they had together. This way was better.

Must be better.

'We've got people standing by to make sandwiches for the volunteers,' she continued as he started pushing the loaded wheelbarrow back towards the road. 'It's going to be big, Jules,' she burst out, having a vision of Elderfield in the sun, with everyone working as a team, enjoying themselves, laughing, helping each other. 'The meeting on Thursday was packed: people are slowly beginning to get what this is all about.'

He grinned. 'You'll like Harry,' he assured her. 'I'll introduce you properly later.'

'And Al is leading a delegation to Mr Sharples – your old headmaster, remember? – to ask if the students can take on one of the empty allotments behind the school.'

'Will old Buggins say yes?'

'I don't know. There's something about monitoring the children when they're off school property. No doubt he'll throw some health and safety regulation at us. He's a tad unimaginative, but the allotments look on to the school playing field, so it's not as if the kids will be trekking across town on their own.'

'"Local gardening writer inspires rebellion,"' he mused. '"Kids clash with Head over allotments." Better. Now we're getting somewhere.'

'I have to live here, Jules,' she cautioned.

'I know,' he replied, but she could see he was already planning the scene in his head.

'Anything else?' he asked.

'The local press are camped outside Bruce Turner's house and the police have been coming and going since yesterday.'

'Oh ho.'

'I don't know what's going on there. I actually feel sorry for the guy. He's such a prig but –'

'Ruth!'

'Well he is, but I saw him coming home yesterday, and he looked thoroughly cowed.'

Jules pulled out his mobile. 'Let me make some phone calls,' he said absently, and wandered back to the house already talking into the mouthpiece. 'Oh,' he called over his shoulder. 'Harry'll be staying here, if that's OK.'

'I'll make up Anna's bed,' she called back.

He turned sheepishly.

'Oh I see,' she teased. 'She'll be staying with *you*.'

He gave her that laughing look of impish wickedness that was his signature, and when she said nothing, he sauntered on to the house talking into his mobile.

I have changed a lot since Rob, she thought. My nephew's bringing home an older woman, and that's OK with me. Ah Rob. She stood gazing over her lilies without seeing any of them.

Downward spiral

That afternoon, as Al arrived at Mrs Mallinson's as usual, a man in overalls was hammering a For Sale sign to the wall beside the gate.

'I don't think you've got the right house, mate,' Al advised him.

The man scratched his head. 'You sure?'

'Definitely.'

'I'll check.' The man retreated to his white van, pulled out a sheaf of papers and went through them one by one until he found what he was looking for. 'This is The Court House where Mrs Mallinson lives, isn't it?'

Al nodded with a sinking heart.

'Then this is the right house.'

Suddenly anxious, Al ran past him up the path to the house. He let himself in with his key and barged through to the sitting room. He found Mrs Mallinson sitting in her nightie in her armchair, gently rocking back and forth. 'Mrs Mallinson,' he began, 'they're putting up a For Sale sign. I thought you wanted to stay here until... for the rest of your life.'

'Georgie flew away.'

Al was stumped. 'Who's Georgie?'

'He flew away.'

'Mrs Mallinson, why aren't you dressed?'

'He won't come back. Birds aren't like cats. They don't come back. They fly away.'

'Mrs Mallinson, you need to get dressed.' He took one of her hands. She was cold and he chafed it, then reached over and switched on the electric heater – although it was early May, it was still cool in the mornings. He found her coat and put it round her shoulders. Upstairs, after a bit of rummaging about, he found her hot water bottle. Hunting through her drawers, he collected socks and sweaters and snatched up a blanket from the bed.

When she was well wrapped up, he made her a cup of tea and liberally spooned in the sugar. The bread was stale, so he decided against making her a sandwich. In the fridge, there was nothing to eat.

So where was all the food he'd bought on Wednesday?

He went back through to the sitting room with the tea.

'Georgie flew away,' she mumbled.

'Here, drink this,' he said and handed her the mug. That's when he saw the strong box lying open on the hearth, and noticed the smell of burning for the first time.

'Oh Christ alive. Mrs Mallinson, what happened? Where is everything?' he said striding over to the box.

'Georgie won't come back. Even if he did, the cats'd get him.'

'Who is Georgie?' he asked again.

'He flew away.'

Al slumped on one of the sofas and watched Mrs Mallinson muttering to herself like an old witch casting a spell. At last he pulled out his phone and called his mother. Vix was round within ten minutes, closely followed by William.

GROWING UP

Ruth was working in her greenhouse when Al reached her on her mobile, and stayed only to wash her hands. She ran into Rob at Mrs Mallinson's garden gate. God he looked good. And so tired.

'Hello Ruth,' he said softly. He reached out to touch her, and then pulled back. She pretended not to notice.

'How are you?' she asked.

'Fine,' he said.

Did he think about her?

'And you?' he asked politely.

'Fine.' Will this always be so hard?

'Mrs Mallinson's taken a turn again.'

'Yeah. Vix called me.'

'So long as they don't call the daughter,' he counselled. 'The old bird's frightened of her.'

Ruth was affronted. 'You can't not call the daughter, Rob.

She's family.'

'Yes, you can,' he insisted, but he didn't sound convinced. He stepped back for her to go through the gate and then they walked to the front door side by side, their hands jammed in their jacket pockets. The gulf between them was like a chasm.

'Al's primulas look great,' he said as they walked past them.

'Don't they?' she replied. So we are reduced to this, she concluded, swapping platitudes.

Al opened the door for them. 'Oh Rob, you came. She's been asking for you. Hello Ruth.'

Rob strode ahead and went to crouch in front of the old woman. 'Hello, Mrs Mallinson,' he said, taking her hand.

'She's gone gaga,' said Vix. She was standing by the window talking with William, and came forward to put a hand on Rob's shoulder. 'She can't stay here. She needs to go into a home.'

'She was fine on Thursday when I left her,' said Al.

'Georgie flew away, Rob,' Mrs Mallinson wailed.

Rob squeezed her hand. 'I know, love.'

'Who is Georgie?' asked Al.

'She had a budgie once,' Rob replied. 'Her daughter left the cage open one day and it escaped.'

'I bet she didn't leave it open by mistake,' muttered Al.

'Al, you don't know that,' said Vix.

'You don't know her.'

'And you do?'

'No, well —'

'For your information, I was at school with her. Yes, she had a silly habit of telling everyone how immature they were and flicking her hair over her shoulder as she did it, but since then she's changed.'

'She bullies Mrs Mallinson,' persisted Al.

'Oh, Al. All you have is Susan's word for it, and everyone knows those two never got on. Jennifer's not my favourite person in the world, but she's definitely not all bad. She's, well, she's nice.'

'Damned by faint praise,' grunted William.

'You're wrong, William. Many people admire her – she's always helping some worthy cause or another. It must have been hard not being loved by her mother. I felt sorry for her and used to give her my sweetie money.'

'Why?' asked William.

'Well, because Susan never gave her any,' Vix responded contemptuously.

'Have you gone soft in the head? Of course her mum gave her pocket money. Why wouldn't she?'

'Because she was mean.'

William laughed. 'Jennifer always was a witch.'

Vix was taken aback by the dislike in his voice. 'How come you know so much?'

'Because the old lady paid me for my odd jobs at the same time as she doled out Jennifer's pocket money. Jennifer manipulated people then, too.'

Ruth shifted uncomfortably. 'Any ideas what we are going to do with Mrs Mallinson?' she asked, breaking the silence and bringing everyone back to the present predicament.

'Call the daughter,' said William.

'What?' cried Al. 'After all you just said about her?'

'Not our job to look after her.'

'No way. No. I could stay here,' said Al.

His mother's expression softened. 'Oh Al, what a nice thing to say, but totally impractical.'

'No, it's not.'

'Who'll be with her during the day?'

He looked around the room at each of them. 'I could be.'

'And school?'

'Stuff school. I want to be a gardener and I don't need qualifications for that.'

'You'll go to school and get your A Levels,' said William.

'Says who?' demanded Al, squaring up to him.

Ruth cleared her throat. 'Exams matter, Al.'

'They don't. You're always saying exams don't matter, Mum,' he said, turning to her.

'They do. I lied,' she replied.

'No, you didn't.'

'Don't talk to your mother like that,' said William.

'William,' said Vix laying a hand on his arm, 'let me deal with this, will you?'

He shrugged and walked back to the window.

Vix turned to Al. 'You're doing your exams and that's an end to it.'

Al drew breath to speak, but Ruth slipped in first. 'Guys, this won't help Mrs Mallinson. She can't stay here. It just isn't practical.'

Again Al drew breath to speak but Ruth went on, 'Al, what happens when she needs the bathroom?'

He backed down immediately. 'Then not her daughter. She can't go to her daughter. She's frightened of her.'

'She'll probably go into a home, but that's for Jennifer to decide,' said Ruth. 'Does anyone have her number?'

Rob moved gloomily. 'I do,' he admitted. 'But I'm not happy about this.'

There was a long moment of dejected silence, and then he pulled out his mobile and punched in the number.

While they waited for Jennifer to arrive, Ruth made them all tea and sent Al out to buy biscuits from the corner shop. He arrived back in time to see Jennifer climbing out of her car. He opened the gate for her and she swept through, ignoring him completely. When he pulled out his key to unlock the door, she held out her hand as it swung open. 'I'll have that, thank you,' she said, pocketing it.

Watching this little interaction from the sitting room window, Ruth realised that she had made a horrible mistake, but it was too late to do anything about it now. Between the front door and the sitting room, Jennifer transformed from someone who radiated spite to a woman gushing with anxiety. She could not thank them enough for watching out for Mother. It seemed she had been worried about her mother's frail grip on reality for some time. Indeed, she'd arrived in time to see her mother burning the contents of her strong box yesterday, and – she spun a finger round her temple – 'I think she's finally lost the plot,' she concluded. 'I was so worried, I've lined up St Mungo's down the road.'

Ruth was appalled. 'St – St Mungo's?' she repeated. 'But that's…'

William helped her out. 'That was condemned last week. It was in all the papers. They're being done for neglect.'

'You really shouldn't believe everything you read in the press,' said Jennifer softly.

'All the same, St Mungo's is…' Even William faltered. He tried again. 'They say it's…'

'Oh, Mr Jones,' breathed Jennifer. 'I've been worried about those reports, too, so I went to visit last week and they couldn't have been nicer. They know about their shortcomings and already have new systems in place. Of course, I'd like her to go to St Benedict's, but the fees…' She left the sentence hanging. They all knew the reputation of the place with its fees to match. 'Thank you all for coming round to help. I can manage from here. Poor old Mother. I'll look after you,' she crooned at Mrs Mallinson, who flinched.

'You let Georgie out. I saw you do it.'

'I did let Georgie out, Mother. You said I could pet him. But as I was putting him back, you had a turn and I was distracted.'

'No. That's not how it was. You left the door open deliberately.'

Jennifer leant over the old woman. 'Mother, get a grip.'

Her mother shrank back in her chair, and then she suddenly started wailing and slapping her head in distress.

This was too much for Al, who stepped forward, but Ruth put a restraining hand on his shoulder, and gripped harder when he seemed ready to resist her.

'It's not right,' he whispered.

'I know, Al,' she replied, equally softly, 'but there are some things in life you can change and some you can't. You've grown up when you can tell the difference.'

'But I know Jennifer bullies her.' He was almost in tears. 'I just know it.'

'Come,' invited Ruth, leading him out. 'You can still visit her.'

In the dark corridor he stopped and punched his fist into his palm. 'She did this to her. Jennifer. Yesterday, when she came. I know she did. I can't just abandon her.'

'You're not.'

'She'll never leave there alive. She'll be buried in there for the rest of her life. It's not right. You can't just force an old woman out of her home because it's convenient.'

'Al, even you must admit she needed more looking after.'

'*I* was looking after her,' he bit out.

'Do you know, I think you've made these last few months the happiest she's had for a long time. I never expected you to stick it out but you did, and I admire you for that. You stuck it out, and I've watched you grow up. Now you have to bow out to Jennifer.'

He pulled out of her grip, and flung himself out of the front door, slamming it hard behind him.

IMPASSE

When Rob walked into his sitting room on his return from Susan Mallinson's house, Emma's mouth was set in a thin line. 'You haven't changed a bit, have you? And you're never going to.'

Rob rocked back on his heels, taken aback by the bitterness in her voice. 'Mrs Mallinson needed me.'

'*I* needed you. This was *our* walk, Rob.'

'Mrs Mallinson took a turn and was asking for me.'

Emma dropped her head in her hands. 'This will never work unless you sometimes put me first.'

'I did put you first.'

'But the moment someone rings, you're off. We'd just finished our walk.'

'So?' he asked perplexed. 'We were back home.'

'I thought… I thought…'

'I wasn't putting you second. The walk was over. We'd returned from lunch. Then Al called about Mrs Mallinson. Emma, this is me. I'm compelled to help people, and if you can't hack it, now's the time to walk away.'

'So you can go to your other woman with a clear conscience?' she sneered.

He sighed, gritting his teeth.

'I hate it when you sigh like that. You sigh as if you're exasperated, which you clearly are, and yet you asked me to tell you when I was unhappy. You said I needed to talk more about things, instead of bottling them up. This is me talking.'

He hesitated in the doorway. The desire to walk away nearly got the better of him. Instead, he sat down on the sofa opposite her. 'I'm listening.'

'I have issues. Things I'm not good at,' she said. 'Waiting at home alone is one of them. Other couples spend time together.'

He took a punt. 'Did you expect me to ask you out to dinner tonight?'

She softened immediately. 'Yeah, I hoped you would.'

He was right. This was not about Susan Mallinson. 'Why couldn't you ask me?'

'You mean, me ask you out?' she queried, astonished.

'Yes.'

'I already did the asking. I asked you to come for a walk with me so we had a chance to talk.'

'You didn't talk.'

'Yes I did.'

'There were huge, long silences.'

'I talked,' she said, her voice rising.

'Then you held whole conversations in your head while you walked in silence.'

She looked horrified, clearly convinced she was right. 'You

remember things way differently from me,' she said at last. 'I told you about the baby. I talked about my new job. I talked.'

'No, you didn't. You mentioned you were worried about the baby, and then you dried up. Emma, I can't spend my life interviewing you. You have to volunteer things. You have to talk properly.'

'But, but I love you, Rob,' she stammered.

He sighed sadly. 'I'm not sure you do, Emma. Not really. If you did, you might let me in.'

'I do,' she said, desperately, scooting out of her chair to kneel at his feet.

'Emma, my beautiful Emma.' He stroked her face. 'I loved you so much but you never talked. You always left me to guess what was going on in that lovely head of yours. And when I couldn't read your mind, you huffed and ran away.'

'I did not huff.'

He ran a hand through his hair.

'What's Susan Mallinson got on you that you had to rush to her side?'

'Now you're changing the subject. That's what you always do. You sidestep anything difficult.'

She sat nonplussed, looking unsure how to proceed. Had she even realised what she was doing?

'I...' she began. 'I'm sorry. I hadn't realised I was changing the subject. We were talking about why you felt you had to rush off to Mrs Mallinson.'

About six lifetimes ago, maybe. He waited stonily for her to go on. When she didn't, he dropped his head tiredly. 'She's a friend and I stand by my friends. I help them when I can. That's what friends do. That's how I hurt my hand,' he said, holding it up. 'I help people.' He stared abjectly at the ceiling. Then he leaned forward and put his lips to the top of her head. 'I'm an ordinary guy, Emma,' he murmured against her soft skin. 'Yes, I want a family but, more than that, I want someone who sees me, loves me. Me.'

'But you always put me second.'

'I'm not perfect either. I can see I might have taken you for granted, and I swear, if we get back together, I won't ever do that again. I, too, learned a painful lesson. But today, walking seven miles in silence was… I found it one of the saddest walks of my life.'

Tears formed in her eyes. 'Oh Jeez,' she muttered. 'I love you so much, Rob. What do I have to do to change?'

He looked down at her hands on his knees and patted them. 'You have to talk,' he said. 'If you want something, you have to ask. If you want me to go out to dinner, you have to invite me.'

'Will you go out to dinner with me tonight?'

He smiled sadly and shook his head. 'I can't do this any more, Emma.'

She stared at him as if the bottom had fallen out of her world. 'Please. Please,' she begged him, grasping his hand and cupping it against her face. 'You have to give me another chance. I can change. I know I can. I just need you to be patient while I do this. Please, Rob. Please come out to dinner with me tonight so I can show you how I am starting to change. Please do this for me.'

He knew he should end this now. He knew he had to be cruel to be kind.

Ah Ruth. She had spoiled him for Emma. He was still feeling through his understanding of his relationship with Ruth, but already he knew what he didn't want. He didn't want what he used to have with Emma any more. Yes, it had been fun, even if it wasn't fun right now, but he wanted to be able to lean on her as he thought he used to, two equals supporting each other like an A-frame in a roof. A relationship was about riding out the ups and downs together as well as enjoying the smooth patches, and she'd broken his trust that she would be there for him when it mattered.

The funny thing was, he still loved Emma. Just not the way she wanted. He'd settled. Now, he couldn't face settling again. At least, not back into the same groove. The prospect chafed him unbearably. The question was, did he want to grow old with her?

Christ, what a mess.

Emma saw him hesitate and jumped in: 'I promise not to get all emotional on you. I just want you to see I can change.'

Emotional was what he wanted. Deep, raw, mad passion. He wanted Emma to hold him, to feel her pressed against him, her breath on his face, her arms linked around his neck, her tongue in his mouth. That's what he missed with Ruth: Emma's rawness and passion. Old Emma's rawness, not this woman who behaved as if she had been kicked, when it had been her who had done the kicking.

'Please, Rob.'

He couldn't bring himself to slap her down. Then he realised her confidence had gone. Had he done that to her, or was she unable to forgive herself for running out? He squeezed her shoulder. 'I'll collect you from Lisa's at seven thirty. Where would you like to eat?'

'Wherever, I don't mind.'

He chewed his bottom lip in disappointment.

She reacted fast. 'But if we could go to the new Thai in town, that'd be great.'

He nodded. 'OK,' he said getting up. 'I'll see you later.'

Emma was clearly expecting a kiss from him. Rob knew it, and walked away. He wanted her to ask for it, and not have to read her mind yet one more time.

Later, on his way to collect Emma from the long-suffering Lisa, he couldn't help himself and detoured via Ruth's house. She was slow in coming to the door and he jiggled on the balls of his feet until he heard footsteps in the hall. He turned as the door opened.

'Hello Rob,' she said calmly.

He couldn't contain himself. Putting his arms around her, he held her tightly. 'I can't do it,' he whispered.

She gently but firmly disentangled herself. 'Go away, Rob.'

'Are you turning me away?'

'Yes.'

Ouch. He recognised that emotion. He'd seen it on Emma's face that afternoon. Still, it hit him hard. 'Ruth, please,' he pleaded. 'I love you.'

'I fell a little in love, too, Rob. But I've moved on.'

'If you're worried about children,' he rushed on, despising himself even as he did so, 'Emma will have the child anyway. I can still be its father. I don't have to be with her.'

'You love her. You always did. Looking back, I can see that now. Meanwhile, you thought you'd fallen in love with someone else and you're angry because she's making you choose. Well, I've moved on.'

'I didn't *think* I'd fallen in love,' he snapped.

'You know why you came here?' she suddenly demanded. 'You came for reassurance because you're not quite ready to burn your bridges. You know how I know? Because if you'd come back to me, you'd have been laughing for the sheer joy of seeing me again. You'd have let yourself in with your key and swung me into your arms. Instead, you're whinging on the doorstep.'

'That's what you think,' he said tightly, misery swamping him. He stalked away without another word.

CHAPTER 14

PHOENIX

Ruth shut the door wondering if she were very shallow. Sending Rob away hadn't been as hard as she had expected. Part of that was down to anger at his 'whinging' although Rob wasn't a whinger. He'd had a moment of weakness and she'd had enough of those herself to want to give him the comfort he craved. And she had most definitely wanted to melt into his arms, but that feeling had lasted a nanosecond before she had felt strong again.

Earlier in the week she'd told Vix she'd fallen hard, but really she was moaning about nothing. A few days in the garden seemed to have centred her again. She'd had time to reflect on her conversation with Vix and see that, while she was hurting, she didn't feel rejected. Yes, it was taking a little while to bounce back, but this was not how she'd felt after Michael's death. This time, she felt pruned, not hacked off at the base. For a short while she had confused pruning with hacking, but now she had recovered her perspective on life.

Rob was lovely. He was sexy and kind. He was as undemanding as he was patient. But he wasn't for her and in her heart she had always known it. Whenever the subject of Emma arose, she came across as a gentle, unaffected yet sensitive young woman who nurtured him. There was a tone of wistfulness in his voice when he spoke of her. He ached for Emma as she had ached for Michael. He had never hidden that; she could never say he'd strung her along.

In a way, he'd been her little piece of therapy. Hadn't Vix

once said you can't be depressed when you're having an orgasm? Oh boy. How right she was. Her breath caught at the memory as she donned gardening gloves and pushed the wheelbarrow along the drive towards the lily bed for her regular inspection for lily beetle.

Through the trees, the evening sun flooded the lawns in Turneresque light and brought her to a standstill. Her breath stilled and she could feel her jaw drop in wonder. It seemed all at once as if her senses could amplify every detail and yet absorb it all, too: the veins lacing a petal, the inky depths of the yellowhammer's eye, the vaulted sky above her, the haughty hoot of the owl in a nearby tree, the silken summer air. Her hands relaxed their grip on the wheelbarrow's handles, and it dropped softly to the ground. In the gateway, movement caught her eye and she and a fox locked gazes before it trotted off.

Radiant joy suffused her, the kind of which she hadn't known for years, and she lifted her arms wide as if offering herself to the sun, its rays like molten gold flooding through her. She had fallen a little in love, and it had been wonderful and fun, but it was extraordinary to assume that the first man she met after Michael would end up as her partner for the rest of their lives.

On the heels of this thought came another: so how do you meet single men?

A month later, this question was still exercising her. Meanwhile, she'd bumped into Rob a couple of times in town, and had given him a relaxed smile, noting as she did so that her heart hardly changed beat. She wasn't indifferent to him; she had simply moved on.

Then, on the first Saturday of June, the day before her garden opened as part of the National Garden Scheme, about a dozen people turned up at her door armed with gardening gloves, spades and clippers. They were there to help her with the millions of last minute things needing to be done to make the Open Day a success. Vix stood beside Ruth at the front door. 'Some new faces,' she murmured, watching them tramp up the drive.

'From the estate,' responded Ruth, thrilled. 'Enthusiasts, though they probably lack knowledge. Even so, I can find lots for them to do.'

'Keen to swap their help for yours in their own gardens, more likely,' said Vix dryly.

'Or Jules's,' agreed Ruth. 'Quite a few people bring up his name and wonder – very loud and often – when he's coming back. I can't say I blame them. Even I can see how charismatic he is.'

'Ah. I spy Laurie and Amanda. Some old hands at least, even if she never stops talking in that shrill voice of hers,' said Vix, losing interest and going back inside. After Ruth had assigned tasks to her volunteers, she wandered back into the kitchen where she found Vix reading the paper. 'Idle so and so,' she murmured.

'I'm helping. Look! The kettle's about to boil,' said Vix.

'When?'

'When I put it on.'

Ruth flipped the switch with an indulgent smile and began setting out lunch for everyone. William turned up soon after and headed straight for the beers, pausing only to greet Vix.

'Darling,' Vix whispered a couple of minutes later, sidling up to Ruth, 'Rob wanted to come, but felt it might be a bit awkward.'

'Tell him to come tomorrow if he wants,' Ruth replied.

'Really?'

'Yes, really. I'm over him and I have a garden to open. Will you man the gate for me in the morning? Lucy said she'd do it in the afternoon.'

'Natch,' said Vix, examining Ruth's face for clues. 'Are you sure you're over him?'

'Quite sure.'

Vix looked disinclined to believe her.

'I'm not being stoical. I'm fine.'

'If you say so.'

'Vix!'

'OK, OK. Just checking. Shall I edge the path to the kitchen garden?'

'And ruin your nails? No. Here are my bestest secateurs. Lose them on pain of death. I need you to deadhead anything going over.'

'What, even flowers only just on the way out?'

'Keep them and make yourself a bouquet.'

'I'll give them to Al. He can take them to Susan.'

'That's a lovely idea. I must go and see her.'

'Don't. It's awful. She won't know who you are and gets terribly upset.'

Across the terrace, Ruth saw William make his way towards Al bearing a couple of beers, and watched hero worship bloom on the boy's face. 'What's with Al and William, by the way?'

'I know, amazing, isn't it? They've been thick as thieves for the last month. I assumed Al would kick up a stink when William officially moved in, but not at all. No sulks. No snide remarks. He doesn't even strop when William hauls him up for being irritating with me. I haven't a clue what happened, but William and Rob can do no wrong in Al's eyes.'

'Rob too?'

'Odd, isn't it? But I'm glad really. William's got him working after school for a couple of hours at the garden centre. I think he suggested it to be kind. Al used to visit Susan at St Mungo's every day, but she didn't recognise him. He got terribly depressed. He only goes once a week now. Did you see her house has been sold?'

Ruth thought a moment. 'Yeah, I suppose I was vaguely aware of it.'

'Guess who bought it?'

Ruth shrugged.

'Actually, no guesses,' said Vix. 'Just tell me.'

'Bruce?'

'He was utterly obnoxious at the committee meeting on Thursday.'

'I didn't go. I was working in the garden.'

'I assumed you were being all quiet at the back. I reckon he's jealous of you. If anyone so much as suggests an idea you might approve of, he kills it instantly, even if it makes sense.'

'How did it go?'

'People want you there. It's not the same with him bossing us around. When you talk, everyone gets excited. When he drones on, all we want to do is run away. He has a real knack for putting people's backs up. His people skills are worse than William's.'

Ruth laughed.

'Well they are!'

'I didn't say a thing.'

'William only lasted two days in charm school and all he took on board was the apology lesson, so he's endlessly buying me flowers.'

'You know the flowers come from the garden centre, don't you?'

'Ooh, cynic! Actually, they come from Lisa's.'

Ruth became reflective. 'You know, it's nearly two months since they last broke her shop window.'

'Really?' Vix looked astonished. 'Goodness, your Bloom thing must be working after all.'

'You thought it wouldn't?'

''Course I didn't. You have such faith in people, Ruth. I think it's really sweet. Actually, I think that's why people work so hard not to disappoint you.'

'For a PR lady, you have a terrible line in flattery,' said Ruth, and then looked round covertly. 'I've had an idea. It's a job for you. Interested?'

'Intrigued, more like.'

Ruth drew Vix over to the window where they could talk without being overheard. 'Now, I refuse to join a website, so don't even mention it.'

'Join –?'

'You know. A website!'

Vix's eyes grew round. 'You mean a dating website?'

'What other websites do people join?' asked Ruth, bemused.

'I can think of a few.'

But Ruth wasn't listening. 'Vix, I don't want to be single for the rest of my life. I need to meet – This is so embarrassing. I thought you might know some business people who weren't too dire.'

'Oh love,' said Vix giving her a bright hug. 'Let me think on it.'

THE PROPOSAL

One evening in late June, Rob invited Emma out for a walk. She had moved back in and ostensibly they were a couple again. Unfortunately, he didn't feel part of a couple. Neither, it seemed, did she: she was being careful of him, as though not quite sure he meant it.

He did. He had resigned himself to doing the right thing. Thus he was, in turn, ultra polite and went out of his way to be thoughtful. This included not working in the evenings and at weekends, although he had had one or two emergency call-outs. She told him that he didn't need to keep apologising for these, but he didn't believe her.

She was beginning to look pregnant, and he found her new curves sexy. Sometimes he just lay with his head against her stomach and waited for the baby to kick. Until two weeks ago he felt nothing. Then came a huge kick. He sat up with a start.

'Jeeeeez! That must hurt.'

She smiled at his wonder and pulled him down beside her again, stroking her distended stomach.

'Do it again,' he whispered to the child, and was rewarded a few minutes later with a smaller movement. He started laughing and leaned across to kiss her. The existence of his child growing inside her suddenly switched from abstract to very real. He was going to be a daddy. That night, in a moment of midnight madness, he cleared his desk out of the spare room, now the baby's room, and carted all his files and paperwork up into the unfinished attic room... where it remained, stacked in boxes.

'One day,' he responded with a shrug the following weekend when Emma asked him when he was going to finish converting the attic into an office.

'What needs doing?' she asked.

'Don't worry, the attic'll be finished before the baby's born,' he said.

'But what are you planning to do with it?'

'I said, you don't need to worry about it,' he snapped. 'I'll sort it.' He was fed up of being doubted and irritated by her nagging. Hadn't he been making a huge effort to keep his promises? Or perhaps she felt he didn't want her involved for some obscure reason that he couldn't comprehend. Why didn't she talk to him, tell him what she wanted, instead of shrinking further into her shell? If she'd genuinely wanted to help, she'd have got stuck in, wouldn't she? So he was still back at square one.

When she had asked if she might have a corner of the garden to grow some roses, he paused in his task of carrying out the rubbish. 'You don't have to ask permission, Emz. It's your garden, too.'

'You know what I mean,' she said.

'No, I don't.'

'Never mind. It's not important.'

'Grow some roses. They'll do well along the back wall. Just pull up the lettuces in your way.'

She smiled and he sighed, knowing she'd do nothing: they were 'his' lettuces. Even when he dug them up himself and gave them away to neighbours, she still didn't put in some roses but solemnly sowed a new row of lettuces, while he watched despondently from the kitchen window.

In this way, the pendulum between politeness and misunderstanding swung through May and into June, with both

Rob and Emma becoming increasingly unhappy. Then one evening in the middle of the week, he took her hand after supper and invited her out for a walk. He found her trainers and waited while she put them on, and they set off through the town.

'Where are we going?' she asked.

'Wait and see.'

Sensing a pleasant surprise, she gave a little skip. 'Go on. Tell.'

'Wait,' he said, amused by her impatience.

'Ah, I'm so tired,' she yawned theatrically.

He raised an eyebrow.

'You might have weakened.'

'Yeah, yeah, yeah.'

'And?'

'I won't,' he assured her.

The excitement bled out of her and she raised dark, wary eyes to his, then she fell in beside him. At last they reached the end of the town and the houses stopped abruptly, as though they were now entering the Great Beyond. Ahead of them lay a hill.

'We're going up Never Ending Hill,' she observed, taking another skip.

'Clever girl.'

'And you have a bottle of wine in that bag.'

'Good guess, but no.'

'Orange?'

'Nope.'

'Juice of any kind?'

'Nope. Keep walking.'

'Water?'

'Don't stop. We've got miles to go.'

'It's not miles.'

'Miles and miles to go.'

'I'm so tired.'

He pulled a cereal bar from his pocket. 'Energy,' he said,

handing it to her.

She laughed. 'OK, I get it. Keep walking.'

'Yep.'

They walked in silence, the evening sun on their faces, until he broke into her thoughts. 'What happened about the promotion?'

She blew out her cheeks. 'I didn't get it.'

'How do you feel about that?'

'It's rubbish. My boss clearly has the baby in mind when he offered the job to Marie, bastard. I could have done it in my sleep and he knows it.'

'So what will you do about it?'

'Nothing, actually. I find I don't mind after all. I'm having a baby and I might not even go back after I've had it.'

Another silence grew between them. Unexpectedly, she was the one to break it. 'Are you going to be rich, Rob?'

He brightened. 'Not especially. What have you got in mind?'

She shrugged. 'I quite fancy being a lady who lunches. You know, like posh women in London.'

'You came across a few, did you?'

'You see them at the Golf Club braying at their own jokes.'

'You can be a mum who does the laundry,' he suggested.

'It doesn't have quite the same ring, does it? Mum who washes. Lady who lunches. Mum who – nah. I can't make it sound sexy.'

'Do you want to be a lady who lunches?' he asked, puzzled.

'Not especially, but I'd like to give it a go. I bet I'd be really good at it. I'd have to change my wardrobe, though – get chic'er clothes.'

He was enjoying her banter. 'You look fine.'

She looked down at her comfortable sweatshirt and jeans. 'You can't Lunch in jeans.'

"Course not. And the baby?'

'We'd have to have a nanny if I Lunched, don't you think? Wouldn't want to cramp my style.'

'Will you marry me,' he asked.

'Jeez,' she exclaimed. 'We aren't even at the top of the hill.'

'We're at the lay by,' he replied.

'O-K.' She sounded bemused.

'I parked up here the night you left.'

'I don't understand.'

'I sorted Mrs Moreton out in two minutes – she was having a right old panic about nothing – but I needed some time to think. You were being a real pain, nagging on about stuff you wanted changed in the house. I was here until midnight.'

'Thinking?'

He looked away, infinitely sad. 'No. I was tired and I just dozed off. I only woke up because I was cold. When I got home you'd gone.'

'Oh, Rob.'

'Biggest mistake of my life, Sweet Pea.'

'You mean –'

'So? Will you marry me?'

Emma smiled up into his face. 'I wish I hadn't lost faith in you that night.'

He dropped a kiss on her nose. 'Do you know what day it is?'

She winced. 'Oh my, is it a special day? Have I missed some anniversary?'

'It's the end of the longest day of the year and the start of the shortest night. It seemed symbolic.'

She gasped. 'Robert Ansell, you old romantic.'

'Well?'

'Well, what?'

'Are you going to get round to answering my question some time soon?'

'No.' She drew out the word softly.

'No, you won't give me an answer, or no, you won't marry me?'

She frowned and looked up at him, frank and sad. 'No, I won't marry you.'

His arms loosened around her neck and then tightened

again. 'No?'

'No, because I want the happy ending.'

'Isn't me asking you to marry me the happy ending?' he asked, baffled.

'Yes, it is. But...'

Rob's heart seemed to stop as the silence went on and on. Then she surprised him by continuing, 'This is me talking, Rob. It won't make perfect sense, because I like to think things out before I say them, but this is me still talking, not having yet another conversation in my head. Argh, come on, Emma, talk some sense.' She pressed her hands together as if in prayer.

'Take your time.' He rubbed the muscles in her neck and her shoulders dropped.

'Right. I'm talking. This is me. Talking. And so far, I've said nothing of importance, especially not about your proposal, for which thank you.' She stood on tiptoe and kissed him. 'Thank you, Rob, for asking me to marry you, for having faith in me, for believing we could make a go of things. See? I'm talking. I mustn't stop. OK. So why won't I marry you?'

She drew another calming breath and he pressed a kiss on her forehead. 'That was reassurance, by the way,' he whispered. 'I'm listening, even though, so far, you've got a painful case of verbal diarrhoea.'

'Yes, I know. It's because,' she looked up at him, 'because I'm not ready for you yet. No, don't get me wrong,' she said, as he started to pull away from her. She scooped up his arms and draped them back over her shoulders. 'I'm not ready because I want you to have a great wife when you marry me. I want you to be absolutely sure you're making the right decision. You see, I love you, but I feel you're still trying to convince yourself that this is the right thing to do.'

He pulled her into his embrace, awed by her courage.

'Besides,' her voice trembled as she spoke, 'I need more practice at this talking malarkey, so, when you do marry me, you know you have a wife who talks to you properly.'

She pushed him away from her so she could see his face.

'You see, I really want that for you. I mean, listen to me. I'm rubbish at it.'

Her determination to be upbeat moved him beyond words. He loved this woman.

'You've endured six weeks of the most terrible blathering and I still haven't got it right. I miss telling you the important bits like my promotion, and you end up feeling you're *interviewing* me again.' She ran her fingers up in the hair at the back of his head, and looked steadfastly at his top button. 'I hate that word.'

He tilted her face up to his and gave her a crooked smile. 'So do I, but you noticed, which is new.'

'I'm trying so hard, Rob. I'm trying to be what you want.'

'It's simpler than that, Sweet Pea,' he said. 'I want you to be yourself. I don't want you to bend yourself all out of shape to be something you think I want. I want you. Just you... and for you to tell me what's on your mind, straight, without always editing it into something you think I might like to hear. Just like you're doing now; giving it to me straight. That's perfect.'

She glowed. 'Kiss me,' she asked. 'Thank you and please kiss me.'

His kiss was gentle. 'So what's the real reason you won't marry me?'

'Because I want you to want to marry me because you can't live without me,' she said in a rush, as if she were afraid she was saying the wrong thing, 'not because you want to give my, our, child a name. And I don't think you can't live without me yet.'

He was taken aback by her perceptiveness. Until this moment she had been right, but now, somehow, she had turned the tables on him, and the hurt went surprisingly deep.

'A part of you still has feelings for this other woman, who ever she is. You've been pretty subtle about that, by the way, and I can't think who she might be. And she's been dead subtle, too. Probably waiting for you.'

'We ended it the night you returned.'

'Then show me how much you want me. I'll marry you

when I believe you can't live without me.'

'You funny thing,' he said, wondering how on earth to prove such a desire. 'I thought you'd be desperate for my proposal.'

'I want more. Like that promotion. I don't want it after all because I want to be a mum. In the same way, I want to be more than just your wife. I want to be your lover. Oh, I know you love me, but I want you to be *in love* with me – as in love with me as I am with you. Am I talking right, by the way? Because you'll have to tell me if I'm doing it wrong, if I'm saying the wrong thing, because I probably have.'

'You're doing it right, even though you're not giving me the answer I expected.'

'There you go. I must be doing it right because I know *expected* is way different from *wanted*. I'm not giving you the answer you *expected*. When you *want* a different answer, then ask me again.'

'OK,' he laughed. He'd think of a way to show her. 'Do you want some champagne?'

'Oh champagne. I never guessed champagne. What, now? You want to drink champagne even though I said no?'

'You said, "Not yet". So let's drink to the baby.'

'Yes. The baby,' she said with the brightest smile she could muster, and he could see she was fighting dejection. She had expected him to discover he couldn't live without her after all, to sweep her up and declare his absolute and unconditional love for her there and then, but he had no idea how to express something he wasn't feeling.

FALLING OUT

All week Rob could feel Emma waiting for him to declare himself. Was she worried he didn't love her? At night she lay rigid with anxiety as if she was expecting him to roll over and say, 'I can't do this any more,' but in truth he was preoccupied. How do you prove love?

Say it with flowers. Diamonds are a girl's best friend. Wine her and dine her somewhere dead romantic. All these clichés he dismissed. Meanwhile, her parents were invited to Sunday lunch. Although Emma was looking forward to it, he was not as sanguine – they had done their best to hamper his quest to find her.

William was unhelpful when he consulted him on his dilemma. 'Just tell the dozy bird you love her and you wanna get hitched. It's that four-letter word that does it. You don't even have to mean it.'

Rob looked at him steadily.

'I don't mean me, you dumb bastard. But you needn't feel obliged to tell Vix that I love her to bits. She'd be all over me like a rash. A man need space while he's out weeding the garden.'

'I get that.' Rob sketched a smile and then sat in a brown study drawing patterns in spilt beer on the table.

William waited. 'Do you love her?' he asked at last.

'Oh, yes,' Rob replied. 'But I'm not very convincing.'

'I suspect you don't fully trust her yet.'

Rob's head snapped up. William's insight often startled him. 'Maybe you're right,' he said, and changed the subject. But the thought continued to go round in his head all week. Could she sense his unease? Maybe she had enough nous not to commit herself until she felt he was sure. Trust took time to rebuild, he realised. What would it take for him to come home and not check she hadn't done another bunk? She'd taken to leaving little notes: 'Out shopping' or 'With Lisa'. Perhaps she understood him better than he thought.

It was in this meditative mood that he hoovered the sitting room on Sunday in preparation for her parents' arrival. They wouldn't recognise it. He hardly did. Besides the new carpet and Emma's stylish curtains, there were cushions on the sofa and prints on the walls. What a little homemaker she was.

'Shall I get you a frilly apron?' Emma asked from the doorway.

'Ha ha. Your mother will be here soon enough to check the ornaments.'

'A little dust won't hurt them.'

He looked at her in disbelief. 'Since when did you get all cocky?'

'Well.' She spread her hands in mock surrender. Then, unable to help herself, she ran a finger over the side table.

'Emma,' he called as she scurried from the room.

She returned clutching a duster and shrugged when he cocked his head in mockery.

'What happened to a little dust not hurting them?'

'You know my mother. Obviously. Look at you hoovering under the sofa.'

He took the cloth from her. 'You sort lunch, I'll do the dusting.'

'Sure?'

He pecked her lips. 'It'll be OK.'

'It's just that I haven't seen them since…'

'They know you're pregnant, don't they?'

'Obviously.'

'I'm serious. They're pretty old school.'

'Don't be silly. They love me.'

He turned on the hoover again. 'Go and peel the carrots.'

As always, Rob wondered whether her parents arrived early and parked up around the corner to enable them to time things to the minute. Her father entered, tall and patrician, while her mother, soft edged and genteel, glided into the house like a ship in full sail. Rob's greeting was degrees cooler than the one at Christmas, the last time they had come to lunch; he was disturbed to find he was angry with them. He didn't actually want to be in the same room as them.

'Sherry?' he offered.

'Thank you, Rob,' said Hilda, ensconcing herself in the armchair. 'You'll have one, won't you, Jim?'

Emma's father nodded stiffly and Rob bolted. Emma found him later leaning against the kitchen counter reading the paper.

'Drinks?'

'Coming right up.' He folded the paper.

'What are you doing?'

'Reading the paper.'

'I thought you were pouring drinks. You've been gone ten minutes.'

'So who's counting?'

She seemed to wither.

'I'm sorry, Sweet Pea. I just…' He didn't know what to say. 'I need a moment.'

'They're being really nice.'

'And I'm being churlish.'

'I didn't say that.'

'No, but I thought it. I just want to shake him.'

'Dad? Why?'

'Let's not go there now, shall we?'

'Go where?'

'They weren't exactly friendly last time I saw them.'

'Ah.' Her mouth twisted. 'Oh.'

'I'll be through when I've made the gravy.'

'It's not something you're ever going to let go of, is it?'

'What do you mean?'

'You're never going to forgive me for running away.'

Her parents were in the next room expecting him to come and make polite conversation. 'Can we talk about this later?'

'If you want,' she said in a defeated voice. The drinks clinked on the tray when she picked it up. As she went by, he gave her shoulder a squeeze. She looked up, hopeful. He snagged the bottle of beer he'd put on for himself. 'I'll be through when the gravy's done.'

She sagged.

Emma's father was still staring out of the window when Rob popped his head around the door to tell them lunch was on the table. They turned as one towards him. Judging by the expressions on their faces, the conversation had not been enjoyable. Now he felt cowardly for abandoning Emma to her parents. So much for being a couple again. Hilda, wedged in the armchair, held out her hand imperiously to her husband to help her up as Rob started back to the kitchen. He was pouring the gravy into a jug when they walked in.

'Quite the domestic man,' said Hilda.

'I do my best,' said Rob. 'Here.' He held out her seat. 'Do you want to stick to sherry or switch to wine for lunch? Emma got a nice red to go with the lamb.' Sticking to the topics of food and wine seemed safer than expressing what was on his mind, which was a welter of confusion, sadness and plain resentment. He felt unbelievably let down by her parents and his anger was growing not cooling.

The inevitable row, when it came, began innocuously enough: Hilda asked when the baby was due. Emma had just a small bump to show for her pregnancy, which she camouflaged with a loose blouse. When she said, 'Late August,' it was as if she had slapped her father.

'What?' he roared snapping back his chair and standing over her at the table. 'You're seven months pregnant?'

'Whoa, whoa, whoa,' Rob soothed, putting his hand on Emma's as she sat frozen in shock. 'Sit down, Jim,' he added quietly.

Jim sat down reluctantly, glaring at his daughter.

Rob was nonplussed. Why was her father so outraged? Surely he'd done the maths? She ran off in early January. It was now the end of June. Consequently she was at least seven months pregnant.

Ah. They thought she was newly pregnant. Well that was going to shake up the bottle of pop.

He glanced at Emma but she seemed to be having trouble finding her voice. Eventually she managed, 'Dad, I told you on the phone.'

Rob seethed at the quaver in her voice. He wanted to demand her father back her up. She would do anything to avoid confrontations, including running away he realised. Her determination to brave it out with her father was so uncharacteristic it made Rob want to spirit her away.

'You never said you were that far gone. I thought maybe a month, but August! When were you thinking of getting married? Or was this something you were going to announce today?'

Emma glanced at Rob, but he wasn't about to be drawn into this discussion. While he would stop her father bullying her into something she wasn't ready for, he didn't want to say something that might cause an irreparable breakdown between Emma and her parents.

'I've... We've –' Emma began.

But Jim wasn't in a mood to listen. 'I never thought I'd see the day. My daughter in a shotgun wedding. None of the family could come, let alone our friends. I'd be too ashamed. No, it'll have to be a small wedding, just the two of us,' he said, indicating Hilda. 'And Rob's father, I suppose.'

This was too much for Rob. 'If and when Emma gets married is for her to decide, and only her. And if she wants a white wedding with all her friends and family, I'll make sure she gets it.'

'If?' thundered Jim. 'What d'you mean, if? Lord help me, but I'll drag you to the registry office and hold a gun to your head if I have to. You will marry my daughter before she gives birth.'

Rob opened his mouth to set him straight, and then shut it. If Emma hadn't told them she'd turned him down, he was not going to make things worse for her.

'I want a white wedding,' announced Hilda. 'I won't be doing with registry offices. They're common. Not for people like us.'

An ally, thought Rob, relaxing back in his chair.

'Are you out of your tiny mind? Look at her, Hilda! She's already showing. You can't organise a white wedding in two weeks and she'll be giving birth on the church floor if you wait any longer than that. Imagine what the cousins'll say. "Jim's precious girl got herself knocked up," they'll say.'

'That's enough,' said Rob.

'They can't come to the wedding. All the people at the golf club. They should have come. My old boss. The Paynes –'

'What do you think, Hilda?' interrupted Rob.

She sniffed. 'Fiona had a beautiful wedding. My sister's daughter. You've never met her,' she said to Rob. It sounded doubtful that she ever meant him to. 'The church was packed and the bishop himself married them.'

'Attended. The bishop attended. He didn't marry them,' barked her husband.

'Afterwards,' she continued, ignoring him, 'they drank champagne in a marquee in the garden. Three hundred people.'

Rob didn't know that many people.

'I don't know what I'm going to say to anyone,' Jim continued. 'We could have got away with it if you were just a couple of months gone. But seven months? You've humiliated us,' he said, his voice full of bile. He got up from the table. 'Hilda? We're leaving.'

'I'll show you to the door,' murmured Rob, dropping his napkin and starting to rise. He had had more than enough of these two. He subsided, however, when Hilda, who suddenly comprehended the size of the rift in the making, backtracked. 'Now, Jim, it'll be fine. We'll just be able to give Annabel a bigger wedding.'

'Annabel? She'll get married in black just to spite us. She's a vegetarian.'

'She's a Goth,' said Emma.

'Same thing,' snapped her father. 'And don't you talk to me. I've nothing more to say to you. So is there a big day?' he demanded, pushing his face into Rob's.

Emma cringed.

Rob smiled. 'Emma's going to be a single mother, aren't you, Sweet Pea?'

'A single mother?' spluttered her father.

'Or maybe I can stick around. Perhaps I should bring my

other girlfriends over with their babies and start a commune, though we might need a bigger place. What do you reckon, Emma?'

Tears were forming in her eyes, but she smiled so brightly up at him that his heart seemed the burst. 'We'd need a larger place, darling, though if you could persuade your other girlfriends to share, we might get away with just two more rooms. I'd need a bigger garden to grow my weed.'

'Good thinking.' He looked down steadily at her, a crooked smile on his face, willing her to stay strong, his heart swelling with each minute she stood up to her father. She would never run out on him again, of that he was suddenly sure. 'You know you'll always be First Wife, so to speak, even though you'll be Number Four.'

'Yeah.' She laughed through her tears, which were flowing freely down her face.

'You won't get a penny,' spat Jim.

Instantly serious, Rob rounded on the old man in a voice that was deathly quiet. 'Do I look like I want your money, Jim? You've just insulted your daughter in every way and now it's time you left.'

'Oh we're leaving. Don't expect us at the Christening. Oh, that's right! There won't be a Christening for the little bastard.'

For a big man, Rob moved surprisingly fast and Jim found himself staring up at him in fright.

'You need to go now,' whispered Rob.

'I'll leave when I'm good and ready,' screeched Jim, squaring up.

Short of physically ejecting him from the house, there was nothing Rob could do. 'Come on, love. We're going for a walk.' He dragged Emma from her chair and propelled her to the door. 'Put the door on the latch on your way out,' he called to her parents over his shoulder.

'Don't you dare walk out on me,' her father shouted. 'Come back here and face the music.' Rob closed the front door behind him, effectively shutting off the old man's voice but Jim was not finished. He wrenched it open and shouted after them, 'You've properly shamed us, you have.'

A couple of boys knocking a football around in the street turned to stare at him, whereupon he slammed the door, only to appear a moment later hustling Hilda in front of him.

'Get into the car,' he bellowed when she stood looking down the road after Rob and Emma. 'We're leaving.'

Hilda seemed inclined to dispute this. She turned to her husband. 'She's my daughter.'

'She's not mine any more.'

'Jim, please stop. You'll regret this.'

'Get in the car or I'll leave you behind.' He got in and switched on the engine. Hilda seemed torn, but climbed in beside him. Jim had no choice but to drive past Emma and Rob as they walked down the street hand in hand, and he affected not to see them. Hilda gave a sad wave. 'I love you,' she mouthed at Emma.

When they had gone, Rob turned Emma into his shoulder. 'I'm here, Sweet Pea. You have a good cry now.'

She sobbed, all the pain welling to the surface. 'I'm so sorry, Rob. I'd give anything to take back running away like I did. I love you so much.'

''Course you do. You just got a little lost. We all get lost from time to time.'

She gave a half-hearted laugh. 'You don't.'

'Oh, I've been lost for weeks.'

'You hid it well.'

'Hm, I think not. You've been very patient. I thought I was being magnanimous, but I was just being angry, wasn't I? Let's get married.'

'Would you like to invite William and Vix?'

'And Lisa and her irritating boyfriend, Patrick.'

'And your friend Mrs Mallinson.'

He grinned. 'Don't forget Mrs Moreton. She started all this. What about your family?'

'Annabel'd love it. We can sneak Mum in the back. Do you

suppose your father would give me away?'

He grinned. 'You already wrap him round your little finger.'

'I'd like a small wedding, if that's OK?'

'Fine by me.'

'After the baby is born.'

Rob pulled her into his chest. 'Are you sure?'

'Absolutely.'

'You know it'll make it harder for your father to come back.'

'Oh, he'll be here as soon as the baby is born. Mum'll make sure of that.'

'You know I love you, don't you?'

'I was never surer.' She raised her face for his kiss.

He brushed the hair back off her face, and studied her. 'You're mine, Emz. Mine,' he whispered at last, and kissed her before they turned homewards. 'Let's drive over and tell Dad the good news.'

CHAPTER 15

REVENGE

Gazzer came home from the Young Offenders Institute without a fanfare. His mother was waiting for him in reception. 'Your father is still livid,' she warned him.

'Did you know they rape pretty boys?' he said getting into the car. She started crying. He was lying but got his reward: her breakdown.

Serves her right, he thought.

He ignored her snivelling and glared out of the windscreen all the way home, consumed by a sense of injustice. They said revenge was a dish best eaten cold. He was as cold as the flipping snows in the arctic.

His father gated him as soon as he got in. As if he cared. He walked right past him to the front door. When Bruce threatened him, instead of backing down, Gazzer made a droll face. 'You got a problem with something, old man?'

Bruce's reaction made him realise that his father had never been outfaced before. 'Fuck. Off,' he sneered and watched humiliation poison his father's whole demeanour. Sweet!

His first day home was hellish for all three of them. Bruce thumped around the house and refused to even look at him, and Gary enjoyed making his mother cry. All day he fed his rage. He alone had been to prison. He alone had borne the brunt of the law for assaulting a police officer. As he lay on his bed before supper, he flushed with anticipation as he texted the crew. They owed him and he'd make sure they paid.

Meanwhile, even his mother was in the grip of this In-

Bloom thing and was doing her pathetic bit to win a gold: there were lame window boxes on all the sills. Over supper he listened in disbelief to her describing his crew painting fences.

'And Adam James rebuilt the roof of the bus shelter,' she went on in an attempt to inject something normal into the conversation. 'The council was never going to get round to it.' She glanced nervously at Bruce but he was ignoring them both. 'Anyway, he got Emlyn and some friends to dig over the flowerbed beside it. Officially the council was supposed to plant it up but they might wait for ever for Bruce – for the council to get round to it. So what do you think Adam did?'

Gary glanced at his father, wondering how long it would take him to put a stopper in his mother's drivel.

'Well,' his mother went on, answering her own question, 'Adam gave the boys twenty quid to buy something from the garden shop. They came back with some trays of red salvia and cornflower plugs, which they planted up like old hands, Adam said to me.'

Later Gary understood the full implications of what his mother had been blathering on about. His crew assembled reluctantly but were not about to see anyone trash the place, not even when he suggested a night on the town to celebrate his release. He couldn't believe his eyes when one or two of the braver ones put their hands in their pockets and slunk away. The rest stood around uselessly under the streetlights in the square. Eleven o'clock struck and a few more snuck off.

'What the fuck has got into you?' he demanded. 'Have they brainwashed you or something?'

The boys studied their feet and the girls picked their teeth as they looked around surreptitiously. Were they admiring the square? He looked around himself. Without anyone really noticing it until then, Elderfield had reacquired its 'quaintness'. It would fit right into a film set for any Austen novel, with its pavements and gutters swept clean and hanging baskets swinging in the breeze.

He jeered that they'd become a load of pussies since he'd

last seen them, and left. As he turned at the corner for one last look, the last of them was scurrying into the night. Impotent rage drove him down the road swinging a long stick at the hogweed that grew along the verge.

Thinking about it as he walked, he realised his mistake. He should have suggested they all go to the pub and get minging. By the time they had barffed up over the pavement in the High Street, they'd have been ripe for some anarchy. Singing and shouting would have escalated into knocking the odd sign. The tinkle of breaking glass would have intoxicated them, and if he'd judiciously handed out a stick or two to the most inebriated, all hell would have broken out.

'Fuck!' he swore, scything at the hogweed.

THE ATTACK

That evening, Ruth was at a party at Vix and William's celebrating their engagement. A few glasses of wine had left her euphoric and bubbly. Rob was there with Emma, who looked breathtakingly beautiful with her titian hair sinuating down her back, and big blue eyes dominating her face. She hadn't put on much weight but she was clearly pregnant, and Rob hovered — there was no other word for it. All evening his hand rested in the small of her back. Ruth could see the way the girl leaned into him, laughing over her shoulder to share a joke. She'd only seen this side of him once before. He had the same uncomplicated smile when he had played football with the boys in Newport. He looked alight.

She was glad for him. As for herself, she was alone but not lonely. She had come to the party determined to sparkle, which wasn't hard. Looking around, she was surprised at how many people had become friends. They had a hug and a kiss for her, drew her into conversation, refilled her drink and brought her food. How cut off she and Michael had become.

Did she miss him? Beyond doubt, but his loss felt like history. Did she miss Rob? In a different way, but that too was easing into history. She could see how much happier he was with Emma. It was extraordinary to watch them. They behaved almost as one person, moving in synch. She rather envied that closeness. It was what she had with Michael.

'You OK?' asked William coming over to pour himself another drink from the bar.

'Congratulations,' she replied.

'Thank you. Marriage, as I see it, means no more cooking, washing or ironing in return for putting out the bins. Seems fair to me. You look a little sad.'

She raised her eyebrows, not used to William being observant. 'Are you keeping an eye on me?'

'Vix was worried you'd make a scene,' he said wistfully.

'And you?'

'I'd have enjoyed it. Nothing like two women fighting over a man, though I'd've preferred it to be over me. All those heaving breasts and strong thighs. Maybe you could scratch each other's eyes out and yank out a few fistfuls of hair.'

'You sound disappointed.'

'I can always tell her who you are.'

'I could walk over and tell her myself. Maybe spit a bit and tell her he loves me really.'

'Now we're getting somewhere.' He sighed. 'I'm sorry it didn't work out.'

'Oh William, you've gone all corny now you're engaged.'

'Seriously, you looked down and I came over to see if I could cheer you up. Here, let me do something about that depressingly empty glass, for a start.'

'No more for me,' she said, handing it to him. 'I'm going to abandon this rotten party.'

'She told me she'd lined up some single men for you. I just met two of them and immediately wanted to vom. Founder members of Accountants Anonymous, I suspect. Mind you, you seem to like dead boring people,' he added, with a nod in

Rob's direction.

Ruth laughed. 'He was never dull. But Wired Hair over there is an auditor not an accountant. He was careful to explain the difference.'

'Are they the best she can come up with?'

'No. I believe one person couldn't make it,' she said pokerfaced. 'He had to attend the Public Regulators Conference.'

'Tell you what, I'll line you up with some of my mates,' he offered with a suggestive waggle of his eyebrows.

'Thank you, William. You've no idea how generous that sounds, but no.'

'They'd be good for a decent dinner at the Pauper's Arms, and a grope in the back of the car on the way home if you were so minded. They'd behave properlike.'

'Vix is a lucky woman,' she said, kissing his cheek. 'Tell her thank you for the party and the… spare men.'

'Are you driving?'

She shook her head. 'It's not far.'

'I'll get someone to walk you home.'

She managed to evade all offers and strolled home alone, still high on the glory of being alive… until she heard something moving about in the dark as she approached her gates. She stopped, her heart tripping as her eyes stripped the dark, trying to make out shapes within shadows. She'd thought the town safe again. What a fool she'd been to turn down an escort.

Later she remembered only a hoodied figure swinging a stick as he ran towards her. Whether he shoved her or she stumbled and hit her head on the ground, she would never know. All she knew was that she woke up alone lying in the road. She managed to stand. The world reeled and she zigzagged up the drive dialling Vix's number on her mobile.

Within minutes Will, Rob and Al screeched up and searched the place, making a lot of noise, but the intruder had long gone. William tried to insist Ruth stay with him and Vix. Holding a bag of frozen peas against the lump on her head, Ruth resisted. In the end, Rob stepped forward and said she was safe enough in the house. She looked up, taking in the deep vertical frown lines at the bridge of his nose and his heavy eyebrows. 'Thank you, Rob.'

'You'll be OK?'

There seemed to be a wealth of other unspoken queries in that question. She nodded. He was a good man.

William argued all the way out to the van but Rob prevailed. They'd left her on the proviso that she would ring William 'if she heard so much as a bat fart'.

BROKEN

Next day Ruth awoke refreshed. There wasn't even a bruise to show for her fall. As she boiled herself an egg, she stood admiring the view of her garden. All her hard work had paid off and the Open Day had raised hundreds of pounds for the Muscular Dystrophy Campaign. That the garden looked phenomenal was irrelevant as far as the In-Bloom awards were concerned. The assessors would be looking at the community not her garden.

Serendipitously her lilies along the road would be at their best when the judges arrived. Most days she spent a few minutes debugging them and nuking the slugs. Meanwhile, William had encouraged other people along the road to pick up the theme by offering them a special deal on lilies. She rejoiced at the way the town was coming together.

A paper was what she needed now. She'd spend a lazy day curled up in a sofa catching up on the world. Before she left, she poked around outside looking for footprints that might have given away the intruder's intentions, but found nothing. With a shrug, she set off… and got as far as her gates, where she stopped as if she'd smacked into a wall.

Oh God. Her beautiful lilies!

Someone had slashed their heads off; the blooms lay where they'd fallen. This was no aimless destruction. Every sweet-smelling head had been decapitated.

Ruth sank to her knees. Who would do such a thing? Spraying graffiti on walls and smashing windows was one thing, destroying flowers that gave pleasure to everyone was mean.

She dialled Rob without thinking but disconnected immediately and phoned William. His voicemail picked up. 'Someone destroyed my lilies.' Her voice wavered.

She took a deep breath. To cry about flowers was too stupid for words.

William called her back within ten minutes. 'Are you sure?' he demanded without preamble in his gravelly voice.

Ruth laughed. 'No, William. I'm sure it's post-party blues or something. Good do last night by the way.'

'Are you all right? No one tried to break in after we'd gone?'

'I'm fine.'

''Course you are. Bleeding obvious, isn' it? You wouldn't be calling me if you were unconscious on the floor. If all you have to worry about is a bunch of bleeding lilies with no heads, life's just dandy. Worrying about running out of scotch, now there's something to get your head around.'

'You ran out of booze last night?'

'Rob dropped us back but we'd pretty well run out of alcohol so he and Emma buggered off home.'

'Perhaps I should be asking how your head is?'

'It'd be better if Vix allowed me some hair of the dog.'

'I'm sorry to have bothered you about the lilies,' said Ruth. 'It's not as though you can do anything.'

'You're right about that, but Vix says women like to talk things through. Not something I've ever gone in for myself. That's for poofters. Rob's your man in the bleeding heart department. Not that he's a poofter.'

'Thank you for that, William,' she said, much cheered by his notion of comfort. 'I'll remember that next time someone slashes the heads off my flowers.'

Vix came round with Al that afternoon. They stood in the drizzle glumly surveying the damage, and then wandered back to the house for tea and biscuits.

'I think I know who did it,' said Ruth.

They both sat up.

'No, no. I can't actually remember. I just have a face in my head. It's not a reliable memory.' She remembered rushing towards the figure who was swiping at her lilies with a huge stick, begging him to stop. He hadn't hit her. He'd pushed past her and she'd tripped. She'd never forget Gary Turner's face contorted with fury in the moonlight. Accusing him at this stage was not going to help anyone.

The local papers were quick off the mark – *President of Elderfield in Bloom tackles thieves; Saboteurs strike down Chair of Elderfield on Bloom* – and theories were rich on the ground. Disturbed thieves had more supporters than the saboteurs hypothesis; there had been no other vandalism, had there?

A HOME FOR A CAT

Al was coming to his own conclusions about that night. Several images kept coming back to him. One of them was of Gazzer stomping off alone down this very road. The timing was about right.

After lunch the next day, he set off to Gazzer's house without any fixed intention just as it started to rain. Despite the wet, dozens of people were out preparing the town for Judgement Day tomorrow. Didn't they have jobs to go to? They couldn't all have taken sickies. The fine rain changed to a mid-summer downpour and everyone looked sodden but it didn't seem to dampen their enthusiasm, though with their luck it would rain tomorrow, too. Unusually he sent up a prayer for sunshine under his breath.

His pace slowed as he approached the Turner's house. Confront Gazzer? His mind boggled. He couldn't even stand up to Neal. He was no Mrs Mallinson. The face that stared back at him from the mirror each morning didn't belong to a hero. It was the man he was going to become – not brave or valiant, just ordinary. Ordinary wasn't enough but he didn't know how to set about being anything better.

He plodded past the memorial and on towards Susan Mallinson's house. There he stopped to look over the gate, his eyes half closed against the rain, water dripping off his nose. It saddened him to see workmen wheeling barrows up a ramp and tipping the contents into a skip. Old chairs, cushions and sofas were ditched. Even the antique kitchen dresser had been hacked to pieces. Stuff that had been in the house for decades. Stuff full of Mrs Mallinson's memories... except she didn't seem able to remember anything any more.

The last time he'd been to God's Waiting Room to visit her, she'd still been dressed in a nightie with fluffy pink slippers on her feet at four o'clock in the afternoon. She was sitting in a plastic chair puddled in pee, staring out at the empty yard. The nurses had told him not to shout, that shouting didn't make anything any better because they were understaffed, and no they didn't know how long she'd been sitting there in her pee but not more than an hour or so.

At the front door of the house, the old woman's daughter suddenly appeared, holding a cat by the scruff of the neck. A workman stopped what he was doing to pick up a sack. She dropped the cat inside. 'The last of the little buggers,' she said, holding the sack out to the man. 'Drown it.'

The workman picked up his tools. 'Not my job,' he said, and went back inside.

'He-llo? I pay you to do as you're told,' Jennifer shouted. When he didn't return, she looked blankly at the sack in her hand, then walked round the side of the house and returned without it. As soon as she went inside, Al leapt the gate and ran to the pond, wading in, shoes and all, hatred for that horrible woman practically steaming out of his ears.

The cat was alive, barely. He wrapped it in the sacking and walked defiantly back down the garden path carrying it in his arms, his shoes squelching muddy water as he went.

When he reached the road, he stood irresolute. The desire to confront Gazzer had waned. Meanwhile, he was holding a half dead cat, and summer rain was coming down in sheets. What was he going to do with it? There was no question of taking it home – cats gave his mother asthma. Who else would want a semi-wild animal?

He walked along aimlessly holding the cat until he found himself at Gazzer's house. Without giving it much thought, he knocked at the door. Gary answered. 'What the fuck do you want? And what the fuck is that?'

'A cat.'

'What's wrong with it?'

'That woman tried to drown it.'

'Give us a look.' Gazzer was unexpectedly tender, cradling the cat in his arm and leaving Al on the doorstep. Sheepishly Al followed him inside, water pooling at his feet. Mrs Turner was half way down the stairs, her hand resting on the banister, her eyes puffy and red. 'Hello, Mrs Turner,' he mumbled, and went through to the kitchen where he found Gazzer crooning softly to the cat and drying it with a tea towel.

'It's pretty wild,' he cautioned.

'Poor babe,' Gazzer murmured. 'Poor half drowned babe. How could they do this to you? You'll be safe here. I'll look after you.'

Al turned to find Mrs Turner at his elbow, her wide eyes fixed on her son.

'Can we keep it?' Gazzer asked, without looking up.

There wasn't a moment's hesitation. 'Of course,' his mother replied. Her breath caught and she looked like she wanted to say more, but Al put a hand on her shoulder. 'I'm not sure how house trained it is,' he warned.

'Doesn't matter,' she said, her eyes on her son and a weird

expression of hope in her face.

'Gazzer,' said Al, 'the Mallinson woman, the daughter, will drown it if it goes back.'

'We won't let you go back there, will we?' Gazzer whispered to the cat. 'You'll like it here. Shh, don't fret. I'll look after you.' The cat stopped struggling and settled under his hand.

'I should go,' said Al.

No one responded.

'I'll call you Kitty. Hey Kitty, Kitty. That's it. You be quiet now and rest.' The cat lay in Gazzer's arms and he seemed content just to sit and watch it. 'She's purring,' he informed them without looking up.

Mrs Turner looked up at Al. 'Thank you,' she mouthed.

Al's eyes widened. He should be thanking them for taking the cat in the first place. Why she would want one of old Mrs Mallinson's half-wild cats, he hadn't the faintest idea. 'I'll go now,' he said inadequately.

'I'll show you out,' said Mrs Turner. 'Thank you for coming round. I – we appreciate it.'

Yeah, right, thought Al feeling relieved and ever so slightly frustrated. He felt he had achieved nothing. As he passed the Seven Eleven, he stopped. The clanking bell announced his entry. He was fortunate to find what he looked for, and paid for it with the loose change in his pocket. Ten minutes later he was back at the Turner's house.

Gazzer opened the door to him once more, the cat asleep in the crook of his arm.

'I thought you might need this,' Al said, holding up a tray and a bag of cat litter. 'I bet your other cat does his, you know, business, outside, but I think you should keep this one inside. Until he learns it's his home. I think that's how it's done, kinda like a homing pigeon.'

'He's a her.' Gazzer walked back into the house leaving Al on the doorstep and the door swinging open.

Guardedly Al followed him back through to the kitchen, passing Mrs Turner who was standing on the stairs again. Her smile, when she saw who it was, looked both pinched and glad to see him. Al went on to the kitchen, and sat down opposite Gazzer. He ripped open the bag of cat litter and poured it into the tray, levelling it out with a shake.

'Where do you want it?'

'By the back door. And for fuck sake get a towel and dry yourself off a bit or you'll ruin my mother's furniture. There's one in the downstairs toilet.'

Al came back still towelling himself off. 'Is she OK?'

'You will be, won't you, Kitty?'

'Does she need the vet or anything? I'd pay for that. She's kinda my responsibility, too, you know?'

'She's mine now. Dad'll pay any vet bills.'

The cat started purring again, deep rounds of rumbling as Gazzer stroked it.

'She's the only one left.' A wave of emotion struck Al as he thought about old Mrs Mallinson surrounded by her cats. 'According to the guy in the Seven Eleven, that woman's drowned the rest of them. She boasts about it in town.'

'Bloody witch. I've a good mind to go and trash her place.'

'I think your dad bought it.'

'Oh, yeah, right. People always get what they deserve in the end, though.'

Al thought Gazzer had been watching too many films. Susan Mallinson was definitely not getting what she deserved. 'Got anything to eat?' he asked. 'I'm half starved.'

'There's some bread in the bread bin,' said Gazzer, his gaze still on the cat.

Al helped himself. 'Got any more jam?' he mumbled a moment later with his mouth full. 'This jar's empty,' he said, putting it on the table.

'In the cupboard.'

'Ruth Dawson was attacked last night,' said Al, spreading jam liberally on a second slice of bread.

'Oh?'

'She got knocked out.'

'And?'

'You were going that way when I saw you last.'

Gazzer looked up, careful not to disturb the cat, but his eyes were burning. 'And you think I hit her. Well, I tell you, I didn't fucking touch her.'

'No, I didn't think you had,' said Al, smoothly.

'Yes you did, but I didn't.'

'I believe you.'

'Like I fucking care.'

'I thought you'd be interested.'

'Well I'm not.'

'Someone destroyed her flowers.'

'You're worried about flowers, now? What is it with you?'

'Nothing.'

'People should thank my dad, you know. He's worked his bollocks off for this pissing Bloom thing, but it's her they turn to, not him. Do you think that's fair?'

Al sniffed. Bruce was a knob but now was not the time to tell Gazzer.

'Just like none of you ever thanked me.'

'For what?'

'I coulda named names.'

Al sat very still.

Gary had assaulted a police officer who had been searching his room. According to the local paper, a BB gun, albeit a convincing replica, had been found along with a kitchen knife – it was no crime to keep such things in your own home. The incident had hardly rated a paragraph in the local paper, despite Gary being Bruce Turner's son. Gary was lucky that the local editor happened to go on holiday the day after the arrest, thought Al, not sure he was comfortable with the coincidence.

'Not one of you stood up for me,' muttered Gazzer.

Al licked his lips nervously. The cat stirred and began cleaning a paw. 'She seems happy here,' he said inconsequentially.

'Happier here than at the old cat lady's,' sneered Gazzer.

Al began to rise to that, and then let it go. Maybe the cat would be: he'd never seen Mrs Mallinson stroke the cats. As he sat contemplating a third slice of bread and jam, the cat jumped onto the table. She sniffed the empty jam jar with little bobbing motions of her head, and then sat washing herself.

Al had a thought. 'That picture you took of me. What did you do with it?'

Gazzer looked blank.

'The one by the car that got torched.'

'Nothing. Why?'

'I thought you'd put it up on Facebook.'

Gazzer gave him a strange look. 'Why would I do that?'

'You put everything up.'

'No, I don't. D'you think I'm thick or something?'

'No.'

'So why d'you ask?'

'No reason. I wondered.'

Gazzer studied him until he looked away. 'Would you have?' he asked Al.

'No.'

'Well, there you go, then.'

The setting sun filled the room with orange light. The rain had stopped and the clouds were clearing. Light from the late afternoon sun hit the jar and a beam reflected off it on to the ceiling. Gazzer sat with his chin in one hand rolling the empty jam jar on the table watching the pattern the reflected light made on the ceiling. He got up and washed it with a preoccupied air. Then he took the new jar of jam, emptied the jam down the sink, and rinsed that, too.

'That was a waste,' Al commented as Gazzer set the jars down in front of him.

'What are they?'

'Er, jam jars?' replied Al, looking askance at Gazzer.

'Duh. What else are they?'

'I dunno.'

'Vases.'

'Oh. Oh!'

'We could put the flowers in jam jars.'

Al picked up one of the jars and held it under the tap, rubbing at the label. 'Better without the label.'

'Whatever. Wadayarekkon?'

'It could work. We'd need more jars.'

'Yeah.' Gazzer was sarcastic.

''Bout a couple of hundred. Maybe more.'

'And?'

'Where'd we get that many jars?'

Gazzer sighed. 'You've got no fucking imagination, that's your trouble.' He took out his phone.

'You texting the crew?'

'Wadayathink?'

'I think…'

Gazzer looked up. 'You don't think they'll come, do you? What the fuck to you know?'

Al affected not to hear the question and inspected the jars in front of him.

Gazzer frowned and pocketed his phone. He scooped up the cat and the litter tray. 'Wait here,' he told Al.

He returned a few minutes later. 'She's on my bed, all curled up and ready to sleep.'

'She seems less wild here.'

'Yeah, well, she's wanted here.'

'Where are we off to?'

'Paddy's.'

Twenty minutes later, Paddy was opening cupboards and emptying jam into the bin. At Caspian's house, he was about to do the same thing, when his sister grabbed a bowl and emptied the jam into that. She waited only to put the bowl in the fridge before following them out of the front door.

At Saskia's house they found a bag of jars under the sink that her mother was keeping for making jam. At Emlyn's place they collected another two jars.

When they returned to Gazzer's house they counted their

hoard. Not enough. Gazzer sent parties round the estate. At each house, the youngsters spoke quietly to the people who answered the door, then waited on the doorstep politely while the people went back inside and invariably returned with a couple of jam jars. By the time it was getting dark they had amassed quite a hoard. At the end of the evening, there were curls of labels all over the floor. Caspian had had to go out twice to find more turps to clean off the glue.

Emlyn mentioned that they needed some of 'that stuff you get from florists' to put in the jars. Lisa lived across the green from Saskia, and though it was nearly midnight, Saskia led a delegation round to her flat. Dead annoyed to be woken, Lisa eventually heard them out, then dressed and accompanied them into town to her shop.

Half an hour later, they returned to Gazzer's house accompanied by Lisa. By now there were several teenagers diligently cleaning labels off dozens of jars. From her van, Lisa unloaded boxes used for transporting flowers, and they started loading the jam jars into these and then into her van.

At first they plonked all the jam jars on the verge in front of Ruth's house, then Gazzer suggested they lay them out like a stream meandering towards the village. They took it in turns to fill the jars from a watering can and then sprinkle a little flower food into each. Finally, they stuffed one lily head into each jar.

By two thirty, everyone was wilting but they were done. Tomorrow... today was Judgement Day.

JUDGEMENT DAY

Early the next morning Ruth was standing in the road with her jaw slightly agape. Before her, lily heads in jam jars threaded into the distance in a colossal river of colour, scent and reflected light from the water. Her throat was so tight she couldn't say a word. Beside her stood three men and a woman with clipboards.

'This is an example,' she said eventually, her voice husky with emotion, 'of how Elderfield in Bloom has changed the town. Before, no one would have dreamed of this... er...' She tore her gaze away from the lilies. 'We had troubles, you see. Youths running wild. You might have read about it. It destroyed property values. Worse than other areas. People were afraid to go out at night.'

The assessors nodded and made notes on their pads.

Their actions brought her back to the purpose of the visit, and she had a momentary vision of Bruce's reaction to their presence at her house. He would be irate. She cleared her throat. 'Bruce Turner, the chair of Elderfield in Bloom, was supposed to greet you officially when you arrived. He'll be put out that I got in first.'

'How many people on the committee?' asked one of the men. 'I'm Daniel, by the way,' he added, reaching out to shake her hand. His was a gardener's hand, all hard calluses and rough. 'Daniel Moloney. This is Robert Gordon, Gillian Ellis, and Chris Johns.'

They all shook her hand.

'Well, there's Bruce, of course, and Mary and Vix and William and Rob. And Lucy and Terry, and, oh, a whole list of other people who've taken responsibility for parts of projects. Like one of the boys at school: Al. He proposed that the school take over one of the allotments next to the playground, and got the headmaster to let students garden in their lunch hour. I suppose Mr Sharples would claim he's running that project, but from what I hear, the kids are organising themselves. Mr Sharples is... nice like that.' She tailed off. It wasn't her business to say how useless Sharples had proved and how many obstacles he had thrown in their way.

'Well, that's cracking,' said Daniel.

Cracking. Ruth had never heard anyone but *Wallace and Gromit* use that word. He said it the same way too.

'We just had to stop and admire the lilies,' he added. 'We've never seen anything like it. There's obviously been some vandalism, but its how you deal with it afterwards that's important in the awards. Sadly, vandalism is a fact of life, these days. I have to say, it's pretty inspired, what you've done here.'

'Oh, this isn't me. This wasn't even here last night when I went to bed, and I was out at midnight looking at the stars,' said Ruth, gazing at the flowers. 'It's like the elves did this.'

'Is that a fact? Well,' said Daniel addressing his peers, 'we could leave the cars here and go into town on foot. It's not far, is it?'

'Not far,' confirmed Ruth. 'I'll show you the way. You're a couple of hours earlier than we expected.'

'We like to arrive early and have a moscy on our own. I must say, you have a beautiful garden here. I hear you had an open day recently, and raised over two thousand quid.'

Ruth was impressed; he'd obviously done his homework. 'I was stunned by how much we raised. Last time I only raised five hundred. Lots of people pitched in – they grew seeds and cuttings to sell in the popup shop on the day; it certainly wasn't just me working alone.'

'I wouldn't mind a quick peep some time, if that's OK.'

'Sure,' said Ruth, still slightly bemused. 'I'd be honoured to give you a tour.'

'Did I read that it's part of the National Garden Scheme?' Daniel asked. He walked beside her and they talked all the way to town. He had an easy way about him. He knew his plants and he had a good eye for design. It turned out he was deep into conservation projects.

She realised, too, that he was subtly milking her for information because he occasionally made notes in boxes on his clip chart. She wondered how many times he'd done this and whether he was this animated about every town he went to. It was not something she would relish, meeting endless groups of enthusiastic worthies. But then, she supposed, isn't this what she did when she went to the committee meetings? People there certainly weren't 'enthusiastic worthies'; many of them she respected and some had become good friends.

Immediately they reached the town hall, Ruth realised how badly she had miscalculated by accompanying the assessors to town. Bruce was red in the face with apoplexy.

'You just can't stop interfering, can you?' he hissed at her.

'Bruce, may I introduce you to Daniel Moloney,' she said, tranquilly.

If Daniel had overheard the exchange – and how could he not have? – he affected deafness and held out his hand. 'A pleasure to meet you Bruce. You have a beautiful town here.'

'Well, I've worked extremely hard to get it that way.'

'Is that a fact?' said Daniel. Ruth could see that he was a natural diplomat because his manner seemed to convey authority mixed with a strange reserve and calm, which had an instantly soothing effect on Bruce. 'Why don't you show us around?' he asked him.

Clearly aware of Jules and his camera crew following them, Bruce guarded the judges all morning and ensured their time with other members of the committee was measured in short minutes. The judges, however, were no pushovers. One of them asked Bruce for a tour of the estate, and Bruce agreed unctuously, until he realised only Chris Johns would be with him. By then it was too late, and he departed blustering ineffectively.

William immediately proposed everyone else adjourn to the nearest beer garden for a pint, which suggestion was greeted with enthusiasm. Away from Bruce's overpowering personality, the rest of the committee blossomed, and they had a long enthusiastic discussion with the assessors about how differently they would do things next year, and what they needed to improve upon.

Daniel let his colleagues run the meeting and sat quietly next to Ruth. Although he did not flirt with her or seem to pay her any special attention, Ruth had the strangest feeling that most of his attention was focused on her as they sipped their drinks and listened to the other committee members talk about the affect of the awards on the town.

'He was very taken with you,' murmured William when every aspect of the town had been catalogued, assessed and photographed, and the judges had finally departed.

Ruth could feel a blush rising up her throat. 'Oh nonsense. We did nothing but talk plants.'

'He could have done that equally well with me.'

'Yes, I suppose. He was kind.' He was lovely, she thought. Articulate, empathetic, intelligent, and far more knowledgeable about plants than herself. He was planning a trip to Kazakhstan in the spring in search of species tulips, together with a group of Dutch bulb enthusiasts. It was the kind of trip she had never even considered, always having trotted along on family holidays to Italy where the family alternated between trips to art galleries and lazing by the pool at a secluded villa. The idea of travelling to somewhere remote and exotic like Kazakhstan to track down new plants excited her beyond measure.

'So you won't mind if he asks you out to dinner,' asked William, breaking into her daydreams.

She grimaced wistfully. 'I shouldn't think he'll do that.'

'Oh, I think he will. He asked for your number. He gave me a lot of tosh about wanting to get an autographed copy of your book, and though I had plenty in the shop to sell him, I conveniently forgot about them.'

'Really?' Ruth went pink. Then she made the mistake of looking up. Rob was watching her. Was he frowning? He turned away to say something to Mary.

I do not feel guilty, she thought, excitement still coursing through her, yet part of her wanted to explain to Rob. 'You don't have to explain anything, love,' said Rob when she caught up with him later.

'No, I don't,' she agreed. 'But part of me still wants to. How's it going?'

'OK. The vegetables are coming thick and fast. Peas, beans, lettuces, that kind of stuff.'

'I meant, with Emma.'

'She's got another month before she hatches.'

'Are you going to marry her?'

'Eventually.'

'Oh.' It was a strange response and she wasn't sure she could ask the next obvious question, do you still love her? The easy camaraderie between them that would once have made such a question straightforward had fallen away.

'She knows about you, by the way. I thought you should know. She knows I fell a little in love with you.'

'I'm going to accept Daniel's invitation... if he does ask me out to dinner.'

This time his frown was obvious.

'What?' she asked indignantly.

'He was the driest, most aloof man I've ever met and I feel sad for you, that's all.'

She swallowed in shock.

'You're settling,' he observed.

Suddenly she was angry. 'Stop it, Rob. You know nothing, and you're not exactly around to do anything about it anyway. Get on with your life and let me get on with mine.'

'He's not right for you.'

He took her breath away. 'That's pretty rich. Look, Rob, I enjoyed my time with you, but life moves on.'

'No, you misunderstand me. I've moved on, too. Em and I –' he shrugged, 'we're good.' There was that uncomplicated smile again – he was truly happy.

'Really?'

'I think it's going to be all right, though it's not plain sailing yet. We have a lot to forgive each other.' He smiled at a memory. 'It's even better than before. I didn't think I could love her more than I did, but I do.'

'I'm glad,' she said, with warmth back in her voice.

He looked down at her for what seemed like an aeon as if to reassure himself that she, too, was going to be all right. Then he must have realised that it wasn't his call any more because he put a hand on her waist and pulled her a little towards him.

'Good bye, Ruth,' he said, kissing her cheek.

All her emotions swam to the surface and she gripped his arm. 'Friends?'

'Always. I'll see you around.'

She nodded, oddly relieved.

'Good luck with the baby,' she called after him. He lifted a hand in acknowledgement, but didn't turn round. Perhaps he was thinking about how Emma was waiting at home for him.

CHAPTER 16

TOGETHER APART

The phone was ringing. Though Ruth strove to pick it up, it was somehow always beyond her reach. She was desperate to hear the voice at the other end. It would be him calling to tell her he loved her. She was almost weeping with frustration as the ringing phone continued to elude her. One last desperate struggle and she would reach it. She put everything into stretching out... and woke up when her hand cracked against the bedside table.

The phone continued to ring. She picked it up. ''Lo.' Her voice was hazy with sleep.

There was a long silence at the other end before a low voice rumbled: 'Hi. Have I woken you?'

'Daniel?'

'I feel guilty now. I thought I'd catch you before you went to bed.'

She yawned as she tried to collect her thoughts. 'This is a surprise.'

'I wanted to thank you for yesterday, for lunch and for showing me round your garden. I didn't mean to wake you.'

'That's all right.' She edged up in bed and blinked in the darkness wondering what time it was. She yawned again. 'I thought you were going away.'

'I'm in Surinam. North coast of South America,' he added. 'Have you been asleep long?'

The bed was warm and comfortable and Ruth snuggled down again, put the phone under her ear on the pillow and curled up around it, pulling the duvet tight around her. She had forgotten to close the curtains and the room was bathed in soft starlight. 'No, not long; I was working in the garden later than I intended and then collapsed into bed.'

'Now I feel really guilty. What time is it over there?'

She reached for her clock and squinted at the hands. 'Close on one in the morning.'

'So late? I'll call you at a better time. Go back to sleep.'

'I'm awake now.' She liked his answering chuckle. 'I thought you were going to Columbia.'

'Surinam first, to kick off a new bio-diversity project. I enjoyed lunch.'

'Me, too. Not often someone more knowledgeable than me comes round and puts me on the spot.'

'Those Latin names are most impressive. You have the edge on me there.'

'Hm. False modesty sits well on your shoulders,' she teased. 'Like one of those magnificent capes that magicians wear.'

This time he laughed. It was a surprisingly genial sound.

'What time is it there?' she asked, at the same time wondering where he was. Was he sitting in some hotel lounge?

'About nine in the evening. I've just had the most boring supper with a well-meaning diplomat and his wife who served me roast chicken. I hate roast chicken.'

'You ate it very politely with me.'

'Ah, but I seem to remember you did something rather special with it.'

'I served it with roast potatoes,' she said in a deadpan voice.

'That's it. It's extraordinary what decent roast potatoes can do to a man's outlook.'

'I was always told to stop digging,' she chuckled.

'Must have been advice from a woman. I'm a man. We're experts at digging holes for ourselves, we forget to put out the bins, we don't do the washing up, and we snore at night.'

'Do you?'

His breath caught at the intimate turn to the conversation

and there was a small hesitation before he replied: 'That's for you to find out.' His voice was like velvet.

There was a pause while she digested his riposte, and then she tried a light come back: 'I don't snore, or sleep with my mouth open.'

'That's useful information.' There was definitely a smile in his voice.

She closed her eyes, picturing him on some verandah looking out over dark forests beneath a starry sky while he talked to her.

'It would be awkward if you snored,' he continued. 'You might keep me awake, and I get snarly with lack of sleep.'

'I'll make a point to let you sleep late.'

'Breakfast in bed?'

'You should be so lucky.' How she liked the way he bantered. Then a thought struck her. 'Is this phone call going to cost you a fortune?'

'Aren't you worth it?'

'It was only lunch.'

'It was roast chicken.'

She resettled in bed, the better to hear his voice. 'I'll cook beef next time.'

'I'd like that. When?'

'You're very pushy,' she joked. 'How about when you get back?'

'Invite me tomorrow and I'll fly back.'

'That's silly.'

'Try me.'

She believed him. Yet listening to the soft silence of expectation settling between them and to her heart beating unsteadily, she had a pang of doubt. 'Daniel, am I, ... it's not just me, is it?'

'Now that depends what you mean.' She could hear that smile in his voice again. 'Do I keep a harem? No. Did we enjoy each other's company extraordinarily?' There was a long pause before he whispered his own answer. 'Yeah.'

She listened to the millions of silent questions batting down the phone at her.

'Ruth, you... I'm... No, you're not the only one feeling this.'

She sighed with happiness.

'We both felt it the first time we met,' he continued. 'It was definitely there when we had lunch together.'

'And when we walked round my garden.'

'And when I kissed you goodbye.'

She brushed her fingers over her lips.

'Sleep now, my sweet. I'll call you tomorrow.'

'Your phone bill will be enormous.'

'That sounds like a promise.'

She laughed quietly. 'It is.'

'I'll hold you to it. Good night then, Ruth.'

'Good night.' She listened to the sound of his breathing, to the stillness blurring the edges between them, and then whispered, 'You have to put the phone down.'

'No, I don't,' he whispered back.

She laughed aloud. 'One of us has to.'

'Not me.'

'Daniel?'

'Mm?'

'I'm... This sounds silly. I like you.'

He grunted. 'I hear a "but".'

'No, you hear me being gauche.'

'Gauche I can handle. To be honest, I'm nervous myself. You're an incredible woman, Ruth. Beautiful, clever, talented. I could easily fall in love with you.'

Her heart seemed to flip within her chest.

'Ah.' He cleared his throat. 'Silence. From a woman, that's never a good sign. Was that the wrong thing to say? Was I too quick? They tell me I'm too direct.'

'It wasn't too quick. Perfect timing, in fact.'

'Do mean that?'

'Oh yes. When do you get back?'

'Saturday on the red-eye from Miami.'
'Would you like breakfast?'
'I like my eggs easy over.'
''k.'

For several seconds they listened to each other's contented silence, at peace. Then he murmured, 'Night night, Ruth,' and the phone disconnected.

AWAITING SENTENCE

Bruce didn't give anyone a chance to relax. No sooner had the In Bloom judges departed than he requested – demanded – that everyone turn their attention to the annual fete, 'Which is ruddy months behind schedule and only two weeks away.'

So instead of lethargy and anti-climax, there was a renewed sense of purpose, and, unexpectedly, everyone was grateful.

It seemed the results to the award were not important, and Al reflected that Ruth was right when she said that the awards had served their purpose. The town was united in a way no one had experienced for years. When people greeted each other in the street, there was warmth in their smiles, not just good manners. There was continual movement in and out of the estate – the community garden scheme was going from strength to strength, and many people from the estate were working hard on stands for the fete, which had, until now, been the exclusive prerogative of the old-town inhabitants.

One sadness: Susan Mallinson died quietly in her sleep. Al only found out when he went to visit her and found someone else in her room.

'Why wasn't anyone told?' he demanded of a nurse he managed to track down in the dining room.

'We informed her daughter five days ago, and she told us to go ahead and bury her.'

Al stared. 'When?'

'Yesterday.'

'Was anybody there?' he said, his voice rising.

'Not as far as I am aware. No invitations were sent out.'

Al gulped. 'Was there even a service?'

'The vicar would have said a few words over her coffin.'

'Dust to dust.'

'Something like that.'

'You don't understand. She had friends in town who'd've liked to've said goodbye.' His voice began to shake.

'I'm sorry.'

The double doors at the entrance banged open violently. 'Al?' It was Rob, striding towards him. 'I just heard. Vix sent me to collect you.'

'She's buried,' yelped Al. 'They buried her and I never said goodbye.'

'I know.'

'No one was there.'

'Come away, Al.'

'No one.' Out in the car park he leaned against Rob's van while Rob unlocked. 'It's so unfair,' he muttered.

'Get in. We'll go and visit her grave and you can organise a memorial service fit for a war heroine.'

'I'd like to do that,' said Al gruffly. 'I know just how I'll begin it. "To you, she was just a dotty old cat lady, a bogey woman who terrified generations of small boys. But before that, she was one of the reasons we won the war."' He climbed into the van.

'That sounds good,' said Rob, climbing up beside him and starting the engine.

'I'll get lots of other people to tell us their memories of her. I bet there are some people who remember her at the War Office or something.'

'Maybe, but she was quite old. It's likely most of her contemporaries are dead.'

'There'll be people who knew her,' Al insisted.

'Yeah,' agreed Rob, and his voice was interested; he wasn't

just humouring him.

'But I won't invite her daughter.'

'There's no need to do that.'

'How did you know she'd died?'

'You're a beneficiary of her will. A letter just arrived at your home.'

'Oh.'

'Do you want to know how much?'

'Will it bring her back?'

'No, but that woman is contesting it.'

'Then I'll fight for every penny.'

'That's my boy.'

'Do you think I'd have enough to build a small bike park outside town? Somewhere me and the guys could, you know, fix up some jumps. She and I were designing one, you see. She was really excited by the idea. I don't know where we'd build it, though.'

'We'll find some land.'

Ruth, when she heard about the search for some suitable land, offered her woods.

'But your flowers?'

'From what you've shown me, Al, most people stick to the path. I think it could be perfect.'

'Wicked.'

'Come round later and have a look. I'm freshly stocked up with chocolate hobnobs.'

'Can we… can we have a hut?' he asked tentatively.

'I think a hut is essential. Kind of like a headquarters.'

'Yeah. Somewhere to hang out. I'd better make sure that woman doesn't get her bloody mits on that money. I was right about her, wasn't I?'

'Sadly, Al, you were,' she agreed.

THE FETE

The day of the fete dawned clear and bright with just a hint of autumn in the air. It was too warm to wear a sweater, but cool enough to want one when the sun disappeared briefly behind one of the dozens of tiny white clouds filling the sky. The fete promised to be a huge success: by eleven o'clock dozens of people from both the town and the estate were setting up stalls and tables. Bunting was hung up, the coconut shy was pegged out, and ponies were saddled and tethered, ready to take anyone with a pound for a ride up and down the length of the playing fields.

Vix was marking out the arena for The Most Obedient Dog, The Best Fancy-Dressed Dog and The Dog Most Like Its Owner competitions. Al was arranging rosettes and small silver cups on a table by the arena entrance while Olivia looked on. When he was done, they walked over to where Emma was setting out the cake stand under an awning Rob was rigging up for her. She looked huge, and occasionally a grimace crossed her face when the baby kicked particularly hard.

Rob noticed Al standing with his hands in his pockets and gazing at the cakes.

'I'm starving,' the boy said.

Emma edged a plate of cup cakes towards him. 'Have one. They're really good.'

'I haven't got any money.'

'So? Vix will buy some later, and besides, William has already snaffled two.'

Al helped himself. 'Thanks,' he muttered with his mouth full. Then, remembering his manners, he asked, 'Want one, Olivia?'

His girlfriend shook her head and patted her stomach. 'Derhahaha. No carbohydrates. I'm on a diet, remember?'

'Oh yeah.' Al looked at her supermodel shape and his brows knitted. Then he lost interest in the whys and wherefores of fads and diets. 'Need any help, Rob?' he asked.

'I'm OK, though you could go and get Emma something to

drink.'

'I'm fine,' she insisted.

As Al and Olivia wandered off hand in hand, Rob climbed down from his ladder and unfolded a garden chair for Emma to sit down on. 'Here,' he said. 'Take the weight off your pins.'

Later, when he was sure Emma was comfortable in the shade and supplied with drinks, dark glasses and sun hat, Rob ambled over to the beer tent, where he found William. 'I thought I'd find you here,' he said.

'Thirsty work, this,' said William.

'Thirsty? You haven't lifted a finger, you idle sod. You've got all your assistants running round putting your stand up.'

'I drove here, didn't I?'

'Yeah, that's really thirsty work,' Rob acknowledged wryly.

'You've met Daniel Moloney, haven't you?' William asked Rob. 'Daniel, this is Rob Ansell, fellow Bloom conspirator. Daniel was one of the judges.'

'I remember,' said Rob, quietly. The other man! He expected to feel a stab of protectiveness but it never came. 'Nice to meet you again,' he added, reaching over to shake the man's hand.

'Likewise,' said Daniel, and Rob had the strangest feeling he was being sized up.

'What brings you here?'

'I'm staying the weekend with Ruth again.'

'Ah.' Again? 'That's nice. You a gardener?'

'I dabble.'

'He's a director of Kew,' interpolated William.

'Good,' said Rob, without a clue what they were talking about.

'The Botanical Gardens at Kew, dunderhead,' added William.

'Got it. That Kew. So you'll know your roses from your peonies, then?'

'Not always.'

Rob liked the man's deprecating sense of humour. Perhaps his assessment on Judgement Day had been wrong. 'She here?'

he asked looking around.

'She's with her nephew. He's got a film crew here and they're capturing "the spirit of Elderfield" for the TV show.'

'Ah. That'll take hours,' said Rob. 'Are you here to make the announcement of how we did?'

Daniel grinned, refusing to be drawn. 'They've nearly finished filming. Just a couple more scenes to get in the bag.'

Rob nodded. He picked up his beer and wandered over to the entrance. At the far corner of the grounds, he could make out Lucy and Terry arranging paintings by local artists under an awning. In front of them, Jules was walking towards the camera, talking in the animated way presenters do, all hand gestures and serious expressions. His producer, Harriet, was watching the action on camera relayed to a small television monitor in the back of a nearby van. Then she peered more closely at the monitor, tutted and popped her head around the van to call out something. Immediately, everyone stopped, walked back fifty metres and began the whole charade again from the top.

A few feet away from Harriet, Rob noticed Ruth watching her nephew, her face full of pride. She looked good, he concluded. Happy. Animated even. Then he saw Daniel walking towards the group and watched Ruth look up at him, her face brightening. Linking her arm through his, she drew him over to where Bruce was standing. Her hold was proprietorial and Rob was happy for her.

Meanwhile, at the entrance to the playing fields, people started arriving for the fete, some tugging dogs on leads. Dozens turned into hundreds and they streamed out over the playing fields intent on enjoying themselves. They toured the stands, bought hog roast for lunch, licked icecreams and watched the first dog show. In the adjoining field, children on fat little ponies jumped coloured fences while, from the ringside, ambitious parents shrieked at them to go faster.

Rob watched all this with satisfaction. He ambled over to one of the tables to pick up a paper that lay there, and absently scanned the headlines just as Gazzer slouched into view. He watched the boy's approach, and suddenly things began clicking into place in his head.

'Hiya, Gary,' he said.

'Wazup, Rob? Your hand fixed?'

Rob held it up. 'Stitches came out weeks ago. How's the cat?'

The boy's face softened. 'Kitty's good. She had kittens in my bed two days ago.'

'Is that a fact?'

'I watched them being born.' There was excitement in the boy's voice.

'Did you see the paper today?'

'Nah.' Gazzer showed no interest.

Rob handed the paper to him. 'Remember that boy, Harris, who got filleted?'

Gary looked momentarily blank and then stiffened.

'It says here, his attackers got ten years for that stabbing,' Rob continued without a break. 'Apparently, they were caught on camera. Funny that, how some people sometimes claim what's not theirs.'

Gary sniffed and ducked his head, wary about being caught in the lie. 'Yeah, well. They had it coming.'

'Yeah,' agreed Rob. 'It looks like they did.'

The boy was stupid not dangerous. Even so, Rob was relieved Al had found a new set of friends, among them, the tearaway Emlyn, who was also biking mad. 'Look after Kitty,' he said to Gary. 'The old girl would be glad to know she escaped and found a new home.'

Later, after the grand parade of all the winners, the PA system squeaked into life one more time and a voice invited everyone to assemble in the main arena for an announcement. Emma sat stubbornly at her stall. 'It's too hot and I'm too fat,' she grumbled. 'Bruce Turner can make as many announcements as he likes but I don't need to be in the audience.'

'Suit yourself,' said Rob. 'I'll wander over. Will you be OK?'

'I'll be fine. I'll hear from here anyway.'

He was making his way over to the main arena when he heard panting behind him. 'Wait up,' Emma called. When she caught him up, she linked an arm through his. 'I changed my mind. I want to be with you when he makes his announcement.'

Everything inside him lifted in love and he knew he had done the right thing in getting back together with her.

THE ANNOUNCEMENT

In the main arena, Bruce Turner was at his most affable. He was shaking people's hands when they arrived, and introducing Daniel Moloney around to all the town worthies and members of the committee. When he finished, Ruth edged over to Daniel and slipped her hand into his. 'Hello, poppet,' he whispered. 'Not long now.'

Ruth felt almost unable to contain herself. Next month, she and Daniel were flying out to Brazil where he was advising a multi-national mining company on how to minimise the impact of their commercial activities on biodiversity. A whole new world was opening up to her. He made her feel excited about each new day. In a month they had become almost inseparable. Ruth reckoned his phone bill must be extortionate because, although he was away a lot, they talked for hours every night. This morning, she'd looked out at her garden and realised that it would never again look so beautiful; Daniel was heavily into conservation projects all over the world and wanted to take her away with him for months at a time. Like the awards, the garden, too, had served its purpose and she was ready to move on.

For now, Bruce was waiting impatiently by the microphone. When he thought he had a large enough audience, he looked over people's heads towards Jules to check the crew were filming. Jules gave him a thumb's up.

Bruce puffed out his chest, reached for the microphone and ostentatiously cleared his throat. 'I'd just like to announce the outcome of the Elderfield in Bloom Awards.' He beamed in the direction of the camera. 'As you know, this was a project I started back in January,' he continued pompously. 'It's had growing support from the town through the months…'

'That's my Brucie,' said William, rolling his eyes as Bruce seemed set to drone on at length. 'Not an outspoken man, our Mr Chairman. No one's ever been able to out speak him.'

Rob's shoulders shook. 'I expect he'll come across as a shining beacon of hope in the TV programme,' he said. 'He's the slithery kind of contortionist who'll live on the reputation of the reputation he might have earned.'

'He's changed since Gary came home,' said Ruth. 'Have you noticed? It's like he's faded – all bluster and no substance.'

'Faded, my eye,' said William.

'He backed down straightaway when I suggested a PA system for today,' she said.

'That wasn't weakness, love. That's because he realised more people would hear him laud it over us. He thinks he carried the whole shebang. I can tell you, it was you and Vix who carried the day.'

'I bet you he forgets to thank the committee at all,' said Vix.

'No bets on that one,' said Ruth. She flushed as Daniel squeezed her hand and pulled her closer to him. 'I know exactly who's responsible,' he whispered in her ear.

She looked up at him and he pressed a kiss to her temple. 'Pay attention, now,' he whispered mockingly, nodding at Bruce.

In the event, Bruce was too excited to ramble on. 'Now, you may remember Daniel Moloney. He was one of the judges of Elderfield in Bloom, and he has turned up today, in person… to announce…'

'Oh Jeez,' Emma suddenly exclaimed over the momentary silence Bruce had left to allow the tension to build up. 'My waters broke.'

Bruce looked scandalised. William burst out laughing. Vix surged forward and put her arms around Emma's shoulders.

'Perfect timing, Sweet Pea,' said Rob. 'You'll have to film that one again, Jules. We're off to the hospital. Somebody mind the cake stand, please.'

Ruth watched them walk away towards the car park, and then felt someone put their arms around her. She twisted round and looked up at Daniel. 'When I've made the announcement,' he whispered, 'let's go home and I'll cook dinner while you pack. Tomorrow, we'll be in Honduras. I can't wait to show you round. Ah,' he said as a huge cheer erupted around them, 'I see Bruce has beaten me to the punch.' Around them everybody was throwing their hats in the air, dancing about and hugging each other as they hallooed and cheered.

Daniel leaned down and kissed Ruth's nose. 'I've got my prize here,' he said, his smile dazzling her.

She felt breathless with happiness.

ABOUT THE AUTHOR

Sophie Chalmers has been a journalist for over 20 years and currently edits magazines for the education sector.

She has won several awards including Welsh Woman of the Year (Small Business).

Made in the USA
Charleston, SC
09 May 2014